SAVING MEGHAN

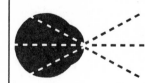

This Large Print Book carries the
Seal of Approval of N.A.V.H.

SAVING MEGHAN

D. J. PALMER

WHEELER PUBLISHING
A part of Gale, a Cengage Company

GALE
A Cengage Company

Farmington Hills, Mich • San Francisco • New York • Waterville, Maine
Meriden, Conn • Mason, Ohio • Chicago

Copyright © 2019 by D. J. Palmer.
Wheeler Publishing, a part of Gale, a Cengage Company.

Wheeler Publishing Large Print Hardcover.
The text of this Large Print edition is unabridged.
Other aspects of the book may vary from the original edition.
Set in 16 pt. Plantin.

LIBRARY OF CONGRESS CIP DATA ON FILE.
CATALOGUING IN PUBLICATION FOR THIS BOOK
IS AVAILABLE FROM THE LIBRARY OF CONGRESS

ISBN-13: 978-1-4328-6358-6 (hardcover alk. paper)

Published in 2019 by arrangement with Macmillan Publishing Group, LLC/St. Martins' Press

Printed in the United States of America
1 2 3 4 5 6 7 23 22 21 20 19

*For my wife, Jessica, and our two children, Benjamin and Sophie.
Love is all we need.*

CHAPTER 1

Becky

Panic gripped her as the airplane's hatch door closed. Her heartbeat skittered against the tightness stretched across her chest. The air tasted stale, harder to take in as her breathing turned rapid and shallow. A thin sheen of sweat dampened her face and coated her body. Her skin stuck to the seat's faux leather upholstery like adhesive. Becky Gerard thought to herself: *I've made a terrible mistake.*

A composed flight attendant, appropriately attired in a blue uniform with a matching silk scarf, spoke through an intercom.

"Ladies and gentlemen, my name is Katrina, and I'll be your chief flight attendant on this six-and-a-half-hour flight from Boston's Logan Airport to Los Angeles. The cabin doors are now closed, so kindly make sure your seat backs and tray tables are in their full upright positions and your seat belt is securely fastened low and tight across your lap. Also, please note at this time we respectfully ask that you power down and store all portable electronic devices until we've reached our cruising altitude."

Becky focused on the portable electronic device clutched in her hand. Instead of powering it down, she held the device low against her leg to keep it out of Katrina's sight. The phone was Becky's lifeline to the outside world, her conduit to what mattered most — her daughter, Meghan.

The plane jolted as it pulled away from the gate and soon after began a slow taxi toward the runway. The pit in Becky's stomach deepened. She waited for a text, some reply from Carl, her gaze fixed on the phone.

Her seatmate, a pleasant fortysomething man, took note of Becky's open defiance with a degree of amusement. "I'll shield you," the man said in a conspiratorial tone.

Becky glanced up to thank him. He gave her a warm, friendly smile, nothing more. It was rare for her to sit next to a man and not feel his desire. She was tall, annoyingly thin to some outspoken friends, with long, flowing blond hair and sharp blue eyes that called attention to her nicely symmetrical face, very much the prototypical California girl — which happened to be her home state.

At forty-eight, Becky could easily pass for a woman a decade younger, but these last few years of Meghan's illness had begun to take a toll on her youthful appearance. There were gray streaks camouflaged in her blond mane, and crow's-feet marked the edges of her blue eyes, deep enough that it looked as though the birds themselves had perched there at night while she slept. Still, men found her attractive, lusted after her, convinced themselves that she could not resist their charms. She understood the sway she held over some men — most men — but she was always strategic in the application of this power of hers.

Her seatmate was the rare breed who gave off no creep factor whatsoever, so she could keep her attention on her phone and not be distracted by him. Carl, her husband of twenty years, should have answered her by now. How hard was it to text *Meghan's fine* or *We're fine* or *No worries, safe travels xo*, anything of the sort, but it had been ages (well, more like thirty minutes) since she'd sent her last probing text, and his radio silence was deeply unsettling. He knew how nervous she was to leave Meghan. She'd been up all night with worry, and he'd

9

promised to respond right away whenever she texted him.

Why isn't he answering now?

The flight attendant patrolled the aisle with the watchful eye of a prison guard. Becky slumped farther forward to block her phone as she typed another message to Carl: *Plane leaving. Where are you? What's going on?*

That voice in Becky's head, the one that had told her not to go to California in the first place, spoke up again to issue stern admonishments of how long the flight was from Boston. She'd be thousands of miles from her daughter. It was stupid to think she could go there without feeling perpetually sick to her stomach. But what other choice did she have? Her mother was dying. According to her sister, Sabrina, her only sibling, it was a matter of days.

"I know you have your issues, we both do, but she's our mother," Sabrina had said during yesterday's phone call. "You should come home."

The truth was, Becky did want to be with Cora in her final moments. She wanted to hold her mother's hand, console her, be there for her despite all the insanity, the layers of hurt that, like geological strata, had marked the epochs of her journey into adulthood.

Even with years and distance between them, Becky could not escape her mother's long shadow. Though the cancer had taken her mother's voice, that voice still rang loudly in Becky's ears. If she wasn't chiding her, she was either critiquing her or ignoring her.

Did her mother have a mental illness? If so, none had ever been diagnosed, but Becky had done plenty of research over the years, not to mention countless hours spent in the therapist's armchair, trying to understand Cora's ambivalence toward motherhood. The bits of wisdom Becky got growing up were not the kind a normal mother would have imparted.

"You have to figure out their doubts and fears, try to use their pasts to your advantage," her mother had once said while explaining how to manipulate people. They were in a doctor's office at the time. Then again, they were always in some doctor's office.

"Look on the wall." She pointed to the pictures that hung in pretty silver frames. "There isn't a woman in any of them, just him and his two daughters. Is he a widow? Divorced? Could be he's lonely, or his

11

confidence has been shattered. That's good for us. We can use it. See how one of his daughters looks like you?" She had pointed out a blond girl who looked to be ten, the same age as Becky at the time. "We'll tell him we're new to town, don't know our way around yet, wondering about schools and such. He'll think of his own daughter when he looks at you, and it'll make him want to be extra helpful. So when we ask for a doctor's note — for my work, I'll say — he won't think twice about writing one, even though he hasn't reached any diagnosis yet."

Her mother did not actually have a job. Her job was getting those notes from the doctors she had taught Becky to manipulate. She did not show Becky how to braid her hair or brush out the tangles. There were no lectures on healthy eating. "You ask around, you'll figure it out," her mother had said when Becky inquired where babies came from. Her mother's love was dished out like food rations, given only in times of great need. And it seemed the only time that need arose was when Becky was with her mother at the doctor's office or a hospital. Becky accompanied her mother on these frequent sojourns as nothing more than a prop — something cute and little to evoke sympathy and dispel suspicion from the doctors and

12

nurses whom Cora had come to depend on for her disability checks.

Like an actress in a play, Becky had her lines down cold, coached by her mother, who was both the director and her harshest critic, which made her so believable when answering the doctors' questions.

Yes, I've seen Mommy faint a bunch of times.

Sometimes Mommy's headaches are so bad that she can't see straight.

Not surprisingly, for all the trips they made to the doctors over the years, nobody could ever figure out what was wrong with Cora, because nothing was ever wrong.

Now Becky was off to say goodbye to this damaged and damaging woman, worried it would be to the detriment of the sick daughter she'd left behind.

Becky bit her lower lip as she stared forlornly at the squat gray buildings that appeared to be rolling past her portal window. Of course, it was an illusion. Becky was the one moving, not the buildings, which meant she was leaving, that this was really happening. She was going to fly, and there was still no word from Carl.

Becky's seatmate sent her another sidelong glance. Perhaps he noticed some color drain from her complexion or her knuckles whiten as she gripped the armrest.

"Nervous to fly?" he asked.

Becky peeled her eyes from her phone, tried to relax and let it all go, but her heartbeat accelerated as the terminal vanished from view.

"No, I'm fine. Thank you," she managed. Her soft voice lacked conviction.

"My wife hates to fly, too," said the man. His capacity to ignore the "don't talk to me" vibes Becky gave off annoyed her, but it was not surprising. Men often had blinders on in that regard — even the non-creepers. "A vodka tonic usually does the trick," he continued. "Anyway, I'm sure you've heard that flying is far safer than driving."

"I'm fine, really. Thank you for your concern."

Becky took a sharper tone and, judging by her seatmate's wounded expression, doubted there'd be any more idle chitchat. She returned her attention to her phone, feeling terrible for the way she'd dismissed the man. Thanks to her mother, Becky was remarkably in tune with other people's feelings.

It made sense she'd be good at it — there had been no better way to get her mom's attention than to show an aptitude for figuring out what people wanted to hear based on their appearance or mannerisms. To see her daughter plying the family trade had impressed Cora more than when Becky made the cheer squad in middle school or got into the National Honor Society her junior year in high school. At the feet of the grand master herself, Becky had learned what to say or do to ingratiate herself with most anyone. With these insights, she could make people happy, put them on edge, or keep the peace, whichever suited her needs. It was shameful in a way, but it was also what had made her such a successful real estate broker. It was all about knowing which levers to pull.

"I'm sorry," Becky said to the man. "I'm traveling for the first time in a long time, and it's hard for me to leave my daughter. She's sick, and, well, I'm waiting to hear from my husband to let me know everything is all right."

"I'm sorry to hear that," the man said sincerely. "What's the matter, if you don't mind my asking?"

"I wish I knew," Becky said. "Nobody seems to know."

Becky was a notoriously private person, except when it came to Meghan's illness. For that, she blared the horns. She talked to anyone, stranger or friend, about the puzzling array of symptoms plaguing her daughter. She sought advice, doctors' names, homeopathic remedies, experimental treatments, diagnoses from the expert and uninformed alike. She had filing cabinets in her office filled with papers, printouts from the web, doctors' reports, lab tests — enough so that a friend once jokingly asked if she was opening up a health clinic.

While Becky avoided the specifics of Meghan's confounding symptoms, she gave enough details to help her seatmate visualize a tense and uncertain situation back home. Muscle weakness. Fatigue. Blinding headaches. Achy joints. Weight loss. Decline in physical coordination. Trouble concentrating. Her daughter's symptoms could change or worsen at any time, making a six-hour cross-country flight feel like an eternity.

"I'm sorry for what you're going through. I'll pray for you," said the man after Becky had dispensed with the background.

It was a kind gesture, not at all unwelcome, and something Becky heard quite often these days. When there were no clear answers or well-defined next steps, prayers seemed to be the only thing people could offer.

Carl finally returned Becky's many texts just as the captain came on the intercom to inform the passengers and crew that they were number six for takeoff. The buzz of the phone surged through her arm like an electric current. Carl's reply was short and simple, four words that made Becky's blood turn cold:

We're at the hospital.

CHAPTER 2

Becky's phone buzzed for a second time.

Carl's next message read: *Can you talk?*

The plane crawled forward a few more feet. Becky did the math in her head: six hours in the air, a layover in California until she could get a return flight home to Boston, six more hours to fly back, and then travel time to the hospital. All of it added up to far too long.

Becky got Carl on the phone.

"Baby, what is it? What's going on?" Panic leaked into her voice.

"I don't know. Holly was over with the twins. The kids were in the backyard kicking a soccer ball when Meghan just fainted. I called 911. The ambulance brought her to Saint Joe's. But she seems fine now, alert, chatty even."

"What did the doctors say exactly?" Becky asked. "And how could you let her run around?"

"She *wanted* to play."

Becky got the subtext. Her daughter may have inherited her father's natural athletic ability, but there was no question she got her strong will from Mom. The twins, Addy and Danielle, were younger kids from down the street. Their mother, Holly, was a neighbor who had become an expert on Lyme disease after Addy contracted it. Becky remembered now that she and Holly had made plans to meet for coffee and talk about the condition, plans she had forgotten about when she'd booked the last-minute flight to California.

The symptoms of Lyme disease are easy to miss or confuse with something else, and half the people who have it don't even remember getting a tick bite. Meghan had already been tested, but Holly knew some rare forms of the disease that she thought worth consideration. It was no surprise she had brought the twins with her. The girls were always eager to learn soccer from Meghan, the older, far-superior player.

But Carl knew better, and it took every bit of restraint not to scream at him. Exercise, exertion of any kind, worsened her daughter's symptoms, which was why Becky had insisted Meghan quit the varsity team, as well as the travel clubs where she was

19

always the star.

The flight attendant, Katrina, stormed down the aisle, glowering as she marched. "You have to put that away immediately."

At that moment, the captain's monotone came over the loudspeaker. "We're presently number three in line for takeoff. Flight attendants, please prepare for departure."

"Now, please!" Katrina barked, pointing at the phone.

Becky ignored the order. "Carl, what's going on? Is she all right?"

This was hardly the first time Meghan had been to the hospital, but it was the first time that Becky had not been with her. Anxiety built in Becky's chest and spread outward as the hard stares of many sets of eyes bored into her from the front and back of the airplane.

"The doctor thinks she became dehydrated. No IV — she wouldn't allow it, of course — but they've given her lots of fluids."

Becky was not surprised. The only tangible result of all the doctor visits seemed to be her daughter's newly developed and incredibly intense needle phobia. Too many failed attempts at venipuncture from inexperienced phlebotomists had deeply scarred Meghan and turned every doctor's visit into an ordeal. Getting an IV into her would have been a miracle.

Despite Carl's reassurances, Becky visualized her daughter on a hospital bed in the ER, the electrocardiogram going flatline. She heard alarms ringing in her ears, and imagined a swarm of doctors and nurses administering lifesaving care.

Becky pinned the phone between her shoulder and ear as she fumbled to unclasp her seat belt. She stood, nearly cracking her skull on the overhead bin as she rose, and clambered over her seatmate, issuing a string of apologies as she forced her way into the aisle.

"Ma'am, you must take your seat this instant," Katrina said while blocking the aisle.

Ignoring the order, Becky shook her head in defiance. "My daughter is very sick. She's in the hospital. I have to get off this plane. Now."

"Ma'am, I'm ordering you back to your seat, right now." Katrina pointed at Becky's empty seat, as though she needed the reminder of how to find it.

Two flight attendants hurried toward the commotion while a third accessed the intercom, perhaps to inform the captain of the disturbance in row 16. The plane continued to roll forward, while Becky, retrieving her bag from the overhead bin, acted as though it had come to a complete stop at the gate.

"Please, I have to be with my daughter. She's in the hospital; she's very sick."

"Hey, sit down, lady!" The angry voice came from some rows back.

Becky's seatmate stood and glowered at the man who had scolded her. "Her daughter is sick," he snapped. "She has to get off the plane. Have a heart, buddy."

"If she's sick, what's she flying for?" the angry man shot back.

Becky paid no attention to him. Her thoughts looped like a recording on repeat: *Get off the plane! Get off the plane! Get off the plane!*

Becky figured she could knock on the cockpit door to get the captain's attention, forgetting what those terrorists had done on that fateful day and how everything about flying had changed since then. As she pushed past Katrina, Becky felt a firm hold on her arm, followed by a strong tug backward.

"Take a seat!" Katrina commanded. She dug her fingers into Becky's tender flesh.

"My daughter is in the hospital with a heart attack or something. Please . . .

22

please . . . don't do this to me. Let me go. I have to get to her."

"Hey, let her go," someone called out. "It's her damn kid!"

"What the hell is wrong with you?" shouted another supporter.

"Sit down, lady!" This third voice, a female's, called out. "I'll kick your ass if you make me miss this flight."

"Ma'am, if you don't take your seat this instant, I'm going to have you forcibly removed from this plane," Katrina threatened.

"Yes!" Becky cried out. "That's what I want. Kick me off right now. I need to be with my daughter. I can't fly to California, don't you understand?"

Becky turned to see a large man approaching her from behind. He had a bushy mustache and thinning dark hair that gleamed beneath the cabin lights. As he flashed some sort of ID to Katrina, his fingers clamped around Becky's left arm, which he then wrenched painfully and awkwardly behind her back.

"I'm an air marshal," he gruffly announced to Katrina. "Please tell the captain we have a situation here, and we need to get this plane back to the gate — now. Ma'am, I'm taking you into custody for interfering with a flight crew."

Becky heard some cheers mixed with plenty of boos. In her peripheral vision, she saw cell phones out, small lenses recording her meltdown for the whole world to see. Soon it would be all over Twitter, Facebook, maybe the news. The air marshal yanked Becky's other arm behind her back with total disregard for tendons and range of motion. A second later, Becky felt the clamp of cold steel biting into her flesh as he secured his handcuffs around her delicate wrists.

She'd never done the "perp walk" before, and understood now the desire for a clipboard or hoodie to shield her face as the air marshal escorted her (and her carry-on luggage) off the gangway and back into the departure lounge. As a woman, she thought she knew what it meant to feel degraded when men groped her, touched her, approached her, catcalled her, but this was dehumanizing on an entirely different level.

It was a short walk from the departure gate to a waiting electric-powered cart that the air marshal had summoned on his radio. People gawked at Becky as the uniformed driver, an employee of the airport, drove her away. They were understandably curious. What could she have done? Even Becky could appreciate the odd sight — a tall, slender woman manhandled by a brute like the air marshal. It hardly made for a fair fight.

Becky tried to hold it together as the driver weaved the cart between clusters of airline passengers all making their way to gates or other destinations. She felt less conspicuous while seated, as nobody could see the handcuffs around her wrists. She was aware of the crime she'd committed, but not the penalties it might carry. All Becky wanted was to get at her purse, which held her phone. Meghan was still in the hospital. For all she knew, her daughter could be gone.

"Please, please," Becky said, willing strength into her voice. "You don't have to do this."

The air marshal answered coolly, "You didn't have to interfere with a flight crew."

Some minutes later, Becky found herself in a stark room constructed entirely of gray concrete bricks located somewhere in the bowels of the airport. Overhead lights reflected harshly off a metal table positioned in the center of the room. She looked across the table at several members of the TSA, all dressed in crisp blue shirts pinned with gold badges. Their shifting glances and nervous looks told her they were not trained to handle a distressed mom in handcuffs.

"Dave, I think you may have overstepped your bounds here," one of the TSA agents offered a bit apprehensively.

Dave.

At least now Becky knew her captor's name.

Just then, the room's only door swung open, and in stormed a strong-featured man in his fifties, with ebony skin and short-cut dark hair. He had on a charcoal-gray suit brightened with a bold red tie, which distinguished him as a person in charge. When he looked at Becky and saw the handcuffs in place, his stern aspect softened. His gaze shifted over to Dave, the air marshal.

"Unlock her," he said. "You went way, way over the line here."

"She interfered with a flight crew," Dave protested in his defense. "She should be charged."

"I can't believe you blew your cover for a situation the flight crew could have handled. Just so you know, I spoke with the captain, who informed me that he would have willingly returned to the gate to let this poor mother off that plane. Now, let her go."

Dave muttered to himself as he complied with the order. Becky rubbed at her wrists, which were ringed red in the matching contours of the handcuffs.

The man who'd come to Becky's rescue pulled over a chair. He sat down beside her. "Ma'am, I'm Reginald Campbell, head of TSA here at Logan. I am so very sorry for what you've been through."

Becky regained her composure. "I know you think I'm going to threaten you with lawsuits and whatnot, but I only want my purse with my phone in it so that I can check in with my husband and make sure my daughter is all right."

"Of course," Reginald said, retrieving the purse from the corner of the room where Dave had tossed it. "If you don't mind, we just need to see some ID for the paperwork."

Becky's hands trembled as she fished her license from her wallet and her phone from her purse. She handed the ID to Reginald and then checked her phone, which showed a series of texts from Carl. The last one eased her anxiety considerably.

Meghan is resting in the ER. Seems stable. She's asking for you. Are you able to get here?

Becky texted back: *Don't let them discharge her. Be there soon.*

"I need to leave now," Becky told Reginald. "I have to get to the hospital. Am I under arrest?"

"Well, Mrs. Gerard," said Dave the air

marshal, taking it upon himself to answer. He stood and exhaled loudly in a way that pushed out his ample midsection like a balloon. "You've created a serious situation for yourself."

"Stop it, just stop it," Reginald snapped. He handed Becky back her license. "No, Mrs. Gerard, you are not under arrest. You're free to go. And we owe you a sincere apology. I also suspect you'll have your airfare refunded and a free trip coming your way."

But Dave was not through. He had to save face somehow. There was a brief, albeit stern, lecture on how to properly engage the flight crew during an emergency, and then some forms to sign, and threats of a stiff fine and possible jail time if she ever disrupted a flight again, all of which Becky said she understood just so they would hurry up and let her go.

Eventually, Reginald took Becky to another dingy room where piles of confiscated luggage languished, each piece representing someone's horrible day. There Reginald explained at least one reason why he'd shown her such compassion.

"I had a son who died of leukemia a few years back," he explained. "Those last moments we had together were the most precious of my life. If I were in your position, I'd have done the same thing."

"I suspect you wouldn't have been on that plane in the first place," said Becky, who had yet to forgive herself.

She felt Meghan's pain, her daughter's illness, as though it were her own. Exhaustion took root inside her bones, where it calcified to make activities once routine (grocery shopping, laundry, cooking, yard work) an effortful chore.

Of course, the brunt of Meghan's care had fallen on her, the mother. At times Becky felt angry for the burden, and immediately afterward she'd be consumed with guilt. How dare she feel anything other than tremendous empathy when it was Meghan who suffered the most? These were things Becky wrestled with in the quiet dark — dreading what tomorrow might bring — while Carl slept peacefully beside her.

Becky's community of online friends, built up over a year and a half through her Facebook group, Help for Meghan, regularly posted positive affirmations, which she'd turn to when in need of a mental pick-me-up.

I breathe in calmness and breathe out fear.
I let go of my anger so I can see clearly.
I may not understand the good in this situa-

tion, but it is there.

She had invited friends whom she knew would want regular updates on Meghan's health to join the group, but word spread the way word does on the internet, and before long, strangers began opting into the public group. Initially, Becky kept the group public, thinking it would be good to cast as wide a net as possible. Members offered advice on doctors, made assured diagnoses, and suggested treatments without ever having met Becky or Meghan, all to no avail.

Becky was never one to turn to God for answers. Cora had instilled in her children no sense of the divine, which left Becky unmoored as Meghan's condition worsened. Her online group had evolved to become her church as well as her religion. It was there she'd turn when needing solace and support. Carl tended to focus more on solutions and answers, at the expense of a compassionate ear. Becky knew not to cast blame. They were both pushing through the dark, and in the process, sometimes, oftentimes, losing sight of each other.

Becky thanked Reginald for his kindness as she got ready to depart. Instead of a handshake goodbye, Reginald pulled her in for an unexpected hug, something she so often wished Carl would do.

She thanked Reginald again before rushing out the door, luggage in tow, in search of a cab to take her to the hospital, praying that if her worst nightmare came true, she'd arrive in time to say a final goodbye to her precious daughter before she was gone.

CHAPTER 3

Becky thrust a fifty through the Plexiglas divider to the driver of the yellow cab — who, at her request, had disregarded the speed limit for most of the trip.

"Thanks," she said, even before her taxi had come to a stop beneath the ambulance entrance of Saint Joseph's Hospital. Saint Joe's did not have the same renown as the Boston hospitals, but it was closest to her Concord home.

The red neon glow of the emergency sign on the portico overhang lit Becky's face as she rushed through the automatic double doors, through the waiting room, and directly to Reception. The opaque sliding-glass window opened on cue, and a receptionist greeted her with a halfhearted "May I help you?"

"Yes, I'm here to see my daughter." Becky huffed out the words, a bit winded from her short sprint. "Meghan Gerard. She's in the ER."

"Just a moment," the receptionist replied, showing no great concern for Becky's obvious agitation.

"My husband is with her," Becky announced. "I shouldn't have to wait out here."

"Just a moment," repeated the receptionist. To punctuate her request, she slid the glass window closed shut, leaving Becky in the company of the ten or so folks in the waiting room.

Becky retreated to a corner, away from the masses, wanting to separate her suffering from theirs. She had just taken out her phone to text Carl when she heard someone call her name. Glancing up, Becky focused on a reassuring matronly woman standing in front of the automatic doors to the ER. She was dressed in blue scrubs and had a stethoscope draped around her neck. Becky raced over to her.

"Mrs. Gerard, my name is Alexandra. I'm Meghan's nurse."

"Is she all right?" Becky's voice carried the weight of her worry.

"She's doing just fine," Alexandra assured her. Her strong accent exposed her Boston origin. "She's resting in bay twelve. It's been a long day, and she'll be very glad to see you. Your husband has been here, of course, but he's not her mother, if you know what I mean."

Becky knew exactly what Alexandra meant, and gave her an extra mark for perception. Carl was certainly a good provider, no question about that, but it was Becky who'd been commander of Meghan's health issues as well as comforter-in-chief for years now.

How many unproductive sojourns to the doctor or the hospital had they endured? How many times had they found themselves frustrated to the point of tears at being dismissed without any answers, without a diagnosis? How many bottles of failed prescriptions remained in the medicine cabinet? How many nights had she gone to Meghan's room, summoned for consolation?

Becky threw open the curtain to ER bay 12 to find a stretcher bearing her fifteen-year-old daughter, who was attached to a monitor recording vitals, oxygen saturation, and heart rhythm. A pitcher of water and a big container of Gatorade were on a tray beside the bed. Carl sat in a chair in the corner of the bay, eyes glued to his phone instead of engaging with his daughter.

He rose from his seat as Becky came to Meghan's bedside.

"Oh, sweetheart. I'm sorry I wasn't there when it happened," Becky said. "I should never have been on that damn plane."

Even though my mother is dying, thought Becky. *Even though I will probably never get to say the three words my therapist told me to say in her presence: "I forgive you."*

Becky reached for her daughter's hand while leaning into Carl, who had come to stand beside her, his strong arm wrapped tightly around her shoulders. He placed a gentle kiss on her cheek.

She fought back tears as she went through the familiar rundown of questions, all delivered with the reflex of a preflight checklist: "Are you feeling all right? Do you need anything? What can I do to help? Tell me what happened."

Meghan answered each question dutifully, but without much embellishment: "I'm fine. No, I'm okay. I'm just tired."

Poor child has to be utterly exhausted, thought Becky.

Carl provided background that Becky already knew, but now, face-to-face, instead of over text and phone, his narration took on new vividness.

"Holly left when I explained you'd gone

35

to the airport, but the twins stayed behind because they wanted Meghan to play soccer with them."

"You shouldn't have let them," Becky said, more sharply than intended.

"It was my fault, Mom," Meghan said, coming to her father's defense. "I didn't even run that hard."

"I heard someone cry out that Meghan fainted, and I came running," Carl continued. "Got there in seconds. Danielle said she went pale before collapsing, and Addy said something about her stiffening up. She was breathing but unresponsive, so I called 911. By the time they got to the house, she was coming around, but she didn't make any sense until she was in the ambulance, and even then she still seemed a bit confused."

"Has Dr. Walker seen her yet?"

Becky knew the name of the head cardiologist at Saint Joe's, same as she did the neurologist and every other doctor who worked there.

"No," Carl said. "Dr. Clemmons said it was dehydration and nothing more."

"Dr. Clemmons is an ER doctor, not a heart specialist. She needs an expert evaluation, Carl. Dammit," Becky muttered. "I should never have left you in charge."

"Becky, come on, don't be like that," Carl protested.

"Just wait a minute," Becky said in a huff. "I'm getting someone who knows what they're doing."

"The doctor said she's fine," Carl said to Becky's back as she was leaving.

There was a subtle bite to the way Carl delivered the word "fine." He had infused it with layers of meaning. At some level, Becky understood Carl's reluctance to accept that Meghan was indeed direly ill with something strange. Test after test and doctor after doctor had failed to yield any meaningful result. But she knew better. There was a time bomb waiting to go off inside her precious daughter's body, spreading disease and sickness in all directions like shrapnel. The fainting episode had to have been scary for Carl, but clearly not terrifying enough to dispel his many doubts. For the first time in his life, Carl had encountered a problem for which money could not buy a solution.

Meghan had stared at her mother from the confines of her stretcher bed, offering nothing more than a weak smile. Pity and sadness consumed Becky. Her daughter was so obviously ill. Her arms too thin, face too gaunt. The ER's harsh lighting had given Meghan's already-pale skin a ghostly pallor.

37

Her blond hair, normally full of body, lay flat against her head, as if no single part of her was allowed to be healthy.

People said Meghan looked like her mother, with the same electric-blue eyes, but there were features of her father's handsome face present as well. Despite her frailty, Becky's daughter was still a beautiful girl, but the smile that lit her face now was just an echo of who she once was.

Becky stepped out of the ER bay with her phone pressed to her ear. She had Dr. Walker's number in her contacts, same as the neurologist, pulmonologist, and various other specialists she could summon like Aladdin rubbing his magic lamp.

"Hello," a man's voice said after the call rang through.

"Gary, it's Becky Gerard. I'm sorry to call your personal number, but you told me to phone anytime I had a problem, and, well, I have a problem."

Gary. Married. One daughter in her early twenties. Cornell grad. Living in New York, working as a lab tech at Mount Sinai Hospital. Thinking about medical school, to her father's delight. He'll probably be tan from his vacation to Costa Rica. Oh, if Cora had had access to social media in her heyday, it would have been like an addict mainlining their favorite drug.

"What's happening, Becky? What's going on?"

Dr. Walker's concern sounded genuine, although Becky knew he'd take great interest even if she called about a leaky faucet. That's because she had helped him by spending a couple of hours reviewing his daughter's rental agreement, and then a good thirty minutes on the phone with her, dispensing advice about getting rid of the application and amenity fee, making sure she had the right to use the outdoor space, and how not to get charged for damages that were there before she moved in.

No surprise, Dr. Gary Walker was deeply grateful for Becky's help. Was she ashamed to use her real estate experience to ingratiate herself? Not in the slightest. By her count, Dr. Walker had examined Meghan at least half a dozen times now for various episodes — scary heart palpitations, shortness of breath, unexplained chest pain — and he always took Becky's calls.

Becky recounted the situation for Dr. Walker's benefit, though he'd already heard about the incident on the airplane. As Becky had feared, cell phone video of her had wormed its way onto the internet, making headlines in the online editions of Boston newspapers, getting minor mention on some national news outlets, and plenty of traction on Twitter and Facebook. Becky's phone had exploded with text messages from worried friends, all of which she would return later.

"Don't worry, I'm actually at the hospital now," Dr. Walker said. "I'll be down in a minute to check on Meghan."

"Thank you so, so much, Gary," Becky said, her voice drenched with gratitude. "I can't tell you how much that means to me."

The curtain to bay 12 parted, and in stepped a slight man in his late fifties with sandy hair, a trim beard, and, yes, a tan. Becky turned her body as she went to Dr. Walker so that Carl would not see her touch his arm. Gestures like this were like deposits into an investment account that over time would pay hefty dividends. Dr. Walker had given Meghan a thorough examination, and returned to give an update on the test results. Judging by the warmth of his smile, Becky relaxed.

"Is Meghan okay?" Becky asked nervously.

"My initial answer is yes; she's fine. But is this the first time Meghan's fainted?" Dr. Walker's penetrating gray eyes hinted at some concern.

"Well, you know she's had spells of feeling very weak and dizzy," Becky said, reliving in her head the many times she'd brought Meghan to see Dr. Walker. "And episodes where she seemed out of it for a moment or two, but she's never fainted."

"That's right." Carl nodded in agreement beside her.

"Well, Meghan's EKG shows a mildly prolonged PR interval. It's probably nothing to worry about, but I think we may want to do some more tests."

"A what?"

Over the years, Becky had acquired an enormous amount of medical knowledge in her quest to help Meghan, but there were always new terms to go along with her daughter's new and puzzling symptoms. Each time Becky heard a new word, it came with a fresh pulse of anxiety.

"The PR interval is the time between the first and second wave on an EKG," Dr. Walker explained. He showed Becky a printout latched to his clipboard illustrating the peaks and valleys of Meghan's heartbeat. "See, here's the P wave, and then this sawtooth pattern is the QRS complex, followed by this hump called the T wave." Dr. Walker stood close to Becky, their shoulders touching, as he traced the line with his

41

finger. Under any other circumstances, the proximity would have made her feel uneasy. This time she welcomed the contact and hoped Carl did not notice.

"The distance between the P wave and the QRS is the PR interval," Dr. Walker continued. "It should be less than point-two seconds. Meghan's is about point-two-four seconds. Not too long, but still, something we should keep an eye on."

"What does that mean?"

Becky asked the question knowing the answer he would give. It was the same answer she'd heard time and time again, the same one she had gotten after countless blood tests that had contributed to her daughter's intense needle phobia.

I don't know.

"I don't know," Dr. Walker said. "I do want to see Meghan in my office for some more tests." *Surprise, surprise,* Becky thought. "Here's the number to schedule an echocardiogram and make a follow-up with me." He handed Becky a card. "Until then, please check with us if she is started on any new medications. Certain ones might need to be avoided if she feels faint again. I'm sure you have lots of questions, but, Meghan, I suspect you're anxious to get back home after spending a full day with us. You're always welcome, but I'd prefer you stay away."

He gave a wink. The anemic attempt at a joke failed to register with anyone.

"Beck— Mrs. Gerard," Dr. Walker said, catching himself. "I was wondering if I could speak with you in private."

Carl was too distracted — or too oblivious — to notice that Dr. Walker had requested Becky, and only Becky. They left the curtained room and found a private corner to talk.

Becky touched his arm again — she was not a touchy person in general, but she wanted assurances he'd answer the next time she called.

"I got a list of Meghan's current medications, but I have to ask this, even though we've already run a tox screen. Is there a history of illicit drug use?"

Oh God, Becky thought. *Must we go down this rabbit hole again?*

"No. Never."

Dr. Walker glanced at the ER bay a bit apprehensively, as if encouraging her to be honest. "It's okay to tell me, even if it's just a suspicion on your part," he said. "It's just that prolonged PR intervals can be a consequence of drug use or electrolyte disturbance, but her electrolytes are normal."

43

"No. I promise you, Meghan doesn't use drugs."

"Very well," Dr. Walker said. "Call my office number, and we'll get Meghan seen right away."

That's all I needed to hear, thought Becky.

"And I'm so very sorry about that episode on the airplane. Wendy called when she saw the video online — thank you again for your help with her apartment, by the way. It was terrible how badly the airline mistreated you. I hope you get some sort of compensation for the trouble and embarrassment."

Becky thought of all sorts of things to say — questions about his trip, how Wendy's medical school applications were coming along — but she did not have the stamina to play any part other than the real one.

"Thanks for the concern, but all I care about is Meghan."

Becky returned to the ER bay to find Nurse Alexandra disconnecting the monitors.

"I don't know what happened to me," Meghan said after Alexandra departed, sounding like she was pleading for answers. "I still feel strange."

"I'll make you some of my chicken soup when we get home," Becky said, which was the only meal Meghan seemed capable of

44

eating these days. "I think I need some, too." That raised a smile on Meghan's lips, but it also brought that look from Carl again, the one that came with accusations. She was glad she had not told him about her call to Michael — aka Dr. Cohen, a.k.a. the neurologist who was coming by — and that Meghan would not be leaving until he saw her. And no way would Becky settle for anything less than a CAT scan.

Three hours later, they were still in the hospital, seeing another doctor.

Dr. Cohen, who had a horseshoe of white hair and sallow skin, would have been headed for retirement if only his wife had not surprised him with a divorce late in life. Becky had learned the sad news months ago, after Dr. Cohen examined Meghan for a persistent headache. She had seen the pictures in his office, studied them closely (thank you, Cora), and thought to ask about his family when she noticed that the photographs of his wife were no longer up. Becky offered to help with his search for a new home, but what he wanted was to have coffee with her, as she reminded him of his daughter who he'd been estranged from since the divorce.

Bad for him, good for me, Becky had

thought at the time, hating herself for feeling anything other than sympathy. But she reminded herself what was at stake, and that had lessened her guilt several degrees.

Dr. Cohen entered the ER bay carrying a small doctor's bag that was so familiar to Becky, she could guess the contents without looking: a reflex hammer, a portable ophthalmoscope, some tuning forks, a broad cloth tape covered with a pattern of black stripes, a number of safety pins, and even a small vial of ground coffee to test for sense of smell if the occasion called for it.

"We're not sure just why Meghan fainted today," said Dr. Cohen, looking alternately at Carl and Becky with an occasional obligatory glance at his patient. "I spoke at length with Dr. Walker, who thinks it may be her heart, but I understand that a friend said Meghan stiffened up when she lost consciousness. I can't rule out a seizure. The good news is that the CAT scan looks normal to my eyes."

Becky let go a sigh of relief. Dr. Cohen looked the way a grandparent might upon receiving good news.

"We had to give a small sedative to get the blood test, but we didn't find anything in her labs that was overly concerning." Dr. Cohen sent Becky a conspiratorial glance, as if to say they should chat in private about her daughter's fear of needles. "Still, I'd like to see Meghan in the office for an EEG and possibly run some more tests, depending on the results. You have my office number. Call first thing in the morning. We'll make sure to get Meghan in right away."

Becky could imagine what Carl was thinking: *More doctors. More tests.*

"Of course. Thank you," Becky said. "It's been a long day. We'll call in the morning."

"I've had it," Carl said after Dr. Cohen had departed.

"Not here," responded Becky.

Carl left in a huff so Becky could help Meghan out of her hospital gown and back into her street clothes.

How can Carl be so cavalier with Meghan's health? Becky asked herself as she helped her daughter get dressed. Didn't he want to make sure they turned over every stone, explored all avenues, and examined every possibility? Why wasn't he willing to do anything and everything in his power so they would not have to endure the unshakable grief and unyielding sorrow of losing another child?

CHAPTER 4

Meghan

I could see it in my father's eyes.

It's not disappointment, though that's there, the letdown because he doesn't have a perfect fifteen-year-old daughter (soon to be sixteen) who is perfectly healthy. I could almost live with that. I knew he missed the rough-and-tumble kid I used to be, a real scrapper.

I'm a soccer player, a battler for the ball. I shove. I push. I elbow and trip my way to that ball — my ball, mine! Knock me down, and I pick myself up by the shin guards, dust myself off, and get back at it again. I've always been the girl who could dress up pretty, but who also loved to get muddy, and that's what I think my dad loved most about me. For a while, before everything changed, I was Daddy's special girl, his spunky daughter. I was tough, a never-say-never, game-on, up-for-anything kind of daughter.

I was like him — a fighter.

When my dad started his home renovation business, all he had was a dream and a lot of determination to see him through the lean times. He'd built his business from the ground up, pushed to make a better life for himself and for us. More than anybody, more than Mom, he understood that you couldn't win every time. Sometimes you got beat. That's why whenever I got beat on the field, nobody was more supportive, more encouraging, than my father. He got that for every peak there'd be a valley. So the look I caught in my father's eyes wasn't disappointment, but something else, something far, far more hurtful.

I could tell by the way he looked at me with sadness and sympathy that he'd do anything and everything to make me well again. But there was a deep sense of loss in that look, too. He was sure he'd lost me to her — to my mom. He feared she'd taken over, planted ideas in my head.

They're so funny, my parents. They thought a closed door was the same as having cotton balls stuffed in my ears. They had no idea how loud they are when they start fighting over me; how their voices rise slowly until hushed talk becomes loud talk.

I've heard them arguing about the doctors, all the tests I've done and specialists I've seen, my mom's obsession with her Facebook group, all of it. He sees that Facebook group as just more people filling her head (and by extension, mine) with nonsense.

Did my dad notice how Mom worked the doctors? Did he see how she gathered personal details about their lives like a squirrel collecting acorns for winter and used them to gain favors? I did. Lord, if it weren't so sad, it would make me laugh. But the outright flirting, well, that's the hardest to take. I've seen her with some doctors, touching their arms, cocking her head to the side, looking at them like they were the most incredible, smartest, most amazing people on the planet. My mom is gorgeous, so it's not hard to see how they can fall for her routine. I just can't believe my dad doesn't notice — or more likely he doesn't care.

Maybe there really is something wrong with me. Maybe I do have some strange sickness, maybe a parasite lurking in my bloodstream, living off me, vampire-like. Granted, it's not nearly so romantic as the vampire from *Twilight,* but that would be just my luck. Instead of landing the handsome and mysterious Edward Cullen, I'd get some wiggly worm swimming in my veins. But after all the doctors and tests, if there were some wormy thing inside me, it would have been found by now. So, sorry, that's not it. Test after test, doctor after doctor, it was always the same story: We don't know what's the trouble with Meghan.

The only thing obvious was that I was getting sicker and losing weight I couldn't afford to give up. It's not like I weighed a ton to begin with. I'm barely a hundred pounds, which puts me in the rare 5 percent range on the doctor's height and weight chart. But despite what my father thought, I don't have an eating disorder.

His browser history was like a window into his worries. I'm not purging every meal, or counting how many ribs I can see in the morning, or popping diuretics the way my mom does her Xanax. I'm just small-boned to begin with. (Yeah, I know that's not a real thing, but people understand what I mean when I say it.) Put more simply, I'm naturally thin, but that doesn't mean I'm naturally weak. A lot of girls misjudge me on the soccer field as some prissy, fragile thing, but their opinions quickly change after the first shoulder-to-shoulder hit. That's when they see I'm no pushover. I'm no weakling. I'm not someone they should take lightly.

But that was the girl from before. Now I don't even play soccer.

Dad drove his Mercedes home in that pukey way, with lots of quick stops and fast accelerations to show his annoyance. It was no surprise to me that Mom and Dad weren't speaking to each other. The whoosh of the wipers was the only soundtrack as they beat away a light rain. I thought of that look in my father's eyes, the one I caught in the rearview mirror, and it made me want to cry. I wanted so badly for him to look at me with pity, or sadness, or worry, or fear, or something other than what I knew he was thinking.

It was dark out when we arrived home. Once again, I hadn't seen the day become night, because I was trapped in a windowless space (not even a room) in the ER. On the surface, our home looks like the kind of nauseating Facebook posts that adults use to make their friends and neighbors feel inadequate. I've seen the crap my mom Likes online: gorgeous families all aglow in a dreamy sunset, or perched on manicured lawns in front of a hotel impersonating a house.

I try to tell myself that we live in a Mc-Mansion because that's the kind of thing my father does — he builds big homes; turns the ordinary into the extraordinary. He's the Candy Man for grown-ups. My dad loves Willy Wonka, the ancient '70s version, which is the only reason I know that dumb song. Instead of pounds of sweet treats, he leaves behind sparkling new kitchens with gleaming marble countertops, state-of-the-art appliances, and fancy-pants cabinets. Instead of taking the sunrise and sprinkling it with dew, my dad can take a shit-shack and turn it into a castle. That's where we live, inside a castle that's big enough for me to have four siblings and still not have to share a bedroom.

I wish I did have brothers and sisters, not only for the company, but also to have someone around to take the focus off me for a change.

Dad pulled the car into the garage, which was so neat and tidy, it looked like we hadn't fully moved in yet. That was another drawback (or benefit?) to being an only child. There wasn't a ton of crap (sports stuff, ski stuff, bike stuff, tool stuff, stuff stuff) to clutter up a space even a quarter the size of our garage. We trekked inside in a solemn processional, Dad in front, me in the middle, Mom behind me, her delicate hand perched on my shoulder as though ready to catch me should I faint again. We passed through the mudroom into a kitchen big enough to double as a ballroom.

"Are you hungry, sweetheart?" Mom asked.

Of course I wasn't. The idea of food made me sick to my stomach, but I knew what'd I get if I refused. I'd get that look from Dad, as if he were saying "Of course you're hungry, but you think you have to say you're not so you can keep up appearances for your mom."

In a strange way, I could take it as a compliment that my dad thinks I'm far more crafty and clever than I really am, that I can think ten moves ahead like a chess player just to keep everyone fooled.

I compromised and agreed to a cup of Mom's chicken soup, the only thing I could stomach these days. Even though I had agreed to some food, I could tell my dad wasn't really convinced I wanted to eat. He knew that after I finished slurping unenthusiastically at the broth, I would send a pile of carrots and chicken down the disposal. It was as though he knew I was doing it to appease him, so he'd think I wasn't playing any games — which, of course, is a game.

While waiting for the soup, I got my phone and checked out the Likes on a "get well soon" Instagram post that Addy had made, alerting the world that, once again, Meghan Gerard had been in the hospital. I noticed the Likes weren't as many as when I first got sick. Same as my father, social media had a limit as to how long it would care.

"Need anything?" Dad said before kissing the top of my head.

Yes! I wanted to scream. *I need you to pull me into your arms and tell me everything is going to be all right. I need your reassurance that someday soon, I'll be able to kick a soccer ball around and not feel the ground drop out from under my feet. I need your love and unconditional support. But, most of all, I need you to believe me.*

Those were my thoughts, but the only words I managed were: "No thanks, I'm fine."

"I'm going to go to bed, then," my dad said, giving me that look again.

As an objective observer, I got his problem. After all this time, there should have been some kind of diagnosis to explain my headaches, muscle weakness, heart palpitations, weight loss, my trouble concentrating, my general malaise — a word my mom uses with pretty much every doctor we see. I should be bedridden in a hospital, but I'm not sick enough to even get admitted. I'm not sick in any measurable way that he could understand. My dad thought if it could be measured, then it could be cut into a recognizable shape, and then, and only then, could it be put into its proper place. But my blood work was fine. My labs were fine. My vitals were fine. Everything about me was fine. But even though my tests said that I was fine, they couldn't tell how I was actually feeling.

Nobody but me could feel what was happening inside my body when my arms and legs went tingly while kicking around a soccer ball. My dad wasn't looking out of my eyes when I saw sunshine one second, blackness the next. But he could judge me based on those damn numbers, those stupid test results. He thought I was trying to get attention, or make my mom happy, or whatever. That's the vibe I got from him. That's the look he gave me. It wasn't disappointment. It was a look of disbelief. He thought my biggest secret was that I was faking it. But we both knew that wasn't true.

My biggest secret was that I knew his.

CHAPTER 5

Becky

Two days after she brought Meghan home from the hospital, Becky was back in her tidy office that could have been a bedroom for another child if only Carl had gotten his wish. He had been open and honest about his desire to have more children, never fully accepting Becky's insistence that Meghan would be the only one.

More children meant more chances of something going wrong, because when you lose a child, no matter the circumstances, every day comes with potential new dangers. Playgrounds cause tetanus. Toys are choking hazards. Pets carry disease. A cough portends the flu. A stomachache signals salmonella. Becky feared life's mishaps and disasters like a child afraid of the dark.

Nobody in Becky's current orbit knew of Sammy. She never talked of him to her friends. They had moved to Concord when

Meghan was still an infant. They bought a quaint colonial, intentionally not sharing their forwarding address or new contact information with former friends and neighbors.

Carl had even changed the name of his business from Gerard Construction to C. G. Home Remodeling to make it more difficult to track them down. Some friends of Carl's remained in the picture, but for Becky, being a transplant from California had made it easy to create an entirely new life for herself.

The years had gone by in a blur, the small colonial regularly upgraded to bigger, better homes as fortunes improved, but time and distance could not erase the dark and painful memory.

Becky had her therapist and her Xanax, but mostly she had her quiet desperation, a gnawing fear that any day could be the day tragedy visited her again. Becky had tried to continue her real estate venture after Meghan was born, but separation anxiety made it impossible to do the job. She felt silent judgment from other stay-at-home moms who had more kids to juggle, but chances were they'd never set foot inside an eerily quiet nursery or experienced that dreadful knowing.

Becky heard a knock at the door. She spun around in her chair to see Holly in the doorway, a thick file folder of papers in her hand. Holly was petite and fit with straight, dark hair like her twin girls, Addy and Danielle. Becky had never been particularly close to Holly until they'd found common ground in the world of difficult-to-diagnose disease. She'd often complained how it had taken more than a year for doctors to figure out that Addy had Lyme, but at least she got a diagnosis.

"Carl saw me coming up the driveway," Holly said, "so he let me in. I only have a minute, but I wanted to drop off the folder in person."

The two women exchanged a quick hug before Becky took Holly's research on Lyme. She thumbed through the contents cursorily.

"Thank you so much," Becky said. "I'll go through this more carefully later."

Pressed up against a wall near Becky's desk stood two large metal file cabinets filled with research on various diseases. Eventually, Holly's folder would find a home in one of those drawers.

"Do you want some wine?" Becky asked.

She probably should have been embarrassed that the bottle was in her office and not the kitchen, but she'd long moved past the give-a-crap stage.

"No, thank you," Holly said. "I can't stay. I've got to take Sarah to soccer."

Sarah was Holly's eldest of her three. She and Meghan used to be good friends as well, but less so since Meghan got sick.

"Any chance Meghan will play next season?" Holly said pleadingly. "The team just isn't the same without her. They only won a handful of games."

"No. Definitely no more soccer, at least not until we figure out what's going on with her," Becky said a bit more forcefully than intended. "We can't risk it."

"Have the doctors come up with anything?" Holly sounded exasperated for her.

"We still don't know," Becky said with a sigh.

Becky was grateful for Holly's help, but now that she had the file folder, there was not much more to say. She had little in common with friends in town anymore — the women with whom she'd once shared chaperone duties, planned birthday parties, attended soccer games, jewelry parties, movie nights, and a host of other experiences that had bound her to them. Their kids were healthy; even Addy had been cured of Lyme. Those kids still played soccer, or did whatever, and Becky often felt the only thing she had in common with her former cohorts was a zip code.

Meghan's illness had dramatically altered the current of their lives. She could no longer care about who made what team, who got how much playing time, what teacher was being unfair, which kid was smoking weed, who was dating whom, or what colleges were on someone's radar.

None of that mattered to Becky anymore. As she had drifted away from those concerns, her local friends had drifted away from her. It had been different in year one of Meghan's still-undetermined illness. Back then, there'd been a flurry of activity surrounding Becky when her daughter became strangely fatigued, started missing school, showed signs of declining skills on the soccer field. The symptoms were insidious and pervasive: muscle weakness followed by an inexplicable decline in motor skills, persistent headaches, exhaustion that weighed her down like an anchor, transforming Meghan from a vibrant kid into one with hardly any vitality at all.

Becky had gone into power mode at home, researching cures for various diseases from mainstream approaches to alternative medicine with a frenzy. Meanwhile, in

Becky's eyes, Meghan's symptoms had worsened, shape-shifted, but stayed vague enough to make it impossible for doctors to pin down. She reached out to friends as each new crisis arose, and they responded with care and concern, along with meals, but the illness dragged on. There comes a time when a person can no longer devote such energy to another's plight. Like her mother's longtime battle with cancer, there comes a time when you just want the pain to be over and done with.

At first, Becky was hurt when the phone calls, pop-over visits, thoughtful notes, and check-ins slowed down before stopping almost entirely. But that resentment did not consume her. Becky could not climb aboard the self-pity train when she had so much to do for Meghan.

Becky's cell phone rang. She glanced at the number and grimaced. It was her sister, Sabrina, calling from California, probably with news of their mother. Becky wondered if her mother had died, if the cancer had at long last run its full course.

She wondered how much she'd care if it had.

CHAPTER 6

Holly departed with a wave goodbye and a pantomimed promise to call. Becky pressed the talk button on her cell phone after swallowing down a generous, get-up-for-it gulp of wine.

"Hi, Sabrina," Becky said. "Is it Mom? Is she gone?" Becky dug her fingers into her leg, awaiting news.

"She's hanging on," Sabrina said.

Becky's tension released. She could put off her conflicted feelings for at least another day.

"The hospice nurse thinks it could be a few weeks, may be longer" continued Sabrina, "but the doctor is giving her a lot less time. It's hard to tell. Her heart rate is elevated, which means her body is working extra hard to keep her alive."

For what? Becky thought. Her mother's life had been a tortured one. Their father had died young, leaving Cora to raise two daughters on a minimum wage job. Their home was dirty — squalid being a more apt description. Becky was that girl, the gorgeous blond who'd come from nothing, the one that some sharp-eyed talent scout might have picked out from behind the diner counter if only she'd been so fortunate.

"Are you coming home?"

Home. Becky wanted to laugh.

"I can't," she said.

"Can't, or won't?" Sabrina asked.

"It's Meghan. She's not well."

Silence, and then, "How's your newfound fame?"

Of course, Sabrina was referring to the airplane incident. She knew better than to question her about Meghan. That conversation had not gone well the last time she'd tried.

"You don't even get fifteen minutes in this day and age," Becky said, sounding a grateful note. "How long do *you* think she has?"

"I can't help you there, Becky." The way Sabrina said it made Becky think she was talking about a lot more than just their mother.

"I feel torn, you know — Meghan."

"Yeah, Meghan. Always Meghan. We all have choices to make," said Sabrina.

"Not all of us," Becky answered, her anger

64

rising. "Not me, or you, for that matter. Cora didn't give us much of a choice, did she?"

"I understand your feelings, but that was a long time ago. I've moved on. You should do the same."

"It's not that easy for me."

Becky hated Sabrina's uncanny ability to make her feel like the little sister again.

"Some regrets last a lifetime. Our mother is going to die, and if you don't fly out here, you'll never get the chance to say what you want to say."

Damn. Why did she tell Sabrina of her intention to make "I forgive you, please forgive me" the final words she'd speak to their mother?

"Now just isn't a good time," Becky said. "We have follow-up appointments with the cardiologist and neurologist this week."

There was a heavy sigh from Sabrina's end, a loud "I don't want to walk this road again" kind of sound.

"There's always a follow-up appointment," Sabrina said.

"This time it's different," Becky said, knowing in her gut that it was not different at all.

"Look, I've got to go," said Sabrina. "I'll keep you posted on Mom. Let me know your plans when you make them."

"Okay. Bye."

Becky heard only the click.

Her sister's call had soured her already dismal mood. To feel better, Becky did what she did most every afternoon around this time: she went online.

She had started her Facebook group, Help for Meghan, out of desperation, back when her daughter's illness went from being a bit player in the family to the only performer in the troupe.

Unwittingly, Becky had created an online oasis of sorts — a place where like-minded people who had taken an inexplicable interest in Meghan's health, or had health troubles of their own, or just wanted a hand in solving a mystery, could gather to share, emote, and hunt for answers.

Becky took great pride in the group. Selfishly, she liked being in the center of things. As the online group broadened, so did its focus. Deep discussions spawned from posts on everything from fibromyalgia to autoimmune disorders. The number of difficult-to-diagnose diseases never seemed to end. Meghan, who was the initial focus of the group, had morphed into a new persona, coming to represent the struggles of many people who sought labels for a whole host of strange and unusual symptoms.

In no time at all, the online group Becky had founded grew from a handful of participants to hundreds. Most of the newcomers had read up on Meghan's struggles, then expressed sympathy and offered advice before pivoting the conversation to personal concerns. Becky found herself researching topics far removed from Meghan's issues so that she could share informed opinions with these strangers who had over time replaced her real friends.

In one of her prouder moments, Becky had helped a woman from Boulder self-diagnose interstitial cystitis that her doctors had initially believed to be a bladder infection. There were other success stories attributed to Help for Meghan, which Becky had since converted from a public group to a private one. It was strangers helping strangers, a collection of people who no longer cared about life's pedestrian dramas, living online with the hope that groupthink could help keep them living in real life, too.

The group shared personal dramas as well as medical ones, which was how Becky knew that certain spouses, some so-called friends, and even a few bosses believed to differing degrees that her group perpetuated sickness. These doubters accused group members of uncovering new symptoms out of fear they'd lose the ties that held them together should they or a loved one become well again. Becky encouraged her virtual friends to stay strong and ignore the naysayers — without revealing that her husband was one of them.

Picking up the glass of wine parked beside her, Becky took a long drink before she began contacting Meghan's teachers. Sophomore year had been considerably less demanding, and she anticipated gathering a daunting amount of makeup work her daughter would need for what appeared to be another missed week of school. Or maybe it would stretch into two. Since returning from the hospital, Meghan hadn't had the energy to do much more than shower and get dressed, and even those simple tasks proved overly taxing. Her daughter risked repeating the eleventh grade if she missed much more school.

Becky took another sip of wine, letting the fruity taste linger before swallowing it down. She moved from corresponding with Meghan's teachers to trading Facebook messages with Veronica Del Mar, a friend from St. Petersburg, Florida, whom she'd never met in person. Veronica had a daughter near Meghan's age who was still awaiting a diagnosis for her chronic gastrointestinal issues. Becky recapped the latest episode with Meghan for Veronica's benefit, typing out in Facebook's Messenger application her terrifying ordeal at the airport and Carl's mounting frustrations with her, Meghan, and the whole damn situation.

VERONICA: They're always frustrated. They don't get us. It's not in their DNA.

BECKY: I'd like to think other fathers wouldn't give up so quickly on their daughters.

VERONICA: Two years is hardly quick.

BECKY: True.

VERONICA: Are you in couple's therapy?? Might need it. I didn't do it and regret it (sort of) . . . It's actually been easier since Don moved out. At least he's not questioning everything I do for Ashley.

Becky knew Don only from Veronica's Facebook pictures. When Don stopped appearing in her albums, Becky got an inkling something was up. Sure enough, Veronica soon posted a status announcing the end of her decades-long marriage. What people did not understand (but those like Becky and Veronica knew all too well) was that chronic diseases spread viruslike to other members of the family, leading to a different sort of sickness.

BECKY: Any new news for Ashley?

VERONICA: No. Treatment options turning into a friggin' "Choose Your Own Adventure" book. "If you want to try neural stem cell transplantation, go to page 61. If you want to opt for another course of intensive antibiotics, turn to page 81." Nobody knows, and Ashley is bad as ever.

BECKY: I'm so so sorry.

She tagged her message with a series of sad-face emojis and prayer hands that seemed a bit tacky given the gravity of Ashley's illness, but to this crowd, it represented a proper expression of her feelings. A ding sounded Veronica's reply, but Becky's attention had drifted to the door of her office, where Carl had appeared holding a tumbler of whiskey in his hand. An avid athlete and all-around thrill seeker, Carl seldom took to drinking, but Becky had noticed a subtle shift as the occasional cocktail became a nightly nightcap, then two.

"Hey, babe. Whatcha doing?" He knew exactly what she was doing, but for some reason, tonight, he did not seem irritated.

"I'm chatting with Veronica."

Carl had come to know Becky's virtual friends with a familiarity usually reserved for people he'd run into at the supermarket.

"Any news for Ashley?" Carl knew the kids' names, too.

"No, nothing," Becky said, resisting the urge to glance at Veronica's last message. Carl had not shown her much attention lately, and it was so surprising and refreshing to receive even a little bit that she did not want to break the spell.

Despite all their recent struggles, the ups and downs typical of any marriage compounded by two volcanic upheavals in their lives, Becky still found her husband to be incredibly attractive. He had on a faded T-shirt that showed off muscles honed on the mountain bike, not in the gym. His jeans had a small hole in the knee, but they remained his favorite pair, comfy like well-worn pajamas. He was barefoot. His wavy hair may have lost some of its body but, unlike Becky, Carl did not bother trying to hide the gray. Carl's jawline was once cut like a piece of polished granite, but had eroded with the years. Even though his smoldering dark eyes had grown lines like hers, and his abs no longer drew glances at the beach, Becky had no trouble seeing the younger man who had captured her heart.

He strode over to her desk and put a hand on Becky's shoulder. His touch sent a shiver through her body. They had sex with the frequency of an eclipse, and fumbled through intimacy as though it were a forgotten college course, but there was tenderness in Carl's touch; she did not just imagine it.

"Listen, babe; I owe you an apology."

Carl knelt beside Becky, evoking a memory of the last time he'd been down on one knee, a diamond in a jewel box and hope in his eyes. She was new to her real estate venture back then; lucky to have one of Carl's homes as her first listing.

"I'm sorry," Carl said.

The apology took Becky by surprise. Usually those were her words, not his. *I'm sorry not to give you the attention you crave, or cook for you, or clean, or make love, or be any fun at all, or do any of the things I used to do. I'm sorry I'm not any of that anymore.*

"I've been unfair," he said, his voice raspy

from drink. "I've judged you, harshly at times, over Meghan, for thinking that you're the reason she can't get well."

This was not exactly breaking news. Carl had made his position clear. If Becky just backed off, pushed Meghan a bit harder, did not hover and worry so much, stopped trying all sorts of new treatments and doctors, their daughter would eventually get well.

At first, he'd been a champion runner, going stride for stride with Becky as they chased down answers. But as the pace and length of this particular race endured, Carl's stamina faded and eventually gave out. *Now he's apologizing? Why?* He had good reason to doubt her — Becky had plenty of experience faking an illness. Her mother was an expert at it, using deception to get her disability benefits. Cora's face flashed in Becky's mind, but faded as she focused on Carl.

"I've left you alone in this fight, and that's not fair. So for the past few weeks, I've been online myself, doing a lot of research, looking for solutions, and I think I may have found one."

"How?" Becky found it difficult to believe Carl had discovered a rock she'd yet to turn over.

"We've seen a dozen doctors at least, but all of them have focused on their specialty," Carl said. "So if they don't see her issues fitting into their respective boxes, they can't see the problem properly. I just focused on the symptoms."

Becky almost laughed. She had been living with Meghan's health crisis for years. Did Carl think she hadn't already plugged their daughter's symptoms into Google, hadn't scoured WebMD, didn't have a warrior army of virtual friends doing the same elsewhere on her behalf?

"You don't think I've done that?" she asked, trying not to sound too annoyed.

"Well, I didn't get anywhere. If anything, it made me appreciate what you're going through. The internet is pretty overwhelming.

"So, I reached out to a doctor friend of mine whose home I renovated. He thinks outside his specialty, and wondered if it could be mitochondrial disease."

Becky squinted, as if that would squeeze out a bit of recognition. For all her scouring and searching, Carl *had* managed to dig up a disease that was entirely new to her.

"It's more commonly called 'mito,' and it's very difficult to diagnose because it affects each person differently."

"What is it?" Becky asked.

Turning back to her computer, Becky googled the disease, and quickly found the answer to her question.

Mitochondrial diseases represented failures of the mitochondria, which are found in every cell and create the energy needed to support organ function. When there is a mitochondrial deficiency, there's less energy in the cell, which causes cells to function incorrectly, even die.

Becky had learned enough medicine to infer what a system meltdown like that could mean for Meghan. It would cause a host of symptoms, depending on how much energy was being depleted from the cells. With so many bodily systems potentially affected, it was easy to see how so many specialists had failed to connect the dots.

"I've found a doctor who specializes in this disease that might be able to help us," Carl said. "He works at White Memorial in Boston."

Becky was elated.

They had a new doctor to try.

CHAPTER 7

Zach

The sunshine was bright. Overhead, the cloudless sky was a special hue of cobalt. The air held no humidity. A gentle breeze rustled the leaves of the trees in the verdant park where Dr. Zachary Fisher sat on a bench with his son, William, at his side.

William scraped the final remnants of his chocolate ice cream from a cup into his mouth. Zach could see big changes in his only child. With each passing day, he was becoming more capable, more independent, and that much closer to moving on with his life.

Zach slid his arm around the back of the bench, but soon enough it was around his boy's shoulders. William slid over, not too old to snuggle up against his father, still working at that ice cream.

"How's the knee?"

William extended and retracted his leg

with ease. A few hours ago, that would not have been so easy. Baseballs don't hurt dirt, but they sure can do a number on a knee-cap. There were plenty of tears at first, but after an inning on the bench, William was back on the field playing the game he loved. And Zach loved him — his boy, his son, the person who shaped his life and gave it meaning.

Zach had never spent much time with his dad, who owned a hardware store that only partially covered the bills. To manage the income gap, Zach's father moonlighted as a home inspector, leaving little time for family but plenty of angst as he incessantly pinched pennies. Early in life, Zach had vowed to pick a career that paid well and afforded him plenty of time with his future family.

His choice to follow his heart and not his head into pediatrics — knowing full well the low pay and high demands on his time — had the full-circle inevitability of a Shakespearean prophecy. Zach found himself scraping by as more and more of his money went to insurance companies and taking extra shifts at the hospital to cover the bills. A few years back, Zach ran a semi-successful private practice, but he'd closed it down when it became more economical to take a full-time job at White Memorial in Boston.

Stacy's income as a teacher was a good supplement, but college was looming, only seven years out, and the 529 plan Zach had intended to infuse with cash would buy half a semester of classes and maybe a few pizzas. Will was a fine baseball player, but the prospects of a scholarship were somewhere on the scale of slim to none.

The sun beat down on their faces, and Zach thought he should apply sunscreen, anticipating Stacy's questions should Will return home redder than when he left. Even though Zach was the doctor in the family, it was Stacy who paid the closest attention to their son's health. She was the one who told Zach that something was wrong with Will. It wasn't like Zach didn't want to hear it. He was a pediatrician, after all.

Zach saw sick kids all the time. He saw terrible diseases — cancers in children, cystic fibrosis, congenital heart disease, type 1 diabetes, and so many others. His son wasn't sick like those kids. He had some stomach pains, which of course was normal for an already nervous kid about to start middle school.

Instead of telling his wife she was being unnecessarily anxious, Zach had another doctor look at Will, because everyone knows a parent shouldn't treat his or her own child. A parent knows the patient too well; knows the little tricks they might employ to get out of some obligation, such as school. A parent would be the first to say an upset stomach was just a case of the nerves. Besides, Stacy would never believe Zach if he told her that nothing was wrong with William. She'd think his need to be right had blinded him to the possibility that he could be wrong.

When Will's doctor could not find anything medically amiss, Zach figured that would be the end of it, but no. Stacy wasn't near done. She was certain Will's ongoing stomach pains were symptomatic of something dire. The medical websites she visited and the mommy blogs she scoured gave her plenty to worry about.

Long before that ground ball had met up with Will's kneecap, Stacy had begun to point out subtle declines in their son's motor skills. Perhaps she had gotten Zach thinking. Maybe that's why he found himself reliving that play in his head, trying to decide if the Will from last year would have gotten his glove down in time to dig out that grounder. Ultimately, Zach decided Stacy was wrong to be so worried.

"What are we going to do now?" Will looked up at his dad with a sweetly earnest expression. Zach's heart swelled. His love for his son anchored him, though lately, he could feel a tug on the line as Will began to pull away. It was subtle, all normal, minor steps toward independence. There'd be times here or there when Will would rather read alone at night. Or there was the day when Will insisted on making mac and cheese himself, and the first time he rode shotgun. Those moments were gentle reminders that Zach's time with Will, his time as the guiding force in his boy's life, would soon come to an end.

Zach wanted so desperately to maximize each opportunity that he sometimes put too much pressure on himself to come up with the perfect father–son activities. So what to do today? They could go ride go-karts, but that was a drive. Maybe they'd take a stroll through the Sculpture Park at the DeCordova Museum, but Zach anticipated the groans and complaints, and today — maybe more so because of that injured knee, or maybe because he felt the fingers of time tapping on his shoulder, or maybe because Stacy had him a bit more worried about Will's health than he cared to admit — he wanted his boy to be completely satisfied with whatever choice they made.

"What do you want to do?" Zach asked, putting it back on Will.

Will gave it some thought while Zach studied his son. He could see traces of himself in the round shape of Will's eyes and the fullness of his lips, but overall, Will looked far more like Stacy's son. He was a fair-skinned boy with wispy blond hair. Zach's complexion was much darker, almost swarthy, and his hair was dark as well, fuller and wavy and with more body than Will's. If Zach failed to shave for a day, he'd sprout a face full of stubble. Two days and he'd turn into a Chia Pet. While Zach had a round face and dark eyes, Will was blessed with Stacy's more fragile bone structure and a far sweeter-looking face, perfectly conjoined with his nature.

Will took his time to answer, and when he did, his request somewhat surprised Zach. "I just want to go home and hang out," he said. "Maybe we can watch a movie or something."

Zach smiled and ruffled his son's hair. "Fair enough," he said, and together they rose.

Being the conscientious child he was, the kind of kid who volunteered for community road-litter pickup, Will tossed his used ice cream cup into the trash basket, took two steps, and then doubled over in pain. Zach let out a gasp and rushed to his son's side. Will righted himself. Fear boiled in Zach's gut. In a blink, his son's coloring had gone from pale to ash, almost gray. The sclera of Will's eyes were bloodred.

"Dad, what's wrong with me?"

Zach's blood thrummed in his ears. He reached for his phone to call 911, but his movements felt languid, oddly constrained, as though he were pushing through molasses.

"Dad . . . help me . . ."

To Zach's horror and utter bewilderment, Will's skin continued to darken. Zach tried to move, to reach his son, pull him to the ground, shield him from this horror, but he was paralyzed. He did not understand why his arms were immobilized. His legs, too, felt encased in cement and could not move. The scream rising in his throat refused to come out.

Will reached for his father. The gray of his face, ever deeper, made his red eyes that much more pronounced. His son's stone-colored fingers were fully outstretched, but he could no longer move them, could not close the short distance that separated him from Zach. It was no use. Hard as Zach strained against whatever invisible force held him in place, overpowering him, he could not move a muscle.

Bits of skin flaked off Will's face and became a fine coating of dust that fell at his feet like gray snow. Zach searched the park for help, but no one was in sight. *Were we alone this entire time?* Zach could not remember. He did not even remember going from the baseball field to the park. It was as though they had just appeared there. Where did he buy that ice cream? What was happening to them?

"Goodbye, Daddy . . . I love you . . . love you . . ."

Will's voice sounded like a faint whisper in his ear. Zach tried to move, tried to snap whatever spell held him hostage, but it was no use. The force that kept him paralyzed was too strong to break. Will's gray face was now covered in strange cracks, his skin brittle like charred paper. *What's happening to him?* Whatever it was — some kind of virus, more like a plague — it had overtaken his son.

"Will . . . Will . . . Will . . ."

Zach stretched until he felt his arm snapping, tendons and ligaments approaching the breaking point. Little by little, the cracks in Will's face began to fade, but the horrifying gray coloring remained. To Zach, Will looked as though he were made entirely of ash, as though someone had gathered up the remnants of a firepit and molded it into the shape of his son's beautiful face. Will's neck, his arms and legs, were made of this mysterious substance. Under his clothes, Zach assumed his boy was nothing but ash, like gray flour.

A strong gust of wind blew from the south hard enough to cause the leaves to show their underside. *No!* thought Zach. *I'm not ready to say goodbye!* The wind blew through Zach's hair, ruffling it like the leaves. But as the wind hit Will, it blew him apart. His head was now a billowing cloud of dust; his body an empty shirt and pants that briefly stayed suspended in the air before becoming a heap of fabric on the ground.

Finally, at last, Zach found his scream. It came out as a loud and mournful wail.

His eyes opened wide.

Zach was bathed in sweat, staring up at the ceiling. It took a moment to get oriented, and when he did, a stab of pain hit him as though someone had plunged a knife into his chest. He was at home, in his apartment on Stuart Street in Boston. Stacy was his ex-wife. Will was dead, gone five years now. He had had the nightmare again; the one his shrink had said was caused by guilt that he had not taken Stacy's worries to heart, not acted sooner.

"I'm the gust of wind," Zach once told his shrink as they tried to understand the dream that always began in the park and ended with Will turning into nothing. "I'm the wind that blew him away."

"You couldn't have known," his doctor had said. "And besides, from what you've told me, you couldn't have helped."

It was true, in fact. Zach could not have saved Will. There was no cure for what Will had back then, and there wasn't a cure now. But doctors often see themselves as all-powerful beings, like lifesaving magicians. Intellectually, Zach knew there was little to nothing he could have done to prevent Will's death, even if he had listened to Stacy, pushed harder for a diagnosis and treatment. Emotionally, he took the blame nonetheless. In Zach's mind, it came down to the simple fact that he was the doctor. It was his job to save lives and, in that regard, he had failed his son. For that failure alone, he would dream of ash.

Zach climbed out of bed and stretched his creaky limbs. In the years since Will's death, Zach had gone from a house to a studio apartment. From his bedroom, he could see into the kitchen, where an automatic coffee-maker had already brewed a pot while Zach was having his heart ripped out — again.

Checking the time on his phone, Zach computed that he had two hours to shower, shave, and get to work. There'd be no breakfast today; probably no food at all. He could never eat on the days when he had the dream. Rubbing his eyes, Zach thought about his workday, something to take his mind off the pain of memory. He reviewed his schedule in his head. A new patient was coming to the office, a girl who might need his help, another chance at a small piece of redemption.

Her name was Meghan Gerard. And if the parents were right, if Zach was her best hope, then poor Meghan was indeed a very, very sick girl.

CHAPTER 8

Meghan

Back at the doctor's office. Again. Lord help me. This was a new doctor, which wasn't a shocker for me. I get new doctors the way other kids get sneakers. His name is Dr. Zach Fisher, and he was handsome in that TV dad kind of way. He seemed nice enough, but there was something about him I couldn't quite put my finger on. He was sort of sad, and I was curious why.

I was more anxious with him than with most new doctors, and I thought I knew the reason. Dr. Fisher was someone that my dad had found, not Mom, which, in all honesty, completely blew me away. My father doesn't try to come up with answers, because he's already made up his mind that my sickness is all in my head, put there by ideas Mom planted like I'm a garden she's tending. Or so I thought.

To my amazement, Dad thought I might

have some rare disease. I say "rare," but I don't know how many people actually have it. I didn't bother to read about it, because every time I research something new, I'm told that it's not what I have, and we have to keep looking. I get attached to my prospective diseases the way I might a boyfriend, and when they're gone I feel a little let down in that back-to-square-one kind of way. So I'm guarded, not diving into any details, not trying to answer any questions but one: Why did my father suddenly think I might actually be sick?

"Tell me how your symptoms began," the doctor asked.

By this point, Dr. Fisher had already taken my vitals, felt around my body, my throat, my glands — not in a creepy way; in a doctor way. I swear I could have done the job for him. I've had it done to me enough times that I have the moves down.

I was wearing a dumb gown — a "johnny," some call it — which had become my sundress these days. If I took off the gown, the doctor would see my breasts that had gotten smaller and count too many exposed ribs. I could guess he was worried I don't weigh what I should. I bet he was thinking *eating disorder,* but he'd be wrong. I don't have a body image problem. I wasn't trying to look like those magazine models with raccoon eyes and pipe-cleaner builds. I had an appetite that had decided to go on holiday for reasons yet unknown. But if the doctor needed to see me naked, I'd let him, and I wouldn't care. That's one benefit of getting poked and prodded by so many strangers. Your body becomes property to be passed around; you become immune to touch.

I told Dr. Fisher about the first time I felt off, which is how I've come to think of my condition. Not "sick," but "off." I told him how I never felt deathly ill, but I knew something was very wrong with me. It started at school, I said, when I got my first headache, that's when the first switch got flipped.

"No, it wasn't then, sweetheart," my mother corrected me. "You had a piano lesson, remember? And you had to stop early because your head hurt too much."

That's right, I thought. *That's when it happened. That lesson was the start of my slow decline.* And then I thought: *How does she know more about my sickness than I do?* I hate to admit it, but it's moments like these when I have doubts about what's going on inside me. Am I sick, or do I just think I am?

Dad said, "She started to have joint pain

soon after, not really severe or anything. More like a nagging, dull ache, wouldn't you say?"

Yes, of course you'd diminish it, I thought, not looking him in the eyes. *But then again, you diminish everything, don't you. Even us.*

"Yeah, that's right," I said while I turned to my mother, as if I couldn't answer without her approval.

"And the joint pain, what was that like for you?"

There was a catch in the doctor's throat, like he got choked up or something, and again I thought of his sadness. It radiated off him like body heat. I was in a typical exam room, not in his private office, so there were no personal effects I could study that might offer clues about his past. I wondered if his whole family was killed in a plane crash. That's the first thought that came to me, and I briefly contemplated the possibility I might be psychic. Maybe he was the sole survivor of this terrible tragedy I'd invented, and I remind him of the daughter he lost. It helped me to imagine other people suffering more than I was. It put things into proper perspective. It reminded me that it could be worse. It could always be worse.

The doctor looked at me funny again,

waiting for me to answer. It wasn't creepy, the way he studied me. It wasn't *that* kind of look. More like he was remembering something, and I'm a reminder of that something for him. I got the sense he wanted those reminders, too, but at the same time, he didn't. It made me think of a boy from school who I had a crush on. Every now and again, I'd catch him staring at me, but he'd always turn away, as if it were okay to admire me from afar, but any real contact between us would overwhelm him. The doctor's looks are sort of the same, but not in a boy-likes-girl kind of way. It's more like I'm overwhelming for him, though for the life of me, I can't imagine why. I settle on my plane-crash scenario and move on. Then I remembered the question about my joint pain, and I tried to think how best to answer.

"It felt like, um . . . like my joints were stiffening."

Oh great, Meghan, I scolded myself. *That's soooooo helpful. That's going to tell him soooooo much.* Part of the problem was that I didn't exactly know what to say anymore. Should I tell Dr. Fisher about how lethargic I've become? How I've lost interest in my friends? My life? I know I'm too young to be going through the motions, but I can't seem to help myself. Nothing holds much interest or appeal for me these days.

I've stopped playing piano. Stopped soccer. I used to love school, never complained about homework, or reading, or even math, which was far from my best subject. I just did the work happily. I had my friends. We talked about boys and teachers, and gossiped the way most girls do. I went to parties and attended school and sporting events and whatnot. I watched whatever shows on Netflix everyone was watching. I posted pictures to Instagram that made me look cool, or pretty, or even better, both. All of that was gone now.

I couldn't concentrate for shit. I didn't care about school anymore, or my friends, or Instagram, for that matter. I wasn't depressed, or sad, or melancholy. I didn't feel like cutting my wrists or legs like some friends of mine did. I wasn't suicidal either. I wanted to live, but I was shutting down. That's the best way to describe how I felt. Meghan Off! It was like switches were flipping inside my body. Instead of running full speed, I was coming to a grinding halt. I didn't want to overshare in front of my parents, so I told the doctor some of this, but not all of it, just enough to give him the impression that I felt utterly, strangely depleted.

"I might start homeschooling Meghan," my mom announced, like that's at all relevant.

I managed to keep myself from rolling my eyes. I don't know if she'd already compiled a full dossier on his life, but I appreciated that my mom wasn't touching this doctor's arms, gazing into his eyes, priming the pump, so to speak, so she can milk him later. For that bit of restraint, I offered a bit of my own.

"She's missed so much classroom time," Mom continued. "I don't think it's going to work out this year."

I saw Dr. Fisher glance at my mother, his eyes lingering maybe a beat too long. I didn't fault him for it. I'd look, too. My mom is gorgeous. She's one of the most beautiful people in the world. Strangers are always checking her out, and before I got sick, some would ask if we were sisters, which always made us both blush before we laughed.

My mom means the world to me, and I wouldn't care if she were ugly as a troll. She's my advocate, my rock, my best friend. I do what she says, and I trust her completely, certainly a lot more than I trust my dad. The fact that he's the one who suggested we see this doctor is probably the reason I'm so guarded, but there's another consideration as well — the tests. Because I don't understand my new disease, I don't know what procedures this doctor might want to perform.

I can't say when it happened, but at some point over the last few years, I've developed an inexplicable, deep-seated fear of needles. You might think it's about the sting; the prickling worry that crops up whenever I hear the fair warning, "You're going to feel a little pinch." Swab on a numbing agent, have me look away, and that should be the end of it. But, no, it's not the end, not by a long shot. There are words for what I have — I know because I've looked them up online. Aichmophobia. Belonephobia. Enetophobia. They sound like rare jungle diseases to me — but, nope, they are morbid fears of sharp things like pencils, even a pointed finger. What happens when you put a needle near me? I feel like I can't breathe. I start to shake like I'm possessed. I'm overcome with an inexplicable feeling of dread. I sweat. I feel like my throat is filling with sand. I can't speak.

It wasn't like this when I was a kid. Sure, I hated shots. I'd throw fits. Produce tears at the mere mention of them. But I didn't feel like I was dying. Imagine someone holding up a sharp object to your eyeball, moving it closer and closer, forcing your eyelids open, making you watch it advance, while you buck and thrash against straps holding you down, and then you'd start to understand how needles make me feel.

We've tried hypnosis, medication, all sorts of tricks, but none of it has worked. Needles are my biggest nightmare, and if this doctor wants more than a vial of blood from me, he's going to have to put me under to get it.

For the next half hour, we talked about my symptoms and all that good stuff. Dr. Fisher listened attentively. I liked him — a lot, actually. He seemed to care, and that made me feel strangely sad. I imagined what it would feel like if my dad looked at me the way Dr. Fisher did, with sympathy and deep concern instead of judgment. I should just say it, put it out in the open, tell everyone what's really going on here. But I stopped myself. I always stop myself. There were enough problems as it was.

"I'm going to be honest," Dr. Fisher said after we'd finished playing everyone's favorite game: What's the Matter with Meghan? There were no more symptoms to review, or issues to discuss, no more *medical* secrets to reveal. "I think you were right to bring Meghan to see me. From what you've described, I'm concerned that she does have mitochondrial disease." My mom covered her mouth with her hands, but I still heard the gasp. "The challenge is going to be proving it."

My dad leaned forward in his chair, eyes boring into Dr. Fisher's. "Why? Can't you just run a test?"

"With mitochondrial disease, testing can be tricky," Dr. Fisher said. "We can do some blood work, but I'd recommend a muscle biopsy."

"What's that?" my mother asked while I was thinking the same.

"It's a surgical procedure where we take a small piece of muscle, usually the size of the end of a little finger, from the upper thigh to test whether or not Meghan's body is producing enough energy for normal function. Recovery is quick, though Meghan will have a scar a few inches long. We'll be able to give a local anesthetic, but for the procedure to work, she'd have to be awake."

From a cabinet in his office, Dr. Fisher produced a needle unlike any I'd ever seen before. It was as long as my forearm, with two plastic loops at the handle where his fingers would go. To my eyes, the needle looked like a machete. Before Dr. Fisher could say anything more, before he could explain the procedure in more detail, or how he'd use that needle on me, I jumped off the table and raced out of the exam room as fast as my weakened legs could carry me.

CHAPTER 9

Zach

Zach awoke at five o'clock that morning, his usual time, grateful not to have had the dream. Thin at forty-two, he proceeded through a series of body-weight exercises — push-ups, sit-ups, several types of planks, various stretches — working long enough and hard enough to get a good sweat going. He showered, shaved, and thought of Stacy. Images of her came to him often, but they always caught him by surprise. The most he had heard from his ex-wife in the past two years was when she would Like something he shared on Facebook, which he seldom did.

Zach found social media a necessary evil — a way to keep in touch with friends and family who would call more often if they did not get updates on his life in some other way. It was not like Zach was avoiding people, but everyone, every single person in his life, was a reminder of Will, and all of it hurt. Going to his parents' retirement home in Florida was like visiting a shrine to their grandson. Framed photographs of Will were displayed proudly on walls and mantels throughout the beachfront condo.

There were two days each year that Zach dreaded more than any others: the day Will was born, and the day that he died. The rest of the time, Zach lived with a nagging ache. He lived like someone who had lost a limb but continued to feel a phantom sensation.

For any parent, the loss of a child was the loneliest, most desolate journey of their lives. Zach knew this all too well. He had been to grief counseling, group therapy, and even tried hypnosis to lessen his pain. He knew he should not run from the reminders of his son, but embrace them, speak his boy's name proudly and often.

"Let his memory be a blessing," a rabbi whose son Zach had treated for mumps told him once.

But Zach could not bring himself to be that person. He existed perpetually in a gray zone, where every day was a struggle for happiness, where guilt grew like bacteria in a petri dish. To make amends, Zach had dedicated himself to finding a cure for the disease that had claimed his son, while doing his best to ensure quality years for those living with the condition.

This was his hope for Meghan Gerard. He was anxious to get to the hospital because pathology should have the results from her blood work and genetic testing. He was confident those results would confirm his belief that she had mito. He wished he could have done an EMG on her, a measurement of electrical muscle response to nerve stimulation, or a muscle biopsy, but the girl's needle phobia forced him to rely on less-invasive diagnostic tests.

He had brought up the idea of conscious sedation — a combination of medicines to help with relaxation and anxiety, but Meghan was not ready to go there yet.

"These medications will help you to relax," Zach had said to a teary-eyed Meghan as they discussed the more invasive procedures in-depth. "We routinely sedate kids for large laceration repairs or putting back dislocated shoulders and the sedation works wonders on patients who are as anxious about their injuries as you are about needles."

"But they're not me," Meghan answered defiantly. "And I don't care if it works for them, it won't work for me. So there's no way I'm going to let you stick me with that damn sword. No. Way."

Zach had sighed aloud, regretting having shown Meghan the Bergström needle, wishing the mother had warned him ahead of time about her daughter's fear.

The nurse who took Meghan's blood sample said she had one of the most intense needle phobias she'd ever seen, poor girl.

"Touch-and-go, hitting the vein," the nurse had relayed to Zach. "If the mother hadn't been with her, I couldn't have drawn a smiley face on that arm, let alone gotten four vials of blood."

Zach didn't need another proof point to tell him getting a muscle biopsy done on Meghan Gerard (consciously sedated or not) was going to be a protracted battle. The mother seemed burdened with guilt, and even implied responsibility for the daughter's needle phobia, and for this reason would not push Meghan to step beyond her comfort zone. Not yet anyway.

After arriving at the rear parking lot of White Memorial at a quarter to seven, early enough to secure a choice spot near the staff entrance of the main building, Zach took an elevator to the third floor. He said hello to several nurses and orderlies as he made his way to the conference room at the end of the hall. A group of young doctors was already gathered, seated around the table, sipping coffees and reviewing charts in preparation for the handoff from night shift to day shift.

This month, it was Zach's turn to serve as attending pediatrician, which meant supervising a group of eight residents and interns. He enjoyed the responsibilities of teaching. It kept him sharp. Mostly, though, he relished the looks of delight and satisfaction he could produce on the faces of this coterie of fledgling doctors simply by imparting clinical insights he had acquired over the years.

Back in his day as an intern, Zach had learned to record all his patient encounters. By the time he had finished his residency four years later, he had amassed a catalog of well over a thousand, all neatly written on three-by-five index cards and classified in diagnostic groups to serve as future reference.

It took extra time, which was in short supply given his near-seventy-hour work schedule, but the discipline was well worth it. Zach had turned himself into something of an expert researcher, which came in handy these days as he devoted most of his spare time to deciphering the secret code of a silent killer.

This morning, like all other sessions of morning report, the group reviewed admissions from the previous night. Zach oversaw his audience of young doctors, a third of them unkempt and sleepy-eyed from their ministrations to patients who had been admitted in the late-night and way-too-early-morning hours.

They discussed patient status and reviewed vitals. Zach took in all the details with practiced efficiency. He was treading on familiar ground, and for a moment at least, Meghan Gerard and the potential for yet another case of mitochondrial disease slipped into the far recesses of his mind to make room for matters more closely at hand.

When it came time for Mary Sayre, a bright third-year intern, to give her debrief, Zach could tell by the tenseness in her face that she had something significant to report. "We got the results of the tests that you requested on the Sperling baby," Dr. Sayre said.

Zach read the lab reports somberly before exhaling a weighty sigh. "I hate breaking hearts first thing in the morning, but let's start our rounds with the Sperlings," he said.

The team of doctors followed Zach down a brightly colored hallway adorned with fanciful murals, but the astringent odors, harsh lighting, and gleaming linoleum made it impossible to disguise that this was the place sick kids went to get well. At least that was the goal, each and every time. It did not always turn out that way, and Zach, and Dr. Sayre, and any resident or nurse working in pediatrics would attest to how personally they took each loss or difficult diagnosis, how deeply it hurt. On this floor, more than most, doctors and nurses openly shed their tears.

Baby Sperling's hospital room was in the neonatal intensive care unit, accessible only through secure double doors at the far end of the pediatrics floor. There were two rows of incubators occupying the wide-open space, about half of which had babies on ventilators, Baby Sperling among them. Zach checked in on the infant with the NICU nurse before making his way to a small room with a twin bed and an armchair that could recline almost flat. A pile of blankets heaped in a corner of the room indicated that the mom and dad had once again spent the night. Both parents had the beleaguered look of soldiers returning from combat.

Baby Roger Sperling had appeared healthy at birth, and his two very proud first-time parents couldn't wait to take him home. But an attentive neonatal nurse had noted that the baby was having some trouble breathing, with periods of blotching and cyanosis, a bluish tinge to the skin that signaled inadequate oxygenation of the blood. At other times, he seemed robust and healthy. When these episodes continued, it seemed prudent to intubate the infant and transfer him to the neonatal ICU.

Zach had deferred the case to an expert team of intensivists, but all were stymied. An ENT got a good examination of the infant's throat but could find no anatomical obstruction of the airway, such as laryngomalacia, in which the airway fails to develop normally. X-rays ruled out pneumonia, and fluoroscopy showed that the diaphragm appeared to work normally, helping to expand the lungs. Blood cultures were negative for infection. Extensive testing for some sort of rare metabolic disturbance turned up nothing. Baby Sperling had two CAT scans of the brain, looking for neonatal hemorrhage, stroke, or some peculiar congenital malformation.

A neurologist performed a nerve conduction test and a needle examination of the baby's muscles to see if that could explain the breathing trouble, but all was normal. A cardiologist found nothing wrong on an echocardiogram but suggested a cardiac catheterization might be necessary at some point.

Roger Sperling was, by all accounts, a very healthy-looking infant. A few weeks ago, Dr. Sayre, who was doing her rotation in the NICU, had casually probed Zach for his thoughts. Why couldn't they wean him off artificial ventilation?

The only thing Zach had noted on his examination was that the baby's pupils were unequal and not very reactive to a flashlight stimulus. Certainly nothing dramatic. But Zach knew that much of diagnosis was in the history, and he was able to get all the information he needed by asking the ICU nurse a simple question: When exactly did Baby Sperling have trouble breathing?

"The neonatal nurse told me that Roger seemed perfectly fine whenever he was awake, but he would tire easily and fall asleep," Zach explained to Baby Sperling's worried parents as they awaited his final verdict.

The mother nodded anxiously, biting at her lip, her body tense as if in anticipation of a coming car crash. Instinct must have told her that in another minute, she'd have confirmation their lives would never be the same.

"The nurse told me when he falls asleep, he begins to turn blue, which is why I ordered a special genetic test."

Zach had exceptional recall, and when the NICU nurse discussed the timing of Baby Sperling's breathing troubles, he remembered one of his index cards detailing symptoms from a genetic mutation in the PHOX2B gene.

"I'm sorry to say that Roger has what we call congenital central hypoventilation syndrome."

The parents' faces were blank. They'd never heard of the condition; no specialist had mentioned it as a possibility. Zach gave them the background.

"CCHS is extremely rare. Only had a handful of cases at White since I've been in practice," Zach said. "In these cases, the brain stem center that controls respiration fails to develop. Affected babies don't respond to rising carbon dioxide in the blood, which normally triggers breathing by acting on the brain stem respiratory center."

Zach decided to hold off on mentioning the disease's former name: Ondine's curse, which sounded even more ominous, though it was named with good reason. In German

107

mythology, Ondine was a nymph, a water goddess, who fell in love with a mortal. The mortal swore that his every breath was a demonstration of his love, but as is so often the case, he proved unfaithful. Ondine punished him by making him remember all his breaths. He was fine so long as he remained awake, but when he fell asleep, he stopped breathing and died.

Baby Sperling had the same problem. When he was awake, his brain remembered to breathe; when he slept, it did not. He would need a ventilator every time he fell asleep, and the condition was permanent; not something he'd outgrow. But the good news, which Zach shared with the shattered parents, was that Baby Sperling would be fine so long as he was awake. He'd require a tracheotomy, of course, and arrangements would need to be made for him to have a ventilator at home, as well as a backup generator. He'd need psychological counseling and social support, speech and respiratory therapy, home health visits and such. Despite his tremendous obstacles, Baby Roger would get to live a relatively normal life during all his wakeful hours. Zach made sure he emphasized that last point to the parents.

After he completed his morning rounds,

Zach was ready to call Becky Gerard. Along with the lab results for Baby Sperling, Zach had in his possession the results from Meghan Gerard's blood work and genetic testing.

The results were inconclusive.

He did not feel compelled to explain to Dr. Sayre or any of the interns the complexities of proving a case of mitochondrial disease. It was notoriously difficult, which was why the hospital CEO, Knox Singer, was beginning to tire of the number of mito cases Zach had been diagnosing of late. Every new case meant more expensive tests and treatments and new battles with insurance companies for the patient and the hospital.

"Are you sure about this case? . . . Are you sure about that one? . . . Are you sure? . . . Are you sure?" That had become Knox Singer's ongoing refrain. But Zach was sure about Meghan Gerard, just as he was about all the cases he had diagnosed over the years, because he knew the symptoms better than anyone. He had lived with those symptoms, and he had watched Will die with them.

Despite the whispers of confirmation bias that were chorusing into shouts, Zach did not particularly care what the administration thought of his penchant for diagnosing new cases of the disease.

He knew mito when he saw it.

Zach retreated to his small windowless office on the pediatrics floor, where his desk lay hidden underneath mountains of journals and research papers devoted to understanding and curing mitochondrial disease. He paused to ask himself: *Am I really doing this again?*

Zach pushed his doubts aside and made the call.

CHAPTER 10

Becky

Becky was in the kitchen, waiting for her world to turn upside down. She hid her real tears among those she cried while dicing onions for the special dinner she was cooking Meghan, who had a new diet to go along with her new disease. Two weeks had passed since Dr. Zachary Fisher had diagnosed Meghan with a mitochondrial disorder, and in that short time, Becky had become something of an expert on the condition. With the help of a dietician at White, Becky had devised a menu for Meghan, one that would hopefully get her body to change food into energy.

Becky now kept a detailed log of everything Meghan ate, with all portions carefully weighed and measured. The number of calories taken in, too many or too few, could be a problem. Meghan's protein intake increased dramatically, and a complex carbohydrate was included with every meal. Meghan went from rarely eating to having four to six small meals every day, including the homemade chicken soup that had been her staple for the past few years.

In addition to the dietary changes, Meghan had begun taking what Dr. Fisher referred to as a mito cocktail. The mito cocktail was a combination of fifteen different vitamins and supplements that a compounding pharmacist combined into a bitter-tasting liquid and then flavored with mint to improve palatability.

"We'll be able to assess her after a few months to determine if her symptoms are lessening to some degree," Dr. Fisher had said. "That'll tell us as much as any biopsy could, if not more."

Becky had reason to be hopeful. Many forms of the disease were shown to be responsive to the high-dose vitamin and supplement therapy. Even better, because of Dr. Fisher's renown with treating mitochondrial disease, Meghan had been placed on a waiting list to receive an experimental medication called Elamvia, which Becky understood to be a peptide agent that helped stabilize the mitochondria, essentially allowing the cells to recharge. The drug showed promise in late-stage clinical trials. For now, as Dr. Fisher emphasized, the goal of Meghan's treatment was to slow the disease progression because there was no known cure.

No. Known. Cure.

Becky retrieved the mito cocktail from the fridge and poured the correct dosage into a glass. The cost of the drink Dr. Fisher had prescribed came in at around $2,500 a month, close to what they paid for their mortgage. Thankfully they had only a small co-pay to worry about. Money was getting tighter, due to a slowdown in the building market. Becky would give up her gym membership in a heartbeat if she had to, even though those two hours she spent working out — on the days Meghan actually made it to school — were her only respite. The rest of her time was spent providing care, doing research, and worrying.

Dr. Fisher had warned that insurance companies were aggressive in pushing back on mito payouts, especially with inconclusive labs like Meghan's. It could mean that Meghan would have to be subjected to far more invasive procedures should their insurance company start to balk at the bill.

Becky blamed herself for Meghan's meltdown in Dr. Fisher's exam room. If she had known the size of the needle, if she had had any inkling whatsoever, she could have given him fair warning. It was a minor miracle Dr. Fisher had convinced Meghan to let him take a cotton swab to the inside of her mouth to acquire the genetic sample. For the blood work, Becky had to employ guided meditation techniques she had learned online to help Meghan deal with the pin-prick sensation needed to get samples.

Since the diagnosis, Becky had watched Meghan like a hawk, observing her every movement, down to the twitch of an eyelash, because she feared her daughter's symptoms would worsen any day. Her research had confirmed Dr. Fisher's dire warning that neurodegenerative diseases were notoriously unpredictable — that a decline could take days, months, or years — hence her vigilance. For Meghan, for the whole family, living with mito meant living every minute waiting for that other shoe to drop.

As was her routine, Becky had also done due diligence on this new doctor. It was far from her usual deep dive, that could come later, but she did gather basic facts from the internet. The most revealing discovery had come when Dr. Fisher shared the story of his tragic past, the death of his son from the disease he had devoted his life to curing.

Her heart broke for him, for what he had endured, because the pain of a losing a child, no matter the age or circumstance, was familiar to her on the most personal, primal, and visceral of levels.

Nothing Becky found out in her quest for answers brought her much comfort, but as expected, the new diagnosis elicited a fresh rush of attention and outpouring of support. She took in every good wish, every hug from a concerned neighbor — Holly included, despite the distance that had come between them — every cooked meal, every phone call, and used them to fill the empty part of her soul that her mother had cratered out. Maybe if Holly still had a sick child, they would have stayed close friends. Becky understood the distance between them was her fault. It was shameful to admit, petty as can be, but it hurt to be around Holly because Becky wanted so desperately to have what she had — a healthy child.

Her Facebook group was full of the sick and struggling, and it was there Becky sought solace. Veronica Del Mar and other online friends helped her ascend the mito learning curve quickly. Though Becky found most of what they shared distressing, she had come to depend on her virtual support network to get her through the day. She felt off-kilter without their messages and regular information dumps.

After finishing dinner prep, Becky decided to FaceTime with Veronica. No one else could understand or relate to her struggles the way Veronica could.

When Veronica's face appeared in the FaceTime window, it looked to Becky as though she'd been expecting to video chat. Her hair, a shade of blond that came only from a box, was styled, full of body, and slightly feathered in a wink to the 1970s. Dark mascara called attention to her blue eyes, and makeup had turned Veronica's sun-kissed skin the reddish hue of Martian rock. A pair of dazzling silver earrings hung low and tinkled like wind chimes every time she moved her head.

Off in the background, Becky could see a pair of tall green plants bracketing a pass-through door into a galley kitchen, as well as a maroon tile floor that kept the apartment cool in Florida's blistering heat.

"Becky, sweetheart, I was just thinking of you." Becky smiled, knowing Veronica would say that even if a man had just climbed off her. "How's Meghan doing? I've been thinking of her and you tons."

"She's doing okay," Becky said. "Sleeping

a lot, probably too much, but I don't know what else to do."

"What about you-know-who?"

The "you-know-who," of course, meant Carl. To Becky's surprise and great relief, he'd been a better husband since the diagnosis. He was more attentive; a real presence around the house, for a change. He'd started looking her in the eyes when they spoke. On occasion, he'd offer to rub her shoulders, or snuggle in bed without asking for favors in return.

"Same thing happened with Don and me when a doctor thought Ashley had celiac disease," Veronica said glumly. "Suddenly, I wasn't Mrs. Crazy. In a day, I went from being obsessive and manipulative to brilliant, dogged, and determined. He got on board with the treatment plan, became Mr. Wonderful for all of three months, and then slipped right back into old habits when the diagnosis didn't stick, denying anything was ever wrong, blaming me for perpetuating the drama."

Becky tried not to let her annoyance show. She had so few good days that any moment there was cause to celebrate needed to be cherished, not squashed. Carl's active role had done wonders for Becky's mood, and nobody — not Veronica, not anybody — was going to bring her down.

"How is Ashley doing?" Becky asked, looking for a change of subject.

"Nothing new to report," Veronica announced with a sigh. "We're going to try this homeopathic healer in New Mexico my friend swears by, but I don't know. It seems a bit nutty to think some shaman across the country could heal Ashley remotely when so many doctors around here haven't done diddly."

"Desperate times," said Becky, reciting a refrain familiar to members of her Facebook group.

They talked at length about Ashley's ongoing stomach cramps, her evident weight loss, and Don's unconscionable lack of compassion for his daughter's plight. Becky suggested Ashley get tested for mito because the disease was nimble enough to fit most any symptom. It was a better plan than some damn fool shaman, and she felt on friendly-enough terms with Veronica to share that exact thought.

"Maybe you're right," Veronica said, sipping clear liquid from a glass tumbler that probably contained more parts vodka than tonic.

Before they could say anything more, Meghan appeared in the doorway. "Mom, I don't feel well," she announced weakly.

Becky swiveled in her chair to focus on Meghan, who looked pale and sweaty. She clutched at her stomach in evident pain, nearly doubled over, shaky on her feet. Meghan's eyes blinked rapidly as though they were trying to adjust to a sudden bright light.

Becky bolted from her chair to go to her daughter's side. "Sweetheart, what's wrong?" she asked, gripping Meghan's bony shoulders.

"I feel sick," Meghan said.

Oh God, no, thought Becky. This was it — the fast decline she most feared.

"Carl!" Becky cried out, her voice drenched in panic. "Carl! Come quick!" He could be anywhere in the house, but Becky was not going to leave Meghan's side to hunt him down. She sent Carl a text. Meghan slumped to the floor, and Becky went down with her.

"I feel wicked nauseous," Meghan said in a weak and raspy voice. Becky checked her daughter over, looking in her eyes. A steely bolt of fear struck her hard. "Carl!" Becky cried out again, but by that point, he was already in the room.

"Call 911," Becky heard Veronica say.

"What's going on?" Carl's tone was more

119

annoyed than worried. He hated being interrupted, especially if he was doing something — either in his office, or working on his mountain bike down in his man cave.

"It's Meghan. She's sick."

Carl knelt down beside his daughter. "Honey, what's wrong?"

Meghan went through her symptoms.

"Get an ambulance!" Veronica cried out.

Carl glanced at the computer, looking mildly miffed. "What were you doing when it happened?" he asked.

"Nothing," Meghan said. "I was in my room, texting some friends."

Like Becky, Meghan's world was mostly confined to what she could do online.

Carl felt Meghan's forehead. Becky knew her skin would feel cool to the touch, and she anticipated Carl would interpret that to mean no alarm was needed.

"Maybe just lie down for a little, see if it passes."

Becky glared at Carl. "She needs a doctor."

"Call 911," Veronica repeated.

Carl rose, stormed over to the computer, and bent down to give Veronica a clear look at his angry face. "This isn't your business, Veronica," he said, his top lip curving into a snarl. With a click, he closed down the Face-

Time application.

While Carl's rudeness appalled Becky, she was not about to confront him. Meghan was in distress, and Veronica was right to consider an emergency response.

"Let's call the ambulance," Becky said with urgency.

Carl huffed. "She has a stomachache. I wouldn't call this a medical emergency."

Becky again touched Meghan's forehead. Maybe she felt a bit clammy, but certainly not hot.

Carl knelt at Meghan's side, his eyes brimming with sympathy. "Sweetheart, do you feel like you can go to your room, lie down for a bit?"

Becky's eyes flared. *How dare he!*

Meghan's nod was near imperceptible. "I think so." She stood shakily, clutching at her stomach, blinking to clear her vision.

Becky went for her phone.

Holding on to Meghan's arm, Carl noticed Becky with the phone to her ear. "Who are you calling?"

"I'm calling an ambulance if you're not going to drive us to the damn hospital."

Carl made a frustrated sound. "Good God, Becky, are you out of your mind?"

"Are you out of yours?" Becky snapped, eyeing Meghan, who swayed on her feet like a sapling bending in the wind. "Does she look right to you?"

Veronica had warned her this would happen, that his support would eventually waver, but she did not think it would happen so soon.

Their eyes met like it was a high noon showdown. Becky said nothing.

"Hang up," Carl eventually said after a few uncomfortable beats of silence. "I'll drive everyone to the hospital. At least I won't have to listen to you fight with the insurance company about the ambulance ride."

Relief washed through Becky as she took hold of her daughter's frail arm. She could feel the bone against the pads of her fingers and wondered how much more Meghan could endure.

"Let's get you downstairs, sweetheart. Can you drink water?"

Meghan nodded as though needing that drink desperately.

"Your face looks blurry," Meghan said as she clutched at her stomach. She sounded on the verge of tears.

Becky glared at Carl as if to say *How could you?*

Carl fell into step behind Becky and Meghan as they descended the stairs. She knew it would be a silent car ride to the hospital, but this conversation was far from over.

CHAPTER 11

Luckily, Becky did not need a lot of background intelligence on Dr. Zach Fisher to convince him to come to the hospital when she called. He came without hesitation, and she and Carl were with Dr. Fisher in the curtained exam bay when he checked Meghan's vitals, looked into her eyes, did everything that did not involve needles. (This time, Meghan would not allow it.) Everything appeared perfectly normal.

Meghan was still having severe stomach cramps, though those had lessened with a hefty dose of Bentyl. She continued to complain of blurred vision, but Dr. Fisher saw no evidence of swelling or irritation in the optic nerves.

Dr. Fisher was off consulting with another doctor, leaving Becky and Carl alone together and yet so far apart. They passed the time in the ER waiting room, both to give Meghan some privacy and because the chairs were more comfortable.

"She looked awful," said Becky, as if needing to justify the alarm she had raised. But she saw it in Carl's eyes, his anger at yet another unnecessary trip to the ER. Becky could read her husband's dark look and sagging body language well enough to know she had pushed him over some invisible edge.

"It's never going to end, is it?" Carl lamented as he bit into a Snickers bar procured from a vending machine. "It was a stomachache. She had a damn stomachache. Why couldn't you have just given it some time?" he asked.

"That's your opinion, not mine," Becky shot back. She tried to look Carl in the eyes, but he refused to meet her gaze.

"No," he said. "It's the opinion of the heart monitor, her oxygen reading, her blood pressure, her temperature, and every other damn measurement they've taken. And it would be the opinion of her blood tests if you hadn't made her so deathly terrified of needles."

"That's so unfair. I didn't make her afraid."

Becky worried Carl would hear the doubt in her voice.

"That's what dealers say when they don't

take responsibility for the addict."

"So I'm her pusher now, is that it?"

A mother seated next to a boy with his arm swaddled in a plastic bag of ice glanced up as Becky and Carl's voices gained volume. Becky knew this timbre well, and seldom did they come away from the ensuing conversation feeling better.

"Stop putting words in my mouth," Carl said. "You know what I mean.

"You brought her here, you called Dr. Fisher in, not me," he continued, going red in the face. "What did it take to get him to do your bidding, Becky? A little flirting? Or did you do a deep dive to get his backstory so you'd really know how to pull the strings? Don't think I don't know how you operate. I'm not a fool."

When they were young and in love, Becky would brag (no better word for it) to anyone who'd listen about how little she and Carl argued. They seemed to agree on everything from movies to ice cream flavors. What Carl thought was cool (back then: grunge, *Silence of the Lambs,* the internet), she thought cool as well, and it was not because of his influence. They were simply compatible. The term she kept returning to was "soul mates."

In bed, she'd locked against Carl like a

puzzle piece. She had waited two months to sleep with him, and when it finally happened, Becky believed she would never be with another man.

"I know you're upset with me, and I can understand why," Becky said now. "But we have to do what's right for Meghan. We have to get answers."

"I don't think there ever will be an answer," Carl said.

Becky eyed him warily. "What's that supposed to mean?"

"It means if we cure one thing, I have no doubt there will be some new illness plaguing her before long. It's your history, you and your damn mother."

Becky bit at her lip, which was the only thing keeping her from slapping Carl's face.

"I can't believe you just said that to me."

But Carl was not necessarily off the mark. Becky hated to admit that her husband's doubts had gotten into her head, burrowed a little hole in her brain, and forced her to ask herself that difficult question for which she had no answer: *Am I crazy?*

Becky knew the mind was a labyrinth of extreme complicity. It twisted and turned like the maze that had nearly swallowed Theseus as he battled the fearsome Minotaur. In her quieter moments, Becky wondered if she was more like Cora than she cared to admit. Was it possible she'd been exaggerating symptoms while at the same time putting ideas in Meghan's head? Had she sent subliminal signals that were helping to perpetuate her daughter's illness?

Cora, who defied all expectations by still being alive, had faked serious illness more than once. She'd complained of chest pain, stomach problems, or even fevers spiked with the help of hot baths filled with pounds of Epsom salts, sipping on hot tea to warm her body from the inside while the bathwater heated it externally. The rise in her body temperature lasted six to eight hours, long enough for the doctors to show concern. Her mother was a grifter — no better word for it. She taught herself to be an expert scammer, and the payoff was government-funded disability benefits that kept food in the fridge. Her phantom illnesses also kept Cora out of work and on the minds of everyone she suckered into caring.

A memory of Cora came to Becky. Her mother moaning in the doctor's office, eight-year-old Becky telling the doctor what she'd been instructed to say: that she'd come home from school and found her mother passed out on the floor. She called

911, just like her mother had taught her to do. The doctor could not find anything wrong, but he wrote her a prescription for some medicine and made an appointment for her to see a specialist. He made sure the disability checks kept on coming.

In one of her rare moments of parental engagement, Cora had taught Becky and Sabrina how to pull off the ruse by lying to the social workers who'd occasionally pay them a visit. In hindsight, Becky had learned how to fake a disease at the hand of a true master. Surely had Cora known about mito, she would have latched on to that illness — with its strange, puzzling symptoms and no known cure — as a means of perpetuating her con.

I'm not my mother, Becky frequently told herself. *And I am not crazy.* But then she'd think of Sammy, and of the nursery where he'd slept for all of three months, eleven days, and fourteen hours before succumbing to SIDS — sudden infant death syndrome. The shock had never gone away. The hurt had never gone away. And her fear that Meghan was next had never gone away. How do you prevent that pain from happening again? You make sure your child has the best medical care in the world, that's how.

Becky never shared her self-doubts with Carl, because she feared he'd question every time she took Meghan to the doctor's for run-of-the-mill childhood stuff: stomach flu, bad colds, and coughs. He'd call her overly anxious. He'd pressure her to admit she was trying to work through her unresolved childhood trauma or the devastating loss of their firstborn, or even inventing illnesses to keep Meghan in the safety of the medical system.

"I'm sorry it upsets you to hear me say it," Carl said, "but I have to be honest. I'm beginning to wonder if you truly want Meghan to get well."

Without her even realizing it, Becky's hand lifted and swung toward Carl's face. She slapped his cheek with her open palm. The smack made a loud sound that brought a deeper hush to an already tensely quiet waiting room. Carl rubbed gingerly at the spot where Becky had struck him with a stunned expression.

"Feel better?" he asked. His hooded eyes grew shades darker.

"You're an asshole."

Carl leaned toward her. Fearing retaliation, Becky pulled away.

"Tell me you don't need the attention, that you haven't become addicted to it. That you're not like Cora."

"That's crazy, and you know it."

"Then tell me. Convince me. Because I think you've learned so much about medicine that it's made you paranoid. You think any cough is tuberculosis and a rash is scarlet fever."

"What about Dr. Fisher's mitochondrial diagnosis? You think he made that up?"

"The tests were inconclusive," Carl reminded her.

"Well, then, do you think Meghan faked fainting?" Becky asked.

Carl gave it some thought. "I think it's possible she believed she had to faint," he said. "Because it's what we've come to expect of her."

Becky had to look away. When she looked back at him, her eyes were flooded with tears. "And you think I put those expectations in her head?" Her voice trembled slightly.

Carl was quiet for a moment. His renovation business had taught him to think first before speaking because often what he said was taken as a verbal commitment. "I think it's a possibility, yes," he eventually offered. "I'm not saying you've done it intentionally. I'm asking if we've created a self-fulfilling prophecy here."

We. Whatever Carl believed, at least he

was implying they were in it together.

"Maybe Meghan believes if she's not sick, she doesn't have a purpose. It's how she gets attention from us. Isn't that what your mother taught you?"

Yes, thought Becky. *She taught me how to get attention. Taught me how to play the game.*

Before Becky could respond, Dr. Fisher entered the waiting room. Becky studied Dr. Fisher's expression as he approached, probing for signs that he was about to break her heart with devastating news. To her eyes, he looked deathly worried, his brow furrowed into deep creases, concern etched everywhere. Her thoughts tumbled with possibilities derived from her vast medical knowledge.

Crohn's disease . . . pancreatitis . . . kidney stones . . . cancer . . .

"Meghan seems to be doing fine," Dr. Fisher began.

Becky blinked, and Dr. Fisher's expression no longer seemed quite so alarming. In fact, his countenance was rather affable and suggested more concern for the parents than for the patient. Carl's accusation continued to worm about in Becky's head. Was she imagining symptoms that weren't really there?

"However, I'm concerned," Dr. Fisher continued. "Let's go where we can speak in private."

They followed Dr. Fisher in silence to a meeting room just beyond the entrance to the ER. On the walk, Becky stopped second-guessing herself and felt a stab of anger for letting Carl get to her the way he had.

He's so selfish, she thought. *He doesn't want a health crisis, because it takes away from him, his time, his business, his damn hobbies. He wants it over with so that his life can cruise along the way it did before.*

Becky kept those thoughts private as she settled into a cushioned seat beside Carl.

"I don't know what's causing Meghan's stomach cramps or blurred vision," Dr. Fisher said. "I'm honestly a bit baffled by the rapidity of these new symptoms. This isn't like the muscle weakness, headaches, and fatigue you'd see with mito. This was an intense gastrointestinal issue. Mitochondrial disease tends to progress more insidiously, a slower burn, and the symptoms tend to be a bit harder to pinpoint. Meghan's complaints are very specific *and* very sudden."

Becky looked anxious. "Meaning what, exactly?" she asked.

"Meaning something else might be going

on with her that's not mitochondrial disease. I've consulted with Dr. Amanda Nash, who heads up our GI practice here at White Memorial, and reviewed Meghan's case with her. I'd like a consult, and I think it's a good idea to have Dr. Nash examine Meghan. It could be we stay the course with the treatment for mitochondrial disease, keep working with the dietician, and continue to give her the mito cocktail, but it could be we have to change tactics altogether, or perhaps we'll have to manage two distinct issues simultaneously."

"Dr. Nash, you said . . ." Carl's voice trailed off.

"You know her?" Becky asked.

He thought a moment. "I think my firm did a project for her a few years back. The name is familiar. Anyway, it sounds like a good idea."

They talked for a time about next steps and made arrangements for Dr. Nash to see Meghan in the morning. Meghan was coming home tonight, but she'd be back tomorrow. Becky wondered if Carl would have supported a second opinion if she'd been the one to suggest Dr. Nash.

She doubted it.

CHAPTER 12

Meghan

I wasn't sure about this new doctor.

Her name was Amanda Nash. My first take was that she seemed powerful in that Wonder Woman kind of way. She reminded me a bit of Mrs. Banes, this hard-ass biology teacher of mine who would have failed me if my mom hadn't intervened.

Dr. Nash had thick, dark hair that I bet was super long when not tied up in a bun. She wore tortoiseshell glasses, but they couldn't hide the fact that her face was really pretty, annoyingly pretty, like, why should she get to be smart and beautiful? She had these gorgeous brown eyes and knew how to use makeup to her advantage. No way did she have a bad side in a photograph.

She was younger than my mom by maybe ten years or so, but I didn't think they'd be friends even if they were closer in age. Dr.

Nash was a bit too cool — not hip, but kind of aloof. If I had to put her in one of my high school cliques, I'd say she was one of the All-Around Girls — you know the type: good at sports, school, involved in a million and one activities, thinking she's got Harvard locked. They were a bit of a rare breed, but we had enough of them to form a group, all of whom were in competition to be valedictorian at graduation.

I hated thinking about graduation because I probably wouldn't get to be at mine. If I did get enough credits, it'd be a miracle, and if I couldn't graduate with my class, I'd probably take my GED and just be done with it. That is, if I could even study. These days, I couldn't remember anything I read. If this new doctor gave me a lot of instructions, she was going to have to repeat it all for my mom because I couldn't concentrate worth shit.

My mom was in the waiting room, more nervous than me. Dad didn't want to come, no surprise there. Honestly, I was fine with it. It was hard to look him in the eyes. Mom noticed, but I thought she figured it was a teen thing, or a sick thing, or a thing thing. I didn't think she gave it much thought.

But I could tell my dad was over it with me — and with Mom. I mean, he pretty much came out and said I was fine, or faking it, or something, when he didn't want to take me to the hospital. I wonder if he thought I was punishing him for what I knew — what I did. I should just get it over with, blurt it out and take the focus off me for a while. But it was one thing to hold on to a grenade, and something else entirely to pull the pin.

A nurse in pale blue scrubs took me to an exam room on the GI floor. I found out that it was short for "gastrointestinal," which didn't make much sense to me. I didn't have any big stomach problems, at least not until I got super sick the other night. But now that seemed to be the big issue for me. I guess I was whatever my current symptoms said I was. So today I was a GI patient. Not sure what that had to do with my blurred vision, but what did I know? I was just a kid.

I was up on the exam table, per the nurse's instructions, when Dr. Nash came into the room. The nurse had made me put on a stupid johnny again — yeah, my sundress. My legs were cold under the thin fabric. I was anxious but not panicked, not yet anyway.

"Do you have to use any needles on me?" I asked as Dr. Nash snapped on a pair of purple latex gloves. My voice trembled, and I hated that I sounded like a scared little girl. No matter how hard I tried, I saw needles as knives, and if anyone had a knife coming at them, I was willing to bet they'd be pretty freaked out, too.

"No needles, sweetheart," Dr. Nash said.

I kind of liked that she called me sweetheart. It eased my worry some. My mom sometimes called me sweetheart, but it always meant the most when it came from my father. I missed him, my dad, the way we were when I was little, when I was his princess, his monkey, which was what he used to call me before I grew breasts and outgrew pet names.

"What are you going to do to me?" I asked nervously.

When Dr. Nash smiled, her nose crinkled a bit. "First, we're going to talk," she said. "I want to understand what happened to you."

What did happen? One minute, I was fine, lying on my bed in my room, the violet-colored walls covered with stickers and posters, a secret hiding place in my closet where I keep something else. The next, I couldn't read a text from my friend Stephanie.

I told Dr. Nash what had happened, and

her expression was kind of a blank. She wasn't giving me much of anything, which made me feel even more nervous.

Dr. Nash studied me. "Are you feeling okay now?" she asked.

"Yeah, I'm okay. Better than I was last night."

"Have you had anything to eat since last night?"

Even though my appetite had flown south, my stomach rumbled at the mention of food, which I figured was answer enough. I told her no, I hadn't eaten per her instructions. I assumed they wanted nothing in my system, but usually that meant blood tests, which also meant needles. I shuddered at the thought.

"Do you ever eat anything that makes you feel sick?"

I thought about it before answering. Some hot stuff, like *really* hot salsa or super-spicy food — Indian food, for instance — didn't feel great, but it didn't make me sick like I was last night. I told all that to Dr. Nash, who made some notes on a paper latched to her clipboard. She went through a list of foods I might not have thought of that could make me feel sick, which strangely enough included broccoli, cabbage, and green peppers. Beans, milk, and cheese were on her list, too, which made sense for an upset stomach, but so was corn. I was dragging my fingers through my hair, teasing out some tangles, when we got to the question about alcohol.

"Do you drink?" she asked.

Should I answer that truthfully? Should I tell her what I had a few swigs of not long before I got sick? Should I tell her why I started?

The first time I got drunk was two years ago at a ninth-grade dance, a few months before I started my great decline. Lily Beauport had brought straight vodka in a water bottle that had passed visual inspection, and Cecilia Montgomery supplied the Gatorade that passed the smell test. The mixing took place in the girl's bathroom on the second floor, and the drinking happened in pretty much every dark corner of the gymnasium.

I was super nervous because I knew if I got caught, I would have been kicked off the soccer team, not knowing then that I'd end up quitting a year later as my sickness progressed. My parents (my mom more than dad) were super-strict about drinking, and I knew they would have grounded me or worse if they ever found out, but I didn't care. I wanted to do what my friends were doing. Besides, I was curious to know how it would taste; how it would make me feel.

I knew I shouldn't be drinking at all, and I didn't do it much. I had to be careful how much I sneaked. I'd definitely watered down more than one bottle of vodka and tequila. And when that extra bottle of wine Mom thought she had in the liquor cabinet went missing, she was kind enough to blame herself instead of asking me. Mom had never found my hiding place in my bedroom where I kept a fifth of vodka. I liked the buzz I got from the booze. It helped me cope with things that I wished I didn't have to cope with. Were my covert trips to the Gerard liquor cabinet what made my stomach sick and my vision go all blurry? I didn't think so, but I did have a couple swigs from my secret stash before I got sick and ended up in the ER. Either way, I wasn't about to find out if it was a possibility.

"No. I don't drink," I said.

Dr. Nash wrote something on her paper. I couldn't tell if she believed me. Not sure I cared.

"Do you go to the bathroom regularly?"

"Yes," I said, stammering, feeling a bit caught off guard.

What does that have to do with anything?

"What about your bowel movements?" She tossed out the question nonchalantly,

141

like it couldn't possibly be an embarrassing topic.

"Um, yeah, sure." I gripped the edge of the table, crinkling the paper underneath the palm of my hand.

"Are your bowel movements firm?"

God, lady! "Um, yeah, I guess. I don't always look."

And that was the truth.

Her pencil scratched something out on her paper. "And are your periods regular?"

Clearly, this doc was not into boundaries. My face went hot and I knew I turned red with embarrassment. I didn't know why that happened. I shouldn't have been embarrassed to talk about my periods with another woman. She had them, too, but I had only a few bits of privacy left, and I wasn't prepared to let another piece go. But away it went.

"Yeah, my periods are regular."

I resisted the urge to add: *Just like my poops.*

"Do you ever have cramping?" she asked.

I nodded slightly.

"Do the cramps happen at school or home more?"

"School, I guess," I said. "When I go." I heard my voice getting softer.

"What about when you're out with

friends?"

"Maybe . . . sometimes . . . but I don't go out much these days."

"That must be hard on you." Dr. Nash gave me a genuinely sympathetic look, and I relaxed a little. I reminded myself that she was just doing her job.

"It's not fun."

That wasn't much of an answer, but I couldn't think what else to say. When in doubt, I usually went with as few syllables as possible. Adults seemed to expect it, or at least they accepted it.

"Have you done any traveling lately? Gone anywhere exotic?"

Maybe she thought I'd just come back from the Caribbean and picked up some bug while I was there. Didn't she see how pale I looked? I had the coloring of an envelope. Didn't I just tell her that I barely left home? I could see the tablet that stored my medical chart on a desk in the exam room. There were probably reports from a hundred doctor visits (and I'm not exaggerating the number) in there. There must be some report about how much school I'd missed, or how I didn't play sports anymore, or how I hardly did anything that didn't involve my phone.

I again explained to Dr. Nash how boring

my days had become since I got really sick, and she seemed genuinely sorry to hear that, but still, I was surprised she didn't know. Then again, those charts told only part of my story — the part that could be explained in numbers and test results, but they didn't tell the whole story of me.

In a way, it was a relief to share the more personal details with Dr. Nash. It made me feel like a whole person and not just the sum of my lab results. I liked this new doctor. I really did. I felt like she might be onto something, that she was going to have some big breakthrough because she was taking a different approach.

I didn't get into the whole mitochondrial disease thing with her. I didn't really understand what it meant anyway. Conceptually, I got it. My cells sucked at making energy. But that was all kind of abstract. This conversation felt more real. For no reason at all, I was overcome with this rush of joy, an uplifting feeling of pure elation. I had a premonition that Dr. Nash, this Wonder Woman, was going to unravel the mystery of Meghan in ways that nobody was expecting.

New hope blossomed inside me. Not only did I think Dr. Nash was going to find a cure, but she was also going to become my friend. More than that, I felt she was going to be someone in whom I could eventually confide my secrets.

CHAPTER 13

Becky

Becky stepped into Dr. Nash's tidy office, which was tucked in a corner of the GI floor. Meghan was on her phone in the waiting room, perfectly occupied, but she should have been with her father. Becky simmered over the fact that Carl was not at the hospital with them, but no, he had too much work and could not bear to pull himself away for even a few hours to talk with a doctor about his daughter.

Damn him!

Their fight had lingered. His accusations continued to sting. Veronica had been right to question Carl's transformation into the man she needed him to be.

Becky purged Carl from her thoughts in order to give Dr. Nash her full attention. She planned to record this conversation on her phone, with Dr. Nash's permission, of course. The audio recordings were extremely

146

helpful when needing to recall information verbatim.

In the back of her mind, Becky thought about the experimental mito drug, Elamvia. After this appointment, she had plans to meet Dr. Fisher to inquire about Meghan's place in the line of patients eager to begin the clinical trial. She wondered if Dr. Nash's diagnosis might bring up the possibility of a new experimental drug or treatment for them to consider.

For some reason — wiliness when it comes to mind games, age, a natural competitiveness — Becky had a harder time working an angle with young female doctors. It was not a question of ability, but her usual approaches often did not have the same effect. Making matters worse, Dr. Nash gave off all the warmth of an iceberg. Becky searched the doctor's pretty face, peered into her muted brown eyes, but could not pinpoint a single trace of empathy or compassion.

She felt a niggling concern that Dr. Nash held her in some kind of contempt. She brushed away the worry as paranoia and nothing more. After so many setbacks, it was easy to see the worst in nearly every situation.

Becky searched the office for a picture of

Dr. Nash's family, a husband smiling in a silver frame, maybe two or three gorgeous kids — clearly, they'd be gorgeous. She wanted something that would give her some insight on the woman, not the doctor, but there was nothing to be found. A few small houseplants were the only clue that Dr. Nash cared for something other than her patients.

"Do you mind if I record our conversation?"

Becky explained the value of the recording to Nash, who had no hesitation in giving her consent. Becky put her phone on the desk, launched her dictation app, and gave a nod to indicate that she was ready.

"I'm going to recommend that Meghan have an endoscopy, specifically an enteroscopy," Dr. Nash began. She took off her glasses, cleaning the lens with a white cloth retrieved from a desk drawer.

Becky felt a stirring of surprise, but not because the procedure was unfamiliar to her. Meghan had already had an enteroscopy last year — certainly Dr. Nash had read that in her medical history. Becky wondered why she wanted to use the specialized instrument to view Meghan's small intestine again.

"Do you think she has giardia?"

Becky knew without having to ask that the parasite was one common reason to order that particular test. It could explain Meghan's stomach cramps, but did it address complaints of blurred vision?

"No, I don't think she has giardia," Dr. Nash replied coolly.

"Well, what, then? Why that test?"

Dr. Nash sighed aloud. "I'll be candid with you, Mrs. Gerard. The test is more for my benefit than for Meghan's."

"Your benefit?"

"Yes, it would be irresponsible of me not to rule out all possibilities. So I'll order the test, knowing in advance that it's going to be negative."

A hot streak raced up Becky's spine. "And how do you know the results without first performing the test?" she asked.

Dr. Nash paused before answering.

Becky folded her arms low on her lap, a defensive posture.

"Mrs. Gerard —"

"Please, call me Becky." Amanda Nash may have been younger, but Becky was not going to be ma'amed by her.

"Becky, then. What I'm going to say may be rather difficult for you to hear."

The spurt of anger Becky had felt was quickly replaced with a fresh stab of fear.

It's cancer . . . it's going to be cancer.

"I've spent considerable time reviewing your daughter's . . . how to put it . . . rather extensive medical history, and there is a problem, but it's not one I think you've considered."

Becky braced herself. Again, the word "cancer" tumbled about her head like a wheel coming free of its axle.

"I'm postulating that there's nothing wrong with Meghan. Nothing physical, anyway."

Becky's eyes narrowed, her expression incredulous. "What are you talking about? You said yourself that you read her file."

"Yes, I read a lot of symptoms that don't have any correlating explanation in terms of Meghan's biology. Her labs, her blood work, all of it is fine."

Becky heard Carl's voice in her head: *I'm not saying you've done it intentionally. I'm asking if we've created a self-fulfilling prophecy here. . . .*

"No, no," Becky said, shaking her head, her body trembling with anger. "Dr. Fisher has diagnosed her with mitochondrial disease."

"Those labs were inconclusive," Dr. Nash said in a matter-of-fact tone. "I understand Meghan is taking a variety of vitamins and

150

supplements as part of her treatment."

"Yes," Becky said. "Dr. Fisher called it a mito cocktail. And she's on a waiting list to be part of a clinical trial for Elamvia, a new drug to treat mitochondrial disease."

"That's all well and good," Dr. Nash said. "But I believe all those treatments are going to perpetuate the problem, which is that Meghan believes she's gravely ill."

"But she is sick!" Becky almost jumped to her feet. "Dr. Fisher —"

"Dr. Fisher's diagnosis, as I said, was inconclusive. I'm the head of GI at White, and very experienced in pediatric care, and my read of Meghan's medical history and my exam of your daughter tells quite a different story. I would think this would be welcome news, to hear that it's not something physical."

"It's . . . it's . . . not something that I believe."

"Have you ever heard the term 'functional disease'?" Dr. Nash asked.

Becky, who thought she'd read about every medical condition under the sun and felt confident she'd do well on a medical school entrance exam if she had to take one, confessed to never having heard the term before.

"What about 'psychosomatic'?" Nash inquired.

Now, that was a word Becky knew quite well, and the implications made her blood burn. "What are you saying? That it's *all* in my daughter's head? That she's not sick in the slightest? That I've been wasting my time and Meghan's, shuttling her from doctor to doctor? Is that it?"

Carl's voice again: *I'm not saying you've done it intentionally. . . .*

Dr. Nash pulled her lips tight. "She's not making it up like a lie," Dr. Nash eventually said, "but I think there are some deep inner conflicts here that need to be explored."

Becky blinked rapidly. " 'Inner conflicts'?"

"I believe Meghan is exhibiting subconscious behaviors. Because of some external stress, those behaviors are manifesting as bodily symptoms," Nash explained. "That's what we mean when we say 'functional disease.' There's a symptom — say, for example, upset stomach or blurred vision, weakness, fainting, general malaise — with no inducer stress, and by that I mean no biological component to explain the symptom."

Becky strained to get her mind around the implications. Countless doctor visits, innumerable tests, endless worry — all because it was in her child's head? She refused to accept that Carl could be right, or that her own self-doubt was anything other than wasted worry.

"I've never for one second questioned my daughter's mental health."

"Well, it's not something you'd have a window into," Dr. Nash said. "Which is why I'm recommending Meghan see a pediatric psychiatrist. Quickly, too."

"A psychiatrist? After she came into my room clutching her stomach, complaining she couldn't see right, you want her to see a shrink?" Becky's voice rose sharply.

"It could help us identify the stress that's causing your daughter's symptoms," Dr. Nash explained.

"It's just your opinion that it's stress, but you're stating it like it's a fact."

"I've read her medical file, and I've examined your daughter."

"And so did Dr. Fisher, and he came to quite a different conclusion."

"No surprise there," Dr. Nash retorted with a look and tone that implied some secret history with Dr. Fisher.

"What's that supposed to mean?" Becky's pulse spiked. She felt protective of Dr. Fisher, the one person she believed could help, and took Dr. Nash's tone personally.

"The stress could be from anything," Dr. Nash said. "Your marriage, for instance."

"My marriage?" Again, Becky found herself having to tamp down her anger.

"Is everything all right at home?"

"It's fine," Becky said, hoping she came across convincingly.

"No issues?" Dr. Nash made it sound like that was impossible.

"Yes, of course there's stress around Meghan," Becky said. "Her health and all we've been dealing with, but we're fine. We've been together a long time."

"Length of time doesn't necessarily translate into a happy marriage."

"Pardon my candor, but I don't really think my marriage is any of your concern," Becky said. "That's certainly not why I took Dr. Fisher's advice to have Meghan come see you."

"No, that happened because Meghan's symptoms don't fit with Dr. Fisher's diagnosis. In fact, they don't fit with any diagnosis — except mine."

"That it's in her head." Becky made it sound ridiculous.

"Precisely. Which is why we need to stop her vitamin therapy and all supplements she's taking immediately. In Meghan's mind, it's reinforcing the notion that she's gravely ill. In the meantime, I'll advise Dr. Fisher to remove Meghan's name from the Elamvia clinical trial consideration. She needs a psychiatrist, Mrs. Gerard, not another drug or treatment."

In a flash, Becky was on her feet, hands clenched into fists at her sides. "That's utterly ridiculous," she said, seething. "We haven't even given the vitamin therapy a chance to work."

"It will never work, because there will always be something until we get to the source of her stress."

A sharp, piercing tone flooded Becky's ears. All other sound in the room — the click of Dr. Nash's nails on her desk, the humming white noise of the hospital — dipped to a nearly imperceptible level. She heard Dr. Fisher's dire warning about early treatment helping to slow the progress of mitochondrial disease; recalled the personal story he had shared about his son, Will — not to frighten her, but to emphasize the importance of early intervention. And now this Dr. Nash, this prissy know-it-all, this god-awful poseur, was making outlandish claims about Meghan's mental health and her marriage, of all things. *How dare she! How dare she!*

No! No! No! the voice screamed in Becky's

head. *This is unacceptable, utterly and completely unacceptable.*

Becky snapped back into herself, fixing Dr. Nash with the kind of angry look Carl had helped her perfect. Of course, Becky was not going to say anything to Nash about her husband's concerns, because the two of them were too closely aligned. She already felt alone in this battle and did not need Carl to have an ally working against her.

"I appreciate your time," Becky said in a calm and even manner. "But I'm not taking your advice, and I don't want to leave here giving you the impression that I might. As for the endoscopy, I do want that done, but I'll find another doctor to perform the procedure. From what you've said, I wouldn't trust you to be — well, let's just say I'd be more comfortable with another doctor, and we'll leave it at that."

Dr. Nash exhaled loudly. "I can see your position. However, I have an obligation to be involved, for your daughter's sake."

"Well, I'm sorry to be rude, but I don't want your help."

Dr. Nash fell silent for a time, making Becky extremely uncomfortable. "I understand how you feel," Dr. Nash eventually said.

With that, Becky collected her things and left the office.

CHAPTER 14

Zach

Zach inhaled half a protein bar after ending a call with the parents of Baby Sperling, the young infant he'd correctly diagnosed with Ondine's curse. They were doing surprisingly well, given the circumstances, and were relieved to finally have a diagnosis to go along with a treatment plan. This fueled Zach more than any protein bar ever could. It was a reminder that every day brought with it the possibility of making a difference in another person's life. But he knew better than to think he could help everyone in the way he had helped Baby Sperling.

He checked the time, anticipating Amanda Nash's imminent arrival. She had called an hour earlier requesting an urgent meeting to discuss Meghan Gerard.

On Zach's desk, camouflaged among the tall stacks of papers and stationed near a half-finished cup of coffee long gone cold, was Meghan's extensive medical history, which he preferred to read in printed form rather than off one of those newfangled tablets. In terms of size, it was the health care provider's *War and Peace.* Zach flipped through page after page of doctor's notes, admission forms, and lab results in search of evidence that would unequivocally refute Nash's conclusion.

He found nothing.

Zach felt foolish for not having considered the possibility that Nash might leap to questioning Meghan's mental health. He should have forewarned Becky that it was a risk with these cases. He'd been a doubter himself, with his own son, of all people. But Meghan was not the only one Nash doubted.

Around White Memorial, few were more respected, or more formidable, than the young, brash, beautiful, and brilliant Dr. Amanda Nash, who, in one of the worst-kept secrets at the hospital, was the CEO's heir apparent to become the next chief medical officer. Her power at White Memorial had no equal, and her nature, for which the word "dogged" did not nearly do justice, made it so whenever she sank her teeth into some cause or issue, it was hard, if not impossible, to coax her into letting go. Zach had a sinking feeling that Meghan Gerard was about to become Nash's newest cause.

Zach heard a knock on his office door, closed his eyes to center himself, then said, "Come in."

Amanda Nash entered Zach's office, maroon blouse peeking out from underneath her white coat, tortoiseshell glasses in place. She looked uncertain where to step as she eyed the overstuffed bookshelves, overflowing wastebasket, and stacks of paper sprouting up from the floor like stalagmites.

"Love what you've done with the place," she said.

Rising from his seat, Zach motioned to the chair opposite his desk. "I've got a requisition order for some guide lights," he said. "Until then, proceed with caution and at your own risk."

Dr. Nash carefully made her way to the empty chair. She smoothed out her coat as she settled into her seat.

"I'd offer you some cold coffee and a half-eaten protein bar, but I'm selfish," Zach said, smiling thinly.

"You're also wrong about Meghan Gerard," Nash said.

"Not wasting any time, are we?"

"No time to waste," said Nash. "I'm assuming you got a tongue-lashing from the mother."

Zach nodded grimly. "She was quite upset when she came to see me. She thinks you've sentenced her daughter to death, which could very well be the case if we take your approach, couldn't it?"

Zach felt good about his retort. It was not too forceful, but carried impact. Then again, rattling Nash was like a wind blowing against a tree — it would take a mighty gust to get her to sway even slightly.

Nash placed a finger to her lips, showing off a strawberry-colored manicure done to perfection. "You're making this worse for Meghan, for the family," she said.

"That's your opinion," Zach said.

"Did she play you the recording of our conversation?"

"She did," Zach said.

"And you didn't find it a bit strange?"

Zach leaned over his desk, arms resting atop Meghan's hefty medical history. "To be honest, I thought you were a little aggressive with her. Not much bedside manner on display."

Amanda attempted a smile, but it could not hide the firm set of her jaw. "To be honest with you," she said, "I was testing her."

Zach appeared nonplussed. "Testing her how?"

Nash said, "A mother is given news that her daughter might not be deathly ill, that it could be something else entirely, that she may not have a devastating disease for which there is no cure — a disease, by the way, that's guaranteed to shorten Meghan's life, perhaps considerably — and it doesn't even register to her that this could be good news? Why, Zach? Why is that?"

"I don't know," Zach said, feeling compelled to take another bite of his protein bar. It was already the end of the day, which meant he was going home to an empty refrigerator and not much of an appetite to do anything about it. He'd probably bang out some sits-ups and push-ups, maybe go for a run, but chances were, he'd put on the TV, grab some journals and his research materials on mitochondrial disease, and read in front of the Red Sox game until he fell asleep on the couch. Rinse and repeat. His mother worried he was losing weight, which he was. Zach worried he was transforming into his father, who had let life's normal hardships prematurely age him.

"Maybe Becky felt threatened by you," Zach offered.

"Spare me. That woman knows as much medicine as we do, which I might add should be a red flag for you."

"Or maybe she's convinced her daughter is sick because she *is* sick. You have no proof of anything, Amanda. You're making a very serious accusation based on some misguided test you devised in your office. I think that's unfair to Becky and to Meghan."

If that barrage flustered Nash even in the slightest, she did not let it show. "I think you may be too blinded by your past, Zach, to see things clearly."

Zach's eyes narrowed. "Watch your step here, Amanda." There was a low rumble to Zach's voice, and he wondered if his warning tone and glowering look might have gotten to her.

Nash shifted uncomfortably in her chair, her eyes flaring momentarily before they cooled. Zach understood he was taking the hard-line approach with Meghan's case. If he were even a little more open-minded, he'd have to give some credence to Nash's thinking. In fact, Zach would bet a million dollars he knew what accusation Nash was about to make next.

"It's Munchausen by proxy, Zach. I'm sure of it."

Zach suppressed a gloating expression. In essence, Nash had fired the first volley in the coming war for Meghan Gerard's future. Munchausen syndrome by proxy, aka medical child abuse, was about to become Becky Gerard's new nightmare — and Zach's, too, because he was not about to abandon Meghan to Nash, not by a long shot.

Unfortunately for the Gerard family, mitochondrial disease, with its array of puzzling and hard-to-predict symptoms, often aroused doubts and suspicion in the medical community. With a case like Meghan's, a medical history as long and perplexing as hers, any physician worth their license would be on high alert. Maybe some would think Meghan was after the attention, but the majority would probably focus on the mother, just as Nash was doing.

Zach knew the etymology of the name was a nod to Baron Munchausen, a literary character from the 1800s who told fantastical stories about himself, lifting the art of exaggeration to new and impressive heights. Nash did not have to be aware of the origin of Munchausen syndrome to accuse Becky Gerard of exaggerating Meghan's complaints or inflicting illnesses upon her daughter for the attention.

As for Zach's diagnosis of mitochondrial disease, his reputation at White would work against him. The belief around the hospital was that Zach, because of his son's death, saw mito where others did not. It was understandable that Nash would think he was too biased to call out a case of Munchausen by proxy even if he walked in on Becky injecting Meghan with poison.

"You have no proof."

"Maybe not, not yet anyway, but I wanted to tell you what I thought to get your take on it."

"Why?" Zach could see the ambush laid out in front of him. Nash was up to something.

"You know the patient better than I do. I want your take is all."

Zach turned his head and bit the inside of his mouth to keep from blurting out the first thing that popped into his mind, which would not have been polite.

"I told you what I think. It's mitochondrial disease."

"Are you sure, Zach?" Nash asked, looking skeptical. "We have a duty to protect this child if she's in danger."

"I don't believe she is. Are you suddenly a psychiatrist?" Zach asked. "I haven't checked on your credentials lately."

Zach knew Nash was too smart to take that bait.

"I feel strongly enough about this case that I'm going to get Meghan seen."

Zach shook his head in dismay. Her teeth

were sunk in. No letting go now.

"Is it a GI issue you're worried about, Amanda? If so, fine, go get that second opinion. But if not, you and I both know you're stepping way over the line here."

"Am I? What line are you standing near, Zach? Because mine has everything to do with the patient, and yours, I'm concerned, has everything to do with your past."

Zach felt his face heat up. "That's unfair and uncalled for."

"I'm not trying to steal your patient, if that's your worry."

"You could have fooled me," he said, his brow furrowing as he forced himself to look at Nash.

"Then you do it. Call in a consult. Get that second opinion. For everyone's sake, you have to be sure."

Zach looked down at Meghan's medical records, which took up a good portion of his available desk space. He wished more than anything that he had found something in those pages to refute Nash's claims.

"How can you be so convinced it's not what I said?" Nash asked, her voice gentle, almost coaxing. "The blood work was inconclusive, and the girl's so deathly afraid of needles, I can't imagine how you'd do a muscle biopsy or EMG."

"I know the disease."

"I don't think that's good enough."

"Well, I do." Zach could not believe how juvenile he sounded. If he was going to help Becky face down this dragon, he most certainly would need to come up with some better retorts.

"Well, I guess if you've diagnosed her with mito the biopsy results wouldn't alter her treatment considerations one way or the other. So go without it if you think it best for your patient, but your case would be much stronger if a psychiatrist supported your diagnosis is all I'm saying."

"I don't need a psychiatrist to tell me anything."

Nash's expression suggested otherwise.

"I understand that you're speaking at a mito conference in Cleveland this week," Nash said.

Zack was surprised she knew his schedule. "I am. And how did you know?"

"I saw the bulletin in the hospital newsletter."

Zack's defenses stayed up. "And your point is?"

"You're the mito guy here, Zach, everyone knows it. You know more about this disease than all of us combined."

"Which is why I'm confident about Meghan's diagnosis."

"You better be, because it's your job on the line," Nash said. "If the mother is harming that girl, and you don't take my advice and try to make the determination, Knox Singer will fire you without batting an eye. You know it, and I know it. We've both sworn an oath to protect the patient. *You* have to protect her. God, Zach, don't be so devoted to the cause that you'd be willing to risk everything for your crusade."

Nash was right, of course. Zach was already off Knox Singer's Christmas list, thanks to the damage his mito crusade had done to White's P&L from a scattering of denied insurance claims.

The file cabinet taking up most of one wall held files of other cases where Zach had suspected mito to be at the root of a patient's diminishing health. Not all the cases were confirmed, but all were strongly suspect. Each file represented a child who counted on Zach to keep coming up with answers to make them better. If he made an enemy out of Nash and ended up on the unemployment line, there could be a lot of losers in the end — including Meghan.

"What do you want me to do?"

"Meghan's your patient," Nash said. "You have to do what you think is right. I'm just telling you as a colleague and a friend what I would do if she were my patient."

"Well, she is your patient, too. You examined her. You have your own files on her now."

"That I do," Nash said, rising from her chair. "But I wanted to give you the professional courtesy of knowing what I thought."

"And what are you going to do about it?"

"I'm going to do my job and safeguard the patient's health. I strongly suggest you do the same."

Nash did not bother with a handshake goodbye before she carefully made her way across the crowded floor. At the door, she turned back to Zach. "Have a good trip," she said.

Zach swiveled in his chair to face her. "I really wish I hadn't involved you, Amanda," he said.

"And I'm really glad you did," Nash said with a solemn expression and one foot out the door. "You're trying to save her from a ghost, Zach — the one haunting you. I'm going to save her from her mother."

CHAPTER 15

Becky

The past two days had been emotionally draining. Becky had still gotten in her daily workouts, but even her high-intensity interval training could not keep her from thinking about Nash's accusations.

She had yet to make an appointment for the endoscopy because the mere thought of the procedure forced her to think about Nash. As for Meghan, she was back to her same old self; no better, no worse. She was still home from school, too tired to attend. The nausea and blurred vision were gone and had not come back, but then again, Becky's research had told her that mito was unpredictable in that regard. There was still no word on the Elamvia clinical trial, but she held out hope for good news.

She also waited for news of her mother's passing that did not come. There was no way she could travel now, even for the funeral.

In fact, when her phone rang, she thought it was Sabrina calling. But no, it was Dr. Amanda Nash. She wanted to see Meghan again, urgently, for a second opinion and asked if Becky could bring Meghan to the hospital ASAP.

"What's the emergency exactly?" Becky asked, hearing the worry worm into her voice.

"We want to run more tests," Dr. Nash said. "I reviewed my findings with a colleague, Dr. Peter Levine, who is also a specialist in pediatrics, and he had some very specific concerns, ones we need to rule out with another exam."

"What kind of concerns?" Becky asked, feeling that familiar tightness returning.

"There could be the possibility of another disease, one we hadn't considered."

Worse than mito, Becky thought.

"Is it cancer?" Becky asked, her voice cracking slightly.

It's cancer . . . it's going to be cancer. Like Cora, it's in our family. It's our curse . . . we fake sickness and get a real disease as punishment.

"We won't know until we examine her," Nash said. "We can do this initial exam without any needles, but if it's necessary, we may have to draw blood. Of course, we'll need your help to get Meghan's cooperation."

"What kind of cancer?" Becky asked.

"Let's take it one step at a time, can we?" Nash asked. "Bring her in now, if you can, and we'll take it from there."

"What about Dr. Fisher? I should call him?"

She didn't say it wasn't cancer, thought Becky, now gripped in a full-blown panic.

"Of course," Dr. Nash said. "But he's away at a conference; you can try his office, maybe his receptionist can get a message to him. But just so you know, he and I have discussed Meghan's case."

Becky did not need a receptionist when she had the doctor's cell phone number. Zach did not answer when she called, so Becky left him a message to call her when he could. She was not going to wait for his okay, not if there was a real concern to address.

Then she called Carl at work, expecting he'd hem and haw, or complain again that they were on the never-ending medical crisis treadmill. Still, she wanted him to go with her to the hospital for obvious reasons. If Meghan had some rare type of cancer, as she believed would be the case, she needed her husband, her rock (or former rock, as she sometimes thought of him) at her side.

"It's Meghan," Becky said when Carl answered her call. "Dr. Nash spoke with another doctor at White about Meghan's case, and she's concerned. Carl, I think it might be cancer."

Tears sprang to Becky's eyes. She clutched the kitchen counter, bracing herself against waves of painful emotions.

"Did she *say* cancer?" Carl asked. "Did she say that specific word?"

"No, no," Becky said. "It was obvious she didn't want to alarm me over the phone. But I know . . . I just know."

"Try to relax," Carl said, his voice bringing her a measure of calm. "I'll be home shortly, and we'll go to the hospital together."

All her upset and anger at Carl for not fully supporting her fell away. She would need to lean on him harder than ever in the coming days. Twenty minutes later, Carl honked the horn to signal his arrival home. He left the car idling in the driveway while he entered through the front door. He went upstairs and got Meghan, who had been resting in her room. She was ready to go. Becky had already told her they were headed back to White for another exam. Meghan protested until Becky assured her there'd be no needles involved.

"What's it all about?" Meghan had asked.

"The doctors are a little concerned about something, and Dr. Nash would like you to see another specialist."

Meghan showed no emotion, which was not entirely a surprise: she'd acclimated to medical uncertainty. As they made their way down the walkway, Meghan pulled away when Carl reached for her arm. Becky noticed the odd exchange but was quick to brush it off. It was tough enough to connect with a typical fifteen-year-old girl, at least according to Becky's friends who had healthy daughters that age. But when you combine teenage hormones with a spirit-crushing disease, you get a profoundly different sort of isolation of parent from child.

For Becky, Meghan's illness had come between mother and daughter like a controlling boyfriend. It tainted everything they did together and it lurked everywhere they went. Fatigue invariably cut short shopping trips to the mall. Tickets for shows were bought and then sold when Meghan could not muster the strength to attend.

Three years ago, Becky had gotten Meghan into scrapbooking. The hobby was far craftier than their skills and imagination warranted, but it was a great way to spend quality time together. They had made collages of vacation photos complete with felt palm trees that had aqua-colored leaves and polka dot–covered bark. There was a page devoted to sports, decorated with an oversize soccer ball and the words STAR PLAYER IN THE MAKING displayed in fanciful letters. The last time Becky had looked at that book, she'd had to brush away the dust.

Becky had vowed to be the opposite of her mother. She wanted to be the mom her kids could come to for advice about love or school, who could help to resolve some conflict with a teacher or a friend. But Sammy's death had cast a pall over their lives, and Meghan's disease had come along later like an uninvited guest who refused to leave.

What she'd give for one day without that selfish guest. What would she give to see her daughter healthy again? Becky did not bother speculating too much, because she doubted that day would ever come.

Dr. Nash was waiting to greet the family when they arrived at the ER entrance a little after four o'clock in the afternoon. Becky felt no residual anger toward the woman, but she did notice how Nash's eyes lingered a bit too long on her husband. Nash had never met Carl before, so her first viewing may have been a surprise. It certainly was not the first time a woman (or a man, for that matter) had taken an extra beat to appreciate her husband's good looks. He was that kind of man, after all; the ruggedly handsome, dimpled-chin, dark-eyes-you-can-lose-yourself-in type. But even Nash's brief, if unintentional, flirtation with her husband did not elicit a rise out of Becky. She was here for a purpose. She was here for Meghan.

After their greetings, Nash took Meghan by the arm and seemed to rush her through the swinging doors into the ER. It happened quickly, too quickly for comfort, and the hasty departure left Becky reeling.

Where was Nash taking her? What test or tests would be performed? When should she expect an update? It was as though Nash were Meghan's handler, ushering her to safety before her fans could converge. But this was no pop concert. This was her daughter, and her daughter was gone now, whisked away in a flash.

Becky turned to face Carl, concern clear on her face. "Did you think that was a bit abrupt? The departure, I mean."

Carl found an empty chair, sat himself down, and proceeded to unfold a magazine he'd brought with him — the current issue of *House Beautiful,* which he read faithfully, seeking design inspiration for his business. Becky sat beside him, annoyed that he did not seem to share her worry.

"It'll be fine."

"But she rushed Meghan off like there was a fire here. How can you say that?"

"Just trust me," Carl said as he flipped a page. "Everything will be fine."

CHAPTER 16

Meghan

Something was wrong with this. I could tell right from the start; the whole thing felt off. This wasn't like going to my other exams or doctor visits. For one, Dr. Nash didn't simply take hold of my arm as she led me away. She gripped it kind of hard, her fingers digging into my flesh as if she was worried I was going to run or something. And then she basically dragged me from my parents while they were still trying to get information from her. She pulled me through the emergency room doors, tugging at me to hurry the entire time like I was a stubborn mule.

We didn't go to the ER like I thought we would, like my mom and dad assumed I would. Instead, we went up an elevator and got off on the fourth floor. We followed a hallway to a glass-enclosed walkway that connected the main building where I was to a different building where I'd never been. We hardly spoke as we walked because I didn't feel like she was being as friendly or warm as before.

"How are you feeling?"

"Fine."

"How have you been?"

"Fine."

"Any new issues or symptoms I should know about?"

"No."

That was the extent of it. It was like we were texting each other. I wondered if she and my mom had gotten into a fight about me or something. Whenever I mentioned Dr. Nash's name, my mom would get an attitude like I'd mouthed off to her. So maybe that's why she hurried me away. Could be she and my mom weren't on the best of terms for reasons nobody thought I should know. I wasn't all that concerned about making small talk with Dr. Nash anyway. I was more worried that I wasn't even in the same building as my parents anymore.

"It's going to be fine, Meghan, sweetheart," Dr. Nash said, perhaps sensing my growing unease. "Really, not to worry. Okay? I'm here to help."

I admit that relaxed me some. Even so, I didn't like how Dr. Nash kept looking at me crookedly, as though I had done something wrong.

While the ER was kind of run-down, everything in this building was sparkling new, very nice looking. Tall glass windows lined a gleaming hallway, and would have let in a lot of light if it weren't so cloudy outside. But I'm not my father's daughter when it comes to architecture and design. I didn't care what this place looked like. I cared more what it was for, which was why I got nervous when I noticed the sign above the double glass doors ahead that read: WHITE MEMORIAL HOSPITAL DEPARTMENT OF PSYCHIATRY.

Why would she bring me here? I asked myself. But I didn't say anything to Dr. Nash as she ushered me through those doors, then down some other hall, and into a room with a single hospital bed and two — I guess I'd call them reception chairs, each with white leather cushions and a black frame finish.

The chairs were positioned next to each other at an angle, to encourage conversation. The walls were bone white. It smelled of powerful cleansers. The hospital bed had no sheets and no pillow. There were no pictures on the wall. No wastebasket. No other furniture of any kind.

I had all sorts of questions swimming about my head, but those would have to wait because a man entered the room. He smiled at me, said his name was Dr. Peter Levine, and told me that he'd be the one giving me my exam. I must have looked nervous, because he assured me it would be nothing more than a simple conversation. He motioned for me to sit in one of the chairs, and then he sat in the other. Time to talk.

"I'll be with you in a minute, Meghan," Dr. Nash said. Her voice sounded sweet, but her smile didn't comfort me. "You'll be fine here with Dr. Levine. Just answer his questions and then we'll take it from there, okay?"

"Okay."

"Why don't you let me hold your phone so that you won't become distracted?"

I pulled my cell phone from my front pants pocket and gave it to her without thinking. She was the doctor, and unless it involved a needle, I simply did what doctors told me to do. But as soon as Dr. Nash had my phone, I wanted it back. It felt wrong not having it pressed up against my leg. That phone was my lifeline. How was I going to call my mother after the exam?

As Dr. Nash slipped my phone into the

pocket of her lab coat, a terrible fear over-came me. My earlier premonitions that something was off came back but even stronger. I imagined myself bolting from my chair, pushing past Nash, grabbing my phone back as I knocked her down.

The fantasy didn't end there. In my mind, I sprinted down the hall, kicking security guards right where it hurt if any of them dared get in my way. And I kept on run-ning, legs churning fast, my arms pumping with purpose, getting back to my parents. But I didn't stop for them, or for anybody. I was out the door and I just kept on run-ning. At that moment, if only in my mind, I was the unstoppable one on the soccer field again. I was the fighter my dad had always told me he admired.

"Don't worry, Meghan. This will be fine."

The sound of Dr. Levine's high-pitched nasal voice pulled me cruelly back to re-ality. Dr. Nash left, shutting the door, tak-ing my cell phone with her. Dr. Levine crossed his legs and fixed me with a curious look. I felt two feet tall. I wanted to sink into my chair and disappear. At that mo-ment, I thought I'd rather have needles pushed into my arms.

Dr. Levine was a lot younger than the other doctors I'd seen. He looked so young that if we'd been out together, people would've thought it was an awkward date. A thin neck barely filled out his shirt collar, while his sport coat hung like a bedsheet across his narrow shoulders. His wire-rimmed glasses magnified a pair of dull blue eyes. He wore his sandy brown hair in a short, convenient style so that he wouldn't have to think about it. A prominent Adam's apple fit his equally prominent nose. In high school terms, Dr. Levine, most certainly, no doubt about it, would have hung with the nerds.

He started talking quickly, like he was nervous or something, but I wasn't paying much attention. I was still wondering why Dr. Nash had brought me to see a psychiatrist when I thought I was getting an emergency exam. "Emergency" to me meant in the ER, and "exam" meant something involving medical instruments. I'm pretty sure that's what it meant to my mother as well, but who'd ever heard of having an emergency conversation?

"So tell me, how are you feeling? Meghan?"

"Huh?" I sounded like I was zoning out in math class when the teacher asked me a question.

"How are you feeling?" he repeated.

I looked at my lap because it was easier than looking at him. "Fine," I said.

"Well, you haven't been that fine. Dr. Nash tells me you're not going to school anymore."

"I'm too sick to go," I said.

I figured he was going to ask me all sorts of questions about what kind of sick, but he didn't.

"Do you like school?" he asked.

"Sure," I said. "Better than being home all the time."

"Do you want to go back to school?"

I nodded, but still wasn't looking at him.

"How come you don't go back to school?"

I shrugged my shoulders. *How do I answer that?* Give him the truth, I guessed.

"My mom doesn't think I'm well enough to attend."

"It must be hard when your mom tells you that."

I nodded. *Of course it's hard,* I thought. *What a dumb thing to say.*

"What do you think about her decision?"

I shrugged again, thinking about what he'd want me to say. I mean, maybe my mom was a little too overprotective. Maybe I could go and just not do as well in my classes. Maybe I could be a below-average student and just get by. But that would have required me to paint a picture that was less black-and-white and more shades of gray. I felt so tired and defeated. I just wanted to give him an answer that would put an end to this conversation.

"I guess I'm too sick to go," I said.

"Because your mom says so, or because you say so?"

What does it matter? I wanted to say, but I told him, "Because my mom says so." I don't really have an opinion anymore. I do what the doctors say. I do what my mother says because I'm the daughter. I'm the child here. I'm the one who still needs protecting.

"Does your mom give you medicine?"

I nodded. "Right now, I take a drink called a mito cocktail," I explained. I expected Dr. Levine to ask me what that was all about, but he didn't.

"Does your mom make you take it every day?"

"Yeah," I said. "I'm supposed to."

"Does she make you take a lot of medicines?"

At that point, I wanted to say, *Why are you asking so many questions about my mother?* but I didn't say anything. Usually, when doctors ask me questions, they're about how I feel, not my feelings. I guess that's why these questions were so much harder to answer.

"Does your mom make all the decisions about what you do?"

"Sure. But I don't really do anything anymore."

"That must be hard for you, when your mom is always telling you what to do or what not to do."

I nodded again, but this time more emphatically because it was true. It *was* hard for me, but a lot of things were hard for me these days. Maybe he could ask me something about my dad. Then I'd have an earful for him. I could tell him all sorts of things I knew, the kind of things nobody would want to know about a parent, but he was only interested in my mom. Too bad for him — we'd have a lot more to talk about otherwise.

"Doesn't seem like you get to do what you want to do."

"I don't."

"Because your mom makes you do things you don't want to do?"

Now I was starting to get annoyed. Didn't we cover this already? *What does he want me to say?* My mom takes me to doctors all the time. She's always trying new treatments to get me better. She doesn't have any real friends anymore. She doesn't go out. She spends more time online than any of my friends do. That's her world now. She's all about my sickness and me. Do I want to see different doctors all the time? No! Do I want to keep trying new treatments? No, of course not. So I said, "Yeah, I don't get to do what I want to do much, if at all."

"Does your mom make you take these drugs?"

"Yes."

"Does it make you upset to take so many different kinds of medicines?"

"It all makes me upset," I said.

"Like the mito cocktail you told me about. Your mom makes you take that, too?"

"Yes."

"And you don't want to take it?"

"No." *Who would?* I'm thinking.

"It must be hard for you, having to do all those things your mother makes you do."

"Yeah, it's hard," I repeated. "When can I go see my parents?"

I bit my nails. Bad habit, like the drinking, but it was a hard one to break, especially whenever I got nervous. Dr. Levine stood. I guess our exam was over. Thank God. He tugged at his jacket, but it didn't fit any better.

"Thanks so much for being honest with

me, Meghan. I'm going to go speak with Dr. Nash, and we'll take it from there."

"What am I supposed to do?" I felt my throat tightening as a trickle of fear traced up my neck. I didn't like the idea of being left alone in here.

"Why don't you sit up on the bed, and I'll be with you in a minute."

Up on that bed I went. I didn't give a second thought to his instruction, because hopping up on hospital beds was something I'd been doing for ages now. It was a reflex, more than anything. But this was a naked bed. No sheets. No pillows. No crinkly paper beneath me. As he left, Dr. Levine took away the chairs we'd been sitting in, and it became a bare room. I was confused.

"I'll be right back," he said.

He closed the door behind him, and I was alone. I sat on the bed, waiting, but after a while, I couldn't sit anymore. I slid off the bed and started to pace the room like a caged tiger. At least I wasn't in a "hospital sundress," but I didn't have my cell phone, so I felt a different kind of vulnerable. After a few minutes of pacing aimlessly, I decided I'd had enough waiting.

I went to the door, turned the knob, and pulled. The door wouldn't budge. Trembling, I turned the knob again and pulled harder this time. My throat went dry and tight. The walls really were closing in on me. I turned and pulled again and again, but it was no use.

The door was locked from the outside.

CHAPTER 17

Becky

She rose from her chair for the fifth time that hour. A check of her phone told her they had been waiting three hours without a word from Meghan or Dr. Nash. Anxiety made it nearly impossible to sit still a second longer. Becky took a single step in the direction of the reception window before feeling Carl's gentle tug on the waistband of her slacks.

"Where are you going?" he asked in a whispered voice. He tossed the magazine he'd been pretending to read on the empty chair beside him.

Becky swiveled at her waist to break free of his grasp. "I'm going to page Dr. Nash again."

"You just had her paged a few minutes ago," Carl said in a displeased tone. "Give it a sec, will you?"

"We've been here for hours!" Becky's

voice rose in anger as she gestured toward the bay doors of the emergency room. "Where is Meghan? Where is she? What are they doing to her? What tests are they running? She's not answering her phone. She always answers her texts. Doesn't that concern you?"

"It's just taking time. They're busy."

Becky's narrowing eyes were a form of censure. "And you're being naïve," she shot back.

Turning on her heels, Becky marched toward the receptionist's window, moving past a mother comforting twin girls, who appeared to have matching ailments to go with their matching pink denim jackets. She knocked on the clear glass window to get the attention of the impassive receptionist, who poked her head out from behind a towering computer monitor. A strained smile appeared when she saw it was Becky summoning her yet again.

"May I help you?" she asked.

"Yes, please page Dr. Nash. I want to see my daughter, Meghan, right now." Becky made no effort to soften her acerbic tone.

"I just did that for you a few minutes ago," the receptionist explained. "In fact, I think we've paged her twice already."

"And what? She didn't respond again?

Does she always ignore her page?"

The receptionist returned a nervous shake of her head. The gesture was meant to be conciliatory, reinforcing Becky's belief that something was definitely amiss.

"Is this unusual?" Becky asked. "Does a doctor often take away a child and not report back for over three hours? Not answer her page? Not even tell the mother what she's doing? What tests she's running? Or even where they are?" Becky sensed Carl's presence looming behind her.

"Sweetheart, she's just doing her job," he said of the beleaguered receptionist. "Go easy on her. We'll sort this out." Carl leaned down to put his face in the window. "I'm so sorry to be a bother," he said, addressing the woman behind the glass. "We're trying to track down our daughter, and we're growing a bit impatient. We'll take our seats, just let us know when you hear back from Dr. Nash."

That's it, Carl, play nice with everyone because that's been working for us so well. Sometimes Becky wanted to scream at her husband to step up and get something done for a change, fix one of their goddamn problems.

He could do it well enough with his business, that was for sure. Contractors weren't delivering on a job? Look out, here comes Carl to give them a good tongue-lashing. Local government wasn't cooperating with a permit problem? It's Carl to the rescue! But when a doctor absconds with his child and won't answer her damn page? *Please . . . and thank you . . . and yes, we'll patiently wait right here.* Becky gritted her teeth because otherwise she might have punched him in the jaw.

Stepping away from the window, Becky let the gentleman with a nagging cough behind her check in with Reception.

Carl followed. "Just relax, honey," he said, taking hold of her arm. "It'll all be fine."

"*You* relax," Becky said to him, pulling free of his grip.

She walked away, not back to their seats, but to stand near the automatic door into the ER. Those doors stayed shut unless the receptionist or someone else with a badge opened them.

"What are you doing?" Carl asked. He eyed Becky with suspicion.

"I'm waiting patiently for our daughter," Becky said, taking a sarcastic tone. "What does it look like I'm doing?"

She did not mean to be so cutting, but he was making it difficult to be kind. Carl exhaled loud enough to express obvious exasperation with his wife.

"What on earth do you think could have gone wrong?" he asked. "It's just taking time. These things *always* take time."

"Plenty could be wrong," Becky snapped. She shook her head in disgust at Carl's inexcusable nonchalance. "There could be a medical emergency, or worse. So until Dr. Nash gets back to us with an update, forgive me for not feeling compelled to sit down and wait patiently."

At that moment, the automatic doors to the ER whooshed open as a nurse exited. Becky slipped past the nurse unnoticed. Carl hurried his steps to catch up to his wife before those doors closed. Becky paused to glance over her shoulder. Satisfied nobody was coming to stop her, she continued her advance. Carl fell into step behind. He reached again for Becky's arm, but she pulled away.

"Stop, Becky! Just stop!"

Becky glared back at him without breaking stride. Soon, she was standing in the actual emergency room. In the background, she could hear babies crying, groans from the sick and injured. She heard doctors shouting orders and saw nurses running to carry them out. The ER was a brightly lit, open space. A curved desk in the center of the room served as mission control for the doctors and nurses who triaged the emergencies taking place behind the curtained bays that lined the walls. Becky wondered which one held her daughter. With the curtains closed, it was impossible to tell.

She tapped the shoulder of a woman dressed in burgundy scrubs who was standing nearby, writing something on a medical chart. "Excuse me," she said. "My daughter, Meghan Gerard, is here being seen by Dr. Amanda Nash. Could you tell me which bay she's in?"

The woman's eyes turned murky with confusion. "I'm sorry, who are you looking for?" she asked.

"Meghan Gerard," Becky said anxiously. "Dr. Amanda Nash brought her here."

The woman — a doctor or nurse, Becky had no way of knowing — took Becky and Carl over to mission control. Carl still looked perturbed, but Becky could not care less how annoyed or frustrated he was with her. She wanted her daughter, and she wanted her now.

The woman with the burgundy scrubs hurriedly typed something into the computer. "I'm sorry," the woman said, sending Becky a sidelong glance. "But we don't have a Meghan Gerard here."

Becky's pulse started racing, and even Carl began to show some real concern.

"What do you mean?" he asked. "Of course she's here."

Burgundy Scrubs shook her head. "No, I just checked. She may be at White, but she's not here in the ER."

Becky's heart plummeted into her stomach. Carl got out his phone.

Becky glared at him hard. "What are you doing?"

"I'm calling . . . I'm calling the hospital," he said, stammering. "I'm trying to find her."

"We are *in* the hospital," Becky snapped at him. Turning to Burgundy Scrubs, Becky shouted: "Where is my daughter!"

Becky's outburst caught the attention of an armed security guard standing nearby. He hurried over. As he approached, Carl moved away, still with his phone pressed to his ear.

"A doctor at your hospital brought my daughter to the ER, and now she's missing," Becky told the guard. It terrified her to think Meghan could be anywhere in the massive White Memorial Hospital complex. With so many buildings, a person could vanish here and never be heard from again.

"When did you last see your daughter?"

the security guard asked.

"When Dr. Nash took her away from us over three hours ago," Becky said, her tone asking: *Where could she be?*

Searching for Carl, Becky spied him as he slipped out of view into the adjacent hallway. She went that way, hands on her hips, taking shallow breaths to force back a tide of rising panic. She stopped halfway to the hall.

"Meghan!" Becky called out, spinning in a circle like a mother who'd lost her child on the playground. "Meghan, baby, are you here? It's Mom. Where are you, sweetheart?"

The security guard approached again, but this time his expression was more severe. "Ma'am, you need to calm yourself."

Becky whirled to face him. "You need to help me find my daughter."

She was bewildered, bathed in sweat. People were coming toward her now, all looking a bit uneasy, as if they were approaching a wild horse. She pulled at her hair as if that could calm the canter of her heart. Every fiber in her being told her something was dreadfully wrong.

"You have no right to keep her from me!" The shrillness of Becky's voice startled even her.

From the direction where Carl had gone,

two additional armed security guards entered the ER. Patients and their worried families began poking their heads out from behind curtains. Becky resisted the urge to go into each of those bays.

"Which doctors were treating your daughter?"

Doctors, thought Becky. *That's right. What's the name of that other doctor Nash mentioned? And where the hell is Carl?* Becky would address him later. She searched her mind, and eventually the name came to her.

"Dr. Peter Levine," she said.

Burgundy's eyes lit up. "I know Peter," she said with a smile that brought Becky a measure of calm. "He's a child psychiatrist here."

Becky felt the air leave her lungs. "He's what?" Alarm bells rang loudly in her ears.

"He's a staff child psychiatrist. Works in the Behavioral Health Unit. I can give you directions there."

Becky vigorously shook her head. "No . . . no . . . she came here to have a medical procedure. It was an emergency exam." Becky cupped her hands over her mouth again and started to pace. "I shouldn't have let her go. . . . I should have asked for more details . . . but . . . I thought, I thought . . ."
She stopped and looked Burgundy Scrubs

in the eyes as though she were a confidant. "I trusted her."

And it was true. When she got the second doctor's name, Becky had assumed he was a GI specialist, same as Nash. And Nash was the one in charge. She was the one Becky had to know about, not Levine. Becky's thoughts had been so fogged with fear, a certainty that it was cancer, stress eclipsing her disciplined approach, that in an unforgivable lapse of protocol, she had lost sight of the other doctor involved.

Just then, Carl appeared, but he was not alone. Nash was with him, as was a man Becky did not recognize. He was tall and broad-shouldered, with a finely coiffed mane of silver hair and swarthy good looks that would make him stand out in almost any crowd. He wore a well-tailored blue suit, and his shoes were shined to a mirrored finish. She figured this was Dr. Levine.

Becky sighed with relief. She shifted her gaze over to Carl and noticed his grave expression. Fear wormed into her gut again.

"Who is that with Dr. Nash?" Becky asked Burgundy Scrubs.

"That's Knox Singer. He's the hospital CEO."

Singer, not Levine, thought Becky. *What the hell is going on?*

199

Carl worked his way through the small crowd of people gathered around Becky. He took hold of Becky's arm, pulling her in close. His touch, the familiar lemony scent of his aftershave, brought her no comfort.

"They want to speak with us in private," Carl whispered in her ear. "There's a serious problem."

CHAPTER 18

Crammed into a room off the ER, Becky, Carl, Dr. Nash, and Knox Singer sat at a round table facing each other. Becky wondered if this was the place doctors retreated to when they had to break bad news. The framed pictures of ships at sea looked cheap enough to grace the walls of a second-rate motel. Equally cheap lighting made everyone look washed out and slightly ghoulish. The tight quarters forced Becky into close proximity with a woman she wanted to pummel with her fists.

Two armed and uniformed security guards stood in a corner, animated as statues. They fixed Becky with sober expressions, an obvious warning against any kind of outburst.

"What the hell is going on?" Becky said, preempting Knox Singer, who appeared ready to make some introductory remarks.

"Mrs. Gerard," Knox Singer said, "let me start by saying how truly sorry I am for keeping you and your husband waiting so long for information."

Singer's imperturbable voice made Becky want to scream. He was smug and arrogant, full of himself, she thought. Nothing about him came across as sincere or honest.

"Where is Meghan?" Carl said harshly. "What the hell have you done with her?"

Becky was pleased to see her husband direct his question to Dr. Nash, whom she blamed for this trouble.

"Meghan is fine," Singer said, still trying out his placating tone. "She's presently in our Behavioral Health Unit."

"Doing what?" Becky asked, now in a stare-down with Singer. "Why is she there?"

"She's resting."

"Okay," Carl said, baffled. "Resting from what? Pardon my French, but what the fuck is going on here?"

Singer and Nash exchanged glances.

"We have a serious situation," Knox Singer said.

"Yes, you told me that in the hall," Carl said. "I'm asking, what situation do we have?"

Carl directed his question at Nash. Becky set her hand on her husband's leg, and soon felt the familiar brush of his fingers as he interlaced his with hers, squeezing tight.

The room door opened, ushering in a man with a troubled expression who looked young enough to be Becky's son. Accompanying the man was an older woman, dressed nattily in business attire. She was in her late fifties, Becky thought. She styled her hair with severe bangs and wore practical shoes that suggested she did lots of walking. Deep worry lines stretched across her forehead, as though she were perpetually dealing with some crisis, seldom getting a reprieve from the tempest of her day.

"Sorry I'm late," the young man said. "There was an incident. Ms. Hope was there to observe."

"What kind of incident?" Nash asked warily.

"Who is this?" Becky said, gesturing to the man. She looked around the room as if everyone should share her outrage at how uninformative this meeting had become. "Is this about Meghan? And who are you?" Becky addressed the woman in a voice loud enough to inspire the guards to take a single step away from the wall.

"This is Dr. Peter Levine," Knox Singer said. "He works with us. And this," he said, motioning to the woman, "is Ms. Annabel Hope, with the Massachusetts Department of Children and Families. And, yes, this is about your daughter."

There was only one empty seat at the table, which Annabel Hope took, leaving Dr. Levine to stand. Whatever rodeo this was, it was obvious to Becky that Ms. Hope had ridden her share of horses.

"We had to give her a sedative," Dr. Levine said, addressing Nash while ignoring Becky. "Five milligrams of haloperidol."

Becky knew all about the antipsychotic medication haloperidol, or Haldol, as it was marketed under its brand name. Becky was outraged. "You can't give my daughter a sedative like that without talking to us first," she said angrily to Levine, who shrank under the weight of her stare.

"Mr. and Mrs. Gerard," Knox Singer said in an affectless voice. "I don't know how to tell you this gently, so I'm just going to have to come out and say it: Meghan is now in our temporary custody."

Carl shot out of his chair like a launched rocket. Pressing his arms against the table, he leaned forward, sending dirty looks at Nash, who did not shrink away. The two guards sprang forward to frame Carl so that if he made any threatening advance, it would be quickly countered.

Becky felt her stomach drop. "What are you talking about?"

Try as she might, Becky could not wrap her mind around what Knox Singer had said, and yet on some primal level, she understood: Her daughter was no longer hers. She belonged to someone else. But why? How could she be in the custody of the hospital? How could they give her drugs without parental permission?

"What do you mean, she's in your temporary custody?" Carl asked, saying what Becky was thinking. He remained standing, while Becky feared she'd topple over if she tried to join him.

Nash removed her glasses and bit at the tip. She looked at Ms. Hope, who seemed perfectly fine with someone else answering. Nash eyed Becky briefly before turning her attention to Carl. "We believe that your daughter's illness is primarily psychiatric in nature," Nash said in a voice that, much like her office, lacked any color or personality.

"No, no, you told me on the phone that you wanted to have Meghan seen to run some kind of tests," Becky said, seething.

Nash shifted uneasily in her chair.

Ms. Hope looked about as surprised at Nash's bait-and-switch routine as someone answering the doorbell on Halloween.

"What I told you on the phone," Nash

said, "is that we had to do an emergency exam. Those were my words exactly."

"Then you tricked us," Becky said, her voice slipping into a harsh whisper. "How dare you! How could you?"

Again, Becky blamed herself for not thoroughly vetting Levine. Why hadn't she looked him up in the hospital directory while she was in the waiting room? It would have done her no good anyway, Becky realized now. Megan was in their custody the moment she let her daughter out of her sight.

Dr. Levine shuffled nervously on his feet, but since there was nowhere for him to sit and nowhere else to go, he took over the spot on the wall that the security guards had abandoned to keep Carl in line.

"We have an obligation to all our patients to do no harm, and that includes making sure nobody is doing any harm to a child," Singer said.

"Are you suggesting that we're abusing our daughter?" Becky was beside herself with anger, though her expression showed only stunned disbelief.

"We have evidence to support that very possibility," Ms. Hope said, speaking for the first time. "A hospital has a legal responsibility to intervene in these matters. Dr. Nash felt strongly enough about her suspicions to order the psychiatric evaluation, which Dr. Levine performed." Ms. Hope nodded toward the rube doc perched against the wall.

"Dr. Levine interviewed Meghan about her experiences," she continued, "and based on her answers to a series of questions, he became very concerned. Given Meghan's lengthy medical history with puzzling symptoms and an endless stream of consults and treatments, all to no avail, there was reasonable cause for the hospital to file a complaint of medical child abuse with my group, the Massachusetts Department of Children and Families. My team acts quickly in these matters, since there's the possibility a child could be returned to a dangerous situation."

"We discussed your case in depth and reviewed all the evidence as provided to us by Drs. Nash and Levine," Knox Singer added, as if that made everything all right.

"Could I see that evidence?" Carl said, speaking through gritted teeth.

"I'm afraid not," Ms. Hope answered. "It's privileged."

Becky scoffed incredulously. "I can't believe what I'm hearing." She looked around the room as if everyone should be sharing her outrage. She looked to Carl, and then to Ms. Hope. "She's our daughter!" Becky shouted, pointing at herself. "Ours! You can't just take her without showing us this irrefutable proof of yours."

"At the moment, Mrs. Gerard," Ms. Hope said calmly, "as a consequence of the complaint, a judge has awarded temporary custody of Meghan to the Department of Children and Families."

"But how?" Becky asked, letting the disbelief ring her voice. "And when? She's been here only a few hours."

"In cases of suspected child abuse, the system has measures for expediting an emergency temporary ruling. We, in turn, have given our permission for Meghan to remain in the care of Dr. Nash and Dr. Levine here at White. Your daughter is now officially a ward of the state, so in legal terms, she's no longer yours to care for."

Chapter 19

Becky wanted to stand up, scream, and throw her chair at Ms. Hope, then pick it up and use it to beat Dr. Nash.

A ward of the state — that made her daughter sound like an orphan. In the eyes of the court, Becky was technically no longer a mother. But emotionally, spiritually, in all the ways that truly mattered, she had never felt more like a mother in all her life.

Fixing a pointed stare on Nash, Becky's eyes grew wide as she rose to her feet. "You tricked us! You tricked us!"

Her vision went black with anger. Separated from her body, her thoughts and actions no longer belonging to her, Becky lunged across the table at Nash. Before she could latch on to the lapels of her lab coat, one of the guards seized a clump of Becky's light knit sweater in his meaty mitt, hard enough to rip a small hole in the delicate thread as he pulled her back.

Carl went on the attack. He grabbed the guard's button-down shirt in his clenched fists, his face snarled with outrage. With a loud grunt, he gave a hard shove that sent the guard backward into the wall. The other guard, who had four inches and a good thirty pounds on his opponent, used a bear hug to pin Carl's arms to his sides.

Carl twisted and turned to free himself. Unsuccessful, he jumped up at the same time he snapped his head backward like a whip. His skull landed a perfect strike against the guard's bulbous nose. There was a sickening crunch and throaty noise, followed by a cry equal parts surprise and anguish. A gush of blood raced out of the guard's nostrils in alarming rivers of red as he spun Carl around to face him. He then uncorked a vicious jab to the midsection that doubled Carl over in pain.

Becky went after her husband's assailant while everyone else moved away. But before she could engage, the other guard clamped his big arms around her.

Becky tried to brake with her heels as he dragged her toward the door. "Why are you doing this to us?" she screamed.

Using the guard's back for leverage, Becky lifted herself high enough off the ground to kick at the one threatening Carl, but her feet bicycled harmlessly nowhere near her target.

"Stop it! Stop right now!" Knox Singer's booming voice brought a halt to the chaos like an irate parent putting an end to a sibling quarrel.

Becky's body went slack as the fight left her. Carl rose shakily to his feet, came to Becky's side, and pulled her into an embrace. The guard with the injured nose, his white shirt soiled like a Rorschach test, fished a cloth handkerchief from his pants pocket, which he then used to stanch the flow of blood. Becky pressed herself against Carl's heaving chest, sobbing uncontrollably. Dr. Nash approached the injured guard. She tilted his head back and examined his bloodied nose, but did not appear overly concerned.

Ms. Hope straightened her business suit after fussing with her hair, which needed no fussing. She stood extra tall in her sturdy shoes, and a self-satisfied grin parted her lips, the outburst seeming to have confirmed her doubts about the Gerards' fitness as parents. The guard who had manhandled Becky unclipped his two-way radio. He was about to call for backup, or so Becky believed, when Knox Singer waved his hands frantically to make him stop.

"Let's not make this situation any worse than it already is," Singer said, his perfectly styled mane now slightly unkempt.

Nobody said a word. Nobody was going to sit down.

Carl glared at Singer with daggers for eyes. "I want to see my daughter," he said with authority.

"I'm afraid at the moment it is not possible to grant you even a supervised visit with Meghan." Ms. Annabel Hope slipped her hands behind her back to signal no negotiation.

Shock replaced Becky's anger. She glared wide-eyed at Ms. Hope with utter bewilderment, as though assessing something alien and wholly foreign to her.

Becky had never seen Annabel Hope before today, had not known that they were in the same city, let alone shared the same planet. And yet this woman had in an instant become an integral part of Becky's world. She, this random person, was in charge of her daughter's life. Becky thought of it like a car accident: two strangers, unknown to each other moments before impact, collide in a life-altering way.

Cora. That was who flashed in her mind. This was her mother's fault. This was karma coming back to get her. Cora had played games with health-care providers for herself and for the sake of her family, and Becky had played similar games to help her daughter. Now both were paying a price — Cora stricken with cancer and Becky confronting a nightmare case of medical kidnapping.

Karma.

"When can I see my daughter?" Becky asked. Her voice came out shaky and soft, weaker than she had intended.

"I can't answer that. Not now, anyway," Singer said.

"When will you know?"

"When I do, you will. I promise," Singer said.

"How can I talk to her?" Becky asked, her top lip stiffening. She felt the tears pressing against her lids again.

"We're not allowing her phone contact or visitation right now," Dr. Nash said, looking to Dr. Levine, who hesitated before nodding in agreement.

"You can't do that!" Becky sensed Carl was going to raise a ruckus again. She tugged his arm to get him to look her in the eyes. The last thing she wanted was for her husband to leave in handcuffs. She needed him now more than ever.

Ms. Hope, perhaps sensing Becky's commitment to de-escalate, came around the table and confidently stood within striking distance.

"When can we speak to Meghan?" Becky directed her question to Ms. Hope.

"Communication with Meghan will be worked out when we've completed our assessments," Ms. Hope said with the same emotion a service manager might use when discussing a car repair timetable.

Becky noticed how she said "Meghan" and not "your daughter," as if the judge's ruling had erased the last fifteen years of Meghan's life, and Becky and Carl no longer factored into it.

"I have only one bit of advice to offer you at this moment, Mrs. Gerard, if you're receptive to hearing it," Ms. Hope said.

Becky returned a slight nod.

"Get a lawyer, and a damn good one at that."

Becky straightened. Anger blossomed in her eyes. "You do the same," she said, pulling Carl's arm to go.

"This isn't over," Carl said, a growl in his voice.

When they were finally out in the hall, Becky counted four guards sent to escort them out. She felt as though she were walking without limbs. She no longer thought of herself as the person she was before. She'd been carved, cleaved, separated from an integral part of herself; cut off suddenly, brutally, from what mattered most; given no clear explanation or even an indication for when she'd speak to, let alone see, Meghan again.

Carl took hold of Becky's hand. They walked numbly out of the automatic double doors into the ER waiting room. Those seated there gawked at the strange processional passing before them — two beleaguered parents trailed by four guards, one of whom wore a bloody shirt. The guards followed Becky and Carl outside into a chilly night devoid of stars. Before long, Becky and Carl were inside the gleaming spotless Mercedes, driving away from White Memorial with no passenger in the backseat — just the two of them, without their precious daughter.

CHAPTER 20

They drove interred in a weighty silence. Becky was too stunned and numb to even attempt conversation. The hostility radiating from Carl distressed Becky because she sensed it was directed at her.

"It's not true," Becky said, willing herself to speak. "None of what they're saying is true. You know that, don't you?"

Carl did not respond, nor did he glance her way. His focus stayed fixed on the road, but his intense concentration was obviously a means to avoid her. Becky shriveled inside. She feared what might be coming. During the fight with the guards, Carl had been her champion, her protector, but now she realized that had been his alpha-male instincts taking over. With time and distance, he was thinking other thoughts. Thinking it might all be true.

They arrived at home not having spoken more than a dozen words between them.

Carl pulled into the garage and came to a hard stop. He got out of the car, slamming his door shut with a bang that made Becky jump.

"I'm going to call my lawyer," he grumbled, heading to his office above the garage. Becky made her way to the kitchen, where she poured herself a generous portion of red wine. It rippled in her shaky grasp. She downed it quickly and poured herself a second glass. She called up to Carl, but he did not answer.

Give him space, she thought as she went up to her office on the second floor, wineglass in one hand and bottle in the other. The large home always felt overwhelming to her, even with the cleaners, landscapers, and various repairmen who kept the place operational without her having to do much more than dial a number. Tonight, it felt profoundly empty.

She walked past Meghan's bedroom, finding it impossible to look inside, let alone sit on her empty bed.

Becky fired up her computer and within moments had Veronica Del Mar on Face-Time. It was after nine o'clock in the evening, but Veronica, draped in a cream-colored cardigan sweater, seemed as fresh and put together as if the day had just begun.

"Sweetheart, it's good to see your beautiful face!" Veronica exclaimed. Becky knew for sure that she looked anything but beautiful.

"It's been a hell of a day," Becky said, taking a gulp of wine.

Becky recounted the entire story in detail, taking her time to get all the details right, starting with Nash's request for an emergency exam and ending with Carl storming off into their silent home to call the lawyer.

"They can't do that!" Veronica sounded shocked. "It's criminal. It's kidnapping."

"That's what I told them," Becky said, feeling the familiar crimp that portended tears. Becky had friends to lean on, a sister she should call, but Veronica was the only one she felt able to confide in. Nobody offered a better shoulder — even if it was virtual — to cry on.

"What now, honey?" Veronica asked, her mellifluous voice full of feeling. Veronica poured a glass of wine herself, a rosé of some variety.

"Carl's going to get us a lawyer. We'll get her back."

"Will we?" Carl's darkly menacing voice came from the doorway.

Becky turned to see him take an unsteady step into the room. Light from the hallway cast Carl in shadows, but she could still make out the glass tumbler clutched in his hand, only a sliver of whiskey at the bottom. She speculated it had been full not moments ago.

"I'll be off in a minute," Becky said, trying to ignore the uneasy feeling creeping through her. Her home should be a sanctuary, and her husband should be her stalwart supporter — yet neither felt true.

Carl took a few more steps into the room. Becky could hear the clank of ice tumbling inside the glass. "Who are you talking to?" he asked, his voice brooding.

"Just Veronica," Becky said, trying to pass it off as nothing.

"Just Veronica," Carl repeated, drawing out the words, slurring them slightly so they blended together. He came closer until Becky could smell the whiskey. "Just Veronica," he repeated almost as an aside. "Did you tell Veronica what happened today?" he asked.

"Yes, of course," Becky said, turning her attention to the camera so she could focus on a friendly face.

"Carl, I'm so sorry," Veronica said through the computer speakers.

"Oh, are you?" Carl came forward to stand behind Becky, looming over her, his face lit strangely in the glow of her monitor. She craned her neck to look up at him.

"I know this is difficult," Veronica said. "But I'm sure it'll resolve itself soon, and Meghan will be home where she belongs in no time." Becky could hear the apprehension in Veronica's voice. Despite being thousands of miles away, her friend knew to be nervous.

"Or," Carl said, crouching low so that his face filled the camera's lens. He put his arm around Becky's chair as if to demonstrate solidarity, though Becky sensed it was a charade. "It won't resolve itself. Maybe I'll have to mortgage the house to pay the legal bills. Maybe our daughter will come back with PTSD from the experience." Carl pointed an accusatory finger at the camera lens and, by proxy, at Veronica. "Or maybe — and here's the big one for you, Veronica — maybe it's *your* fault." Carl took the final drink of whiskey and licked the liquid from his lips.

Veronica reflexively, or anxiously, brushed some platinum hair from her face. "I'm sorry, I don't follow?"

"You don't?" Carl asked, his voice taking an even darker turn. "Have you ever fed a stray animal, Veronica?" Becky hated how Carl said her name with such simmering contempt. "Do you know what happens when you do?"

"Carl, I don't see how a stray —"

"The animal comes back for more food," Carl said before she could finish. "Do you know why?"

"Please, Carl," Becky whispered.

Carl turned slightly, sending Becky an uneven smile that made her shiver. "Do you know why?" Carl asked again.

Veronica let out a sigh that could just as easily have been a groan. "Because it's hungry, Carl," she said snippily, stating the obvious.

"And now it doesn't have to look for food, because the food is right there, at your doorstep. So it gets conditioned to come to you, to visit, because you've made it need you."

"Are you implying that I'm feeding your wife ideas like she's some stray cat?"

"No," Carl said, removing his arm from the back of Becky's chair, his hard jaw set even tighter than usual. "I'm not implying it; I'm telling you that's what you're doing. You and all your little cohorts here on social media are nothing but a never-ending spin cycle of nonsense. But you don't think about the repercussions or the consequences. You don't think about how your actions affect real lives, do you? *Do you!*" Carl's face contorted with raw rage.

"I think you've had a long, traumatic day, and maybe a little too much to drink," Veronica said calmly enough, though Becky could see the strain on her friend's face.

"And I think you've put ideas into my wife's head. I think you're feeding off her worry and anxiety like some kind of vampire. Just because you screwed it up with your kid, doesn't mean I'm going to let you screw it up with mine." Carl picked up the laptop from Becky's desk, the magnetic power adapter coming free of its port. He held the laptop at eye level, peering angrily at Veronica.

Becky watched him warily. "What are you doing?" Becky said with some bite. "Leave us alone, Carl. You're being an asshole. Go somewhere else, please!"

Carl stepped away from Becky, but kept the computer's camera held up to his face so that Veronica could still see him. "The hospital is convinced that my wife is intentionally making my daughter sick. Did she tell you that?"

"I was getting the full story when you interrupted us," Veronica said.

Becky rose from her chair. She stormed over to Carl, trying desperately to pry the computer from his grasp, only to have him turn his back to her. "Give it to me," she said, jaw clenched, pounding away on Carl's back with her fists.

Undeterred, Carl took a few steps toward the window. He cradled the laptop in his hands while Becky landed blow after blow against his back. "I'll tell you what I think," Carl said, his voice flat. "I think you're poison. I think you've filled my wife's head with so much crap, she doesn't know what to think."

"I'm a big enough girl to think for myself, Carl!" Becky shouted. "Now, give me back my computer!" She pulled on his shirt but managed only to free the fabric from the waistband of his jeans.

Carl whirled.

Becky took a step back, afraid for a second he might smash the computer on her head. In all their time together, she'd never once feared him. He was strong, but never violent.

"You want to keep chatting with your virtual pal, is that it, Becky?"

Becky reached for the computer, but Carl pulled it away as her fingers brushed the outer casing.

"Or maybe you want to call your mother. Get some pointers on how to fool the system. You're obviously nowhere near her level of mastery."

Becky looked away, unable to stand the sight of his face.

Veronica cried out: "Carl, stop it! Stop it right now!"

"I told you," Carl said, narrowing his eyes at Becky. "I told you what was going to happen if you kept up your search, kept pushing for more tests, more treatments."

"Your daughter is sick, Carl," Veronica said, trying to keep an even tone.

"You took my daughter from me!" Carl shouted at the computer, at Veronica. "You did this! You!"

Becky rushed at Carl, reaching for him, but did not see the chair in her way. Before she knew it, she was on the floor, landing hard on her knees. On her way down, Becky's arm clipped the wineglass on the desk, shattering it to pieces on impact. A pool of red liquid seeped into the rug like a gruesome stain.

Carl moved toward the window. "No more feeding my wife your cracked-up ideas about our daughter," he told Veronica. "Leave us alone. You're not welcome here. Not now. Not ever."

Carl opened the window. He used the computer to push out the screen as Becky yelled for him to stop.

"It's for your own good," Carl said impassively. "And mine."

Without another word, Carl opened his hands and let the computer fall from his grasp. Becky heard Veronica scream as though she were the one he'd tossed out the open window.

CHAPTER 21

Zach

When Zach heard the news, he knew he'd be cutting his Cleveland trip short.

He'd already given his speech about childhood mitochondrial disease to a packed room of doctors, researchers, and parents, all of whom had a stake, some bigger than others, in finding a cure for the incurable.

Zach's presentation had gone over quite well. As expected, he had fielded a number of questions about the Elamvia clinical trial he was helping to coordinate. He'd also facilitated a lively Q&A focused on the mito cocktail, which some believed had little scientific data to support its effectiveness.

There was also considerable discussion around coenzyme Q_{10}, a substance similar to a vitamin, which segued into a somewhat contentious dosing debate that Zach knew was coming and would have preferred to avoid. There were no clear answers with this disease. Every potential solution had drawbacks, including high dosing of coenzyme Q_{10}, which offered evidence of improvement in muscle fatigue for some but also led to muscle breakdown in 10 to 20 percent of patients. With mitochondrial disease, it always seemed to be one step forward and five steps in reverse.

For Zach, it was another year at another conference, attending lectures, dinners, and breakout sessions as he endured the discomfort of a stiff back from his sagging hotel mattress. And, as usual, he'd be leaving with no new medical breakthroughs or hints of a cure. In essence, it had been another year with nothing much gained but the renewed promise of a better tomorrow. But it was time away from Boston, from home, from memories he could not, would not forget. And oddly enough, whenever Zach left the Boston area, the dream left with him. Zach kept his phone in his hotel room so he would not be distracted during the lectures, but when he checked his voice mail for the first time that day, he found a different sort of nightmare waiting for him: an extremely irate message from Becky that had made him shake with anger at Nash.

He had called Nash, of course, but the call was sent directly to voice mail, probably intentionally. If he were in her shoes, he would have done the same. Still, he had left a rather angry message that implored her to call him immediately. He did not expect his phone to ring anytime soon. He could hardly fathom the number of lines Nash had crossed, but the deed was done, the bomb had gone off, and what was left for Zach were the pieces of a shattered family he'd have to try to put back together.

Zach checked out of his hotel a day early and caught a late-night flight back to Boston, incurring a rather hefty fee for the last-minute change. He instructed his office manager to reach out to the Gerards and set up a meeting at White first thing in the morning. He knew he was being a bit of a coward not addressing the family right away, but figured everyone would be better off after a night's sleep, assuming anyone would get a wink.

Zach could hardly imagine Becky Gerard's anguish, though he knew the source of her pain would be staring right back at him anytime he peered into a mirror. As antici- pated, Zach had a hard time falling asleep that night, but when he finally did, he dreamed he was sitting next to his boy, on a park bench, under a bright blue sky, eating ice cream, waiting for his heart to get ripped out.

Becky and Carl sat across from Zach in a room a few doors down from his cluttered office. Outside, the early-morning sun sprinkled prisms of light across the windows of the tall buildings comprised in the White Memorial medical complex. Off to the north was the Mendon Building, home to the Behavioral Health Unit.

Zach saw Becky glancing out the window repeatedly. He got the feeling she knew exactly where her daughter was being held. After this meeting, Zach planned to go to Mendon to try to see Meghan and get an update on her condition, but first he had to face the parents.

"It's your fault," Becky said, her voice packing a lot less punch than Zach had expected. Exhaustion may have taken its toll, zapping Becky's fight.

"I understand you're angry," Zach said, "but I promise you I'm going to do everything I can to help."

Becky had on a black sweater over a paisley-patterned blouse and dark jeans that showed off her slender physique. Carl was equally put together, dressed in a white oxford shirt and dark jeans as well, the glint of a gold Rolex peeking out from beneath a cuffed sleeve. Zach suspected people were often jealous of them, the perfect couple who seemed to have it all, but if they knew the daunting situation they faced, he doubted any of those envious souls would trade places with the Gerards.

Carl Gerard sent Zach a look of pure contempt. Zach's one and only fight had been on a school playground at the end of sixth grade against a boy he'd had no business battling, but who'd needed a punch in the nose to put an end to his bullying. It looked to Zach like Carl was ready to make it fight number two.

Becky Gerard was seated next to her husband, but Zach observed no real connection between them. They did not make eye contact, or hold hands, or do any of the little things that he and Stacy might have done before everything fell to pieces. Whatever had come between husband and wife was pronounced enough to feel like a fourth person in the room.

"What has Nash said?" Becky asked. "How long are they going to hold Meghan here? When can we bring her home? When can we see her? Talk to her?"

Zach looked down at his hands. He did not have any answers and said as much.

230

"Well, when are you going to know?" Carl asked, leaning forward, encroaching on Zach's personal space the way that playground bully had done so many years ago.

"I've left messages for Dr. Nash, and I have calls in to Knox Singer. I'm sure they'll meet me later today."

"And what are we supposed to do in the meantime?" Becky said, tossing up her hands in distress. Her body sagged forward as tears sprang to her eyes.

To Zach's utter surprise, Carl made no gesture to comfort his wife.

"This is a process," Zach said. "Not one I'm very familiar with, to be honest, but it's happened in mito cases before. This disease, unfortunately, has unusual and inconsistent symptoms. Parents, like yourselves, often become strong advocates for their children, pushing for consults with specialists and sophisticated tests. Some doctors misinterpret these efforts as a bid for attention and label the condition Munchausen syndrome by proxy."

"Where have you heard that term before, Becky, huh?" Carl asked.

"We both know that answer," Becky replied coolly.

Zach knew not to tread on the obvious marital strife as he knew to avoid a downed power line. "From what I understand of this situation — and, granted, I haven't been able to do a deep dive here — it's a temporary custody ruling, so we have time to plan our next moves."

Color rushed into Becky's pale cheeks. "Time? These people have my daughter!" she exclaimed. "They took her phone. I don't have time to wait. I'm going up there now, right now, to get her." Becky pointed out the window. "They've kidnapped her! Don't you see? We need the goddamn FBI here!" Becky smacked her hand against the table, the sound punctuating her decree. "I don't think I've made myself clear, Dr. Fisher. I'm not leaving here without my daughter."

Carl shot his wife a hard look. "Maybe you should have thought all this through before you set off on your quest to make Meghan a medical cripple."

Becky snapped her head around so fast, Zach thought he heard vertebrae popping. "You know what, Carl, fuck you." Becky looked away in disgust.

Carl pushed his chair back. "I told you this meeting was going to be a waste of time," he hissed, rising to his feet with a scowl. "I'll meet you at the lawyer's office." He tossed his car keys onto the table with a clatter. "I'll take a cab. I have a few hours to kill, so I'm going to go check on the condo job in Beacon Hill."

"Aren't you going to try to see your daughter?" Becky remained in her chair, her gaze directed once more out the window at the Mendon Building.

"We can't see her, Becky," Carl said, "or do you think the judge's ruling is all bullshit?"

Zach thought if Carl's voice carried any more bite, Becky would have suffered a puncture wound. "Listen, I understand you're both extremely emotional right now, and that's understandable, but I think for Meghan's sake it's important we form a united front here."

"Really," Becky said, glaring at Carl, who was putting his sport coat on. "Because our united front involved my husband throwing my computer out our second-story window."

Zach thought it best not to press for details. "Listen, can we please sit and talk?" he implored.

"You sit. You talk," Carl answered cuttingly. "But don't you think you've done enough damage already? Stay out of this, Dr. Fisher. This isn't your fight anymore." And with that, Carl was out the door, the stamp of his heavy footsteps fading down the hallway.

Becky sat quietly for a moment. "I'm sorry," she said. "That wasn't fair of him — or me, for that matter. I know this isn't your fault."

"What's happened between you?" Zach's instincts told him not to press for information, but curiosity beat out his better judgment.

"Are you married?" Becky asked. She caught herself, embarrassed, as if she had remembered something, and decided against saying it aloud.

Zach wondered if he had told her about Stacy and Will, but could not recall.

"That's personal, I shouldn't have asked," she said.

It took a moment or two for the tension to leave his body, and when it did, Zach shared, in brief, the worst moments of his life.

"Oh God, I'm sorry," Becky said. "You did tell me that and it completely slipped my mind when I asked my question. I feel terrible for bringing it up."

"It's not a problem. And, hopefully, it helps to know that I understand all too well how a marriage can suffer under extreme stress. You have my sympathy."

"I lost my son, too, you know."

Zach didn't know. His heart broke for her.

"SIDS," she said. "I put him down for a nap, and when I went to check on him, he was gone."

"I'm so sorry," Zach said.

"It was eighteen years ago, but I still think of him all the time. I wonder where he would be today, what he'd be doing. He'd probably be off to college."

"I can relate to everything you're saying," Zach replied, holding Becky's gaze, feeling a long-forgotten tug on his heart.

"Even today, all these years later, just seeing a crib can send me back into that darkness. That's why we had to move, to escape the reminders that were everywhere, that covered every inch of the town where Sammy died."

"You and Carl have been through an awful lot," Zach said, finding his words empty and unhelpful.

"What I need is to have my husband at my side," Becky said.

"What happened last night?"

"Carl found me chatting with my friend Veronica over FaceTime, and he just lost it. He started screaming at me, well Veronica mostly. Blaming her for everything because she's part of my online support group, but really he was blaming me for letting the group fill my head with a nonsense fantasy, nonsense in his view at least, that Meghan is actually sick. Then he tossed my computer out the window."

"He's wrong," Zach said. "And Nash is wrong, too."

To Zach's complete surprise and astonishment, Becky reached across the table to put her hand over his hand. His body froze up like an engine grinding to a halt. He was not at all accustomed to touch.

Did the contact comfort her, or was she flirting with him? Zach was not sure, but he did notice her looking at him in a different way, and it made him feel incredibly uncomfortable. He pulled his hand out from underneath Becky's, hoping his slow withdrawal would be viewed less harshly than if he had jerked his hand free, which was his initial instinct.

"How can you be so sure of me?" Becky asked.

Zach cleared his throat and recomposed himself. "I don't believe for one second that you'd hurt your daughter intentionally. We're going to get this straightened out."

"What if I was doing it unintentionally?" Becky asked. "What if I'm sick and I can't help myself?"

Zach found Becky's calm demeanor eerily unsettling. "I don't believe that's true," he said, worried his answer might have sounded forced.

"Why so confident?" Becky asked. "You don't know me well at all. How can you be so sure of yourself?" The coolness in her voice set a chill against Zach's skin. If he'd just met her, if this were a police interview, he'd think her quite capable of the charges.

"I guess I can be confident because I believe Meghan has mito," he said.

"But you're not positive, are you, because we don't know for sure it's mito?"

Zach shook his head, rubbing his facial scruff with the hand newly freed from Becky's touch. "That's right, I'm afraid. We haven't confirmed a diagnosis."

"So you see, Carl might be behaving like a complete jerk but, in a way, a part of me understands why he'd have his doubts. Nash, too. But what I don't understand is how they can take my daughter without having the proof. Why does Nash's claim trump ours?"

"Because you don't return a child to a dangerous situation," Zach said flatly.

Becky's body tensed. She got it. If mito were harming Meghan, then it would be blamed on bad luck and nothing more. But if Becky were to cause harm, everyone from the hospital down to the doctors who had treated the patient would bear the responsibility. For this reason alone the burden of proof shifted, arguably unfairly, onto the parent.

"Carl's attitude isn't helpful. It's going to work against you," Zach said.

"Be honest, Dr. Fisher —"

"Please, call me Zach."

Becky leaned back in her chair, hands folded primly in her lap. Her eyes were again assessing him, making him feel strangely vulnerable. "Be honest, Zach," she said, tilting her head, looking at him coquettishly. She could start a fire with that smile, thought Zach. "If you weren't so close to the situation, you'd probably blame me, too."

Zach did not like the way Becky kept planting these doubts. Did he see Meghan as having mito because it's what he wanted to see? Was it possible Becky was something more than a devoted mother? Zach looked at Becky with renewed intent, forcing himself to see past her beauty, searching her face for assurances that were not there, looking into eyes that were clouded with grief, anguish, or perhaps something else — perhaps, as he now feared, malice.

Zach knew something of the psychology that makes a parent do harm behind closed doors. He knew that in such cases, the parent had usually suffered an unpredictable childhood, one of abuse or neglect. And while he knew nothing of Becky's upbringing, he thought of the baby she had lost, and what it might have done to her. He knew what the loss of Will had done to him.

No . . . no . . . no, Zach thought to himself. *It can't be true. It can't be.*

And yet, try as he might to reason it away, the doubts remained.

CHAPTER 22

Meghan

I woke up not sure where I was. I didn't remember falling asleep, but as soon as my eyes opened, I thought for a second I'd been in a car accident and this was an operating room. I'd never had an operation before, but the walls of the room were painted white like the operating rooms I'd seen on TV, and the overhead lights burned my eyes the way I figured powerful operating room lights would burn. I panicked because I knew I wasn't supposed to wake up during surgery. I wondered if maybe my stomach was cut open or something. I waited to feel sharp jolts of pain, hear doctors screaming: *She's awake! She's awake! Get her back under!*

But as my mind cleared, I saw there weren't any doctors in the room with me. In fact, I was alone. *But where am I?* I drifted in and out of consciousness, feeling woozy and dazed, but little jolts kept jabbing me back to alertness.

The feeling of coming in and out of focus reminded me of the time I'd woken up still drunk in Shelly Stevenson's basement last year. A bunch of my girlfriends had crashed out in sleeping bags after we'd polished off the rum punch that Tanya Carmichael had made from her parents' stash. We had huddled together and watched horror movies until we'd passed out, having laughed and screamed ourselves to exhaustion.

When I came awake on the basement floor, my head was throbbing, buzzing. I eventually made it to the bathroom, where I sent that good time into the toilet with a splash. I stayed in a fog for most of that day. That's how I felt now. My brain was clouded and I'd swear someone had stuffed cotton in my mouth. *But where am I?*

I tried to swing my legs off the bed to stand, but my knees connected hard with a plastic guardrail raised along the side. *Who has a bed with guardrails on it except old people or sick people?* Directly across from my bed was a television built into the wall, but the screen was covered in thick plastic, like someone was worried I might try to steal it or break the glass. I slumped back onto the mattress and began to count to ten, trying to rid myself of that doped-up feeling. My eyelids grew heavy, and it became dark again.

When they opened for a second time, I had no idea if a minute, an hour, or a day had passed. But I was more alert now. I could see clearly that I was in a mostly empty room with a hospital bed in the center. There was a second room across from the bed, the door slightly ajar. The lights were off, so I couldn't see inside, but I guessed it was probably a bathroom.

Off to my left was a sort of couch, more like a bench built into the wall, with a couple of long cushions to make it comfortable for sitting. There were three square windows above the couch, but I couldn't see a latch, or handle, or any way to open them from the inside. There were no blinds or curtains on the windows, and light poured in from the outside. Daytime. What did I last remember? Day or night? I couldn't think clearly enough to recall. I wasn't entirely sure what my last memory was.

I realized there wasn't a sheet or a pillow on my bed. *How come this hospital doesn't believe in sheets?*

I managed to get myself out of bed. There was a second door to my right, with a square portal window built into it. I went to that door and tried the knob, but it was locked. I turned the knob several times; it wouldn't budge. Then I remembered pulling on a doorknob just like this one and it, too, had been locked from the outside.

A second memory came to me, and I shivered. I recalled screaming, crying for my mom — not my dad, no, not him — pleading for someone to come get me. People came, all right, about four of them. They grabbed me and pushed me down on the bed with force. Someone came at me with a needle. Yes, I could see it in my mind's eye like it was happening all over again. It was sharp and long, coming straight at my arm, some liquid inside the syringe. I bit the arm of somebody who was wrestling me, tasted their blood as it seeped into my mouth. Whoever it was screamed and gripped my arm hard enough to break it.

Was that a dream?

Glancing at my arm, I noticed a big purple bruise above the elbow, so I knew it wasn't just my imagination. Around my wrist was a hospital bracelet. On my other arm, someone had secured a small square piece of gauze to my skin with a few strips of medical tape. I peeled the tape back, felt the pull against my skin as it came free, and saw beneath a tiny dot that was probably the spot where a needle had sunk into my vein. Who had put that needle in me?

I tried the doorknob again, this time banging against the door for somebody's attention. I peered out the portal into an empty hallway with splashes of color on the wall. Color or not, every fiber of my being told me this place was my worst nightmare.

I stumbled back to my bed, feeling like the floor was made of water. My stomach rumbled as I slumped onto the mattress. I drifted off for a second, then jolted awake when I heard the door slam into the wall. A stout nurse in blue scrubs with dark hair to match her dark expression barged in, and behind her were two large men who could easily have played the entire offensive line for my high school football team. They came at me fast, surrounding me.

"You shouldn't be up, Meghan," the nurse said. "Guess we didn't give you enough."

"Enough what?" I asked. My voice was soft in my ears. "Where am I?"

"The hospital, Meghan. You're a patient here. I'm Nurse Amy," said the nurse. "I'll be looking after you for a few hours."

One of the large men came out from behind Nurse Amy. He had mocha-colored skin and a mustache like a pencil line. He

244

also had a big bandage on his arm, which could explain his angry look. I thought of the bite I'd given someone and wondered if he might have been on the receiving end.

"How are you feeling?" Nurse Amy asked me.

"I don't want to be here," I said, tears springing to my eyes. There were flashes of Dr. Nash and Dr. Levine. I had met with them at White. My parents were here somewhere, in the waiting room probably. I had to get to them. I didn't know how long I'd been here, but something told me it was a long time.

I jumped off the bed and rushed for the door. Well, in my mind I was rushing. It was more like I threw myself off the bed and fell into Nurse Amy, connecting hard enough to knock her to the ground. I heard a muffled grunt when she hit the floor. Spinning, I managed to avoid Bite Mark, but ran straight into another one of the goons Nurse Amy had brought with her. This guy grabbed my shoulders and, in reflex, my knee went up to his groin. I connected with something there, because he doubled over in pain. Adrenaline surged through me, bringing me back to my senses. I knew the feeling well from the soccer field. Everything was in sharp focus, clear as a glass of water.

I sized up my opposition in a fraction of a second. He was the last defender I had to beat before I'd square off with the goalie — only this goal was the open door out of here.

As I neared the door, I could see Bite Mark in my peripheral vision, lunging at me. I gave a little juke move, one I'd practiced countless times with a ball at my feet: a shift to the right before rapidly decelerating and shifting to my left. Bite Mark fell for it, dived to his right, and tackled only air. I spun the other way and was on the move again, headed for the open door that was maybe five or six strides away. I glanced behind me the same way I would if a defender were on my heels.

I made a few quick assessments. Wherever I had kneed Mustache Man, I must have hurt him, because he was still on the floor, groaning. Also, Nurse Amy wasn't very athletic, because she, too, was slow to get up. I had Bite Mark beat, and even though I was feeling funky from whatever drug they'd put in me, I thought my chances were good to get away.

I'd made it to the door and was deciding if I should run left or right when a mountain-size man appeared in the doorway. He grabbed me in a bear hug, hoisted me off my feet. I squirmed to try to slip from his grasp, but he tightened his grip around my waist until I started to have difficulty breathing.

I twisted my body to free myself, and that's when I saw Nurse Amy coming at me with a needle the size of a bayonet attached to a large syringe. I whirled back around and tried to sink my teeth into the chest of the guy holding me. Before I could latch on, he used one hand to push my head away. He was strong enough to keep hold of me with one arm, but then again, he outweighed me by at least a hundred pounds.

"No!" I screamed. "I want my mom! I want my mom! I just want my mom!"

I kicked and thrashed wildly in the giant man's arms, but couldn't break free of his hold. I couldn't look at the needle coming my way either.

"Mom!" I screamed.

I felt a sharp pain in my arm and saw the needle being pulled out of my flesh like the fang of a snake having deposited its venom. Almost immediately my blood felt hot as my skin started to tingle all over. I felt this incredible warmth swimming through me.

The tension in my muscles let go. My legs went still. My head was buzzing, but I wasn't scared anymore. A peaceful feeling washed over me like I'd been set free. I was a fish now, swimming up a river. Water rushed through my gills. I was a bird taking flight for the first time, soaring high into the sky, turning before making a dive. I was a cloud floating. A tunnel appeared before me, darkly ominous. I was being dragged toward it. I pushed against the feeling, but it was no use. I wasn't strong enough to resist. A thought came to me as I slipped inside that dark space, one single, final thought that was as clear as if I'd spoken the words aloud.

I'm getting out of here. I'm getting out of here, and you can't stop me.

Chapter 23

Becky

She rose from her seat at the booth in the back of the diner to greet Dr. Levine. They shook hands tentatively before settling across from each other.

"Thank you so much for making time for me," Becky said.

"I don't have long," Dr. Levine answered.

"I have to be at the lawyer's office soon," Becky offered as a way of assuring him she'd keep it brief. "But I would have dropped everything to make this meeting happen." She peered over her grease-splattered menu and caught Dr. Levine looking at her, his eyes lingering a beat too long to avoid notice. Becky had her strategy worked out in advance, thinking she could pit Nash against Levine — use the younger doctor's ego to her advantage. But now she wondered if there was something else that might give her an edge.

Did she remind him of someone, an unrequited love from high school, perhaps? The cheerleader he could only admire from afar? Aside from LinkedIn, which offered scant clues about the man, Levine kept his social media accounts private. But the way he'd looked at her made Becky wonder if there was a girl who had rejected him years ago.

As a precaution, Becky had come dressed for that possibility. She looked more like she was going out on the town than having breakfast at the Moonlight Diner — a hole-in-the-wall kind of place that Dr. Levine had suggested for its proximity to White Memorial, but not so close as to risk being spotted by Nash or worse. She'd let her hair down for the occasion, and her bronzy blond mane that draped past her shoulders was full of body, thanks to the extra conditioning treatment she'd applied. To enhance her tawny complexion, Becky had used her Giorgio Armani foundation, and her perfume scented the air with a touch of seduction. She wore a formfitting black turtleneck sweater, and the shape of her body in jeans as she strode to the back of the diner drew glances from the male and female patrons alike.

It had taken her almost as much effort to

get ready as it had to get Levine to agree to this hastily arranged rendezvous. On the phone, Levine had held all the cards, but that one look he sent her, an innocuous little tell, provided Becky a clue as to how to play him. He was so young and simple, many years and burdens away from having complex channels burrowed into his psyche. The same could not be said for her husband, the man she should feel closest to, her rock, her true north, who had let their current struggles cloud him with doubt and angst.

"Why don't you come right out and say it," Becky had snapped at Carl earlier that morning as he was tying his blue tie in the hexagonal mirror that hung above a custom double vanity in their bathroom.

"Say what?" Carl had mumbled to his reflection.

"That you think I'm abusing Meghan. That you believe I'm intentionally harming her."

"I don't think that," Carl said in a detached manner that lacked all conviction. "Like I said, I think you're confused. I think you've become confused."

"What's the difference?" Becky asked as she painted on a truffle-colored shade of lipstick. *Why isn't he asking why I'm getting made up?* Becky had wondered. *What does he think I'm doing today before our meeting with the lawyer? Why doesn't he care?*

The bathroom where Becky and Carl had readied themselves for the day was nicer than their first apartment. Hell, it was nicer than their first home. Cool and chic, designed in a luxurious gray, the master bath featured mixed marble with natural stone elements. Becky could not remember the last time she and Carl had made love in the freestanding tub, but there was a time not too long ago when he'd make her a bubble bath, scent it with rose water, and kneel at her side as he washed her back. When Meghan got sick, Becky began taking baths alone.

She knew her marriage was on rocky ground, but Carl was still her husband, and Becky could not turn off her loyalty like a light switch. She'd done that with her mother for valid reasons, but also with lasting consequences. Despite her best efforts to hold on, her marriage had turned into something utterly unfamiliar. She was no longer a wife, but she wasn't a widow or an ex-wife either. She was trapped in something akin to marital purgatory.

On occasion, they'd still have sex, but Carl had grown distant and disconnected. Sometimes she'd get him to look her in the eyes, but those looks never lasted for long. Their lovemaking went from being intimate to a check-box item that they had to make sure got done because it seemed the only thing that bound them as husband and wife.

When he became angry with her over Meghan, when innuendo turned into accusation, they had stopped having sex altogether — unless they had enough wine and whiskey to make it possible to forget who they were and what they were going through. In that way, they'd become intimate strangers. Maybe that was all they could manage. Maybe that's why she had decided to keep two secrets from Carl that day, her breakfast meeting with Dr. Peter Levine being one of them.

At first, Dr. Levine would not even take her call, but Becky guessed right how to bait him. His LinkedIn profile showed membership in Alpha Omega Alpha, the national medical honor society, along with other academic achievements. Levine might not have had a lot of experience as a doctor, but a scan of his curriculum vitae revealed him to be competitive and determined to succeed. He was also professionally green as a newly sprouted sapling, having completed his residency only a year ago, which meant he was still out to prove himself, leaving his ego vulnerable to attack.

Becky's instinct told her that Levine was under Nash's thumb, so she put that assumption to the test first by getting him on the phone, and again after he'd rejected her breakfast invitation.

"I understand your reluctance to meet," she had said on the phone to him. "I'm sure Dr. Nash wouldn't approve."

"Dr. Nash doesn't manage my schedule," Dr. Levine said in a sharper tone. Becky could not suppress her smile.

"Oh, I'm sorry," she said. "Dr. Nash gave me the impression that she was the one in charge, that you were . . . inexperienced. Her word, not mine."

Even though Nash and Levine worked in different departments, Becky knew enough about a hospital's inner workings to play up the turf war angle. She had been careful to keep her tone friendly while making sure Levine knew she thought less of him because of Nash. It was a delicate mind game, and Levine was too inexperienced in the ways of life and women to realize he was being played.

"I don't work for her," he had said. "She's not my boss. I'm a doctor, same as she is."

Becky knew then and there the battle was won, but she still had to seal the deal.

"How about this, Peter," she said, using his first name. "Meet me for a cup of coffee, just the two of us. There's something you should know about Dr. Nash. Something my lawyer told me that you'd want to hear. I promise I only want to talk. Unless, of course, you're not allowed."

That was it all took. They spent another five minutes setting up the meeting place and time with all the intrigue of an espionage novel. Levine's objections were numerous: *That's too close to the hospital. I don't want anyone to see us. It has to be discreet.*

Now that they were finally together, Becky had high hopes of emerging victorious once again. For her, victory was an easy mark to define: Meghan had to come home. Manipulating and maneuvering the green doc gave her no joy, but Levine and Nash had given Becky no alternative.

Dr. Levine set his menu down on the red laminate table. "I'm just going to have coffee," he announced.

"Me, too," said Becky, setting her menu down as well.

She was careful to keep her eye contact brief. She did not want to do anything that would come across as blatantly flirtatious, but she did not want to seem unavailable either. It was a delicate balance, and while she tried to exude confidence, underneath she was as nervous as a new driver. Levine was the way out of her nightmare, but one misstep would close that exit for good.

She appraised him thoughtfully, hoping his eyes would do the talking. Should she play the Nash angle as she had planned? Or try the Mrs. Robinson approach: the older, more experienced woman, piquing his curiosity?

By the time the waitress came to take their coffee orders, Becky had settled on her strategy.

"How is Meghan?" she asked.

It had been almost forty-eight hours since she'd last seen her daughter. Almost two days without hearing Meghan's voice, seeing her precious face.

"She's fine. We're taking good care of her. I promise."

"Peter," Becky said, aware of the effect using his first name would have now that they were in person. "Peter, please, look at me — just look."

He did. He could not help himself.

"I'm not who you think I am."

Levine's boyish face took on a newfound hardness. "Is that why we're here? I thought you had something to tell me about Dr. Nash."

"I do, and I will share it. But I want you to see me, really see me, to get to know me. I want you to believe that I'm not the person you think I am."

"I didn't make my assessment based on you, Mrs. Gerard. I did it based on Meghan. That's my job."

"Please, please, call me Becky, and I understand. I honestly do. But now that we're here, together, do I strike you as someone who'd harm my daughter for attention, or to fill up some dark hole in my soul? Yes, I have real knowledge of medicine, especially of Meghan's illness, and I've made relationships with her doctors. And, yes, I've been intensely involved in her care, but I'm asking you — what mother wouldn't?"

"I understand what you're saying."

Becky sensed a coming breakthrough. She pressed ahead. "I've studied the illness, Munchausen. I know that mothers with this sickness had an insecure or ambivalent relationship with their own parents — often the mother — and as a result had a hard time forming attachments. Then they'd overcompensate with their own children. That's not me. That's not me at all. I love my mother dearly. In fact, she's dying of cancer, and I can't fly to California to be with her because of Meghan's illness and this situation we're in."

While it was true Cora was still alive, Becky doubted Levine would track down Sabrina to get the real story there.

"I didn't grow up in a chaotic, unstable household," Becky continued, referring to yet another characteristic commonly found in perpetrators of Munchausen by proxy. "I'm not a compulsive or controlling mother. I'm not suffering from some inconsolable grief that I've projected onto Meghan. I'm just extremely devoted to my daughter, my only child."

That was it. Those were all the symptoms of Munchausen by proxy that Becky knew about. If Levine were a dogged detective, if he were to go digging, truly hunt, he could refute every claim she had made, checking every box for the condition markers in the process. Becky was counting on him not being all that thorough.

"I'm not in a position to do a psychological evaluation of you, Ms. Gerard," Levine offered in response.

"Becky, please. I may be a good deal older than you, Doctor, but don't make me feel it."

"Becky, then."

"Do I strike you as insecure?"

"Like I told you, I'm not here to do a clinical evaluation of you. I'm interested to know what you've heard about Amanda Nash."

Becky knew it would come down to this.

"She has it out for Dr. Fisher. Do you know that? She thinks he sees cases of mito where there is no mito because of what happened to his son. That's why she got it in her head that I was doing something to Meghan. No other explanation worked for her — certainly not the truth, of course, which is that Meghan has mito."

"She doesn't make the psychiatric diagnosis," Dr. Levine replied. "I do."

"Then you can undo it," Becky said in a pleading voice. "Let's exhaust all diagnostic possibilities before you accuse me."

"That would go against my clinical judgment."

Becky reached across the table and placed her hand over Dr. Levine's. She sensed him slipping away. Time to switch tactics. His skin felt soft, new, and receptive to her touch. He did not pull away. He held her gaze. He was trying so hard to be a man — it was almost endearing. Would she do it? That was the question tumbling about her head. Would she sleep with this man to get her daughter back? All he had to do was change his clinical opinion. All she had to do was surrender her soul.

"You're wrong," Becky said. "Look at her again. Examine her again. Nash wanted this, not you, Peter. She's got it out for Dr. Fisher. She and Knox Singer want Zach gone from White because his mito diagnoses are costing big bucks, and they're using my daughter as the puppet to make that happen. They're using you, same as they are using me. Don't you see?"

Becky saw a flicker in Levine's eyes. The shift was so slight, it was almost imperceptible, but it was there, a nascent fear bubbling below the surface that maybe, just maybe, she was right.

"I appreciate what you're trying to do," Levine said. "I'm not a parent, but I can understand your struggles here. However, I'm afraid there's nothing I can do to help. I firmly believe Meghan is where she needs to be. In fact, I think I'm going to take a pass on the coffee." He started to rise. "It's not right for us to be together."

Becky reached across the table, taking hold of his arm, applying enough force to get him to sit back down. The sweet look in her eyes drained in a blink, replaced with something far darker and more sinister.

"Peter, listen to me, listen very carefully."

Becky's voice turned low and strangely ominous. "I'm not someone you want to cross. Believe me when I tell you that."

Dr. Levine jerked his arm away. He stood, his bravado retreating like the tide. He dropped a five-dollar bill on the table and left without saying goodbye.

The law office of Leers and Hall was located on the second floor of a two-story brick building in Wellesley, Massachusetts. It was a tony town like Concord, populated with its fair share of rich people with secrets, but none like the kind Becky was carrying.

A sweet-faced young receptionist, who stole more than a couple of glances at Carl, escorted them to a meeting room off the main hall. Inside, Becky and Carl found a long mahogany table surrounded by plush leather chairs. Seated in one of those chairs was the attorney Andrea Leers, whom Becky had met only once before at yesterday's brief get-to-know-you meeting. Thanks to a sidebar conversation Becky had with Leers it was not an inconsequential face-to-face either, as Carl was soon to find out.

Leers, a woman in her late fifties, had on sensible shoes like the kind Annabel Hope from the DCF might have worn. Her navy blue suit jacket and skirt were understated and could have been bargain priced, lest one think her hefty hourly fee was frivolously spent on a fancy wardrobe. Her hair was cut short above the ears and rounded into the shape of a period, as if she herself were the last word anyone would need to hear. Her dark eyes were kind but serious, reflecting not only compassion but also an understanding of the monetary value of every second. Nothing about her, from her gestures to her words, was wasted.

Normally, Carl would have put on the charm, sending Leers a smile big and bright enough to cover his worries. Instead, he seethed when he set his eyes on Dr. Zach Fisher, who was seated across from her.

Carl gripped Becky's arm and pulled her in close to his body, putting his mouth up to her ear. "What the hell is he doing here?" Carl whispered.

Becky's second secret was now out in the open, but she had no plans to reveal her breakfast meeting with Dr. Levine.

"Excuse us a moment, will you please?" Becky said, addressing both Leers and Zach as she led Carl out into the hallway. They moved farther down the hall to get out of earshot, but there were offices all around them. If Carl raised his voice, it would cause a scene — which was how Becky had planned it.

"I'm sorry, I should have told you," Becky said.

"You invited him?" Carl asked, with disdain.

"Dr. Fisher offered to come as our medical advisor, and I said yes."

Becky left out that it was Leers who had suggested Zach's involvement for fear Carl might fire their attorney on the spot.

"God!" Carl tossed his head back, throwing his arms up in the air as if all were lost now. "That's great," he said with sarcastic bite. "That's just great, Becky."

"What is your problem?" Becky asked, knowing full well what his problem was. She might as well have invited Veronica to join them. "We need him," she said, imploring with her eyes. "And if I told you I wanted him here, you'd have said no."

"I'm walking out. I'm going to the car."

"Don't." Becky sputtered the word. "Don't you walk out on me, on us." She took hold of his hand. Carl held her gaze. She wanted so desperately to have her husband at her side. She wanted that man who'd fight for her, for his family, the way he had fought against the guard who'd grabbed her that day in the hospital.

263

"Please just hear what the lawyer has to say," she begged him. "I wouldn't have invited Dr. Fisher if I didn't think it was essential. If I'm wrong, I promise, I won't mention Zach Fisher's name ever again, I swear it."

Carl folded his arms as he looked away. When he looked back, his eyes were red. The last time she'd seen him on the verge of tears was after Meghan was born.

"I just don't want to lose her," he said, his face tightening as the raw emotion set in.

Becky wrapped her arms around her husband in a firm embrace. She knew he was thinking not only of Meghan but of Sammy as well. Carl stiffened at her touch. She could sense him holding on to those feelings, afraid of letting them go.

"It'll be all right, baby," Becky said, rising up on her toes to speak in his ear as she caressed the back of his head, keeping him in a loving embrace. She felt him lean into her, needing her, and this opened her heart so wide, she forgot all about the laptop, the accusations, and his distance.

In that single moment, he was her Carl again, the handsome developer who had built one of the first houses she'd ever sold. He was the man who'd held her as they wept for their son, who'd given her a daughter. He was her companion, her champion, her friend, lover, and husband. He was the person she remembered and missed so dearly.

"We're going to get through this," Becky said, still holding on tight. "Together, we'll do it together."

Carl leaned harder into her embrace, and Becky could feel him letting go. As he did, he began to cry, tears thick as raindrops streaming down his face. His heaving chest worked for each breath. His body trembled in her grasp as the emotion came pouring out of him.

"Together," she whispered.

Carl gripped her tighter. "Together," he whispered back.

CHAPTER 24

Zach

Becky and Carl returned looking drained and depleted, but Zach noticed something else about them. They were standing close to each other now. This was good, thought Zach. They needed to form a united front to get through the storm ahead. But it was also a bit unsettling to see Becky acting cozy with her husband after she'd been so strangely flirtatious with him in his office. Could she turn her emotions on and off like a faucet? People with Munchausen were master manipulators, which was why Zach reminded himself to be cautious and on guard.

While he did not feel swayed by Becky Gerard's charms, he was not made of stone either. He could not help but notice Becky, finding something compelling and alluring about her. He'd be lying to himself if he denied that her attentions had opened a door of sorts, and he was having a damn hard time shutting it again.

Zach had hardly dated since his marriage came to a crashing end. He'd gone out a couple of times, forced by friends to try to "get back on his feet," but the evenings were dimmed by his heartache, his memories and regrets. His past was always a third wheel at the dinner table.

Zach had tried antidepressants but, in an unfortunate bit of catch-22, found that they only compounded his guilt. He felt guilty for feeling happy, or at least not depressed. He strangely missed having the weight of Will's death to carry around, like Atlas forced to hold up the celestial spheres. Zach held no doubt that making a breakthrough in the disease would help him far more than any pill ever could.

He noticed the heart-shaped diamond-encrusted silver pendant standing out against Becky's black turtleneck and wondered if it had been a gift from Carl. Maybe he'd had it engraved with something personal, touching. Zach thought of the last present he'd bought for Stacy, some meaningless scarf picked up at an airport gift shop on his way home from some meaningless conference. He was never good with gift giving, planning surprises for birthdays or anniversaries and such. He could see now what he could not see then: that time was finite, and every day a gift not to be taken for granted.

Zach could tell the Gerards were holding hands beneath the table and was genuinely glad they had reconciled. In fact, his heart broke for them.

"Who is looking after my daughter?" Becky asked.

"The woman's name is Jill Mendoza," the attorney said.

Zach poured water from a glass pitcher and tried not to make eye contact with Carl. It was possible Carl had reached some new understanding with Becky, but that did not parlay into a new acceptance of Zach. It was obvious Carl would rather have any other doctor at this meeting — even Nash.

"Who is Jill Mendoza?" Becky asked.

"She's the guardian ad litem, appointed by the court to make decisions in loco parentis, in place of the parent, regarding Meghan's best interest," Leers answered. "Legally, she's the one who makes decisions for Meghan now."

Zach watched the color drain from Becky's face, while Carl looked as though he'd swallowed something bitter.

"What kind of decisions?" Becky asked.

"Medications, treatments, who Meghan gets to see, what she does."

"Basically, she's us," Becky said, her voice on edge.

"Well, in a way. Yes and no," Leers said. "She's authorized to make recommendations and decisions regarding Meghan's well-being, including medical treatments. But she's not her parent. You are."

"What does that mean exactly?" Carl asked.

"In short, all the decisions you would normally make for your daughter, Jill Mendoza now makes. You lose the right to visit or talk to your child unsupervised. You don't have the final say about how your child is raised or treated. But it's temporary. Our fight is just beginning."

As the meeting progressed and the Gerards absorbed the devastating news, Zach learned a lot more about the process White Memorial, and Nash especially, had gone through to take Meghan from the family. It was not a process Knox Singer had entered into lightly. In fact, removing a child from a home was viewed, according to hospital policy, as being a measure of last resort. Somehow Nash had convinced Singer to act, and hastily at that, which meant Dr.

Levine's report must have been truly damning.

Citing her legal duty to report suspected child abuse and neglect, Nash had gotten the DCF wheels in motion. The 51A Nash had filed then led to a 51B, an investigation of said claim, which DCF did with its own doctors taking consult from Nash and Levine, who presented compelling evidence to get an ex parte hearing with a judge to gain temporary custody of Meghan. All this ran counter to how big bureaucracies functioned, but in cases where there is a risk of severe abuse or neglect, when the child could be in danger should they return home with the parents, the typically slow-moving processes churned with startling rapidity.

"How could a judge just give our child away?" Becky asked, letting go of Carl's hand to slam hers on the table.

Leers did not flinch. "The threshold to find reasonable cause to issue temporary custody is fairly low," she explained. "But we have our second hearing, and that's why Dr. Fisher is here."

Known as a seventy-two-hour hearing, this was perhaps the most critical step in the process, the attorney emphasized. During that hearing, the judge would determine whether DCF should retain custody of

Meghan until the next hearing could take place, that one on the merits of the petition. A hearing on the merits typically occurred within twelve to fifteen months from the time the case began. The Gerards were potentially facing a full year, maybe even longer, without custody of their daughter.

"Why does Dr. Fisher need to be here?" Carl rolled up his shirtsleeves, again reminding Zach of that bully from his school days.

"We need a medical consult to prove that mito is a medical possibility and Nash and Levine were wrong to discount it," Leers said.

"So DCF is supporting Drs. Nash and Levine?" Carl looked a bit confused.

"Not exactly," said Leers. "The good news here is that the Department of Children and Families has an obligation, a *legal* obligation, with a mandated timeline of at least six months, to try to get Meghan back home to you. They *want* reunification."

"Well, then, why don't they just return her to us?"

"It's not that simple," Leers said to Becky. "They also have a duty to protect the child."

"What if we can't convince DCF we are fit parents?" Carl asked.

Zach was wondering the same.

"They have the ability to pursue perma-

271

nent custody and also termination of your parental rights."

Becky gasped. "Just make her not ours? They can't do that!"

"I'm afraid they can," said the attorney. "But we have our opportunity to present our case tomorrow, which I feel is very strong. This is a fluid process, and the hearing of the initial petition on parental unfitness will take time. But we have to cooperate. We have to play by the rules. If we lose the seventy-two-hour hearing, we'll have other chances to get Meghan back. We can't look at any defeat as a final blow. Is that understood?"

Everyone nodded. To himself, Zach pondered the significance of losing the hearing. Meghan would remain at White, a prisoner of the Behavioral Health Unit, and a clock would be set for the permanent termination of the Gerards' parental rights.

"How do we win this case?" Becky asked.

Leers turned to Zach.

He cleared his throat. "This is a matter of 'he said, she said,' " he began. "We're trying to prove Meghan has a disease that we haven't yet confirmed."

"How do you confirm it, Dr. Fisher?" Carl asked. Zach detected more than a trickle of exasperation in his voice. "Because we've been down this road before. And there's never an answer. There's never just one test. There are lots more tests, followed by more guessing, like my daughter is some fucking science experiment."

"She's hardly that!" Zach felt his blood surge. "There are other tests. There are things we can do that we haven't done, that we should have done."

"Well, why didn't you!" Carl demanded.

"Because your daughter is terrified of needles!" Zach tossed his hands in the air. "I couldn't do the tests I wanted. She had a panic attack in my office, or do you not remember? We need to do that muscle biopsy and maybe an EMG, but both involve a lot of needles."

"Well, if *she* hadn't made her so afraid of them, maybe we'd get that done." Carl sent Becky a look that put a quick end to reunification hopes. "But that needle you showed us was the size of her damn arm. She'll be scarred forever if you try to put that in her."

"Better that than she doesn't come home?" said Becky through gritted teeth.

Carl's shoulders slumped forward. "So that's what it's come to. That's our only hope to get her back. My God, Becky, what have you done?"

Becky looked stunned. "I've been trying

to help her!"

"Next time, don't do her any favors."

"Please, please," Leers said, pleading for calm. "This would be a disaster for us tomorrow. Okay? A disaster. The seventy-two-hour hearing is always rushed. We don't have proper time to prepare a big defense as it is. Dr. Fisher is our star witness. He's the best hope we have for getting Meghan back where she belongs. Is that understood?"

Carl gave a reluctant nod, but only after Becky sent him a scathing sideways glance.

"When we go before the judge, Zach will present medical evidence to show that Meghan has mitochondrial disease," the attorney continued.

"How's that going to work when you haven't proved it yet?" Carl asked. "You couldn't convince Dr. Nash; how are you going to convince a judge?"

"Let's let Dr. Fisher handle that," Leers said.

Carl threw his hands up. "Well, then, I guess I'll prepare myself for the worst."

"You need to do more than that," Leers advised, somewhat forebodingly.

"How so?" Carl asked, nonplussed.

Leers scanned the room as her expression turned increasingly tense. "These cases, from my experience, tend to get very emotional. Oftentimes it's difficult to maintain a unified front."

"Meaning what exactly?"

Zach sensed the attorney's reluctance to answer.

"Meaning that while I represent your interests as a couple, I strongly suggest that you each retain your own counsel individually."

"Why would we need that?" Becky asked.

"Don't be dim, Becky," Carl said in a dark voice that made Zach wonder if he'd ever been violent with her before. "We need it because we might be forced to go up against each other," he said. "A judge may have to decide if one of us is fit to parent Meghan, but not the other."

"Oh my God." Becky looked the way the parents of Zach's patients did when he had to deliver bad news. For the remainder of the meeting, Becky did not say another word.

CHAPTER 25

The courtroom was nothing special. The judge sat at an imposing wood desk bracketed by two American flags in heavy-duty stands. To one side was the witness box, and on the other stood a smaller desk for a court clerk. A bailiff in a brown uniform, gun holstered around his waist, hovered near the table reserved for the Gerards' attorney, Andrea Leers. The opposing attorney, representing the Department of Children and Families, sat directly across from Leers. A wood partition separated the lawyers from the section reserved for the public, but there was no jury box. This was a civil matter, and Meghan's fate rested solely with the judge.

The room was divided like a wedding, with those supporting White on one side of the aisle and the Gerards on the other. Zach sat in the row behind Becky and Carl. Across from him sat Nash, Knox Singer, a very nervous Dr. Levine, and the people from DCF, including someone named Annabel Hope, whom Becky had pointed out with contempt. Jill Mendoza, Meghan's new decision maker, was in attendance as well. Nash would not meet Zach's gaze, though he noticed she seemed to have no trouble glancing over at the Gerards.

Zach felt a heavy tightness in his chest, not only because he was Becky and Carl's best hope for getting their daughter back but also because he was facing off against the hospital CEO. Zach and Knox Singer had already exchanged a few tense words in the hallway before the hearing got underway. Zach replayed that exchange in his mind, trying to decide if his employee badge would still get him access to the pediatric floor tomorrow. It was fifty-fifty at best. The memory faded as the judge entered the courtroom.

"All rise for Judge Trainer!" the court clerk announced as a thin-boned woman draped in a black robe climbed a short flight of stairs to her sacred perch. She had an angular face that enhanced a severe look. Her wavy hair, brindled with a variety of dyes, was graying at the temples. Wire-rimmed glasses dangled from a lanyard draped around her wiry neck.

"Please be seated," Judge Trainer said as she got settled. "All right, good morning, everyone. I've read the DCF affidavit, and I have reviewed some of the exhibits including the DCF 51A and 51B reports and all of the medical records. Is there anything to add before we get underway?"

Ms. Leers stood first. "No, Your Honor," she said before retaking her seat.

The opposing attorney stood as well. "No, Your Honor," she said.

And with that, the hearing was underway.

First to go to the witness stand was the DCF investigator, Annabel Hope. She recounted her conversations with various witnesses for the court, as well as her consult with White's in-house medical experts. From that alone, she had made her decision to file an affidavit in support of the request for temporary custody. In her cross-examination, Leers made the point that Annabel Hope had never spoken to the parents or Dr. Fisher, so her decision did not take into account other critical viewpoints.

"I was obligated under law to act expeditiously based on the information I could obtain. With Dr. Fisher being out of town at a conference, it was not feasible for me to conduct that interview. In regards to the parents, we were concerned the mother might try to" — Ms. Hope cleared her throat — "act in a way that would not be in the child's best interest."

And with those final words, Ms. Hope was excused from the witness stand.

The lawyer representing DCF, a young woman who spoke with more confidence than her years or experience should have allowed, called Dr. Nash to the witness stand. Zach noticed Becky tense up as Nash took her seat, but Carl showed no outward signs of hostility toward the woman who for all intents and purposes had kidnapped their daughter. In fact, he showed no real emotion at all. His eyes weren't red from crying. His jaw was not tense from clenching. He looked strangely relaxed and equally detached from his wife — not even an arm placed in comfort around Becky's back, no hand holding hers. As far as Zach could tell, there might as well have been an aisle separating the two spouses.

Nash sat primly in the witness box, looking reserved, as if somehow that conveyed her impartiality. She began with the case history, starting with Meghan's referral from Dr. Fisher's office.

"She presented with new and unusual symptoms — nausea and blurred vision —

that did not fit with Dr. Fisher's initial diagnosis of mitochondrial disease."

Nash described those symptoms in more detail for the record. The opposing attorney's next questions covered Dr. Nash's growing suspicion.

"In a typical situation, a mother would be relieved to hear that her child might not have a life-threatening disease. It would be akin to a parent thinking a child had cancer, only to find out later the tumor was benign. But Mrs. Gerard was not relieved. In fact, she was extremely agitated and pushed hard for more tests."

Nash then recounted her contentious meeting with Zach, which had led to her decision to bring Dr. Levine in for his consult. Her testimony took most of forty minutes.

Andrea Leers delivered her cross-examination to a tension-filled room. Across the aisle, Zach spied Dr. Levine gnawing on his fingernails like a beaver takes to a piece of wood.

"Did you know Dr. Fisher was going to be out of town for a mitochondrial conference when you phoned Becky with this request for an emergency exam?"

"Yes, I did."

"And why didn't you wait until Dr. Fisher

returned before making that call?"

The opposing attorney was on her feet in a flash. "Objection, immaterial," she said.

"Your Honor, the question shows fore-thought on the parts of Drs. Nash and Levine in that they knew without Dr. Fisher, it would be easier to lure Becky Gerard to the hospital for that emergency exam. That sort of planning suggests the possibility of bias prior to Dr. Levine's exam."

Touché, thought Zach, who was mightily impressed with Leers's thinking.

"Overruled," the judge said, directing her attention to Nash. "You may answer the question."

"I was concerned for Meghan's well-being," Nash replied, calm as could be. "And I did not want to wait for the consult."

"But you waited two days until Dr. Fisher went out of town to make that phone call to Becky."

The call record had been officially submit-ted to the court as evidence.

"Dr. Levine's schedule did not allow for an earlier consult."

"Even though it was an emergency in your mind, even though you believed Meghan was in immediate danger, did you intention-ally wait until Dr. Fisher was away at the mitochondrial conference to call Becky

Gerard and request that she bring Meghan to White Memorial for an emergency consult.

"No, I did not," Nash answered with authority.

Zach did not believe her for one second.

The next person to take the stand was Dr. Peter Levine. He managed to stop fidgeting with his hands long enough to place one on the Bible and swear he'd tell the whole truth and nothing but the truth. The opposing attorney reviewed Dr. Levine's exam of Meghan in great detail, including the questions he had used to determine she was a victim of medical child abuse. It was here that the opposing attorney introduced the term "Munchausen syndrome by proxy."

"Did Meghan talk about the brother she lost to SIDS?" the attorney asked Dr. Levine.

A heavy pall settled over the room. Zach saw Becky's head bow slightly.

Dr. Levine looked uncomfortable on the witness stand. "No, she did not. To be honest, I didn't know."

"Now that you do know about the Gerard baby, who died at around four months of age, does that influence your opinion of Meghan's case?"

Levine glared at Becky for reasons Zach

could not understand. If anything, he should have been sympathetic.

"It would make me even more certain of my diagnosis. The loss of a loved one, especially a child, can trigger subconscious fears which can then manifest as pediatric symptom falsification."

"Could you state that in less clinical terms?"

"In the case of extreme grief, a mother can believe a child is sick, or make the child sick and try to get him or her well, as a way of healing a grievous wound from the past."

"And is that your opinion of Mrs. Gerard and her relationship with Meghan?"

"Yes. Even more so now."

To Zach's ears, Levine's testimony was like the *Titanic* brushing up against the iceberg. The ship had not yet sunk, but he knew it was headed in that direction.

When Ms. Leers got her chance to cross-examine, she strutted forward like a lioness coming upon a wounded gazelle.

"Dr. Levine, how long have you been a licensed physician?"

"I finished my residency last May."

"So, not long?"

"I was a doctor when I graduated medical school six years ago."

"So again, not a very long time," Leers said.

"Objection, immaterial," the opposing attorney announced.

"Your Honor, I'm attempting to show that Dr. Levine's inexperience is what led him to ask leading, not open-ended, questions of Meghan Gerard, which opens the possibility of misdiagnosis."

"Objection, that's an unproven fact purported to be true."

"If I may, Your Honor, have the opportunity to continue my line of questioning, I intend to show that Dr. Levine's inexperienced questioning resulted in what I believe to be a misdiagnosis of medical child abuse. It's my intention to show that the tragic loss of the Gerards' first child has no bearing whatsoever on the health issues facing Meghan."

The judge hesitated momentarily before answering. "Overruled. You may proceed."

Leers straightened her suit jacket, a reset of sorts. "You spoke at length with Meghan about her views of her mother."

"Yes," Levine said.

"In the course of that conversation, you determined that Meghan harbored negative feelings about her mother."

"I did."

"You asked, and I quote here: 'Because your mom makes you do things you don't want to do?' Are those your exact words?"

Leers had cited Levine's statement — documented in Meghan's medical record — from memory.

"Yes. That's what I said."

Again, Zach thought Levine looked and acted extra nervous. Perhaps it was just being on the witness stand, though Zach thought it more likely he knew the attorney had him dead to rights.

"Is that a standard question you would ask?"

"Yes."

"Do you think that question is a bit leading? I'd go so far as to say unsophisticated."

"No. I think the question helped me paint a picture of Meghan's home life. It's unlikely you find a smoking gun with these sorts of cases. It's not like if they answer in a certain way, we can say for sure it's a case of Munchausen by proxy."

"And you have a great deal of experience determining Munchausen by proxy?"

"No, this would be my first case."

"But you are sure there's no smoking gun?"

"It's called research," he said.

"But you didn't know the Gerards had

previously lost a child?"

Levine shifted in his seat. "No, I did not."

Zach resisted the urge to pump his fist in triumph.

"Do you think the leading manner in which you questioned Meghan led her to give you the answer you wanted her to give as opposed to what she was trying to say?"

"No."

Ms. Leers went over Dr. Levine's questions to Meghan for the court, taken from the affidavit. The more Zach heard, the angrier he became. There was no doubt in his mind that Levine's questions had been incredibly naïve, and could have confused Meghan in her fragile state.

"If Meghan had known one possible outcome could be her being placed in DCF custody, do you believe she would have given you the same answers to your questions?" Leers asked.

Dr. Levine's leg stopped bouncing, and his fidgety fingers went still as a trace of a smile came to his boyish face. Even the opposing attorney looked pleased. A pang struck Zach as he realized Leers might have made her first mistake of the day.

"That's why we're careful in how we word the questions," Dr. Levine replied with an almost cocky grin. "And why my medical

training isn't, as you put it, unsophisticated."

Becky cupped her mouth with her hands.
Carl went rigid. He had to know, as did
Becky, that even more damage had been
done. The question was, how much?

CHAPTER 26

It was Zach's turn to testify.

This was not Zach's first time on the witness stand. He'd been an expert witness in malpractice cases before, but this time felt more nerve-racking, either because his job could be on the line, or because he did not want to fail the Gerards — Becky, especially, whom he viewed as a deeply devoted yet shattered mother. Even Carl, who'd shown him nothing but contempt, had his deep sympathies.

"What makes you think Meghan has mitochondrial disease?" Attorney Leers began.

"The main symptoms of mitochondrial myopathy are muscle fatigue, weakness, and exercise intolerance, also called 'exertional fatigue,' which refers to the unusual feelings of exhaustion brought on by physical exertion," Zach began. "The mitochondria contain DNA with some of the genes needed for mitochondrial function. There are other genes needed for proper mito-chondrial function found on chromosomes in the nucleus of the cell. Meghan's cells have a deficiency in processing mitochondria. Her lack of endurance and declining skills as a soccer player, I believe, are attributed to her cells' inability to produce the required energy as a result of a genetic deficiency."

For the record, Zach recounted Meghan's fainting episode that had led to Becky's embarrassing removal from the airplane. The opposing attorney had already cited that incident as an example of Becky's instability.

"How did you come to your mito diagnosis?"

"There are no published consensus-based practice parameters for clinicians to initiate diagnosis or patient management," Zach said. "Instead, I rely on a set of internally established guidelines and personal anecdotal experience."

"Which is why this disease is notoriously difficult to diagnose?" Attorney Leers asked.

"Yes."

"And even if you do certain lab tests, such as a muscle biopsy or electromyogram, or EMG, to detect abnormal muscle electrical activity, many cases still do not receive a specific diagnosis?"

"That's correct," Zach said. "This is a very wily disease to pin down."

"But you have a lot of experience in this area, don't you?"

Zach listed his credentials: medical school at Case Western Reserve. Residency at University of Massachusetts Memorial Medical Center. Fellowship in pediatric neuro-oncology at New England Medical Center. Board-certified in child neurology. Membership in the Mitochondria Research and Medicine Society. Attorney Leers did not bring up his numerous publications in respected journals.

"And, in your opinion, was there any harm in treating Meghan with the mito cocktail that you had prescribed?"

As Zach looked over at Singer and Nash, a cold feeling swept over him.

"No. But we didn't give her enough time on the treatment to properly assess the effectiveness."

"By removing the child from the parents' care and stopping treatment, it's your opinion that Meghan's health and well-being are being jeopardized?"

"It is, strongly," Zach said.

Strongly.

He guessed what Singer was thinking:

Zach felt strongly about every mito case he diagnosed.

"No further questions."

Attorney Leers returned to her seat as the opposing attorney came out from behind her table to face off with Zach.

"Dr. Fisher, you have a personal history with mitochondrial disease, do you not?"

Zach braced himself. He knew this was coming. He and Attorney Leers had prepped for it. But that was in the abstract. It was different when the question was being asked of him in court.

"Yes, I do," Zach said solemnly.

"Can you tell us about it?"

You know damn well about it, he seethed.

"My son, William, had the disease. He died from it."

"How long ago?"

Screw you, thought Zach as he tried to rein in his emotion.

"He died five years ago."

"That must have been devastating for you."

Attorney Leers was on her feet in a flash. "Objection, Your Honor. This is not about Zach's son. This is about Meghan Gerard."

The judge sent a stern look to the opposing attorney.

"Your Honor," she said, "I intend to show

291

a predictable pattern with Dr. Fisher of frequently diagnosing cases of mitochondrial disease that may have origins in his tragic past."

The judge thought for a beat. "Objection sustained," the judge said. "Limit your questions to the topic."

"Yes, Your Honor," the attorney responded demurely. "Dr. Fisher, how many cases of mitochondrial disease have you diagnosed since your tenure at White began?"

"Maybe two, three dozen," Zach said.

"And is that more or less than the rate of diagnosis at comparably sized hospitals?"

"I don't know," Zach said, sensing a tickle of worry dancing at the base of his neck. "Conservatively, I'd estimate the prevalence of mitochondrial disease in children is approximately one case per five hundred. So every minute, there's a baby born somewhere that will develop the disease by age ten."

The attorney returned a puzzled look, as if to say Zach's numbers and her findings did not quite jibe.

"Your Honor, I'd like to move to introduce a document which shows that Dr. Fisher's rate of diagnosis is double that of hospitals with a comparable patient population."

The attorney presented the evidence to

the judge, who glanced at it before setting it aside to allow the cross-examination to continue.

"Dr. Fisher, have you ever been accused of confirmation bias?" The attorney pulled her lips tight as she waited for an answer.

"Some have expressed concern that my past might be clouding my judgment, but those are accusations I've vehemently denied."

"In Meghan's case, did you do a muscle biopsy?" The attorney glanced down at her notes, making Zach think she had a laundry list of diagnostic measures to throw at him.

"No. It's a somewhat painful procedure, and the patient has a severe needle phobia."

"What about an electromyogram?"

"No, for the same reasons."

"Did you do cerebral imaging?"

"No. I didn't see it necessary to subject her to unnecessary radiation."

"What about blood work?"

"Yes."

"Even with Meghan's needle phobia?"

"It wasn't easy."

"And the results?"

"Inconclusive," Zach said regretfully.

Zach could not avoid a long discussion about heteroplasmy, a unique feature of deleterious mitochondrial DNA that was not present in Meghan's samples, and why that was not a tell-all. He worried about losing the judge in technical jargon.

"Did you order genetic testing?"

"I did," Zach said.

"And those results?"

"Inconclusive," he said. "The gold standard here, if it could be called such, is the muscle biopsy, with which we would do additional genetic testing, as well as microscopic evaluation, enzyme testing, and so forth."

"So why did you diagnose her with mito?"

"Given the patient's needle phobia, I opted to rely on my clinical findings and other noninvasive observations to pursue a diagnosis. Oftentimes that's equally as effective as other diagnostic measures. I was looking at a patient with a progressive disorder that involved multiple organ systems, fitting the disease criteria."

"But then Meghan got new symptoms."

"Yes, she did."

"In your opinion, were those related to mito?"

"Mito is an unusual disease. The symptoms can be extremely variable from person to person, so it wouldn't be out of the question, but my thought at the time was that it did not seem to fit the disease pattern as I know it."

"What is the disease pattern as you know it?"

"Mitochondria produce ninety percent of the energy our body needs to function. The symptoms depend largely on which cells are affected, and the range of symptoms can be from mild to severe. Typically, the disease presents with muscle weakness, exercise intolerance, maybe some vision problems, fatigue. There can be GI issues as well, but what Meghan experienced at home was unusual given how the symptoms tend to occur more insidiously over time. But when Meghan came to the ER with sudden severe gastrointestinal issues and equally sudden vision problems, I became concerned."

"So you referred the patient to Dr. Nash."

"I did." Zach flashed Amanda an angry look.

"And she came to a different conclusion?"

"I think that's obvious," he answered.

"Please answer the question yes or no," the attorney stated flatly.

"Yes."

The attorney scanned her notes. "One more question, Dr. Fisher," she said. "Has an insurance company ever denied your claim for a mito cocktail with an inconclusive or negative result on a genetic panel for mitochondrial disease?"

Zach swallowed hard. "Yes. On a few occasions."

"Could it be ten?" the attorney asked.

Zach thought before answering, though he did not need to. "It could be that."

"And who paid for the continued treatment you prescribed despite the insurance company's objections? The hospital or the patient?"

"Um —" Zack felt the full weight of Becky's stare without having to look at her. "I explained to the parents the risks of stopping treatment. In most cases, the parents agreed to cover the cost."

"But not all?"

"No," Zach said. "Some of the patients' parents were not able to meet the cost burden."

"In that case, who paid?"

"The hospital, I believe, had to absorb the cost." Zach thought he could see Knox Singer grinding his teeth.

"And why did the insurance companies deny payment for your prescribed treatment?" the attorney asked.

The microphone broadcast Zach's heavy inhale. "They didn't believe my diagnosis, because I had made too many of them," Zach said.

"No further questions, Your Honor," the attorney replied.

CHAPTER 27

Becky

Becky and Carl made their way down an austere hallway until they reached the entrance to the Behavioral Health Unit, located in the newly constructed Mendon Building. Becky trembled with excitement. It had been four days since she'd last set eyes on her daughter. Questions of how much Meghan had been eating, how thin she'd be, how frail she'd look gnawed at her. When she thought of the possibilities, she was overcome with sadness and grief.

The door to the unit buzzed open, and there was Nash in her white lab coat, arms folded, waiting. Zach had forewarned Becky that Nash would be running the show, even though the Behavioral Health Unit was Levine's territory. He speculated, correctly so, that the social workers and Meghan's new guardian would take a supporting role given how this case had the potential to be high profile — and Nash, who could be as ego-driven as any surgeon, would see an opportunity to raise hers at White even higher.

"She's going to want to control the situation as much as possible, and she's got the clout with Knox Singer to do just that," Zach had said. "So whatever she tells you, best to play by her rules."

Becky took the advice begrudgingly.

Nash's penetrating gaze shifted over to Carl, and her forbidding expression softened. Becky felt outnumbered. It was as if those two were in cahoots, having secret conversations about Becky's unfitness as a parent.

As much as she wanted to, Becky and Carl had not reconciled. There was no big "aha moment" after the trial when rose petals tumbled from the sky, trumpets blared, and all was forgiven. There was only nervous anticipation.

They had arrived at lunchtime. Becky observed a large food cart parked near the secured entrance. A group of young people, as diverse as any city high school, dressed in comfortable street attire, retrieved trays of hot food from one of two open compartments below. A stout woman, her dark hair stuffed inside a hairnet, oversaw the self-serve process, repeating that the mac and cheese was in the left compartment, and turkey and gravy in the right. Everyone called her Loretta. She was friendly and greeted each patient by name. She called them "dear" and "sweetheart" and "darling."

"Meghan's very excited to see you," Nash said. "I'll take you to her in a moment, but first, I have to ask if I can see what's in your purse. You do understand that you can't give your daughter anything, no gifts, no items from home, nothing of the sort, unless it is approved."

Becky snarled in disgust, and even Carl looked mildly annoyed.

"It's utterly ridiculous," she scoffed. "Do I need to go through a metal detector as well?" Becky asked, her voice drenched in sarcasm. "Want to pat me down for weapons?"

"No need for that," Carl said, addressing Becky reproachfully.

"It's a safety issue," Nash answered, taking the high road there. "I apologize."

"You have the soup ready?" Becky asked.

Attorney Leers had found out during a conversation with a social worker that Meghan had not been eating much, so at Becky's urging, she requested that Judge Trainer grant Becky permission to bring chicken soup from home — a food that Meghan was certain to eat.

Judge Trainer, citing safety concerns, had denied the request, but made a concession to have the kitchen staff at White Memorial prepare the soup to Becky's exacting recipe. The soup was then to be served in a metal thermos that Becky had provided to Attorney Leers so as to give it the appearance of coming from home. Becky worried that Meghan might reject the meal if she thought it was not homemade, but secretly she did not want her daughter to know that her mother was not permitted to give her anything from the outside — including soup. Thankfully, Judge Trainer had agreed to this further concession.

"Yes, we do," Nash said. "But you know we do serve three hot meals a day." Nash directed her attention to Loretta's food cart. "Meal times are eight A.M., noon, and six. We offer two choices for hot meals and can accommodate special diets."

"That's all well and good, but Meghan is a very picky eater," Becky said softly. "And her disease has diminished her appetite considerably."

"I understand."

"I'm afraid as a policy we need to search your purse, or to make it even easier we can

301

just keep it at the nurse's station until your visit is through."

Becky held on to her purse a beat too long, as though clinging to the last shred of her dignity.

"Give it to her," Carl said snippily.

"I can't believe this is happening," Becky said as she handed over her purse, which Nash took with all of the fanfare of a TSA screener.

"Meghan is waiting for you in Charlotte's Web."

"Charlotte's Web?" Becky said.

"Yes, we named all our meeting spaces after famous children's books," Nash explained.

"Are we going to be alone?" Becky sounded a hopeful note.

"No," Nash replied. "Dr. Levine is in with her, as are Annabel Hope from DCF and Jill Mendoza."

"So, a big family reunion, is that it?"

Nash seemed unmoved. "Please, if you'll follow me," she said with a wave of her hand.

Nash led them down a hallway painted sky blue — a color chosen perhaps because the children kept here were not permitted access outside — to Charlotte's Web.

Becky paused at the door to exhale her

302

anxiety. She turned to face Carl, biting her lower lip. "We're here for Meghan," Becky said. "Whatever we're going through, we have to put it aside. We have to be united for her."

Carl said nothing. He opened the door.

Becky stared into a big open space with comfy chairs scattered throughout, a television, artwork on the walls, and that distinct hospital smell clinging to the air.

When Meghan saw her parents, she sprang up from a green armchair and came running, though at a far slower pace than she could have done if healthy. Becky quickened her strides, and soon she and her daughter were locked together. Meghan broke into tears, clutching her mother, sobbing. Becky was crying as well, caressing the back of Meghan's head, while Carl wrapped his arms around mother and daughter as though sheltering them underneath a cape. When they finally broke apart, Becky and Meghan were dabbing away tears with their fingers.

Carl gave his daughter a close inspection the way he might a rental car, checking her over for dents or dings. "You look well," he said.

You look well? Is that all he can think to say? Becky sent him an irritated glance as she

303

took hold of Meghan's hand. In fact, their daughter did not look well at all. She was too thin. Her gorgeous blond hair lay flat against her head, dull, without luster. She wore gray sweatpants and a blue top that Becky had sent from home. Her sleeves were rolled up, and Becky could see bruising on her arms — along with marks that looked like needle punctures. Had they been drugging her?

"Sweetie, I can't tell you how good it is to set my eyes on you," Becky said, wondering when the tightness in her throat might ease.

It was then Becky noticed her audience, seated nearby at a round table, coffee mugs set out in front of them like it was a teachers' lounge: Levine, Mendoza, and Annabel Hope — three of the four horsemen of the apocalypse.

"Can we have some privacy, please?" Becky asked in a curt, albeit pleading, tone of voice.

Mendoza approached. She was a stout woman with dark hair and dim brown eyes. Her manner was detached — not discourteous; not congenial. "We'll stay out of your way," she said, "but I have to remain in the room."

Meghan looked confused. "Why? Aren't I going home?"

"Baby . . . let's sit and talk," Becky said, taking hold of her daughter's too-thin arm, feeling the bone in her grasp.

Becky led Meghan to a table on the opposite side of the room, as far from the hawks as she could get. The only thing missing to make it a scene out of a prison visitor's lounge, thought Becky, was a glass partition.

Just as they were getting settled in their seats, Dr. Nash came into the room. Becky got up to meet her before Meghan could see what Nash held in her hand — she wanted to be the one to give Meghan the soup, not Nash. Taking the thermos from Nash with a perfunctory thank you, Becky returned to the table where her daughter and husband sat.

"Look, sweetheart, I made chicken soup for you," Becky said, grinning through the tears as she unscrewed the lid. "Your favorite."

Meghan took the thermos, seeming pleased with the familiar smell wafting upward, and said again, "I'm going home today, right?"

Becky and Carl looked at each other like two people worried about drawing the short straw.

"Right?" Meghan repeated, more a statement than a question.

"Sweetheart —"

"No! No!" Meghan vigorously shook her head from side to side. "I'm leaving. I'm getting out of here today. Today!" She pointed at the air, putting an invisible exclamation mark on her decree.

"We had a hearing with the judge about your case, and she's decided to give it some more time to investigate what to do next."

"More time to investigate what?" Meghan said. She got up from her chair and drew worried glances from the observers, who held their ground.

"Some of their concerns," Becky answered slowly, searching for the right words.

"What concerns?" Meghan's sweet face crumpled. Tears flowed down her face.

"Please sit, baby," Becky said as she coaxed her daughter back into her chair. "They want to make sure that you're . . . that you're —"

"They want to make sure that when you come home with us, you'll be safe," Carl said with a whiff of disdain.

Meghan looked utterly confused. "That's — that's ridiculous," she stammered. "Of course I'll be safe. It's home."

"The judge isn't so sure," Carl said.

"What judge?" Meghan said, her voice rising with anger. "Who do they think is going to hurt me? Mom? You?"

Meghan's eyes flared when she looked at her dad, and Becky picked up something unexpected in her daughter's face, her voice. *What was that?* Was there something between him and Meghan she didn't know? Some secret between father and daughter? She had noticed the distance, but shelved those concerns to focus on more pressing issues.

"It's complicated," Carl said.

"I don't get it," Meghan snapped at him. "I want to go home. I want to go home now!"

Levine was up in a flash, approaching with quick strides. Mendoza came over, as did Nash.

"Is everything all right?" Dr. Levine asked in that boyish, high-pitched voice of his.

"Yes," Becky said sharply. "Meghan is just going to have some soup. Isn't that right, honey? You're going to relax so we can talk."

Under the table, Becky gripped Meghan's leg, forcing her daughter to meet her gaze. With her eyes, Becky pleaded for Meghan to calm down. She did not want to give the doctors any more ammunition, and certainly did not want Meghan dragged away to have Lord knew what done to her. *What are those pinpricks in her arm anyway?* Becky had planned to confront Mendoza and Levine about Meghan's treatment, but not now. She bristled at the thought of losing even a minute with her daughter. They were only giving her an hour as it was.

Meghan picked up on her mother's cues and managed to regain her composure. She sipped the soup, which seemed to soothe her.

"We have help coming our way," Becky said after Levine and the others moved away to let them talk privately, but still remained in the room.

"Help how?" Meghan said, her lower lip quavering. "I don't belong here. I should be home with you. They stick me with needles." Meghan showed her mother her marked-up arm.

"What are they putting in you?" Becky asked. "Carl, what the fuck are they doing to her here?"

Carl seemed horrified. Finally, a reaction from him. He bolted from his chair, stormed over to Dr. Nash, and gruffly pulled her aside. He spoke to her close enough to whisper in her ear. He returned to the table, glowering. "I'm going to speak with Dr. Nash in private," he said. "I'll be back in a minute."

Meghan watched Carl and Nash depart Charlotte's Web for the hallway beyond.

"It's so weird how they name these rooms after children's books," Becky said, turning her attention back to Meghan, wanting to change the subject until Carl returned with more information. "Why ruin my memory of them? I used to read that book to you when you were little. You loved it so much."

"Well, I don't have any friends here; no spiders looking out for me," Meghan said, offering Becky a little flash of the spirited girl she loved and treasured.

"What's it like here?"

Meghan fell quiet. Then she said, "I haven't had much interaction with the other — what are we? Patients? Prisoners? But I'm guessing they're all crazy because this is a locked floor, after all. Did you know that? Like, I can't just walk out the door."

"How do you spend the day? What have you been doing to keep your mind off things?"

A thoughtful look came over Meghan's face. "Everything here happens like clockwork," she said. "I have room checks every fifteen minutes."

"What for?" Becky asked.

"To make sure I'm breathing. And I get off easy. The suicidal kids get checked every five minutes."

Becky had noticed a big chart out front near the nurse's station and realized it was a running record of each room check.

"Most of the time it's like I'm living in a dream," Meghan continued. "I'm fuzzy and tired all the time."

Becky looked again at her daughter's arm. Were they keeping her sedated? Maybe Carl would have some answers when he came back.

"When can I get out of here?" Meghan asked again.

"There's a woman, a special investigator the judge has appointed, who's going to help make that happen. Her name is Kelly London. Your father and I are scheduled to meet with her very soon. She's going to help us prove that you have mitochondrial disease, and then the judge will let you come home with us."

"Why can't I go home now?" Meghan's watery eyes were pleading.

Even though there was hope Kelly London could rule in their favor, Becky decided now was not the time to reveal the outcome of the seventy-two-hour hearing. Meghan had found her appetite at last, and Becky worried she'd stop her daughter from eating.

The truth would be much harder to swallow. According to Attorney Leers, they may have lost the hearing, but they'd won a decisive part of the ongoing battle. Not every case gets appointed a court investigator, and Kelly London's impartial opinion would go a long way to swaying the judge's decision. There was a chance they'd get Meghan home before the next hearing on the merits of the petition, which could be some months away, but a lot depended on what the investigator had to say.

"It's a process, sweetheart," Becky said, reaching across the table to stroke her daughter's hand, hating how dry her skin felt. "Are you showering, baby?" she asked.

"No. I've refused to take one until they give me a shower curtain," Meghan said with disgust. "What do they think? I'm going to hang myself?"

Becky forced the gruesome image from her mind.

"I do," Meghan said. "Because I'm getting out of here." Her eyes narrowed into a determined expression.

"In time, yes, you are," Becky said.

"That's not what I mean," Meghan said with conviction. "Who is this Kelly London person again?"

"She's the special investigator the court appointed. You see, we wanted you to come home with us, and we went to court to make that happen, but the doctors and the judge want to give it some more time."

"Here? In a mental hospital? Are they nuts? Or am I?" Meghan almost cracked a smile.

"Nobody is crazy, sweetie. We all just want what's best for you."

Meghan looked deep into her mother's eyes. "You're as bad at lying as I am, Mom," she said.

"I promise you — we're going to get you home." Becky felt herself cracking under the strain. She was trying so hard, so very hard to hold it together for the sake of her child.

"It's you, isn't it, Mom," Meghan said softly, breaking eye contact. "Dr. Levine keeps asking me about you. They think you're doing something to me. Is that it?"

"Baby, no. No."

"Don't lie to me, please."

Becky almost caved. "It's not true."

Meghan looked ready to say something but stopped herself. "Dr. Levine asked if I thought you needed me to be sick, Mom. What's that all about? Why would he even ask that?"

"I don't know, honey. I don't. But . . . but" — Becky wondered how much to share, and decided to take at least one step over the line — "but if you *are* sick, I mean really sick, you *can* get out of here."

Meghan looked confused, even a bit disoriented. "So you *want* me to be sick?"

"No, no," Becky said, maybe so quickly that it sounded defensive. "It's just that if you *are* sick, with something the doctors can diagnose, then we'll be able to bring you home. Dr. Fisher is going to help us with that."

"Figure out if I'm sick?"

"Yes," Becky said. "That's all we have to do. You just have to be patient, okay, baby. Just be a little more patient."

And be sick, thought Becky.

They spent a few minutes talking about life at the hospital, routines and such, when Meghan clutched her stomach. She bent over in extreme pain and groaned as her pale lips pulled tight across her mouth. When a second rush of agony hit her, all color drained from her face. Meghan's eyes began to water. She blinked rapidly, similar to the way she had done the night she'd stumbled into Becky's home office complaining of severe stomach cramps.

"Meghan, honey, are you all right?"

"I don't feel so good," Meghan wheezed as she clutched her stomach again. Meghan pushed her chair back and tried to get up. Carl and Nash came into the room just as Meghan struggled to her feet. She managed to stand, albeit shakily, until her legs buckled beneath her.

Becky rose out of her chair in a flash, knowing she was too far away to catch her in time. But Carl was there, and he grabbed Meghan by the shoulders a second before she hit the ground hard.

"Honey, what's wrong?" Carl laid his daughter gently on the floor.

Nash came over, showing deep concern. With her stethoscope, she listened to Meghan's heart and checked her pulse with her fingers. "Her heartbeat and pulse are normal," she said, sounding a bit confused, perhaps because Meghan's sudden symptoms were so severe.

Meghan kept holding her stomach, groaning.

"Did you do something to her?" Carl asked Becky. His voice turned threatening.

"Me?" Becky said while she knelt at her daughter's side. "How dare you. Please, she's sick, can't you see?"

Soon they were surrounded: Nash, Levine, Annabel Hope, Jill Mendoza, all of them crowded over Meghan.

314

"Everyone give us some space," Nash ordered.

They all took two giant steps back. Meghan made another plaintive, pained sound.

"Let's get her to her room," Nash said. "I'll examine her there."

Meghan moaned even louder as Nash and Levine pulled her to her feet.

Becky grabbed Dr. Levine by the shoulder. "This is your fault," she said, her teeth bared like fangs. "You did this to her. You put her here. You made this happen, you son of a bitch. I warned you what would happen. I warned you."

Levine's eyes were wide, uncomprehending as he moved away from Becky. With Nash's help, they dragged Meghan toward the door.

Becky went to follow, but Jill Mendoza got in her way.

"It's best that you leave Meghan to the care of her doctors," she said.

Becky pushed past Mendoza, shoving the much heavier woman aside like she was not even there. Carl fell into step behind, but as Becky reached the door, a large man with a thin mustache appeared to block her way.

"Let me out of here," Becky said to him in a growling voice. "I need to be with my daughter."

Jill Mendoza approached from behind. "I'm afraid I need you both to leave the premises now," Mendoza said sternly. "Whatever happened here has upset Meghan. I promise there will be another opportunity to visit."

Annabel Hope was off in the background, looking on with a grim expression. Dr. Levine had left in a rush to help Dr. Nash triage Meghan.

"Another opportunity?" Becky said, whirling around to glare at Jill Mendoza with disgust. "She's my daughter! She's sick! I want to see her now! Right now!"

"I'm afraid you don't have that authority."

"She's my daughter," Becky said, her voice now breaking.

"Becky," Carl snapped at her. "Don't make it worse."

Becky spun around and punched Carl in the shoulder with a closed fist. "Do something!" she screamed at him. "Do something! I want to be with my daughter! I want to know what's happening to her!"

The man with the mustache came forward menacingly. "Ma'am, please come with me. I'll escort you out," he said, his voice thick with authority.

Becky sank to her knees. She looked at all the faces staring down at her. "It's Dr.

Levine, dammit!" Becky cried out in a help-
less voice. "Don't you see? He's got it in for
us. He's trying to destroy us to protect his
career, his reputation. He's staked too much
on this. He has to be right. Don't you get
it? Don't you see?"

Nobody said anything, not even Carl.

"Damn you all," Becky said, crying now.
"Goddamn you all."

But even as she cried, she knew one thing
was true: Her daughter had been taken
away, sick as could be, so maybe now,
maybe after this episode, they'd finally
believe Meghan's illness couldn't possibly
be inside anybody's head.

CHAPTER 28

Meghan

"How are you feeling?" The muffled voice pricked my ears before it faded. At first, I thought I was dreaming until I heard the voice say, "Open your eyes if you can."

I tried, but it felt like someone had stuck tape across my eyelids. Eventually, I got them open. Light flooded my eyes, but for a time my vision stayed blurred. As things began to come into focus, I could make out Dr. Nash leaning over me, studying me. Her concerned look was the kind someone might give you if they'd seen you take a fall.

"How are you feeling?" she asked again.

The heavy smell of astringent cleaners acted like smelling salts, bringing me more fully to my senses. At that moment, I knew exactly where I was. Turning my head slowly, I glanced out the window expecting to see daylight, but instead confronted a darkening sky. The slight bit of movement sent a shattering pain ripping through my skull.

What happened to me?

The last thing I remembered was being with my parents in Charlotte's Web, and my mom complaining about how silly those room names were because it spoiled her good memories of the cherished book. I was upset because they weren't taking me home. For a second, I put my hopes on this being a dream, and that I was home, in my comfy bed, but the pain in my skull was too real — and even my nightmares weren't that cruel.

I tried to swallow, but my throat was so dry I could have choked on air. Dr. Nash noticed and gave me a plastic cup filled partway with water. I propped myself up on one elbow and drank, slowly, savoring the wetness coating my throat. A chill went through me despite the sweatpants and sweatshirt I had on.

"What happened?" I asked, my voice raspy and weak.

It was then I realized Dr. Nash was not the only one in the room with me. Dr. Levine was there as well.

"You gave us quite a scare," Dr. Nash said.

I stretched my mind, bending and flexing it, trying desperately to remember, but I came up blank.

"You got very sick," Dr. Levine said.

"Sick?" I said, confused, while Dr. Nash refilled my cup of water.

But then, in a flash, visions came at me like headlights speeding my way, slicing through the void to illuminate all sorts of unpleasant memories. I remembered my stomach burning, cramping, and my vision going blurry. I couldn't see straight, couldn't think straight either. My mother was there, scared for me. I could see her panicked face anticipating the worst. And that was the last memory I had before waking up.

"Do you feel up to talking?" Dr. Levine pulled over a rolling chair, then settled in beside my bed.

Talking? God no. What I felt like doing was crying, but I didn't think I had a single tear left inside. I felt empty and useless as a flat tire. The deep ache in my heart simply wouldn't go away. I thought of my room at home. If I closed my eyes, I could go there, see the lights I'd draped around the mirror over my dresser. I could touch the Himalayan salt rock on my nightstand, which my mom had bought for me because she'd heard it had healing properties.

I thought of my closet jammed with clothes that no longer fit right and my hiding place, too, where I kept my secrets. My little stash of booze. Letters I wrote but never gave to a boy I thought was cute in middle school, who to this day doesn't know it. There was a letter I'd written to my mom about Dad that I hadn't had the courage to give to her. But I'd written it. I'd put those words down on the page, wrote out everything I knew. Afterwards, I felt somewhat better, though no less burdened. My room was my safe place, where I could keep those secrets. It was my sanctuary. Not here. Not in this strange place with this strange man who studied me strangely.

"Meghan," Dr. Levine said, his voice gentle as a breeze. "Do you remember what your mother said to you right before you got sick?" he asked.

"Said to me?" I asked, repeating his question because I found it so odd. "No, I . . . I don't."

"I'm going to be very blunt with you, Meghan. Did your mother say something that made you think you were sick?"

"What?" I scrunched up my eyes, looking at him like he was speaking a foreign language.

"Did she say something to you that triggered your reaction? Something that might have encouraged you to be sick?"

Encouraged me? My eyes became slits as I tried to wrap my brain around that one, but it was like bending steel with my hands. It couldn't be done.

"I was sick," I said, sounding quite sure of myself because, fuzzy as I felt, that memory was vivid and real.

Dr. Nash looked at me with these dewy, sympathetic eyes. *You poor, poor thing,* she was saying without having to say it.

"Your vitals were completely normal, Meghan," Nash said, her voice now coolly detached and clinical. "No fever. No irregular heartbeat. We did blood work on you — and, yes, before you ask, we used needles, but you were quite confused and didn't even notice. With symptoms as severe as those you presented, you'd think there'd be something to clue us in as to the cause, some biological marker that would help us come to a diagnosis. But there was nothing, no markers, no indicators. All your test results were perfectly healthy and normal for an almost-sixteen-year-old girl."

I was less surprised that she knew my birthday was coming up than I was confused at what she was trying to tell me. "Are you saying . . . are you saying I was faking being sick?"

"No, dear," Dr. Nash said, her tone dipping into condescending territory. "I'm saying that you were sick, that you felt sick, that you acted very, very sick. But without a biological indicator, something that tells us your system was compromised — a fever, a dip or rise in your blood pressure, an accelerated heart rate, something of that nature — we have to look at the possibility that your illness was triggered by something psychosomatic. Do you know what that means?"

I wasn't an idiot. I did pretty well in English even though I didn't attend school regularly anymore. I knew what that word meant. That's when I remembered my mother saying something like: *If you're sick, you can get out of here.*

I wasn't sure what she'd meant at the time, because of course I was sick. I'd been sick going on two years now. But was my mom suggesting I might not have been sick enough? Is that why my stomach had cramped? Why my vision had turned blurry? Was it like some weird hypnotic suggestion she'd given me? How would that even be possible? I felt like I was going to die, and that's not exaggerating.

As my thoughts continued to crystallize, I felt oddly detached from my body. From the start of this ordeal, as I've been ferried

323

from one appointment to another, a walking, talking episode of *House,* there has never been any real diagnosis — not with Dr. Fisher, or Dr. Nash, or with any of the countless doctors my mom has taken me to see. I've been a great mystery, as unknowable as Stonehenge or the Bermuda Triangle. But now they think they've solved me like the Sunday crossword puzzle: Meghan Gerard is either sick in her head, or Meghan's mommy is the crazy one. That's it. That's the answer. But I knew that couldn't be true. Not my mother. Not her. Nobody loved me like my mom. Nobody.

A little voice in my head spoke up, asking me over and over again: *What if it is true? What if it was "psychosomatic,"* to use Dr. Nash's word? What if my mom had triggered some kind of a strange, subconscious reaction that even I couldn't understand or control? If so, it would mean I might never get out of here, because every time I'd see my mom, I'd get sick like I did, and they'd run all sorts of tests on me again, and those tests would show nothing wrong, and they'd say it was all in my head, and they'd keep me here, locked up in this shit-hole prison for the rest of my life.

"I don't know what you're all talking

about," I eventually said. "I just know how I felt."

Dr. Levine studied me anew. "Your reaction was pretty intense, Meghan," he said. "What we're trying to figure out here is if your symptoms were psychologically rooted, or if there are other symptoms we can't measure in some way," he said. "That's what we need to answer. So, can you help us?"

"I'm not faking," I told him.

"You can trust me, Meghan," Levine said. "I'm not here to hurt you."

"I did tell you the truth."

I swear he looked like he believed me.

"You saw the labs, Peter," Nash said.

"Yes, yes I suppose I did. But still —"

" 'But still' what?" Nash asked, as if I wasn't even there. "What else could it be? Is there another psychiatric condition here we should discuss?"

"No . . . no, not that, it's just . . ." Dr. Levine sounded concerned about something. But what? "Meghan, this is a strange question," he said, "but I need you to be very, very honest with me right now. Okay?"

"Okay," I answered, feeling more than a little apprehensive.

"Has your mother ever been violent before? Has she ever hit you, or threatened to hit you?"

"No," I said with conviction. "She loves me. She'd never."

"What about your father?"

"No."

Dr. Levine rubbed his chin, studying me, and I panicked, thinking he could see right through me.

Chapter 29

Zach

The restaurant was upscale for a pizzeria, but the moody décor, black-clad waitstaff, eclectic artwork, and obscure pizza toppings helped to justify the obscene prices demanded for a ten-inch pie. No doubt Zach's boy, Will, would never have suffered such a hipster joint. He could not wrap his mind around why someone would actually *request* pineapple on a pizza. Will liked his pizza plain and cheesy, and his pizzerias a little more on the greasy side. Zach could never predict what things would make him think of his son, which was why he seldom varied his routine. But tonight, on account of Dr. Peter Levine, Zach was willing to make an exception.

Dr. Levine had sent an email near the end of the workday, requesting an off-campus sit-down about Meghan Gerard, claiming to have some big revelation that might change everything. The restaurant was Levine's choice — neutral ground, he'd called it, away from White, Nash, and other inhibitors to an open dialogue.

Zach sat at a table in the back, scanning the menu halfheartedly while keeping an eye on the front door for Levine, who was nearly twenty-five minutes late. Checking his phone, thinking he'd missed Levine's call or text, Zach saw only an email from Jill Mendoza. She was responding to a message Zach had sent earlier, an electronic missive of the "ready, aim, fire" variety — an email typed in haste, layered with emotion. While he grimaced slightly at the tone of his correspondence, Zach stood by every word. Even so, he hoped it would not end up in Knox Singer's in-box.

In Zach's mind, the Gerards had been hit with charges simply because they disagreed with the diagnosis of two doctors. "You're using a sledgehammer to try to force a square peg through a round hole," Zach had written in his email to Mendoza. "The peg may go through, but only if it breaks."

The system was the problem. The state could not investigate even the suspicion of medical child abuse until doctors formally declared the parents unfit. The parents not only endured the trauma and indignity of losing custody to the state, but they also lost their rights to govern their child's medical care.

Zach had written:

The medical capacity of DCF is nil. The entire agency has one half-time pediatrician, one half-time psychiatrist, and a handful of nurses on staff. You're making a very dangerous assumption based on scant medical evidence, and I fail to see why these drastic measures are even necessary. By bringing in all these subspecialists, you've clouded the situation with value judgments from egos that cannot accept the possibility they've made a terrible and potentially tragic mistake. I suggest we convene a meeting with the clinicians involved, try to reach a consensus on a plan, and work with the parents instead of treating them like criminals. Let DCF take the lead on coordinating the key players if that will satisfy them, but once all the views get aired, it would help immensely if you and the others holding Meghan hostage would take a damn humility pill.

In her reply, Mendoza did not seem to take offense. She thanked Zach for his suggestion and promised to explore the idea of a consensus meeting. She then went on to detail how Meghan had gotten violently ill during the mother's visit, but her doctors could find no physical cause.

It sounded to Zach like Meghan had experienced some type of a somatoform disorder, in which her bodily symptoms present in a disproportionate level of distress, including pain, but the source cannot be traced to a physical cause. It was a telltale marker of Munchausen syndrome, and the fact that the mother was present during the episode lent credibility to the proxy accusation. Zach had no doubt Meghan had experienced real distress, real pain, but the incident served only to reinforce the notion that Becky Gerard might be so deeply enmeshed in her daughter's mind, her psyche, that a single suggestion could be enough to trigger a profound somatic reaction.

Zach wondered if that frightening episode was at the heart of Dr. Levine's surprise dinner invitation, but the mystery seemed destined to remain unsolved. Almost thirty minutes late now, Levine was still MIA.

Zach approached the hostess at the front of the restaurant. "Do you do deliveries?" he asked.

The curly-haired hostess said they did. He explained his dinner companion's tardiness.

"I'm a fellow doctor at White Memorial," Zach said, showing her his license with the MD stamped at the end of his name. "I'm a bit concerned. It's not like Peter to be late." Zach knew they could not call him on this embellishment. "If he's ordered takeout from here before, perhaps you have his address on file. I'll pop over and just make sure he's all right. He's not answering his phone or texts."

There was some hesitation on the hostess's part, a brief conversation between her and the manager, but eventually, the MD won their trust. Zach set off into a humid spring evening in search of the missing doctor.

Zach used the address the pizzeria had given him to locate Dr. Peter Levine's home four blocks away. He lived on the first floor of a classic three-family dwelling in Roslindale, an established residential neighborhood of Boston. It was not the fanciest of places, but Levine was a newbie doc with plenty of medical school debt to pay down. There was no garage or driveway, but ample street parking made it so that Zach did not have to drive around searching for a place for his car. Zach did not know if Levine lived alone or if he was married, straight or gay, happy or sad — he knew nothing about the man other than that he was wrong about Meghan and very late for dinner.

All three floors had some lights on, but Levine's home was lit up as though someone else were paying the electric bill. Zach strode up the front stairs. He rang the buzzer to Levine's unit and waited. No answer. The houses here were nestled closely together. Zach could see into the window of the adjacent home. A family was sitting down to eat — mother, father, and two young children. There were smiles all around as the father scooped food from a baking dish onto waiting plates. Such a mundane, ordinary moment, one the family did not, could not fully appreciate. Meals like this one happened most every night for this family and others like them. But not for Zach, who felt a profound ache at seeing the ordinary in motion.

He could not recall the last good day he had had with his son. It had passed as uneventfully as every other day, but at some point, there was the drop-off, akin to going over a cliff, when the subtle changes he had failed to notice congealed into a more pronounced sickness from which Will would not return. The more vivid memories Zach retained were also the cruelest — the hospital bed, his boy's moonlight pale skin, his tears and Zach's mixing as they embraced, the arguments with Stacy, the longing for that one good day.

Zach rang the bell again, waited for a response, but none came. Moving to the other side of the porch, Zach leaned his body over the railing to get a good look in the first-floor window. Through the gauzy curtains, he saw the outline of a man seated on a sofa, but could not tell if it was Levine.

Perhaps the door buzzer was broken, Zach thought. Perhaps Levine had his phone powered off and he'd forgotten all about their dinner. Zach leaned his body out a bit farther and rapped on the window to get the occupant's attention. There was no movement, so Zach knocked a bit harder. Still nothing. Sirens approaching from the direction of Main Street worried Zach. Someone may have called the police, thinking he was a burglar. Zach resumed knocking, louder this time. *How can he not hear?*

Concern pinged at Zach — something was not right. He returned to the buzzers, but this time went for the floor above, where there were plenty of lights on as well. There was no intercom system, but soon enough Zach heard heavy footsteps descending the stairs. Moments later, a large man in dungarees and a work shirt appeared in the foyer, looking quite perturbed. Perhaps he thought this stranger on his front porch was from Greenpeace or Jehovah's Witnesses, come to disrupt his evening ritual. He opened the door partway, stuck his face in the crack, and growled, "No solicitors."

"I'm a doctor," Zach explained, and introduced himself. "I'm trying to reach Peter Levine, your downstairs neighbor. I think he's in the living room, but he's not answering his phone and won't respond even when I knock on the window."

The door opened fully, and the large man stepped onto the porch. He was the size of an NFL nose tackle. The porch floorboards creaked slightly under his weight. "Show me," he said.

Zach leaned over the railing, knocked on the window, and made sure the big man could see that the figure seated inside did not budge.

"What's your name?" Zach asked.

"Doug Griffin," said the man.

"Doug, do you have a key to the unit?" Zach asked.

"No," he said. "The landlord does. I can call him."

Zach thought it over while a fresh stab of

concern hit him. Something was terribly wrong. "How far away is the landlord?"

Doug ruminated on it. "I don't know. Usually takes twenty minutes to get here when the damn sink starts backing up. I'd fix it myself, but it's a matter of principle."

Zach did the math in his head. Twenty minutes for the landlord to show with a key, ten for the police to let him in. If there was a medical emergency, it could be too late. Zach thought of another way. He descended the stairs and searched around until he found a good-size rock from the garden.

"Do you have a stepladder?" Zach asked.

"Yeah, there's one in the shed."

"Get it!"

Doug went to the shed while Zach launched his rock through the window adjacent to the one where the still figure sat. Glass splintered noisily, violently. Shards fell like plinking raindrops. The person inside did not move. Doug returned with the ladder and positioned it underneath the broken window.

Zach went up quickly. Using his elbow, he broke away more glass until he could get his hand inside to undo the latch. The window opened easily and Zach slipped inside, careful to avoid the broken glass littering the hardwood floor. He popped to his feet, heart hammering, gripped with nervous anticipation. He went to the sofa. There, with his back straight, eyes open and blank and hands resting on his lap, sat Peter Levine. There were no visible wounds on his face, neck, or hands.

"Peter!" Zach yelled, giving gentle slaps to try to rouse him. Levine's skin felt cool to the touch. "Peter!" Zach shouted again.

From outside, Zach heard Doug cry out, "Is everything all right?"

"Call 911," Zach said, sitting on the sofa next to Peter. There was an empty teacup on the coffee table before him. His body seemed perfectly intact. No blood. Levine was like a wax figure.

One look at Peter Levine's pale skin, and Zach knew there'd be no radial pulse in either arm when he checked. He did not have a blood pressure cuff on him, but soon enough, the EMTs would show up. They'd try to get a read but would come up short.

Zach stared into Peter Levine's murky eyes, seeing infinity there. He put his ear to Dr. Peter Levine's chest, positive of what he'd hear. Nothing. The sound of silence.

CHAPTER 30

Becky

"You have to do it," Veronica said. As usual, she sounded quite sure of herself.

Becky, who had bought a new computer specifically to have this FaceTime chat, did not share her conviction. "I'm worried what it will do to Meghan . . . to our case," Becky said. "I'm on shaky enough ground as it is with that judge."

"Don't fret, *chica*. Call in the cavalry," Veronica insisted. "Fight fire with fire. The press has to know about Meghan. They'll be all over this story. Trust me, I know."

One look at Veronica's LinkedIn profile would be proof enough. She was a PR professional with years of experience working for one of the world's largest public relations firms. She had helped Fortune 500 clients navigate bad press, led crisis response campaigns, and generated enormous attention for her efforts. She was the Olivia Pope of PR, a dam with floodgates that could be opened or closed at her whim, and she wanted those gates open to draw media attention to Meghan's plight.

"If they took Ashley like that, you best believe I'd have the media on my side," Veronica said. "And then I'd have the hounds barking at the gates of White until I got her back."

Becky felt a sharp pang of guilt that she was not doing enough to help Meghan. She also understood her daughter's sudden sickness might not have helped her cause, as she had hoped it would. Veronica was right: She should rise up and meet the challenge head-on. Thump her chest, beat her drum, bang on those doors until she got back what they took from her. Becky's shame burned like a flame against her skin. For Meghan's sake, she would be better. She had to be better.

"Help me do it," Becky said.

Veronica smiled, her ruby lips parting to reveal a bright white smile that had convinced more clients to trust her than Meghan had doctors. "That's my girl," Veronica said. "I'll take it from here. Any news on your mom?"

"She's still alive, miracle of miracles," Becky said with no evident emotion. "But

I'm not going to see her. Not until Meghan's home safe."

"Does your sister have anything to say about that?"

"Sabrina has something to say about everything, but I don't care. I don't care what anybody thinks. I just want my daughter back."

"The story writes itself," Veronica said. " 'Big, faceless hospital rips sick girl from mother's arms.' Seriously, Beck, you're going to need to supply refreshments for all the poor reporters who will be camped out on your front lawn."

"Do I want that?"

"Of course you want that!" snapped Veronica. "You need it if you're going to get Meghan back."

"But the judge —"

"I have bad news for you, sweetie. The judge is not going to be on your side. Nobody is. Except, of course, for the public at large."

"What about Carl?"

"What about him?"

"Shouldn't we at least consult him before . . . you know, we release those hounds?"

"He's your husband. I can only tell you what I would do."

Becky knew exactly what Veronica would do. She thought it over, anticipating Carl's outrage, then decided to let Veronica operate from the shadows. Just because the media had learned of the story did not mean Carl had to know she was the source of the leak. A little jolt of excitement tingled in Becky. Veronica was right. It felt good to take charge.

Damn good.

Carl was around the house somewhere — his office, perhaps — but what did it matter? They'd barely spoken since coming home from the hospital yesterday. He was still stewing in his anger, marinating in dark thoughts, facing an impossible choice: Whom to believe? The doctors or his wife?

But Becky felt no sympathy for him. None whatsoever. He could think what he wanted. It made no difference to her either way. There was no question in her mind that Carl wanted Meghan back home. She could see the ache in every new worry line carved in his beleaguered face. But would he be willing to go to the same lengths as she would to make that happen?

She'd find out soon enough.

The doorbell rang at exactly three o'clock that same afternoon. Becky opened the front door, hoping that the attractive dark-haired woman standing on her front step was simply lost and in need of directions. She seemed far too young to be Becky's best chance at getting her daughter back. But no, she was, in fact, Kelly London, the court investigator appointed to make an influential report to Judge Trainer.

Carl emerged from somewhere. If he had any decency or tact, he would have made his head-to-toe scan of the young Ms. London a bit less apparent. But it was hard not to look at Kelly. She had a youthful beauty, and a body that appeared to have endured every workout ever devised. She wore a tight-fitting sweater, hip-hugging gray slacks, and pumps that gave her a few inches of extra height. The day was warm, so no need for a coat, which gave Carl even more to ogle. Becky held her tongue.

She always held her tongue.

"Thank you for making time to see me," Kelly said, her voice melodious as a song-bird's.

A pit opened in Becky's stomach. If Kelly London was over twenty-eight, then Becky was related to Mary, Queen of Scots. How could the courts have assigned such an inexperienced person to head up this investigation? Becky wanted a do-over. She wanted to call Judge Trainer, tell her a mistake had been made, that they'd sent a law school student instead of a seasoned court investigator to her house. Rather than make that call, Becky invited Kelly inside. She offered her something to drink or eat, but Kelly and her hyper-thin physique declined.

They set up shop at the dining room table, where Kelly had plenty of room to spread out the file folders and notes she carried in her leather bag. Carl and Becky each gave consent to let Kelly record the conversation. Carl was especially accommodating, nodding obsequiously, seemingly smitten with her.

Becky was used to women checking Carl out, but she'd seen the opposite before, too, and had even talked with him about it on occasion. She noticed how he looked Kelly in the eyes longer than was strictly appropriate; saw how his posture straightened, how his arms stayed in a state of perpetual flex. Carl often complained about getting older, so perhaps it was Kelly's youth that he found attractive. Maybe she reminded him of a time when life was far simpler.

"Let's start by getting an update on Meghan. What have you heard?"

Carl did most of the talking. He recounted

for Kelly's benefit how the doctors had essentially dragged their deathly ill daughter away from them. He sounded aggrieved, but his anger was directed at White, not Becky. It had been the reverse on the car ride home. Carl was convinced Becky had said or done something to Meghan to make her sick. When Dr. Nash called with news that Meghan's test results had come back normal — that there was no physical cause for her profound and rapid-onset illness, that the blood work was perfectly fine — Carl's doubts had found new, stronger footing. There was a fight — another damn fight.

"And we still don't know what made her so sick?" Kelly asked in a honey-dipped voice. There was no edge to this woman, because the years had yet to hone one. She did not, could not, appreciate Becky's struggles — she was probably still cruising the bars with her girlfriends.

"There's been no official diagnosis," Becky said before Carl could interject his point of view. "But I'm not sure they tested her properly. I haven't seen any of the labs. Nobody has sent me any reports."

"Well, that's because Jill Mendoza would need a court order to release them," Kelly explained. "That would be her decision to make." Kelly tossed this out rather thoughtlessly, as if Becky were not fully aware of the guardian ad litem's power.

"I know it doesn't look good that we were together when she got sick," Becky said. "But I'm not intentionally making her sick, if that's what you're thinking."

The look Kelly returned made it clear she'd need more than an impassioned plea in order to get Meghan back. "I guess that's what we're here to figure out," said Kelly. "The question is how to prove it."

"That's simple," Becky said emphatically. "She needs to have a muscle biopsy done, and maybe an EMG test — that's electromyography. It measures the energy in her muscles and nerve cells, or something like that. Dr. Fisher can explain it all better than I can."

"Dr. Fisher, yes," Kelly said, glancing at her notes. "I have an appointment to speak with him later today."

In the cracks of time when her mind drifted away from Meghan, Becky sometimes thought of Zach. She imagined he had been an amazing father, kind and attentive. It made her wonder what sort of husband he'd been to his ex-wife, Stacy was her name, wasn't it. Most likely he had been kind to her as well, with a big heart, always peppering her with sweet little surprises. It had disappointed Becky how unreceptive Zach was to her coquettish behavior, but she had to try. Bonding over their dead children would dredge up too much pain for them both.

She researched him the way she always did — relying heavily on social media and reports from the mitochondrial community for which he was something of a hero — but found little joy in his life or his past that could be used to ingratiate herself to him. He worked and he grieved, and that was the extent of Dr. Zach Fisher as far as Becky could tell. She figured he was lonely, as she could find no evidence of a girlfriend, wife, or lover. Maybe he was still pining for his ex, or it could be she needed to turn up the charm factor a few ticks higher. She'd do that if she thought it would be of benefit to Meghan — unlike Carl, whom she'd watched flirt aimlessly, with no justifiable goal in mind.

"How do we get this procedure done?" Kelly asked.

"We need Jill Mendoza to authorize it," Becky said bitterly. "She's the one in charge."

"It's an invasive procedure," Carl said with evident reservation. "Meghan's in a fragile state. She has a terrible needle phobia because of all the treatments she's received." He turned his attention over to Becky — and no, he did not look at her the way he did Kelly London.

"If I may be very candid," Kelly said somewhat tentatively, "it sounds to me, Carl, that you doubt your wife."

Becky perked up. *Well, now,* she thought. This girl had more fight in her than it would appear.

"I do," Carl admitted, slightly sheepish.

"Why is that?" Kelly asked. "If I'm going to be of value, I need everything put on the table. No secrets, no hidden agendas. Those won't help your cause."

"What do you know about Munchausen syndrome by proxy?" Carl asked.

Kelly gave a rote answer, a textbook definition of the mental health disorder.

"What do you know of the psychology — the background of the illness?"

Color flushed across Becky's cheeks, as she knew exactly where this was headed — to Sammy, Cora, to her life.

"Not as much as you, I suppose," Kelly offered.

"You see, I didn't know much about the condition myself until my wife was accused of it," Carl said harshly. "But I went online, did my research, and found some common characteristics."

"Such as?" Kelly's eyebrows were raised.

"Grief," Carl said. "The loss of a loved one. We had a son, Samuel. He died at fourteen weeks of SIDS."

Kelly's hand reflexively went to her mouth. "I'm so very sorry," she said. Becky noted that her sympathy came across as genuine.

"But that's not all," Carl continued. Becky clenched her jaw. "Mental health professionals have compiled something of a profile of these mothers — it's almost always mothers, you see — who use their children to gain attention from medical professionals. And — surprise, surprise — these women had childhoods not too dissimilar from my wife's."

"Carl, please." Becky pursed her lips, feeling the blood throbbing in her veins.

"No, sweetheart," Carl answered coolly. "Ms. London encouraged us to be honest, so let's try that for a change. Let's be honest."

Kelly shifted uncomfortably in her chair. "It is important," she said, directing her attention to Becky. "Better the issues come out here than some other way."

But there would be no other way to find out, thought Becky, not without Carl volunteering it.

"All these mothers have attachment issues," Carl continued unabashed. "They have an insecure or ambivalent attachment to or are estranged from a parent. Becky's mother is dying in California, but my wife won't go to visit her."

"Because of Meghan," Becky said.

"No, it's because of Cora," Carl shot back. "She was a terrible mother — abusive, if you ask me."

"My father died when my sister and I were very young," Becky said, unsure why she felt a sudden compulsion to defend her mother. "It was difficult. We didn't have much money. My mother, Cora, did the best she could."

"She faked disability to get money from the government," Carl said flatly. "She taught her kids how to lie for her, how to trick the system, and when the kids didn't live up to her expectations, she hit them."

Becky's face burned as if Cora herself had reached across the country to smack her with the cane she pretended to need. She could see her mother in that ratty, pit-stained nightgown she always wore; heard her voice, coarse from the cough she'd been feigning for years.

"If they don't believe you, we don't eat,"

Cora had said prior to the social worker's arrival. "Make them believe. Make them believe!"

Becky snapped back into herself as Kelly pursed her lips, perhaps in an attempt to hide a grimace. Becky nervously pulled her hair back into a ponytail. She hated talking about her mother, but she hated even more that Carl had shared her painful secrets so willingly.

"When you add it all up," Carl said, "why wouldn't you suspect my wife? Becky stopped working when Meghan was born because she got physically ill when someone else looked after her daughter. To call her an attentive parent would be like saying the Secret Service pays attention to the president.

"When Meghan got sick a few years back, my wife took her to see doctor after doctor, never getting any diagnosis. Mito is just the latest in a string of possibilities that have all been disproved."

Becky returned a strained smile. "Do you feel happy getting all that off your chest?" she asked, making her resentment clear.

"It would all have come up in my investigation," Kelly offered, making an effort to dress the fresh wounds. "I'm honestly glad you shared. The question now is what to do going forward."

"We have to get Meghan tested," Becky said with authority. "It's our best hope."

Kelly took down some notes on her legal pad while Becky sent Carl a withering stare.

"And you, Carl," Becky said, "need to decide whose side you're on here. Don't make me choose, because it won't be a choice."

Before Carl could rebut, the doorbell rang again. He looked at Becky, confused.

"Are you expecting someone else?" Kelly asked.

"No," said Becky, wondering if Veronica had gotten word out to the media, if it might be the press already chasing the story. She got up to find out, with Carl falling in behind her while Kelly London waited in the living room. Becky opened the front door, and was mildly surprised to see two men in suits who looked nothing like reporters.

"Becky Gerard?" one man said.

"Yes?"

Both men flashed official-looking badges.

"I'm Detective Richard Spence, and this is Detective Howard Capshaw of the Boston PD," said the thinner of the two.

Spence had the more hard-bitten face, along with a full head of hair. Capshaw's thinning hair had fewer grays, while his plump cheeks held a ruddier complexion.

"What's this about?" Becky asked nervously.

"Last night we were called to the home of Dr. Peter Levine. I believe you know him," Spence said.

"I do," Becky said, glancing anxiously back at Carl.

"He's dead," said Capshaw. "And we'd like to ask you a few questions about that, if we may."

CHAPTER 31

They gathered in the living room, the detectives seated on the comfortable chairs last used years ago, when Becky and Carl had still hosted parties. The furnishings, in general, all of it oversize dark wood pieces, went together because it had come — down to the lamps and throw rug — from a showroom at the furniture store. Becky had come from nothing, had never dreamed of having anything, which was why she'd never cultivated any style or flair for interior design. She sold homes, not the furniture that went in them. She went for the largest pieces, not the prettiest ones, but even then, the massive room looked spare and lifeless to her.

Becky and Carl sat on the sofa, holding hands — something they used to do that no longer felt natural or even authentic. Kelly London kept to the dining room, reviewing her notes, checking her phone, and most likely eavesdropping on the conversation.

"How did Dr. Levine die?" Becky began.

"If you don't mind, we'll ask the questions," the heavier Capshaw said, returning a tough guy stare.

"Very well," said Becky, removing her hands from Carl's to fold them on her lap. "Ask away."

"What's your relationship with Dr. Levine?" Spence began.

News of the man's death had cleansed Becky of much of her anger.

"He and Dr. Amanda Nash have been . . . examining and looking after our daughter."

"Can you be more specific?"

"He was assessing her mental health," Becky said, unsure how much she should share.

Spence wrote something in his little black notebook.

"When was the last time you saw Dr. Levine?"

"That would be yesterday afternoon," Becky said, a hitch in her voice. "When he and Dr. Nash took Meghan away from us after she got sick while we were visiting her at White."

"What was she sick with?" Capshaw asked.

"We don't know," Carl said, eyeing Becky in an unloving way. "It's been . . . let's just say . . . difficult to figure that one out."

"We have some background, but feel free to elaborate for us," Spence said.

"Happy to," Becky said, sounding a defiant note. "The doctors at White believe I've been abusing my daughter, medically speaking — making her act sick, or fake an illness, or just putting ideas in her head so that she feigns sickness for the attention. None of which is true, but I'm having a hard time convincing anyone of that fact, my dear husband included. The hospital took her from us, and they are keeping her there against our wishes."

Becky sat up straighter, as if unloading her emotional burden had physically lightened her load as well.

Spence jotted furiously in his notebook like a beat reporter getting a scoop. "And I'm guessing you haven't been criminally charged?"

"No," Carl said. "We're in court. Trying to figure that one out."

"So with Dr. Levine —" Capshaw said.

"Are you going to ask if I think he got what he deserved?" Becky said, interrupting Capshaw while drawing Carl's ire. "Or if I had something to do with his death? The answer is no, to both. If you ask if I'm broken up about it, well, yes, only because he was so young. But he's also put my family through a bit of hell, so forgive me if I don't display the expected degree of shock and sorrow. Now, are you going to tell me how he died?"

"We don't know," Spence said, glancing at his notebook. "A Dr. Zachary Fisher was supposed to meet him for dinner. When he didn't show, Dr. Fisher went to the house and broke a window to gain entry."

"No evidence of trauma, no sign of forced entry, just a guy sitting on a sofa like you're sitting on now, only he was dead," Capshaw added.

"What was Dr. Fisher meeting with Dr. Levine about?" Carl leaned forward, thumb pressed to his chin hard enough to leave the skin bloodless underneath.

"According to Dr. Fisher, it was about you, Mrs. Gerard," Capshaw said. "Did you happen to have a sit-down with Dr. Levine at the Moonlight Diner a few days ago that did not go particularly well?"

Carl whipped his head in Becky's direction. Deep creases sank into his furrowed brow. "You met with him? Without me? Without telling our lawyers?" Carl was seething. "Dammit, Becky, what are you trying to do here? Sabotage our chances?"

"I was trying to get my daughter back,

which I don't believe is against any law," Becky answered imperiously. "So what? We had breakfast, a very short breakfast — what does that matter? How do you even know about that, anyway?"

"Because Dr. Levine mentioned it in an email to Dr. Fisher; said something about you threatening him. Did that happen, or do you think that doesn't matter, too?"

Becky replayed that day in her head. She had said something, hadn't she? A warning to Levine not to cross her — or else. It came out sounding overly dramatic, she remembered thinking, even a bit silly, but she'd meant every word of it. She was about to confess, to explain it away, when her mother's voice came to her like a whisper on the wind. *Deny it until the day you die. Deny it and never admit to them you were lying.* Of course, that little bit of parental advice had been in reference to the scam Cora had been running, but the lesson applied across a broad spectrum of life's travails. Here it was rearing its head once more, goading Becky back into a past she had tried so hard to leave behind.

"I did nothing of the sort."

"So he made up that you threatened him?" Spence asked incredulously.

"I don't know what he did or didn't do or

say," Becky replied. "I just know that I never threatened him."

The "I've heard that one before" look that Spence gave Becky showed his cop's seasoning.

"Can you tell us where you were last night, Mrs. Gerard?" Capshaw asked.

Becky's hand went to her chest. "Am I a suspect or something, Detectives?"

"Just answer the question if you can," Spence said impatiently.

"Well, I was . . . I was home, I suppose."

"All day, all night?" Capshaw asked.

"No, I went out for a while — the grocery store, the gym — the owner can vouch for me if you want to call him."

"What time did you come home?"

Becky glanced up at the ceiling, as if tilting her head back would dislodge some stuck memory. "Maybe four, five that afternoon. Around that time, anyway."

"And was anybody home with you?" Spence sounded distracted, like he was putting together the time sequence in his mind.

Carl shook his head glumly. "I worked late that night," he said. The suspicious look he gave Becky made her want to disappear, but not before she left him with two black eyes.

"What time do you think you got home?"

"It was after midnight," Carl said. "Why?

Do you have a time of death?"

"Medical examiner thinks it was between three and six o'clock, but we're still trying to narrow that down."

Becky looked confused about something. "Did you say there was no foul play? No break-in, no struggle, no apparent injury? That he just died, suddenly?"

Capshaw nodded. "Yeah, that's what we said."

Spence chimed in. "But when a young person like Dr. Levine dies suddenly, with no apparent cause of death, and he's involved in a contentious situation — and I think it's fair to say this situation can be called contentious — then, you know, we get a bit curious."

"Well, did you do a toxicology screen or something like that?" Carl asked.

Capshaw shrugged. "Let's just say that's a work in progress."

"Well, I had nothing to do with it," Becky snapped. "I may not have liked him, but that doesn't mean I wanted him dead."

Spence's thin smile adequately conveyed his disbelief. "In that case, we're hoping you'd be willing to provide us with elimination fingerprints, as we call them, and a DNA sample, just so we can check those boxes."

"Fine," Becky said with a curt nod.

Capshaw added, "And we're wondering if you mind us taking a look at your computer; let us borrow it for a few days to have our forensic guys comb through it."

"Don't you need a warrant for that?" Carl asked.

"Not if we get permission," Capshaw said.

"Carl, let them take it," Becky said, giving a dismissive wave. She had painstakingly restored her files, research, and bookmarks from her backups, which provided confidence that if something were to happen to this computer, she'd be able to recover her data with little trouble. "I've nothing to hide. It might look bad in Judge Trainer's eyes if we're not seen as cooperative. It's terrible what happened, and I'm happy to assist with the investigation, even though it'll be a waste of everyone's time."

Capshaw stood, and Spence did the same.

"Great," Spence said. "You show us where the computer is; we'll bag it up and give you a receipt. I promise we'll get it back to you in a few days' time. Home delivery, so it won't be a further inconvenience. Thanks again for your cooperation."

"It's no problem, really," Becky said. "I can use Meghan's computer in the meantime. Obviously, she's not using it."

"Oh, one more thing," Capshaw said. "Does this look familiar to you?" From the pocket of his sport coat, Capshaw retrieved a clear plastic police evidence bag with a single diamond pendant earring inside. "We found this on Dr. Levine's living room floor, not far from his body. Just curious to know if it looks familiar to you before we send it off to the lab for DNA analysis."

Becky studied the earring closely. "No. I don't recognize it," she said firmly.

Spence gave a nod that was neither a show of approval nor disapproval, just the acknowledgment of a claim that was not yet a fact.

Carl did not buy Becky much jewelry these days. His last purchase was a diamond-encrusted pendant from Tiffany's with her initials engraved on the back, which she wore more than any other piece she owned. He probably would not remember those earrings even if he had bought them for her.

A knot formed at the base of Becky's neck. She grew quite anxious, rethinking her decision to willingly give the detectives her computer and submit to their forensic tests. But there was no easy way to back out of the arrangement now. After the detectives were gone, Becky would go to her bedroom. She'd rifle through her jewelry box, even though she had little doubt that she'd find only one of her pair of diamond earrings inside.

CHAPTER 32

Meghan

Happy stinking birthday to me.

What a joke. Never in all my life did I think I'd be celebrating my sixteenth birthday in a psych ward, but here we are, so let the festivities begin. There were a lot of tears when Mom and I saw each other, but that was nothing strange. People cried all the time here. They hollered at empty space or stared blankly at their feet the same way they did at the television in the common rooms. There were always odd noises — weird gurgles, grunts, cries. One girl was convinced she was a horse. She'd gallop down the halls neighing and snorting at people so they'd know to keep away. It worked.

Mom and Dad were barely speaking to each other. It's like they've already split up and I'm to blame. But that's not really true. It's my father's fault, and he knows it. It's not like we ever had the big happy family to begin with. I've only seen my Grandma Cora a couple times, and it's been years since I've been out to California. Not that I want to go. She's old and smells like bark, something decaying. Her fingers are always yellow and nicotine-stained, like her teeth. I don't miss seeing her, or going to her jam-packed trailer home, which looks like a rundown flea market to me.

Aunt Sabrina could visit if she wanted to, but clearly she doesn't. Which leaves my dad's side of the family. I don't know many kids with divorced grandparents, but I've got a pair. Nobody ever told me the reason they split up, and I never bothered to ask. My father always said he'd never end up like them, which is why he took great pride in holding his marriage together after Sammy died.

He'd talk about it at parties, which made Mom furious. But his drinking sometimes made it hard to keep his voice low and his thoughts to himself. I overheard him say that most marriages couldn't have survived that kind of strain, but not his. You see, my dad can't have weak things in his life. That's why he can't have a weak daughter. But he's the weakest man I know.

There's music at my lamest birthday party

ever. It's the first time I've heard music since I've been here. Somebody brought cheap Bluetooth speakers, so Taylor Swift sounds like she's singing from the bottom of a tin can. Normally, I listen to music on my phone, which I haven't had in days. Actually, I don't know how long I've been here, because I've completely lost track of time.

But my phone! I just want my phone! I want to talk to my friends. I want to scroll through Instagram and see what they've been up to. I want to type in my familiar second language, the code of the teenager. J/K — just kidding. BRB — be right back. NP — no problem. But there are other codes, too. Codes my parents don't know about that I could type right now and mean every bit. KMS — kill myself. TIME — tears in my eyes. VSF — very sad face. And then there's KPC — keeping my parents clueless, which is exactly what I'm doing, keeping them clueless, or at least one of them.

Somebody (for sure not Mustache Man, who I bit) put up balloons and even hung a few streamers, but it's like that old "lipstick on a pig" line. Today, we were in A Wrinkle in Time. I guess they wanted to see if a different room would lead to a different outcome. Things are different, all right, but not because of the room change. Evidently, I'm now the talk of the town. I've been on TV, in newspapers, Facebook, Twitter, blogs — everywhere there's media, there's Meghan.

My friends must be freaking out. I guess I'm something of a celebrity. I'm sure they're posting to social media about me all the time. My mom came to the party armed with presents, but she'd say her biggest gift to me is all the attention she's drummed up about my case. She's super proud for making it happen. I don't know how she got the ball rolling, but whatever she did, it's supposed to put pressure on the hospital and make them let me go. Who knows? Maybe it will work, but I'm not holding out hope.

My mom said she had something important to tell me, but we were going to talk about it after I opened my presents. Speaking of presents, what the heck happened? They all looked like they'd been opened already. My mom was a damn fine present wrapper, but this job was whack. The paper was torn at the edges. The tape had been put on crookedly. I didn't get it at first, but then Mom explained: "They had to open the presents first to see what I was giving you."

I squeezed Mom's hand and thanked her.

I told her I loved her, which I did, more than anything. Then I opened my gifts. Of course I got books, because what else am I going to do in here? Dad got me Beats by Dre headphones. There was jewelry, a Go-Pro camera (which I couldn't have, because I'm not allowed to film anything on this floor), a cool hat that would be great for the winter — unless I'm still in here. Kids on this floor don't get fresh air.

I told the doctors they could tie me up, put shackles on my ankles, staple me to Dr. Levine if that's what it would take, but please, please, let me breathe some fresh air, let me get out of this sterile rat maze even for just an hour. But there was no place for me to go, or so they said. I kind of understood. This was a city, after all. But if they were trying to keep me from being anxious or depressed, it sure would help if they gave me some natural sunlight instead of that stupid lamp. And *no* — yoga and Wii tennis don't make up for having zero time outside.

Like I said, I'm a prisoner here.

What looked like a big pile of presents seemed a lot smaller after I'd finished opening them all. That Jill Mendoza lady looked on approvingly, as if I'd invited her to the party. Dr. Nash hung out in the back, near this attractive young woman who got a lot of *those* kinds of looks from my dad. Her name was Kelly London. Apparently, this Kelly lady was the special investigator who could help us out, which explained why Mom pulled me aside to tell me she was super important and that I should be extremely nice to her, so that's what I did. I smiled and tried to act not crazy.

Mom's words came back to me: *If you're sick, you can get out of here.*

We'll see about that, I thought.

Despite this being the worst birthday celebration ever, and I do mean ever, there was this really strange vibe in the air. I thought maybe it was because I'd obviously lost weight and basically looked like a dirty stick mop, stringy hair and all, which maybe is why Mom came armed with a thermos of her chicken soup. But no, my raggedy appearance wasn't it. There was something else going on, something that nobody was telling me, but I didn't bother to ask. You spend enough time here, and you learn to lose your voice.

I slipped on the new Beats headphones and used my mom's phone to listen to Pandora, which, to be honest, sounded totally sick. I was just getting into the good part of a song when this big, important-looking guy came storming into the room, all red-faced and super agitated. I turned the volume of the music all the way down but continued nodding my head to the non-existent beat. I heard somebody call the angry guy Knox Singer, and I remembered he was the hospital CEO or had some mega job like that.

"Have any of you been outside?" he yelled. "It's a goddamn circus out there. There must be a dozen news trucks. More! I don't need to tell you that we can't run a hospital like this."

Dr. Nash and Jill Mendoza went over to Singer, and so did my mom, but not me. I was just bobbing my head, pretending I couldn't hear every word they were saying.

"What's the matter, Knox?" I heard my mom say. "You don't like it? Well, you better get used to it, because those reporters are going to be around for a long, long time unless you want to relinquish my daughter back to our care. If not, I'll keep getting more press." Mom poked her finger at Singer like she was stabbing him in the chest.

"You do realize you are putting us in a very difficult position," Knox said. "And it certainly won't help your case with the judge when she learns how uncooperative you've been."

"I had nothing to do with getting the media involved," I heard my dad say, which made me sad. I mean, he's always been the alpha, the big dog in the family. He's the kind of guy I never thought would let anyone push him or us around. But that was all an illusion. Everything about him is an illusion.

"Let me be clear about something," Knox said. "This attention you're drumming up is a safety issue for my patients and staff. I can't accept this."

"Well, I can't accept what you've done to Meghan," my mom shot back.

This guy didn't intimidate her. Not in the slightest. I wanted to stand up and hug her, but I didn't dare.

"I want to transfer Meghan to a residential treatment center where she can get the kind of specialized treatment and support she needs," Knox said. "She could even go outside. I think it's especially important we make this move in light of what happened to Dr. Levine."

Dr. Levine? I thought. *What happened to him?* Only now did I realize he wasn't in the room with us. *Where is he?*

"Let me tell you something," my mom said. "I will sue anyplace that agrees to take

Meghan in, and all the news crews outside your hospital will move there, so I highly doubt any residential treatment center from here to Missoula is going to accept your generous offer to house my daughter."

I managed to swallow the gasp rising in my throat.

"You have a dark soul, Mrs. Gerard," Knox said. "And what you're doing to your daughter is unconscionable."

"I assure you, you and I share the same sentiments about each other," my mom said.

"Becky, please, constrain yourself," my dad chimed in. "Think about how this will look to Judge Trainer."

"Meghan is a sick girl," I heard my mother say. "She's sick, and soon enough you're going to realize it."

I glanced out the window, looking into the hallway at the other patients, who carried lunch trays back to their rooms. It was noon, which meant in fifteen minutes Loretta would wheel her empty food cart away. I'd seen the menu that morning and was grateful to sip Mom's homemade soup and not the sock dipped in broth that Loretta was serving for lunch that day.

I honestly couldn't have been prouder of my mother. She was amazing, standing up against the CEO like that. And then I was overcome by a terrible sadness. She was battling for me, fighting doctors and courts, facing off against my father, coordinating the press, all for me. And what was I doing to help? Nothing. But there was something I *could* do. Something I *would* do. Yes, I would have to do it. For my mom, for me. I knew what had to be done.

I stood up. I took off my headphones.

"I'll do it," I announced in a loud voice.

All conversation came to a grinding halt.

"Do what, darling?" Mom asked.

"The muscle biopsy," I said. "I'll do it. I want it done. I want it done now. I want to show you all just how sick I am. Because I am sick! You just don't see it."

My mom closed her eyes and pressed her hands together like a thank-you for answering her prayers. We had talked about getting the biopsy before my kidnapping, but obviously, it had taken on new importance. Honestly, I should have demanded it the first night I was here, but I'd been a little out of sorts and was holding out hope for another solution because they couldn't sedate me during the procedure.

I'm not entirely sure why I had to be awake, but it had something to do with how anesthesia messes up the sample. I do know that I could have refused to have the biopsy, created a big fuss, and since it wasn't going to save my life, I probably would have gotten my way. Maybe not, maybe my parents would have gone to court, or they could have restrained me, held me down, but that's irrelevant now because I was all in.

Cut me. Get it done, and get me the eff out of here.

Mom started toward me looking happier than I could remember as I felt a familiar cramping in my stomach. My head began to tingle, too.

Oh no, I thought. *Not again.*

My insides tightened as if a pair of hands were squeezing my organs. Even my lungs felt compressed. The room began to spin. I took a staggering step toward my mother and sank to the floor, clutching at my abdomen. Dad looked at me oddly, almost detached, as if he was not surprised to see me on my knees and in distress.

Mom's walk became a run, and eventually Dad came over to me as well.

"Baby, is everything all right?" she asked, caressing my hair. Her voice sounded so far away.

"Get her some help!" my mom screamed at the room.

Another violent spasm rocked me. I groaned in pain. Knox Singer, Jill Mendoza, and Dr. Nash looked at me like I should be getting an Oscar for this performance. None of them came to my aid. Through a haze of tears, I saw the Mendoza lady holding Kelly London back. A fresh cramp came on so intensely that I couldn't breathe through the pain. I fell over onto the cold linoleum floor, curling into a fetal position, clutching at my stomach. My heart was beating funny — too fast, and then too slow. I was dizzy. Everyone looked blurry.

"Get her some help!" Mom screamed as she cradled me in her arms. "You think she's faking? You think she's making this all up? Look at her! Look how goddamn sick she is, you monsters! *Do something! Do something!*"

Dr. Nash looked to Jill Mendoza, not my mom. "I suggest our protocol," I heard Nash say.

"Yes, that's fine. Get her back to her room."

I had no idea what their "protocol" was, but then I saw two big orderlies, including Mustache Man, coming toward me with purpose. One of them pulled Mom off me like he was breaking up a street fight. He held her in his massive arms. She was kicking, screaming, spitting wildly. The other orderly picked me up like I weighed nothing.

"We planned for this, Mrs. Gerard," Dr. Nash said to my wailing mother as the orderly carried me away. "If Meghan experienced another crisis with you in the room, we agreed to examine her, but we're not going to treat her. We are not going to feed her delusion or yours, is that understood?"

My mom broke free from the orderly's death grip. I managed to resist being taken away, dragging my feet to delay departure, just long enough to see Mom get in Nash's face.

"My daughter is sick, and you won't help! We're in a hospital, and you won't do anything! How can you?" My vision may have been blurred, but I could see Mom looking at Dad to do something.

"Leave it be, Becky," he said.

And that's when I knew. That's when all doubt left me. My dad was gone. He believed them, not me. It was just Mom and me now. We were a duo. We were in this alone. I guess that's how it's always been.

I cried out for my mom one last time. One more time the pain came, like fire burning inside me so hot and intense, I thought my heart would melt. Weak as I was, I managed to lift my arm. I stretched it out as far as I could. My mom came toward me, but everyone blocked her way, including my dad.

She blew me kisses with tears in her eyes. "We'll do the test," she said.

I blew a kiss back to her, and then everything went black.

CHAPTER 33

Becky

Tomorrow was the big day: Meghan was scheduled to have the muscle biopsy done. Becky wondered if she was as nervous as her daughter. She was in her upstairs office, online as usual, using Meghan's computer to answer a reporter's questions since hers was still with those detectives. She startled when her cell phone rang. Sabrina. Becky thought of sending the call to voice mail, but had a feeling her mother might in fact be dead this time.

"Hi, Sabrina," Becky said flatly. "So?"

"Hi to you, too," said Sabrina. "And no. Mom's still with us."

Becky was not sure how she felt, but relieved was not one of her emotions. "Any change?"

"No, not really," Sabrina said. "Seems like you've been busy. You can't seem to stay off the news these days."

Of course, Sabrina was referring to the airplane incident and to CNN, the first national news outlet to pick up Meghan's story. Others soon would follow. Since the CNN story came out yesterday, producers from the *Today* show, *20/20,* and *Dateline* all wanted exclusives, and all were willing to pay to get them. Veronica's advice to Becky was to say no across the board.

"Think of the media like a man," Veronica had said during their last FaceTime chat. "Play a bit hard to get, and they'll keep the story alive, which is really what we want."

So Becky had fielded dozens of calls and sent dozens more Veronica's way. They cherry-picked the best outlets to keep intense local pressure on White Memorial, while at the same time did what they thought was most effective to help the story slowly spread westward.

"It's not me, it's the damn hospital," Becky said to her sister. "If they'd just let Meghan go, we'd be done with this."

But would you be done? Sabrina was probably asking herself.

Becky did not feel like getting into it with her sister. Certainly, she was not going to bring up the missing earring, or how she had willingly handed over her computer to the detectives without a warrant. She knew how Sabrina would see it. She had learned from Cora just as Becky had.

Meghan's latest medical crisis at her birthday party was also a topic to avoid, knowing Sabrina would press her about the exam results. Becky was not surprised the doctors had been unable to pinpoint a physical cause for her daughter's sudden distress. *No real diagnosis, that sounds a lot like Cora, doesn't it?* Sabrina would say. *You've taught her well. She's learned from the best. Maybe it's just in our damn DNA.*

Becky switched topics and told her sister about the death of Dr. Levine.

"Mom would say he got what he deserved," Sabrina replied coolly.

"Well, he was very young. It's still tragic."

"Tragedy follows us like a shadow, doesn't it, Sis?"

"We've done all right," Becky said. "Despite the circumstances."

But they hadn't done all that well, had they? Sabrina had never married. Never had children. Never dated, for all Becky knew. She lived a sheltered life, working as a CPA, counting other people's money, lonely as Ebenezer Scrooge himself. Becky may have put physical distance between herself and Cora, but poor Sabrina had put in an equal number of emotional miles by distancing herself from everyone. The only obligation Sabrina felt was to the mother who knew nothing about mothering, who had left the two sisters to fend for themselves and deceive the social workers who circled the dilapidated trailer Cora still called home.

Becky did not know how long Sabrina would want to talk. Sometimes it was five minutes; other times it could stretch on for a good while, with lengthy periods of silence tucked in between painful reminiscences. But the doorbell rang, giving Becky good reason to put a quick end to the call.

Becky headed downstairs, her footsteps echoing in the cavernous home. It had been an extra lonely day for some reason, and not because Carl was off somewhere. These days, Becky did not even bother asking where he was going. They were an LLC, not a married couple. They were running a business, and the business was getting Meghan back. After that was done, well, maybe so were they. The marriage had nothing to give her. No support. No loving embrace. No tender kiss. Maybe that's why Meghan's absence felt so huge lately. Maybe that's why Becky had spent a good hour under the covers of Meghan's bed, inhaling her daughter's fading scent, feeling the stiffness of the sheets that had not been slept on in ages.

Soon, she thought. *When the biopsy is done, we'll have all the proof we need, and then it will be over.* Becky was confident they would have done the biopsy even if Meghan had not volunteered to undergo the procedure. White would not want an "oops" moment in denying a potentially life-saving treatment because they did not run a test that could help prove/disprove the condition. But there had been no urgency on the part of the hospital because the mito cocktail only inhibited disease progression slowly over time. Still, Becky wondered if she had pushed Meghan harder to have the test done sooner would that have helped avoid this entire ordeal altogether. Would that one test have been enough to reverse the charge of Munchausen syndrome by proxy? Maybe. Maybe not. But it certainly would not have hurt her cause.

Now, a treatment, as well as the clinical trial, was at risk, and the tragedy that had befallen Zach Fisher's son was never far from Becky's thoughts. At least Becky had Zach on her side, and she trusted him implicitly. She believed he'd find something, some root cause, but if not, she was prepared to keep looking. Because looking for the answer was her identity. More than

Carl's wife, or Sabrina's sister, or even Meghan's mother, Becky was the woman who hunted for a cure.

Opening the front door, Becky was once again surprised when Detectives Capshaw and Spence, dressed in near-matching blue blazers and red ties, greeted her on the front step. In his hand, Spence held an oversize clear plastic evidence bag with her computer inside.

"Sorry to drop in unannounced," Capshaw said. "But we thought we might catch you at home. We wanted to bring this back to you in person."

Becky took the computer but did not invite the detectives inside. She caught a hard-edged stare from Spence, the thinner of the pair, that made her feel uneasy.

"Thank you," Becky said. "I appreciate that."

"Is your husband at home?" Spence asked, leaning his body forward in an effort to peer inside.

"No, he's out," Becky said curtly. "Is there something else I can do for you, Detectives?"

"Mind if we ask you a few more questions?" Capshaw said.

"I'm a little busy at the moment," Becky lied.

Capshaw pursed his lips and appeared to be chewing on a thought. "If you've seen cop shows before, then you'll know this is the part where we tell you we could have that chat downtown," Capshaw said with only the faintest of smiles.

Becky took a step to the side. "Please. Come in," she said, motioning them inside.

The detectives stepped into the foyer and looked around as if expecting to find Carl at home. She got the feeling they did not trust much of what she had to say.

"Shall we go to the living room again?" Becky asked.

"Here's fine," Capshaw said. "We won't be long."

"What can I do for you, Detectives?" she asked, setting the computer down on an antique console table she and Carl had bought on a "get away from it all" drive to Vermont, made maybe a month or two after Sammy died.

Capshaw blew on his hands to warm them from the unseasonably cool spring afternoon. "Well, according to your browser bookmarks, you seem especially interested in . . . poisons."

Her earlier nugget of worry grew into a knot. "Poisons?"

"Yeah, hemlock, popular with the ancient

Greeks," Spence said. "Aconite aka wolfsbane. Though that's not what killed Levine, in case you were wondering, or at least we don't think it is."

"The medical examiner has to order specific tox screens for the more exotic poisons, so maybe if Levine had died of asphyxiation, then wolfsbane would have been on someone's radar," Capshaw tossed out. He was a little too nonchalant for Becky's liking. It was as if they were two cats playing with a cornered mouse.

"There were other poisons in your browsing history," Spence said. "Belladonna, which means 'beautiful woman' in Italian — or in the case of the plant, a good option for a spear tip."

"Plan on doing any hunting in the Amazon?" Capshaw inquired half-jokingly.

From the pocket of his sport jacket, Capshaw retrieved a piece of paper and read down a list.

"Polonium. Mercury. Cyanide. Arsenic."

"Either you have a morbid fascination, or the BBC hired you to write for *Sherlock*. Which is it?" Spence folded his arms and eyed Becky.

"It's my daughter," Becky said assuredly. "Come up to my office. I'll show you file drawers filled with research on all sorts of conditions. It's what I do, Detectives. Since my daughter got sick, all I've done is research. I'm trying to find out what's wrong with her. I assume that's not a crime."

Spence and Capshaw exchanged glances.

"No, of course not," Spence said. "How is Meghan doing? She's been all over the news."

"That's because she's a prisoner at White. She's a kidnap victim. Which, by the way, is the only crime I'm aware of that's been committed here."

"Point taken," Capshaw said, shuffling his feet, heavy shoes threatening to mark up the softwood flooring underneath.

"Tomorrow is a big day for us, actually," Becky said. "Meghan is having a muscle biopsy done, and we have high hopes that it's going to clear up this whole mess by proving she has mitochondrial disease."

"Not often you hope someone has a disease," Spence said.

Becky broke eye contact. "I assume you made no progress in figuring out why Dr. Levine died so suddenly?" she asked.

"No, we haven't," Capshaw said.

"I just hope for your sake it wasn't arsenic or belladonna that did him in," Spence said. "Thanks for your time, Mrs. Gerard. We'll leave you be."

Capshaw nodded his head almost as if he were tipping his hat goodbye.

Becky called for their attention as they turned to go. "Detectives, did you get the DNA on that earring back yet?" she asked.

"Not yet," Spence said with a sigh. "The lab is always backed up. Hopefully soon."

Soon, thought Becky, trying her best not to bite her lip. While she was something of an expert at manipulating doctors, Becky could not parlay that particular skill to the police. These detectives could read body language. They'd know she was nervous about something. She needed that biopsy done now, and she needed those results to come back positive. She needed to get Meghan back home. Because soon, very soon, everything was going to get a lot more complicated.

CHAPTER 34

Meghan

I was trying not to scream. *It's minor surgery,* I told myself. *Minor. No big deal.* So this procedure was no big deal, or NBD in my texting parlance. But it *was* a big deal. The only surgery that's minor, my dad told me before getting his knee scoped for the third time, was surgery done on somebody else.

My breath quivered like I'd just exited the water after a chilly ocean swim.

You can do this, I tried encouraging myself. *There is nothing to be afraid of. Think of what Mom's been going through. Do it for her.*

I gripped the thin sheet covering the surgical bed, balling the fabric up in my fists. I tried to clear my thoughts, but it was no use. All I could think about was Dr. Fisher sticking a needle the size of a spear into my right thigh. *No,* I said to myself. *It's not my right thigh. It's the "vastus lateralis," the largest muscle of the quadriceps group.* Dr.

Fisher had taught me that name. I don't know why it helped me to think of the incision point in anatomical terms. Maybe because I thought of my thigh as belonging to me, but that vastus lateralis didn't even sound like a body part. Whatever. I didn't want to analyze that one too much, because it was working. We had talked about conscious sedation again, but I decided against it. I was worried about having to deal with two unknowns at the same time, and resigned myself to get through this experience without the added help.

There were no bright overhead lights in this small operating room, no specialized equipment. It was a simple procedure, after all. Minor surgery, right? There was a tray with some sterilized instruments on it, but I made sure not to look at the needles — or the scalpel, for that matter.

I had my mom with me, which was probably the only reason I wasn't crying hysterically. I unclenched the bedsheet to hold her hand. I felt so stupid for being this afraid. It's just a dumb needle, after all. You'd think after being pricked and prodded for two years straight, I'd become immune, but the brain gets what the brain wants, and mine wanted fear. I know there's nothing to be afraid of. It's a prick, and then it's over. I should be over it. It's childish and stupid. It's pathetic. It's weak.

I tried to reason it away — *won't hurt, little pinch, I'll have anesthetic, yada yada yada* — but my anxiety was up in my throat. The room spun like I was inside a tumble dryer. Mom held my hand tighter. My dad was somewhere nearby. I didn't want him with us, but he'd insisted on being there. I knew it had to have hurt him when I told him not to stand too close because it made me feel worse.

Good.

"You ready, Meghan?" Dr. Fisher asked.

Tears sprang out of my eyes. My body shook so badly that the line Dr. Fisher had drawn with marker on my vastus lateralis must have come out crooked.

"This is that first pinch we talked about. I'm going to infiltrate the incision point with a local anesthetic containing adrenaline. You'll be fine. You're doing great."

I liked hearing Dr. Fisher's voice. It was comforting. I could wrap myself in his sadness like an extra layer of protection. His hurt took away some of my own. I squeezed my mom's hand harder.

The needle went in. I felt the pinch. Dr. Fisher didn't warn me, or did he? I couldn't remember. I screamed, that much I knew. I screamed because I knew I was that much closer to getting the giant needle.

My father came over to my bedside. "You did this to her," he said to my mother.

"Not now, Carl," Mom said. I could tell without looking that she was clenching her teeth.

"You're doing great," Dr. Fisher said again, which I knew was a lie.

He swabbed my leg with antiseptic solution and covered the area with a surgical cloth containing an oval-shaped cutout centered over the incision point.

"I'm going to test you first. Does that hurt?"

I lifted my head off the bed and could see Dr. Fisher's hand dragging a scalpel across my leg like he was painting a line with a thin brush. I didn't feel anything, but my mind told me it hurt like hell. I swear I could feel my skin being ripped apart.

It's a trick . . . it's all a trick. Your mind wants you to be afraid.

I thought of my mom. I wouldn't let her down.

"No, it doesn't hurt," I managed.

And just like that, the pain went away.

I closed my eyes. I could feel pressure as Dr. Fisher cut, but couldn't feel the clamps he used to keep my skin pulled apart. Dr.

Fisher talked me through the next phase of the procedure.

"The first layer I'm going through is the subcutaneous fat, then we'll get to the Scarpa's fascia and then the subscarpal fat," he said. "Okay. I can see your fascia. Looks great, Meghan. You're doing great. I'm going to make a little more incision."

A hornet the size of a small pony was buzzing around my head, its stinger dancing in front of my face. "Go away, go away," I said.

"It's okay, Meghan," Dr. Fisher said. "Nobody is going anywhere."

I knew I'd sound ridiculous if I confessed to imagining an oversize insect buzzing near my face. I didn't need it getting back to Nash, who'd have yet another reason to think I was crazy. It was bad enough she couldn't find any medical reason why I kept getting sick every time my parents came to visit.

Reason or not, every day my body felt like it was shutting down a little bit more. More switches inside me kept getting turned off. Everything I did — from showering to eating to talking with my therapists — felt like a series of impossible tasks, or what my English teacher would call a "Herculean effort." Just opening my mouth to say "I'm fine" takes a lot out of me.

"I've incised the underlying fatty tissue," Dr. Fisher said, "and I can see the muscle tissue underneath. No wonder you're so good on the soccer field. That's some great-looking muscle you have there. I'm now mobilizing a short section of your muscle and applying a stay suture to both ends so I can manipulate the area."

I focused on Dr. Fisher's voice, used it like a lighthouse beacon to guide me through the fog of fear.

"I've got the sample clasped in the forceps between the suture ties. I'm going to take it out now. You won't feel a thing. Everything is going so well."

My tears didn't think it was going well.

Breathe . . . breathe . . . breathe . . .

"She's terrified," I heard my dad say, like he couldn't believe how scared I was.

"Quiet," my mother growled.

I heard a high-pitched whine followed by a zapping sound, as if my imaginary hornet had flown into a plus-size bug trap.

"That's just electrocauterization," Dr. Fisher said, sensing my distress. "It lets me seal off blood vessels that are bleeding. Nothing to worry about. And I've put some extra freezing in the fascia. You probably didn't even realize I used a needle on you,

391

did you?"

I hadn't.

"All right, Meghan, we're almost done. But now I've got to get the sample with the biopsy needle. There aren't many nerves in the muscle, so it won't hurt, but it won't feel like nothing, either. Okay?"

Jagged energy shook my body.

"Okay," I said, trying to sound brave while failing miserably. The only saving grace was that I couldn't see the needle.

"Here it comes."

A darkly ominous voice spoke up in my head: *It's gonna hurt. It's gonna hurt soooooo much, Meghan. You're going to scream your head off. Get ready. Get ready to bleed!*

I knew the voice wasn't there, but that's what you get with irrational fear. I took in breaths like Mom always reminded me to: through my nose, then out my mouth, slowly and deeply.

I braced myself. There was an uncomfortable tugging sensation, like a hand pulling at something that did not want to let go. Pain followed. It was sharp, dull, and burning all at once, an indescribable sensation, unlike anything I'd ever felt before.

I cried out.

I cried.

I thought, *Thank God, thank God Almighty that I'll never have to experience that again.*

CHAPTER 35

Zach

Dr. Lucy Abruzzo, head pathologist at White Memorial, put a rush on Meghan Gerard's biopsy, both to accommodate Zach and to address Knox Singer's concerns. Singer had made it quite clear he wanted anything pertaining to that particular patient at the top of the "get it done" list. The relentless bombardment from an insatiable media had turned White into a nightly news item, and Knox into a target for relentless criticism. This did not bode well for Zach's future at the hospital, but he had other, more pressing issues to address.

"It's the wrong stain," Dr. Abruzzo said matter-of-factly to Zach. "That's the issue."

When Dr. Abruzzo first broke the news over the phone to Zach, he understood what using the wrong stain meant for Meghan, but he felt compelled to see the ruined biopsy sample for himself.

They were alone together in her path lab. Zach had limited experience with Dr. Abruzzo. She was a bit of a mystery around White — an extremely fastidious, committed, dedicated physician who was much better at working with tissue samples and dead people than with the living.

An avid marathoner, Dr. Abruzzo brought the kind of focus it took to train for races to her lab. Everything about her was precise and intense, which was why this mistake was so uncharacteristic, not to mention inopportune.

The lab was a big, open, airy space hidden in the subbasement of White. It was well stocked with the best equipment, including the microscope Zach was looking through. He adjusted the coarse focus to get a clearer picture of the stained sample on the microscope stage.

"It's a regular H and E stain," Lucy said, sounding frustrated. "If we'd known we were looking for a specific diagnostic condition, we'd have stained it differently. I'm so sorry, Zach."

A routine H&E stain on this muscle-tissue biopsy was fine for showing the histological anatomy, the cells, and the nuclei, but that's not what Zach had requested.

"How did this happen?" Zach produced a

copy of the order sheet for the lab test. He thought he'd been extremely clear: he wanted a Gömöri trichrome stain that looked specifically for ragged red fibers as a marker of mitochondrial disease. The diseased muscle fibers stand out a bright red, making it obvious when the result came back positive.

"I know it's not done routinely," continued Zach, "but I specifically ordered it. And now the specimen's lost, and all we've got is this routine everyday stain that doesn't give me a hint of what may be going on metabolically within the muscle."

"Data entry error, I suppose," Lucy said. "It used to be that we'd do all the stains regardless, to cut down on errors like this, but you know how Singer is with his budget. He sucks out more fat than a plastic surgeon. So now, unless it's for a very specific reason, we do the minimum required, which in this case is a basic H and E stain."

"But I *was* specific," Zach said, trying not to groan. "I filled out the paperwork myself."

"The lab tech must have entered it wrong," Lucy explained. "That's why the old system was better. It cut down on these sorts of errors."

"It happens a lot?" Zach asked.

"From time to time, yes," Dr. Abruzzo said.

"This was one really bad time for it to happen, Lucy."

There was nothing more for them to say. The damage was done. Now Zach had the difficult task of breaking the news to the parents.

"What do you mean, you have to redo the procedure?" Carl Gerard, veins throbbing at his temples, jaw firmly set, looked ready to reach across the cluttered desk to put his fist through Zach's teeth.

His clear intention was a far cry from the confusing exchange Zach had had with Becky in the hallway outside his office moments ago while they were awaiting Carl's arrival. She had taken hold of his hand, leaned in close so that he could smell her perfume, whatever that scent was, and whispered in his ear, "Thank you for all you're doing for us, for Meghan. You're a godsend, Zach Fisher."

For a second there, Zach had thought she was going to try to kiss him. Of course, he would have resisted. Even as it was, he was shocked into near paralysis. Her hair was free from the ponytail she often wore, flowing like a golden waterfall across her slender shoulders. She wore a formfitting white blouse with French cuffs and dark slacks. He saw the way she looked at him. It was not the normal doctor-parent interaction he had had thousands of times.

He thought *It would be so easy to fall for her charms.* She was seductive, incredibly alluring, and he was lonely. But what was she really all about? After all this time, he still wasn't sure. Jill Mendoza had made it a point to keep in touch with Zach ever since he'd sent her that somewhat biting email about DCF's medical incompetence. She told him about the alternative placement option for Meghan that had fallen through because Becky threatened to sue anyone who took in her daughter.

"Does that sound like a mother with her child's best interest at heart?" Mendoza wrote in her email. She also mentioned the pattern of Meghan getting sick whenever Becky came to visit. Zach did not have to cast a wide net to catch a lot of doubt. A crazy thought came to him about the ruined sample. *If Becky Gerard is willing to use her feminine allure to charm doctors, is it possible she used it on some guileless lab tech?*

More than possible, Zach thought.

"What do we do now?" Becky said, her voice strained.

"Like I said, we have to redo the biopsy."

"No," Carl said defiantly.

Becky snapped her head around to appraise him harshly. "What did you just say?" Her voice shook with anger.

"I . . . said . . . no!"

"You can't," she said. "I'm her mother."

"And I'm her father!" Carl stood. "I have rights, too. And I say *enough.* Enough of this! Enough tests. Enough procedures. Enough. Enough. Enough! I'll make sure Jill Mendoza refuses to honor any request, including if it comes from Meghan."

Carl slammed his fist into a towering pile of Zach's research papers.

"You and you," Carl said, pointing an accusatory finger first at Becky and then at Zach, "are in on this together. That's what I think. Are you screwing my wife?"

Zach's expression widened with surprise. "What?"

"Careful with her," Carl said, sneering. "She knows how to get what she wants."

"Carl! How dare you!" Becky snapped.

"Dr. Nash has been right all along," Carl said. He paced the room, not minding the stack of papers he tipped over with his foot. "I should have listened from the start. I should have . . . I should have paid more attention."

"Carl, calm down right now," Becky said. "We're going to redo the biopsy, and we'll prove that Meghan has this condition. It's that simple."

Carl looked strangely calm. "I see it now," he said, his voice turning softer. "So clearly. I mean I've always known, but now, now I have no doubt. It's you, Becky. You're the problem. I don't know how you've gotten inside Meghan's head the way you have. I don't know why. But everywhere you go, bad things happen when it comes to our daughter. I, for one, am done."

"That's crazy talk, and you know it," Becky said.

"I'm not subjecting Meghan to any more torture," Carl said flatly. He put on his sport coat. "I'm not doing it."

Becky rose from her seat and followed Carl to the door. "Where do you think you're going?" she asked.

Carl turned and looked back, his eyes haunted, his face showing the strain of years of difficulty, of all he'd endured, all he'd lost. "You want this procedure done again for *you*, Becky," Carl said. "Not for Meghan, but for you, and for Cora, and Sammy, and whatever shit you've carried around all these years. It's poisoned you. It's made you not right in the head. You need help. But I can't be that person anymore, because I don't believe you. I don't honestly believe Meghan is sick at all."

"You saw her the other day," Becky said, sounding panicked.

"What I saw was a girl *acting* sick, like Dr. Nash explained. They examined her and found no physical cause for her distress. Nothing to explain it! Whatever is wrong with you, you're passing it on to our daughter, and I won't stand by and watch it happen. I won't. I'm done, Becky. I'm done with this whole charade."

"It's not a charade," Becky said. "Meghan has mito, and Dr. Fisher can prove it."

"Dr. Fisher," Carl bellowed, "is as fucked up as you are!" His face contorted with fury. Zach tensed, ready to defend himself if need be, but Carl stood his ground. "His kid died from this disease, and he's trying to make it right. Don't you get it, Becky? You may think you're playing him, but he's playing you. He's playing us all. He's as deluded as you are." Carl's arms fell limply to his sides. His head bowed.

"What are you going to do, Carl?"

"Do? I'm going to talk to my lawyer — and I don't mean *our* lawyer, Becky."

"What are you saying?"

"I'm saying there is no way I'm going to let you cut open my daughter again."

CHAPTER 36

Becky

Becky was amazed, and more than a little sad, to discover that everything she needed, the essentials to survive, could fit into a single suitcase. Her house — this palatial, often overwhelming abode, with its too many rooms filled with oversize furniture, shelves stocked with knickknacks, walls graced with photos and paintings — all of it she now saw as an illusion. It was a cold veneer applied to cover cracks in a marriage that had broken open the day Sammy died and was never properly repaired.

Meghan's illness may have been the tipping point, but Sammy was the beginning of the end for her marriage. Becky was now ready to take her life in a new direction, one without Carl, or this house, or the memories it contained. The hard part would be leaving her daughter's belongings behind because that was Becky's center, her grounding.

In Meghan's room, Becky rifled through the closet, searching for clothing to take to White, hoping to get approval to give them to Meghan, when she noticed a freestanding bookshelf pressed up against a wall, partially hidden by a colorful array of hanging clothes. It was an odd sight, Becky thought, to keep a bookshelf tucked inside a closet, but even stranger to see the unit was turned around so that the shelves were up against the wall.

Becky ducked low to avoid the tangle of clothes overhead and spun the bookshelf around. The unit was lightweight, easy to move, but the dark closet made it difficult to see the contents of those shelves. Using the flashlight built into her phone, Becky illuminated a fifth of vodka and two unopened bottles of wine. There was also a wooden box, held shut with a clasp. Becky eyed the alcohol, dumbfounded. She had no idea Meghan had been drinking. Maybe it was the stress of her sickness, pressure from her peer group, or the strain in her and Carl's marriage. Whatever the reason, Becky blamed herself. She should have been more attentive, more aware. As a teenager, Becky had done the same — stolen from the liquor cabinet and hid her boozing from

Cora, who probably would not have noticed if she had kept a bottle on her dresser.

Becky opened the box and peered inside, expecting to see drug paraphernalia. Relieved to find only papers and trinkets, she sighed aloud and spun the bookshelf back around, leaving the items undisturbed as though they were part of an archeological find. It was a shock to discover her daughter's secret hiding place, but Becky did not dwell on it for long. She had more pressing matters to address, namely, leaving her husband and her home for good. *Everybody has secrets,* Becky thought as she backed out of the closet.

Becky carried her suitcase downstairs. Filled with slacks, blouses, undergarments, toiletries, and probably too many pairs of shoes, it weighed a good deal more than she'd anticipated. She had made a reservation at a nice hotel in Boston, not far from White Memorial, where she could be alone with her thoughts and regrets.

She did not want to have a failed marriage, but she could not abide Carl's hardline approach, his doubts, or his accusations. He had not returned home after storming out of Dr. Fisher's office. His only communication had been a cold text informing her that he'd be working late and would probably crash on the sofa in his office, something he had done often over the last few years. In response, Becky had left him a note on the kitchen counter saying only that she was staying at the Copley Plaza Hotel for a few days, doing some soul searching. If Carl did not get that "soul searching" was a euphemism for irreconcilable differences, that was his problem.

Carl might think he had all the power, the best lawyer, the strongest case, but Becky was not about to keel over in a fetal position, or hide out in her hotel room, sipping Sprite Zero. She had someone to see, an appointment she had made, someone to tip the balance of power in her favor.

Java du Jour was a coffee shop equidistant from White Memorial and Becky's hotel. Becky found a table facing the door and waited for Kelly London to arrive. At five past the hour, Kelly came breezing in. She scanned the crowd for Becky, who saw her first, stood, and waved to get her attention. Kelly looked put together as always, with a blazer, a dressy blouse unbuttoned to an alluring degree, and hip-hugging gray slacks. If they weren't potential adversaries, if Kelly did not hold tremendous sway over Meghan's fate, the two women might have hugged briefly instead of shaking hands, which they did with a degree of formality.

"Thank you for meeting me," Becky said.

"You made it sound important."

They ordered lattes at the counter and returned to the table Becky had saved with her coat. The spring was getting warmer, and soon summer would be here, but this would be a summer like no other. Assuming Meghan was sprung from the hospital like a prisoner making bail, there'd be new issues to address. Where would Meghan live? How would she and Carl split time? How could Becky be sure Carl would look after Meghan the way she would? Her daughter's health would complicate the already complex dynamics of divorce. But those were questions for another time. Step one in Becky's grand plan was to get Meghan out of White, which meant getting the biopsy redone against her father's wishes.

Becky spent fifteen minutes catching Kelly up on recent events, including the biopsy mishap, Carl's war declaration, and her decision to leave him.

"I'm deeply sorry," Kelly said, sounding genuinely empathetic. It was strange for Becky to confide in someone so young, who could relate to her struggles perhaps only in terms of a jilted boyfriend, who knew nothing of the profound, soul-seismic jostling of ending a long marriage.

"I need your help," Becky said.

"With what?"

"We have to get Judge Trainer to mandate a second biopsy."

A glint in Kelly's eyes dimmed, confirming Becky's fear that it would not be a simple request of the court. "It'll require an evidentiary hearing in open court with counsel for all parties and witnesses," Kelly said.

"Then call for it. We need it, and we need it now."

"Judge Trainer will be concerned for Meghan's emotional welfare. From what you described, her needle phobia is quite intense."

"It is," Becky said. "But if I don't prove she has mito, I might lose her."

Becky's breath clogged as tears flooded her eyes. She wiped them with the palms of her hands, and Kelly gave Becky a napkin to dab away the moisture still clinging to the corners.

"I'm sorry," Becky said, her voice quaking. "It's so hard. It's all been so hard. It's been going on and on and there's no end in sight."

Sympathy flooded Kelly's innocent blue eyes.

"It kills you as a parent," Becky said, "when your child is hurting and you can't do anything to make it better. It absolutely crushes you. You feel . . . so horribly guilty, no better word for it. And Carl, how does he live with himself?" Becky's expression soured. "All those mornings when Meghan didn't have the energy to get out of bed, and he just brushed it off as nothing. He'd tell her she was lazy, but she'd insist it wasn't in her head, and he didn't listen. He's still not listening.

"I'm looking for an answer, Kelly. When I'm in the waiting room, headed for the next appointment, and I see all those kids with their worried parents, I think *Some of those kids aren't going to make it. Some of them won't get the help they need. But not us. We're going to figure this thing out.* That's what I tell myself, because I *have* to get the answer. That's my only job."

"And my job is to help the judge make the best decision for Meghan," Kelly said.

"She needs to be with her family . . . or what's left of us. She needs to get out of White."

"It's frustrating. I get it," Kelly said.

"You might look at us, our big house and

nice car, and think we have it all together, but I'll tell you, money and connections don't shield you from heartbreak," Becky said. "I need your help desperately. Don't let Carl get in the way."

Kelly peeled her gaze from Becky, and seemed momentarily lost in thought. "When you opened your front door and saw me for the first time," she said, now looking Becky in the eyes, "I knew what you were thinking: *This girl is too young, too inexperienced, to be of any help.*"

Becky laughed, embarrassed for having been so transparent. "You got me," Becky said, holding up her hands in mock surrender. "So tell me, how old are you?"

"I'm twenty-seven," Kelly said. "I have student loans I'll probably never be able to repay on my salary. I drive a ten-year-old car that's on its last axle. I bought a gym membership instead of cable. My mom was a pill-popping drug addict who died of an overdose five years ago, and I don't know who my father is. I have no family to lean on. I won't hook up with a guy just to make my life easier, and I don't trust men easily, for reasons we don't have to get into. I'm telling you all of this just so you know that on the outside, I may seem a certain way, that you may judge me as a certain type —

the pretty, outgoing, carefree girl — but I'm not that at all. I'm struggling in my own right, with my own demons, so I get the heartache and pain more than you know."

Becky could not help but think of her own hardscrabble upbringing. She had done to Kelly what so many people did to her: she had judged her without getting to know her, or the facts around her circumstances, first.

"I'm sorry," Becky said. "We have a lot in common, you and I."

"I suspect we do," Kelly said.

"Will you help me?" Becky asked.

She reached across the table and touched Kelly's hand. Countless times, Becky had touched a doctor on the arm or hand just to manipulate him, but this time it was different. This time Becky was seeking a deeper connection.

She looked into Kelly's eyes, pleading. "Please help me," Becky said.

"I'll go to Judge Trainer, we'll get that hearing," Kelly said. "And we'll get that biopsy done."

CHAPTER 37

Zach

It was never a good sign to get an email from Knox Singer's personal assistant at any time of the day, but Zach found it especially ominous to receive one first thing in the morning. The email invited him to an emergency meeting in the conference room adjacent to Singer's palatial office. It would seem the situation with Meghan Gerard was reaching a boiling point, fueled in part by the omnipresent media coverage.

It had not been a good night for Zach. He had had the dream again, but this time it was different. Instead of a strong wind blowing Will to dust, there was no wind at all, leaving Zach's fingers outstretched, inches away from touching his boy, inches that were actually miles — infinity, really — because he was stuck in the limbo of grief.

When Zach arrived, Knox Singer and Amanda Nash were already seated, talking together. There was an empty chair that would have been occupied by Dr. Peter Levine if only fate had taken a different turn. Questions took the place of his presence at the table. How did a seemingly healthy man die so suddenly and inexplicably? The medical examiner said the cause of death was cardiac arrest, but what had caused his heart to stop beating? So far, toxicology had turned up nothing.

The best guess was death from ventricular fibrillation — a disturbance in the heart's electrical system whereby the lower chambers quiver and the heart can't pump any blood, causing cardiac arrest. A sizable portion of White's cardiac patients get admitted due to some type of arrhythmia, and while the condition is common, it's far from fatal. Most of the fatal cases occur in association with other heart conditions, like valve problems, blockages, or coronary heart disease.

An autopsy of a young, seemingly healthy person who had died from the condition would most likely reveal other, congenital heart problems, ranging from hypertrophic cardiomyopathy (thickened heart) to unusual branching of the coronary arteries coming off the aorta. Such was not the case with Dr. Levine. His heart was perfectly normal, leaving doctors to speculate that an underlying genetic problem had caused his untimely death.

The police had another theory, though, namely Becky Gerard.

Detectives Spence and Capshaw had grilled Zach in his office for the better part of an hour, asking all sorts of questions about Becky's behavior, her motivations, her state of mind. When they dived into the dark subject of poisons, Zach got a clearer picture of their thought process. But what kind of poison could cause a massive malfunction of the heart's electrical system? Toxicology tests were not conclusive. There was no grand panel that covered all known toxins, but in Levine's case, it was unclear what to even look for. Only the standard tests were ordered, and they had all come back negative.

Zach had promised to contact the detectives should he think of anything that might be useful to their case. In his off-hours, he had begun doing research, trying to match Levine's autopsy to the known effects of various exotic toxins. He was asking himself a most difficult question: Could Becky Gerard's commitment to her daughter have driven her to kill? Would he have killed if he felt that Will's life was in danger? Both answers frightened him.

"Thanks for making the time, Zach," Knox Singer said as Zach settled into his chair.

"Happy to be here," Zach said — as if he had had some choice in the matter, as if he could have refused the CEO's meeting request.

"We're going to get right to it," Singer said. "Becky Gerard is causing us serious difficulty."

"Well, you did take her daughter by court order," said Zach.

"For good reason," Singer said. "That woman is a menace."

"Or she's just a very committed parent."

Amanda Nash leaned forward with a look suggesting Zach was being naïve. "Would a committed parent threaten to sue any other facility that agrees to care for Meghan?" she asked.

"If that parent believed in her convictions enough, then, yes, I suspect they would. *I* would."

Knox Singer interrupted. "I've talked this over with Amanda and Dr. Levine, God rest his soul, during several private conversations. You understand as well as anyone the medicolegal environment we're subject to these days. We all have to be extremely cautious, but after those meetings, and they were contentious, I assure you, I'm more convinced than ever we have an obligation, a legal duty, to protect that child from her mother.

"Now, what we need is for you to reach out to Mrs. Gerard. She trusts you. Listens to you. Tell her to back down, for Meghan's sake. This media attention has got to stop. Let's have a sit-down, see if we can come to an arrangement."

"You don't honestly think she's innocent in all this, do you, Zach?" Nash asked.

"To be honest, I'm not sure what I think."

Zach knew better than to bring up his extracurricular research into toxins. Doing so would only add confusion to an already confused situation. But there was another theory Zach had been considering, one he felt the timing was right to share.

"What about Carl Gerard?" Zach asked.

"What about him?" Singer said.

"It's my understanding that he's been present both times Meghan has, for argument's sake, experienced some yet-to-be-determined medical event during their visit."

"Are you suggesting that Carl Gerard, not Becky, has some sort of sway over his daughter?" Dr. Nash sounded incredulous.

Zach returned a half shrug. "I'm merely suggesting that the father's behavior is something to consider."

"How so?" Nash asked.

"We have a tainted sample from the muscle biopsy. These things happen. We need to repeat the procedure. He won't grant his consent. Now it's headed to court. Becky Gerard has met with Kelly London and convinced her to push for a special hearing to force the second biopsy. Carl's not budging. Does this sound like a committed parent who has a child's best interest at heart?"

Nash did not appear convinced. "Isn't Meghan deathly afraid of needles because of all the tests and treatments she's received? Tests and treatments, I might add, that were wholly unnecessary and driven entirely by the mother."

"It's your opinion they were unnecessary," Zach said.

"And that of the court," Singer added.

"It's not an official opinion yet, Knox," Zach countered. "There's been no formal ruling. I'm merely postulating that while it's rare for a father to have this particular mental health problem, it's not unprecedented. For someone with Munchausen's, the attention Meghan's case is generating would be highly addictive, which could explain why he seems so keen on perpetuating the conflict, fighting against a test that could prove a mito diagnosis rather than being open to exploring all treatment possibilities."

"It's always a mito diagnosis with you, Zach."

"Are we going there, Knox?" The dream had put Zach on edge, and he was not sure he could restrain himself if pushed. "I'm not going to question my findings or talk about my other patients. This isn't the forum."

CEO or not, Knox Singer was not someone to openly challenge. Zach had done more than tread on thin ice; he had stomped on it, begging for it to give way.

"Zach, let me be very clear about something," Knox said, his hooded eyes deepening. "Becky Gerard is our problem, not her husband."

"You're not even going to consider the possibility?" Zach asked.

"I think your judgment here, if I may be so forward, is a bit suspect," Nash said.

"In what way?" Zach asked.

"Becky Gerard has a certain sway with male doctors," Nash said flatly.

Zach's eyes narrowed into slits. "Are you

implying that I'm . . . what, smitten with her?"

"Are you?" Singer's tone was serious.

"No," Zach said.

"As part of their investigation, DCF has spoken with nurses elsewhere who have had interactions with Becky. They've found a pattern with her. She gains favors by being, let's just say, generous with her attention."

Zach sent Amanda a look of pure disgust. "You really think that little of me?"

"You may not even be aware," Nash offered.

Singer rolled back his broad shoulders. "What I think," he said, "is that we've got a real shit storm on our hands, Zach, and it's partly your fault. You've filled Becky's head with this idea that Meghan has mito."

"Excuse me, Knox," Zach said, his voice a few ticks more than he had intended. "But I didn't fill anybody's head with anything. I'm using differential diagnosis to come to a conclusion, and I've yet to rule out mito as a possible cause of Meghan Gerard's symptoms."

"Either way," Knox said dismissively, "we've got ourselves a major distraction, and you're doing nothing to ameliorate the problem. Now, you can either make a concerted effort to get Becky Gerard to back off her crusade and let the courts do their job, or you can pull your résumé together, because you won't be working here for long."

Singer stood and left the room. With that, the meeting was adjourned.

CHAPTER 38

Becky

It was just after ten in the morning when Becky entered the busy lobby of the Edward W. Brooke Courthouse in Downtown Boston. After passing through security, Becky took the elevator to the fourth floor, where she paced the gleaming granite-covered hallway outside the judge's chambers, waiting for Kelly London to arrive. Becky grew more anxious as the minutes passed.

All of the courtrooms were booked for other cases, but Judge Trainer, aware of the urgency, had made special arrangements to hold this evidentiary hearing in her private chambers. Few judges conducted lobby conferences these days — the legal term for a type of sidebar conference typically done in open court with the involved parties only. The private nature of a lobby conference, Kelly had explained to Becky, is what made it possible to conduct the hearing outside a courtroom. That was all well and good, but Kelly was running late, and the door to the judge's chambers would open at any moment. Becky was not prepared to make her case for the biopsy without Kelly's help.

Andrea Leers had recused herself from these proceedings due to a conflict of interest. She represented the unit of Becky and Carl, not Becky's interests alone. Becky had given some consideration to hiring an attorney but saw no reason. She had the ultimate weapon on her side: Kelly London, the person Judge Trainer herself had appointed to head up the court investigation.

The elevator chimed and out stepped Carl, dressed to impress in a tailored gray Armani suit. It was the first time in two days Becky had seen her husband, and the unsparingly harsh look he sent her way erased any lingering doubts about her decision to leave him.

Instead of withering under his stare, her resolve was strengthened by Carl's overt hostility. Even so, it was difficult for Becky to reconcile the man she had once loved with the determined adversary he had become.

How have we come to this? Becky asked herself. She thought they'd weathered the harshest storm possible with Sammy. If they could survive that, she'd believed, nothing could tear them apart.

She'd been wrong.

Carl had exited the elevator alongside a petite woman with auburn hair and a fine-featured, doll-like face. She, too, was dressed sharply, in a one-button seamed jacket and matching navy-colored slacks. Becky quietly took in her oversize black leather briefcase as well as her too-big-to-be-missed diamond ring. With another glance, she saw that Carl no longer wore his ring. As he came toward her, Becky twisted off the rings on her finger, managing to slip them into her purse without his noticing.

"How are you?" he asked. The flat tone of his voice suggested he did not care how she answered.

"I'm fine," Becky said. "You?"

"We don't have to go through with this," Carl said. "You need help, Becky. Professional help."

Becky peered over Carl's shoulder, grateful to see Kelly step out of the elevator. "Not a chance," she said.

"Is it Zach?" Carl asked. "Is that why you left me? For him?"

It took great restraint for Becky not to roll her eyes like a teenager. "It's not about you,

Carl. And it's certainly not about another man. It's about Meghan, and your lack of faith in your daughter and in me."

Kelly came over to Becky and Carl, appearing unsettled.

"Is everything all right?" Becky asked nervously. "I was worried you weren't going to show."

"Becky —" Kelly began, but Carl interrupted her.

"Tell the judge you've changed your mind, Becky," Carl said. "Tell her we talked it over and agreed we don't need a second biopsy."

"No chance," Becky repeated, turning to Kelly for solidarity, but she did not receive a reassuring glance in return.

The door to Judge Trainer's office opened at 10:30 on the button. The judge, wearing a white blouse and slacks but no robe, poked her thin, weathered face into the hallway.

"I'm glad you're all here," Judge Trainer said. "Please come in; we'll get started right away."

Judge Trainer's sizable office was warm and inviting. Towering bookshelves filled with legal tomes took up a good portion of the available wall space. The surface of the judge's massive oak desk was kept as neat as a soldier's bunk. Light poured in from a pair of south-facing windows, which explained the faded colors on the ornate oriental rug in front of Judge Trainer's desk.

Four chairs had been set up in front of the desk, awaiting the meeting's occupants. A trial court officer, imposing in his uniform (black slacks topped with a white shirt and a black tie), stood emotionlessly near the door, looking ready to pounce if these proceedings got out of hand. Nearby stood a small table where a court reporter and court clerk had set up temporary shop, prepared to handle the administrative duties of the hearing and document every statement as part of the official record.

As everyone else took their respective seats, Judge Trainer settled her slender frame into the plush leather chair that bore the imprint of her body. Appropriately enough, Carl and Becky bookended the two women who would be arguing different sides of the biopsy issue. Everyone was sworn in so that anything said would, at least in legal terms, be the truth, the whole truth, and nothing but the truth.

Judge Trainer slipped on her wire-rimmed glasses to glance at the brief laid out on the desk before her. "Good morning, everyone," she said in a crisp, officious tone. "I've read through the brief Ms. London sent over. I also have a written statement from Jill Mendoza, Meghan's guardian ad litem, who apologized for not being able to attend this hearing in person. I understand the mother would like me to authorize a second biopsy for Meghan after the previous test was tainted due to a lab error, and the father is opposed. Is that correct?"

"Yes, Your Honor," Kelly said.

"And is it true that Meghan's psychiatrist, Dr. Peter Levine, died suddenly from still-undetermined causes?"

"That's true," Kelly said. "The autopsy is inconclusive at this time."

Judge Trainer sent Becky a leering look clouded with suspicion. "Very well," she said solemnly. "Let's talk." Judge Trainer leaned forward, elbows resting on her desk. Her open expression, her whole demeanor, boosted Becky's confidence.

But something about Kelly still seemed off.

The opposing attorney spoke up. "Judge Trainer, we've met before. I'm attorney Erin Haze from Coleman and Wells, attorneys-at-law. I've recently been retained by the Department of Children and Families to represent their interests in this matter."

"Yes, Ms. Haze, I do remember you."

"Mr. Gerard was present when Meghan

had the biopsy done, and saw for himself how truly distressing the procedure was for her, both physically and emotionally. It should be noted that the Department of Children and Families, along with several prominent doctors at White Memorial, are against the procedure and believe the mother to be engaged in medical child abuse in the form of Munchausen syndrome by proxy.

"Since Meghan is not currently receiving treatment for mitochondrial disease because of a belief that a psychosomatic disorder — a psychiatric condition — is the cause of her symptoms, there is no reason to subject her to the emotional trauma of further testing. Furthermore, a positive test result from the muscle biopsy will not, at this time, change the current course of treatment because there simply is no gold-standard test for diagnosing mitochondrial disease. Much of that diagnosis comes from clinical observation, and the diagnosing physician, Dr. Zach Fisher, is compromised due to confirmation bias resulting from his tragic connection to the disease, which has led to him overdiagnosing this condition in other patients. All of this was brought up in court already.

"I have letters from Dr. Nash and Ms.

Annabel Hope from DCF substantiating their positions. They'll be happy to come to court and testify under oath if that's what's required."

Ms. Haze unclasped her brief to produce the letters from a file folder and handed copies to the judge, who read them in silence.

"Well, Ms. London?" Trainer asked as she set the letters on her desk. "You're the court investigator on this case. Have you had a chance to delve into this issue?"

"I have, Your Honor," Kelly said.

"And?"

Becky's thoughts flickered. She prayed Kelly's support would be enough to sway Judge Trainer's opinion over that of Nash and DCF.

"On this issue, I agree with the Department of Children and Families," Kelly said. "A second biopsy is unnecessary and potentially damaging to Meghan's mental health."

Becky's jaw dropped. "What?" she cried out, staring dumbfounded at Kelly.

"Very well, then. Since Meghan's in DCF's care, I don't believe that there is anything the court needs to do. Thank you for your time."

"No," Becky said, rising to her feet. "That's not what we discussed. That's not what we agreed to."

Kelly London rose quickly and headed for the door before Becky could stop her.

"Is everything all right, Ms. Gerard?" Judge Trainer asked. "You've gone pale."

Becky did feel faint, rattled and torn apart.

"No, no, it's not all right," Becky blurted out, repeating the only thing she could think: "This isn't what we agreed to."

"What who agreed to?" Judge Trainer asked, confused.

Becky gave a moment's thought to chasing after Kelly, but a voice in her head told her it would be wasted effort. The same voice also told her who was behind Kelly's stunning turnabout.

Becky stormed over to Carl, her eyes ablaze. "How much, you son of a bitch?" she snarled.

Judge Trainer came out from behind her desk. "Mrs. Gerard, you must restrain yourself." As if on cue, the court officer took one threatening step forward. "Now, I understand this is emotional, but please refrain from any outbursts while in my personal chambers."

Becky centered herself. She eyed Carl like a prizefighter intimidating an opponent. "How much did you pay her?" she asked in a far softer tone.

"Becky, I don't know what you're talking about," Carl said.

But he knew. She could see it in his eyes. She'd accused him of other things in the past, which he'd denied with all his heart. She didn't believe him then either.

"How could you?" Becky asked him while Erin Haze looked on with alarm. "How could you do that to your own daughter?"

"Becky . . . I don't —"

"Spare me," Becky said with disgust. She turned quickly and fled the room. It was obvious what she had to do now. It was not her fault. She had to see Meghan. They had much to plan.

They'd left her no choice.

CHAPTER 39

Meghan

I woke up at six thirty. I hadn't slept more than a couple of hours. My mind did somersaults all night. Would it work? Could it work? My stomach cramped with worry. I thought about how many ways my mom's plan could go wrong, and what would happen if we got caught. What would they do with me? They'd bring me back here, that's what. Nothing would change, except my mom would never be allowed to see me again. Nothing would change, except the judge would rule that I couldn't be my mom's daughter anymore. Nothing would change, except that I'd lose my family because there was no way I was ever going to live with my father.

Not after what he'd done.

So what were we risking? Everything.

I dreamt about Dr. Levine in the little bit of sleep I got. He stood outside Charlotte's

431

Web, staring at me, blame in his eyes. I'm ashamed to admit that I'd wished him dead plenty of times. Maybe wishes really did come true. But the last thing I needed was more guilt to lug around. I felt guilty for being sick, for making my mom suffer, for freaking out about needles. I felt guilty for being alive. But I felt only partially guilty for breaking up my parents' marriage. Someone else owned a big chunk of that blame.

Someone named Angi.

The day had started like all the others. Breakfast at eight. Group at nine. Individual therapy at ten. It was getting close to lunchtime. Almost noon. If Mom's plan worked, it would be the last lunch I'd have here.

Thank God for that.

Maybe this place was good for some people, but not for me. I wasn't crazy when they locked me up here, but I sure as shit was going to go nuts if I stayed much longer. That's why I agreed to the plan. Mom and I went over it yesterday when she came to visit, but that wasn't the only thing we talked about.

I couldn't believe it when she told me she was leaving Dad. I cried. I'm not sure why. He doesn't deserve her. But I know what he does deserve. Soon as I'm out of here, I'm going to tell Mom all about him. At least I can get one secret off my chest.

I heard all about the meeting with Kelly London and Judge Trainer, so I guess the battle lines have been drawn. It was Mom, Dr. Fisher, and me on one side, and my dad, Dr. Nash, and DCF on the other. They don't believe that I'm dying. They think I faked it every time I got sick in here — faked the stomach cramps, the blurred vision, the intense pain. But it's not just the sudden attacks that are killing me. Something is picking away at me bit by bit, going at me slowly, methodically. My little vampire, whatever it is, is living off me, and nobody can see it happening. That's why I have to go along with Mom's crazy idea. It's the only real option we have.

I figured we'd have to get new identities like they do in the movies. Then we'd need to find a doctor who believes us, a doctor who can make me better. But a question tumbled about in my head, whispering to me in the dark, roosting in my gray matter. What if I was leaving with the very person who was making me sick? What if the doctors were right and my mom was all screwed in the head? What if she was the sick one, not me? What if she had me so convinced I was sick that my body was acting the part, taking her cues and turning them into something physical? But those doubts were no match for my desire to get the eff out of here.

At first, I told Mom no, I couldn't do it. Maybe it was all those unanswered questions that gave me cold feet but, honestly, I think I was just scared half to death. But Mom was smart. She knew I'd be too nervous. That's why she came at lunchtime yesterday, so we could plan and prepare. She didn't bother bringing me soup from home, and instead told me to get the hot lunch, so it wouldn't look out of the ordinary when I did it again today, and also so I could see for myself how her plan would work. I paid real close attention to every detail she pointed out to me. I thought the timing was a bit tricky, but I saw what she was talking about.

There's no *easy* way out of here. I couldn't just slip out during a shift change. The doors to the unit were locked and always guarded. My room check happened every fifteen minutes. I had thought about pulling a fire alarm, trying to make my break in the chaos, but hospitals don't evacuate. I found out during a fire drill that they use fire doors to keep patients safe without moving them. I honestly couldn't see a way out of here until Mom came up with one.

And in forty-five minutes, we'd find out if it was a good plan or not.

I was on my bed, distractedly flipping through a magazine, when Mom showed up. She looked gorgeous in her jeans and black knit sweater over a white top. She also looked really tired. I had a feeling she hadn't slept much either. Mom gave me a big hug. I sank into her embrace. When we broke apart, I checked the time on her phone. Ten minutes before lunch. Today they were serving mac and cheese (again) and salmon (gross), but I wouldn't be eating. I would be leaving.

I wanted to use Mom's phone to check Instagram, but I couldn't do that. In fact, I'd never do that again, because soon I was going to be gone, not just from here, but from everywhere. Meghan Gerard was going to die. She'd be born again as somebody else. She'd have a new name. A new address. A new life.

"You can do this," Mom whispered in my ear, stroking the back of my head. "I know you can do this, sweetheart. We have no choice, okay?" Mom pulled away so I could look her in the eyes. "We don't have a choice."

I nodded, showing her that stiff upper lip I had perfected as a youth soccer player.

"You know where we're meeting?"

I gave Mom the address that I'd committed to memory.

"You take the first cab you find." She handed me four twenties. I shoved them into the pocket of my sweatpants. "Pay cash. Don't talk to the driver after you give him the address," she said.

I nodded again.

Mom unzipped her tote bag. She took out a fuzzy blanket from home that covered a long navy trench coat I recognized from her closet. She removed both items, tossed them on the bed, and then showed me the empty bag. Using her fingers, Mom pried something loose from the bottom of the tote. She held up the edge of a false bottom for me to see.

"Holy crap," I said. "You're like James Bond."

"Jane Bond," Mom said with a wink and a smile. "Yesterday, I went to a sewing store and bought some Peltex; cut it to the same dimensions as the bag."

I held the false bottom in my hand. It was sturdy, nonpliable. I brushed my hand over the dark fabric Mom had fused to the Peltex with a hot iron. "I had to risk seeing your father to get my sewing machine, but I needed the fabric tight. I didn't want Nash to find it."

"Did she search your bag?"

"She did. Even checked the pockets of the coat. Since there was nothing else in the bag, I knew she'd have no problem letting me bring you a comfy blanket from home. What harm could a small blanket do?"

Mom smiled wickedly. Nash was always there when Mom came to visit. I didn't understand all the dynamics, but I knew I was important enough to Dr. Nash for her to keep a close watch over things.

Hidden underneath the false bottom was a small backpack. Mom unzipped it to remove two wigs, one blond and one brown, as well as a pair of tortoiseshell glasses. The blond wig was long like my hair, which would come into use later. The brown wig was short. In less than an hour, the police would be looking for a girl with long blond hair who didn't wear glasses. They wouldn't find her. Mom stuffed the coat, the brown wig, and the glasses back into the backpack, which I then slid underneath my bedsheets. Yes, I had bedsheets now. Someone, maybe Nash, had decided I wasn't a suicide risk.

I jumped when a nurse, not much older

than me, poked her head into my bedroom. I shifted position quickly so that I was sitting on the backpack, worried the nurse might see a lump and decide to investigate.

"Hello, Meghan, Mrs. Gerard," the nurse said, friendly as can be. "Just making a room check. Is everything okay?"

"We're fine, thank you." Mom's harsh tone sent the nurse scurrying away with a frown. After the nurse left, Mom checked her watch for the umpteenth time. "It's twelve fifteen," she said. "Go get your lunch and bring it back here. Hurry, hurry!"

The urgency in her voice sent me darting out into the hall with the other inmates — or what the doctors here called patients. I got in line behind a suicidal girl, another with an eating disorder, and this schizophrenic chick who I think tried to drown her sister in the bathtub. Those three always whispered to each other whenever I passed them in the halls. They didn't like that I was the floor celebrity. They were jealous the local news was still hot on the Meghan Gerard story — the only kidnap victim who wasn't actually missing. Soon I wouldn't have to think about them. I wouldn't have to think about anybody here.

I listened to Loretta, who must have said a dozen times that the right side of the cart was the mac and cheese, and the left was for the salmon. The mac and cheese side went the fastest, but I got the tray with the fish to keep to the plan. I paid close attention to the cabinet space underneath the cart, which kept growing larger as more trays were taken away. Once all the trays were gone, Loretta would wheel the cart away, only to return an hour later to collect trays from each room. It was an efficient process, but more important, a predictable one.

I brought the food back to my room. The salmon smelled disgusting. Mom put the tray on the side table and removed all the covers. Then, she mashed the salmon with a fork to make it look like I'd eaten some of it. She took a few bites of the mashed potato and peas to enhance the illusion.

"Don't forget the shower," Mom said.

"Right," I said, glad she'd reminded me. My nerves made it hard to keep all the details straight.

Mom checked the time on her phone. Ten minutes past twelve. Five minutes to go.

"How long is the lunch line?" she asked, tension hardening her face.

"Probably almost done by now," I said. My legs shook like Jell-O.

"Go check," Mom said.

I poked my head out of my room. There was only a handful of kids waiting for meals. When the last tray was gone, Loretta would be, too. I told Mom she had to hurry. Mom gave me another hug.

"You can do this," she said, kissing my forehead softly. "You can do it."

Mom stepped out into the hall. I went to the bed to get the backpack out from under my sheets.

There was no turning back now.

CHAPTER 40

Becky

There was fire in Becky's eyes as she stormed down the hall, channeling all the anger and resentment she'd built up since the start of Meghan's forced confinement. Behind her fierce exterior lurked fear, uncertainty, and doubt in spades. There were holes in her plan — gaping ones, at that — and she'd yet to figure out how to close them. But the other option was even more distressing. If Zach Fisher had done anything, it was to convince Becky that Meghan needed to resume her treatment ASAP.

Yes, it would take time to sort everything out — plug the holes, so to speak — but at least it would happen on her timetable, not the court's. No plan was perfect, Becky had decided. Even if the publicity would make it impossible to find another doctor to treat Meghan, she could, at a minimum, mix a mito cocktail herself. The ingredients were listed online, and these days there were plenty of sources for buying most any vitamin or supplement. She was confident, though not entirely certain there'd be a way to get a compounding pharmacist to fill in the gaps in her knowledge.

Again, no plan was perfect. But doing nothing was not an option for her or, more important, for Meghan. Every day she'd be locked in here, getting sicker, for months, until she hit the same point of no return that Zach's son, Will, had reached. Even if the court eventually released Meghan back into her custody, there'd be Carl to contend with. She highly doubted he'd support her taking any kind of supplements, let alone one as complex and pricey as the mito cocktail. The only way to save her daughter, Becky believed with every fiber of her being, was to go at it alone.

Even if alone meant far from perfect.

She came to an abrupt stop in front of Loretta's food cart, her canvas sneakers squeaking slightly on the linoleum floor.

"May I speak with you a moment?" Becky said in a clipped tone. She folded her arms across her chest, deepening her sour expression.

Loretta, who had a sweet and innocent

face, looked utterly confused. She glanced around, perhaps seeking approval before taking direction from the parent of a patient, but the nurses were down the hall.

Nash was nowhere to be seen. She'd already done her duty by searching Becky's tote bag for contraband. Jill Mendoza, who had to personally approve each of Becky's visitation requests, had been present while Nash conducted her bag check.

Mendoza had arranged for Becky and Meghan to have lunch together in A Wrinkle in Time, but Becky had put her foot down.

"Could I please, please just have some time alone with my daughter in her room?" Becky had asked Mendoza. "We need privacy to talk about what's going on between Meghan's father and me. We're getting divorced, and it's very hard on her. She blames herself."

Mendoza and Nash held a sidebar conversation. Would they let her be alone with Meghan in her bedroom? The entire plan hinged on that happening. While awaiting a decision, Becky focused on the sounds of the hospital floor: the whimpers, grunts, and strange noises Meghan often complained about.

At one level, Becky understood this was a place of healing — sick people really did get better here. But her daughter would not be one of them. Meghan's illness was something else entirely, something only Zach Fisher understood. Now they'd have to find a new doctor, one like Zach but in California, where they were headed. Nash and Mendoza had pushed Becky toward the ledge, but Kelly London was the real tipping point. That bitch — and Carl. *Screw them both,* Becky thought.

How had he paid her off? How much had it taken?

Becky had checked their bank accounts but did not see any large cash withdrawals. That did not mean Carl could not have gotten Kelly money some other way. She had her debts, her bills, her obligations, and Carl had corporate accounts he could have pilfered with no way for Becky to check. In retaliation, Becky had pilfered an account on her own — a fifty-thousand-dollar withdrawal from a joint savings account she hoped Carl would not notice until later. The question was how to get to California, where she and Meghan could hide out with Sabrina for a while, though her sister was unaware she'd soon be harboring a fugitive. Becky knew that law enforcement would look for them there, but presently that concern was nothing more than another hole in a plan that, if given shape, would have the recognizable look of Swiss cheese.

As it was, Sabrina had her hands full with Cora's final days, or maybe final month. Her mother was being as unpredictable with death as she had been with life. Becky was confident Sabrina would not turn them away — or worse, turn them in — but she was less certain how Meghan would react to leaving her father. She could lie for a time, say it was only temporary but, eventually, the truth would come out. Carl was going to fight for full custody, and his refusal to believe Becky would be a death sentence for their daughter. In time, Becky knew Meghan would come to see that all this was for her own good.

First, they had to get away, and that meant finding a place to hide out until they could get new IDs. There were ways to buy them or fake them, but it would take time to get that done. One thing was for sure: they could not purchase cross-country bus tickets without showing identification — and that would be a big problem once the police issued an Amber Alert.

The hideout was actually the easy part of the equation to solve. Becky had used one of Carl's corporate credit cards to create an Airbnb account under a false name. Carl's company often rented places for work crews when they had lengthy jobs to do. The comptroller would pay the Airbnb bill with no idea that it was Becky and Meghan who occupied the residence. To keep the account a secret, she had used a new email address created on the public Wi-Fi at a Starbucks. Good luck to the police with tracing that.

Loretta looked nervous about facing off with the well-known, seemingly volatile mother of the floor's most notorious patient.

"Yes, Mrs. Gerard?" she stammered, her accent coming on strong.

"I need to see you in Meghan's room right away. I need to show you what you're serving my daughter."

"But . . . but, Mrs. Gerard, I no make the lunch. I just serve."

Loretta's English was far from flawless. Becky guessed she was Brazilian, but where she came from was irrelevant. What mattered was that she came to Meghan's room. Now.

"You listen to me," Becky snapped. "I want you to see what you people are trying to feed her."

Leaning in close, Becky felt no compassion, no shame, no regret for intimidating — really terrifying — this lovely woman who had absolutely nothing to do with Meghan's saga. But Loretta was a means to an end, and Becky meant to end this nightmare right here, right now.

Spinning on her heels, Becky took a single step before whipping her head back around. "Well, are you coming, or should I call your supervisor?"

Loretta slunk out from behind her cart, shoulders sagging forward as she followed Becky down the hall, leaving her station untended. Meghan's room was empty, but the bathroom door was closed with the shower running.

Becky took hold of Loretta's arm, essentially dragging her to the portable table positioned over the bed, where the salmon lunch was laid out. She stabbed at the salmon with the fork.

"Do you call this cooked?" Becky asked.

Loretta leaned forward, peering at the mashed salmon warily, as if the fish might magically reanimate itself to jump at her. "The fish is fine, Mrs. Gerard," Loretta said calmly. "Lots of people eat it, no problem."

"No, the fish is not all right," Becky said sternly.

"You want a different lunch?" Loretta asked. "I get for you in the kitchen."

"You think I'd trust you to feed her after this?!" Becky's powerful voice carried. "This

447

food isn't fit for a dog!" Outside, she heard footsteps approaching.

"Please, please, Mrs. Gerard, calm down."

At that moment, several nurses burst into the room, eyes wide with worry. Joining them were two well-muscled orderlies who looked ready to calm the situation using any means necessary.

"What's going on?" asked the nurse who'd done the room check moments ago.

"This food is what's wrong!" Becky yelled. "My daughter wanted to try something different for a change, took a bite and got so sick, she threw up all over herself. Now she's in the shower cleaning herself up."

Becky pointed to the bathroom door before waving everyone over to the bed, where they could view the food issue up close. All came willingly, including the orderlies. Loretta stepped to the side to make room. Soon everyone was gathered around the bed, bodies leaning forward, examining the tray as though it were a crime scene.

"You call this edible?" Becky shouted. "This is absolutely disgusting." Becky stabbed at the food with a fork. People leaned in even closer to get a better look.

Becky risked a peek toward the open door. She gave what she hoped was a near-imperceptible nod. A moment later, Meghan slipped out of her hiding place behind the door. She looked briefly at her mother, eyes swimming with fright, before she darted unnoticed into the hallway.

Almost there, baby, Becky thought.

She stabbed at the food, yelling and cursing, accomplishing only one thing with her antics.

A distraction.

CHAPTER 41

Meghan

The hallway was empty. Mom was right —
as usual. The nurses and orderlies were busy
handling my mother, while everyone else on
the floor was busy eating. I moved at a brisk
walking pace down the quiet hallway, alert
for any witnesses. I had the backpack on. I
felt the pockets of my sweatpants for the
cab money Mom had given me. Check. I
made sure I remembered the address where
I was going. Check. We wouldn't have cell
phones to communicate. Mom was shutting
hers off and throwing it away. That was my
suggestion. I saw a *CSI* episode where the
police had tracked down the killer using cell
towers to pinpoint his location, even though
he didn't make any calls.

I stood in front of the food cart. First I
looked left, then to my right. All clear. From
down the hall, I heard Mom still ranting
about the lunch. She sounded like one of

those crazy people I'd seen in videos freaking out at a fast food restaurant because of soggy fries or something.

It was now or never, I thought. Now or never. Pushing all fear aside, I opened the cart's right compartment, where the mac and cheese was kept. It wasn't hot inside, not like an oven, but there was plenty of lingering warmth from all the meals that had heated up the insulated space.

I squeezed my body into the compact opening by pulling my knees to my chest. I had maybe two inches of headspace. My back scraped against the metal slots used for holding food trays. I let the steel bite into my spine without making a sound. I closed the door shut, plunging myself into complete darkness. Eyes open or shut, I couldn't see my hands in front of my face. The lingering smells of salmon and mac and cheese made my stomach flip.

Mom's voice was muffled but intelligible. "You know what, forget it!" she shouted. "Just forget it. Please leave us alone, will you?"

I couldn't hear the water running in my room, but I knew that it was. The nurses would think I was in the shower. Even better, this impromptu gathering would count as a room check. It didn't matter if the nurses saw me or not, because they believed I was in the bathroom — naked, wet, and sick from that gross lunch. It would be good enough for them.

Timing was critical to our plan. We would have fifteen minutes before the next room check. By that time, I'd be out of the shower and lying in bed, my head turned away from the door so they couldn't see my face. At least that's how it would look to the nurse who came to check on me. In truth, there'd be one of my shirts stuffed inside the blond wig Mom had brought to form the shape of my head. The blanket Mom brought and a bed pillow under the sheets would create the illusion of my body.

Mom would stay in the room until the second room check was over. She'd tell the nurse to let me rest. No reason for her to come inside just to look at my sleeping face. Then, Mom would say she was going to get some coffee in the café and she'd be back soon. But she wouldn't come back. By the time the staff figured out it was a wig and pillows in the bed, we'd both be long gone.

Sometime later — maybe a minute, maybe more, it was hard to track time in the dark — I heard footsteps approaching. Terror gummed my thoughts as I tried to concentrate on relaxing.

Please don't open the cabinet . . . please don't open the cabinet . . .

"*Que puta*," I heard Loretta mutter. I felt a sudden jolt, followed by a squeak of wheels. The cart was moving. "*Que puta*," Loretta repeated. I knew what that word meant and figured she was talking about my mother.

I worried my weight would be noticeable, that Loretta would have a hard time pushing me out the door, but that wasn't the case.

"Bye, Loretta," I heard a nurse say.

Bye, all of you, I thought.

Being cramped up was hard work. My stomach muscles were burning. My legs ached mercilessly. My hip joints started to scream, but I worried about shifting position even a little, so I lived with the discomfort. I heard the elevator doors chime open. Loretta gave a little grunt as she wheeled me inside. Before long, I felt myself going down. I thought of myself finally being free from this place, of going home, but not home. I was going someplace new. I let go of all doubts about my mother. It didn't matter if she was making me sick or not. It didn't matter if she was crazy or not. It didn't matter if I was making myself sick. I was getting out of here.

I would be free.

Closing my eyes, I did the rhythmic breathing exercises Mom taught me and began to think of all the good things in my life. I used to keep a gratitude journal, and the entries came back to me vividly.

My bedroom . . . my friends . . . my mother . . . my soccer . . . but him? Was I grateful for him? I gave it some thought as we went down, the elevator stopping to let people on and off. Yes, I decided, I was grateful. But could I forgive my father? That was the bigger question. I believed I could. But first, he'd have to own up to what he'd done. If he could do that, then he could join us wherever we were going.

That's what I wanted, what I imagined as Loretta wheeled the cart out of the elevator and into a room that smelled like hot soapy water. I heard shouting in a foreign language. The cart stopped moving. I listened for Loretta's footsteps, but I couldn't hear anything over the hum of appliances and loud talking. I snapped my eyes open, but it didn't make a difference. The pain in my joints intensified. I had to get out from under here. But what if Loretta was standing nearby? What if she saw me? I listened as best I could. I had the sense I was in a big, open space, maybe the kitchen. I heard running water and lots of commotion.

I imagined my freedom. *Please, God,* I prayed. *Please protect me.* I asked God to tell me when it was safe to go. I waited for a feeling — a kind of knowing, the sort I'd get on the soccer field when I'd send a ball into open space, believing in my heart of hearts that a teammate would be there to receive the pass. Almost always, I was right.

I let maybe five minutes go by. By that point, my joints were on fire, but I could block out the pain. I pushed open the cabinet door just a crack. Light flooded the compartment. I peered outside but saw nobody. I pushed the door open some more. I could see now that I was in an industrial kitchen. The floor was lined with square red tiles. The walls were made of beige brick. The room held some stainless steel tables for food prep along with several industrial-size refrigerators. There were tall rolling carts holding trays of cooking supplies. Other carts carried stainless steel mixing bowls. The lights were bright, and the food smells overpowered each other to create an odor that could hardly be called appetizing.

I crawled out of the cabinet onto my hands and knees. Scurrying like a cock-roach, I took shelter behind one of those tall, rolling cabinets. I poked my head out just a little to see Loretta and a group of kitchen staff all huddled together, not more than fifteen feet away from me. They were talking animatedly in a foreign language — Portuguese, I think — and from the angry look on Loretta's face, I was pretty sure the conversation was focused on my mom.

Loretta was doing a great job of keeping everyone distracted. I noticed a lit EXIT sign on the wall farthest away from the kitchen staff. I slipped out from behind one rolling cart and crawled to another, praying I hadn't made a sound. Nobody looked in my direction. I followed the EXIT sign to a set of swinging doors. Keeping to the ground, I pushed a door open wide enough to slip outside.

At last, I could stand. I looked for the nearest stairwell. I was dressed normally enough, in sweatpants and a zipped-up sweatshirt, so I wouldn't attract attention on the upper levels, but I clearly didn't belong down here. I took the stairs to the main level. There were people now, lots of them, going about their business. For a second, I thought they were all looking at me. I worried they'd recognize me from the news reports, start pointing, calling for the police, but I was invisible to them. I was nothing. They had their own concerns.

Eventually, I found a bathroom, went into

a stall, and moments later emerged a brunette with short hair, tortoiseshell glasses, and a long navy coat. I followed the lit EXIT signs like each was my north star. My legs were still stiff. My heart pounded so hard, I worried I might need to be resuscitated. That would be ironic — having a medical emergency while I was escaping the hospital. I followed the hallway to a revolving door that opened onto a busy street with lots of cabs. The urge to run was overpowering, but I managed to keep my cool and remain inconspicuous.

I entered the revolving door and began to push. I was like a skin diver on her way to the surface, my lungs quaking with their hunger for air. Before I knew it, I was standing outside, and I took that big beautiful first breath. The air was cool on my skin — familiar and yet strangely new. Clouds covered a slate-gray sky, blocking out the sun, but I knew the smells of a spring afternoon, a fragrant vibrancy that made me feel reborn.

I stuck out my arm, and a cab pulled curbside. I got in, closed the door, and gave the driver an address in Cambridge. Just like that, we were off, snaking through clogged traffic on unfamiliar streets. I kept my eyes open for the police — every siren was like a needle stabbing me.

Something happened on that drive to Cambridge, to the Airbnb Mom had rented under a false name, something that brought the doubts I'd been repressing to the surface. For the first time in ages, I was on my own. I wasn't under the watchful eye of my mother, father, or any of the doctors who were supposedly looking after me. And, finally, I didn't feel so terrible. No fatigue. No headache. No switches going off. No intense cramping. No sick feeling. In fact, I'd never felt so alive. My body hummed with renewed energy. I felt a hundred times better than before — make that a million. Maybe I wasn't sick. Maybe it was all in my head. Maybe someone had put the idea in my head.

There were only two people in the whole world who could have done that — my mom . . . or my dad.

CHAPTER 42

Becky

Even with light traffic, the cab ride from the hospital to the rental in Cambridge felt interminable. On her way out of White, Becky had kept on the lookout for clusters of security, or a disturbance of any sort that might be a preamble to her capture, but there was only typical hospital commotion, business as usual.

As the cab drove on, the next steps of Becky's plan continued to weigh on her. How would they get new IDs? Would they need more disguises? When could they leave Boston? What about her mother? How would she know if Cora had died or not?

Without a cell phone and no access to email, there was no easy way to contact her sister to find out. Becky thought she could safely make a call from the landline at the Airbnb, but perhaps the police, who'd soon be working an active Amber Alert, would coordinate resources even across the country. They'd certainly be able to figure out who Becky's sister was and where she lived. Putting a wiretap on Sabrina's phone seemed a logical thing to do. Becky had learned quickly that crime was easy to commit but harder to get away with.

She decided to play it safe and not try to contact anyone. The worst thing that could happen was that Cora passed and Becky would not know. If that was a must, so be it. She could still grant forgiveness to her mother's spirit, same as she could ask forgiveness for herself.

The cabdriver, a stout man with a goatee and tweed cap, talked on his phone, earpiece in one ear, not listening to the radio. Becky wondered if they had discovered the ruse yet. Was the hospital going crazy, looking for Meghan? Had the Amber Alert been issued? Sunlight sparkled across the dappled water of the Charles River as the cab traversed the Longfellow Bridge en route to Cambridge. It was during this crossing that a thought came to Becky, another potential pitfall in her plan that she may have overlooked.

Cameras.

Becky was sure there were plenty of cameras inside the hospital, but she had no idea if there were any outside. If so, it was possible the police could pick up the license plate of the cab she'd hailed not far from the hospital's main entrance. And that meant they could do the same for Meghan. Like most Boston area residents, Becky had sat glued to the television during the hunt for the Boston Marathon bombers. She knew how determined and thorough the police could be. The fact that they could identify the bombers in a crush of spectators by piecing together security camera footage from different storefronts was nothing short of astounding. The safe harbor Becky believed she'd steered her and Meghan into no longer felt quite so protected.

Becky did not let the new worry consume her. Again, no plan was perfect, but this one appeared to be working well despite how quickly she'd put it together. The cab turned onto Memorial Drive, a two-way road that followed the snaking contours of the Charles River. Becky looked out the window at a crew boat tearing through the water, thinking God would keep her and Meghan safe, that there would not be any cameras that would lead the police to their hideout. She'd cash in all those prayers that her online community had sent for so long.

Eventually, the cabbie dropped Becky off

at a three-story apartment building tucked in a quiet street near Inman Square, a populated neighborhood in Cambridge that was within walking distance of the better-known Harvard Square. Becky paid her cabdriver, leaving a generous tip but not one that would stick in his mind.

At the other end of the street were two grocery stores — a Trader Joe's and a Whole Foods — but Becky and Meghan might be living off takeout for a while. She could probably shop for food wearing Meghan's brown wig, but the risk might not be worth taking. During the planning stage, she'd found out that home delivery services like Peapod did not accept cash. Later, Becky would see if she could figure out a work-around so that they could subsist on something other than pizza and pad thai.

Turning the dials on the portable lockbox attached to a bike rack outside the apartment to the code the owner had sent her over email, Becky retrieved one set of keys. She headed up a short flight of stairs to the second-floor unit. The door at the top of the stairs was closed, but not locked. Becky opened that door with her heart in her throat. Would Meghan be there?

"Sweetheart?" Becky called out as she stepped inside.

Meghan jumped up from the living room futon. She threw her arms around her mother, tears in her eyes.

Becky held on tight, as though Meghan might float away should she let go. "I told you you could do it, baby. I told you."

Meghan's body trembled, but soon relaxed. Becky stepped back so she could peer into Meghan's eyes, checking her up and down to make sure she was perfectly fine. Both mother and daughter were overcome with an uncontainable giddiness, like a pair of bank robbers who realized they'd escaped with the cash and their lives. They laughed and they cried while fading sunlight filtered through the windows overlooking the quiet street two floors below.

Becky acclimated herself to her new surroundings. It was one thing to see a place online, but something else to be there in person. True to its description on Airbnb, the apartment was very private, which suited them perfectly. The place was furnished with an eclectic eye — country chic, Becky thought of it, with funky chairs, plenty of houseplants, and interesting art on the walls. Nothing here could be found in a Pottery Barn catalog. For sure it was nothing like Becky's former home.

Former. The thought of never going back

to where she had once lived, abandoning those memories — including a box of Sammy's baby pictures and clothes — struck Becky with force. She understood they'd taken but one step in a long journey.

Becky and Meghan swapped stories from their respective ends of the escape. Meghan recalled crawling out of the kitchen, while Becky described her anxiousness descending the elevator, fearing a nurse would check the room before she made her getaway.

"Should we see if we're on the news?" Becky asked.

Meghan figured out how to turn on the TV. They sat together on the futon, drinking water from tall glasses found in a well-stocked kitchen cabinet. The police had issued an Amber Alert. Becky's and Meghan's names scrolled along the bottom of *The Ellen Show*. At five o'clock, Meghan's daring escape was the lead story on all the news outlets. Police formally named Becky as a suspect in the kidnapping of her daughter and mentioned that she was a person of interest in the mysterious death of Dr. Peter Levine. Reporters harped on the fact that Becky was also accused of Munchausen by proxy.

"God, Mom," Meghan said. "They make you sound like a crazed killer or something."

Becky said nothing.

Both Meghan's and Becky's pictures were broadcast on TV. Meghan groaned when she saw hers.

"Did they have to use that shot?" She rolled her eyes. It was a candid pic Becky recognized from her daughter's Instagram page. Meghan's hair was pulled back into a ponytail. Her smile was a little crooked. "And who sent them that anyway?" she hollered. "My account is private."

Becky was eyeing the picture they had chosen for her — a nice enough headshot taken from her Help for Meghan Facebook page, but somehow what could have been a flattering image looked to her like a mug shot.

"It doesn't matter who sent it," Becky said. "Nobody can find us here. And I have more than enough cash to get us to California. We're fine."

Meghan nodded but did not seem convinced. Poor darling had so much to worry about on top of being sick.

Meghan shut off the TV at the commercial break. "I lived it; I don't need to see it," she said, slouching low on the futon.

Becky turned the TV back on. "We need to keep updated on the police progress. The news will leak any information they have."

"What now, Mom?"

"We have to be patient," Becky said. "We'll get caught only if we're impulsive. If we take our time, think things through before we act, there's no chance we'll be found."

Meghan's eyes brimmed with worry. "But what if they do find us?" she asked. "They'll take me away from you. They won't let you be my mom." Meghan broke into tears as Becky pulled her into an embrace.

"Never," she whispered in her daughter's ear. "They will never take you from me. Do you hear? Never."

Meghan sniffled away her lingering sadness while Becky inventoried the small one-bedroom apartment. She and Meghan could share the queen bed, or Becky could sleep on the futon. There were sheets for both. She'd prepaid two weeks, counting on being here for at least that long, knowing she could extend the stay if necessary.

"We need to rest," Becky said. "Get our strength back. I don't want you off your treatment for too long."

"For mito?" Meghan asked.

"Yes, of course, what else?"

Becky sensed her daughter had something more to say, maybe on the subject of mito, but she was holding back. She decided not to press the matter. Her daughter had been through enough for one day.

They ordered a large cheese pizza and three large salads, with bread and dressing on the side. There was no food in the fridge. No cheese. No milk. Nothing. Becky decided she'd risk a trip to Trader Joe's in disguise. Crappy, nonnutritious food could exacerbate Meghan's mito symptoms. She'd pay cash. Nobody would think anything of it.

As they cleaned up after dinner, the news recycled the same report, with the exception of an interview with Detectives Capshaw and Spence, who reminded the public not to approach Becky, as she could be armed and dangerous.

" 'Armed and dangerous'?" Meghan scoffed. "Do they even know you? Have you ever even fired a gun?"

"Never," Becky said. "What's dangerous was not treating you for your disease."

"Exactly," Meghan said, though she did not sound nearly so adamant.

"Don't worry," Becky said, gazing out the window at the quiet street below. "You've gone a long time without treatment. You'll be okay for a bit longer. Dr. Fisher told us mito is a slow-moving disease."

"It's not always slow," Meghan said.

"What do you mean by that?"

"It came on fast when you visited me at the hospital," Meghan said. "Or did you forget?"

"Of course I didn't forget."

"Why do you think that is, Mom? Why would I feel sicker every time I see you?"

"I don't know," Becky said, trying not to let her hurt show. Did Meghan now doubt her? That could cause all sorts of unforeseen problems, far worse than the possibility of cameras.

"Never mind that," Becky said. "The good news is that we're safe and you feel okay now. We're together — that's all that matters. We'll watch movies and bad TV. We'll make the best of it. But we are going to have to pool our wits to figure out how to make those IDs. I don't think we can hitchhike across the country without raising suspicion."

"What about Dad?" she asked.

Becky's eyes frosted over. "What about him?" she asked.

"How will he find us?"

Becky hoped her silence was answer enough.

"He's my dad," Meghan said, her lower lip quivering.

"He doesn't want to get you better."

"And you do?"

Becky wished that had come out as a statement of fact, not a question. "Yes, of course," she said.

Meghan went quiet. She looked like she wanted to say something else, but had to ponder repercussions first. Becky could almost see the crushing weight of whatever burden she was carrying.

"Talk to me, Meghan. What's going on? Are you scared? I understand if you are. But, trust me, I've gotten us this far. We'll make it the rest of the way. Do you trust me?"

Meghan gave it some thought. Becky hated that her daughter could not answer immediately.

"I do . . . but . . . but —"

"But what?"

"Nothing."

"Talk to me," Becky said, forcing Meghan to look her in the eyes. "I'm your mother. I will always love you. I will always protect you."

Meghan seemed to be working up her nerve. Becky thought a newfound resolve had blossomed on her daughter's face.

"I trust you because you're the only one I have left," Meghan said. "So, please, Mom, please don't be messing with my head.

Okay? I won't be able to take it if you are."

"Those news reports are lies," Becky said. "Don't believe them. I will never lie to you. I will always be honest. That's a promise. Okay?"

Instead of a hug, Becky held out her hand to shake, like they were making a deal.

Meghan hesitated. "In that case, we should both be honest," Meghan said.

"Okay, then let's. You can tell me anything. Whatever's troubling you, it's all right. I promise. You can tell me."

Meghan inhaled deeply. She looked at her mother with terror in her eyes, visibly distraught.

"There's something you should know about Dad," Meghan said. "He hit me. Hard."

CHAPTER 43

Zach

Zach rode the elevator up to the executive floor, feeling certain he was getting fired. What other reason could there be for summoning him to a meeting with Knox Singer? They blamed him for Becky Gerard. They blamed him for all the negative press White had been receiving. They could blame him all they wanted, but Zach had never told Becky to break her daughter out of a locked floor.

Those who wished to point fingers, however, were right about one thing — Zach was the one who had put the idea of mito in Becky's mind, and from there the spark had turned into an all-consuming conflagration, which showed no sign of dying down. Zach may have felt responsible — hell, guilty even — for what had happened, but nothing had changed his mind about the diagnosis. Meghan had mito, same as Will had had mito. Without treatment, her symptoms would worsen, and eventually she'd be gone, just as Will was gone.

That's how Becky had come to see it. That's what had driven her to act. It's also what crushed Zach all over again. If he had been like Becky — more determined, more convinced that something was direly wrong with his son — if he had listened to Stacy, acted sooner and with urgency, the outcome might have been different for them. He might have slowed down the disease, bought himself another day, or month, or maybe even years with his boy.

Zach understood that the truth was more complicated and nuanced than that. Doctors had learned a tremendous amount about mito since Will's death, but there'd been no breakthroughs, no proof that early and aggressive intervention would have given his son a longer life. Even so, Zach took any chance he got to cast blame on himself, like a pious man convinced self-flagellation was the only way to repent.

Zach entered the crowded executive conference room expecting an ambush, not the police. But there they were, Detectives Capshaw and Spence with the Boston PD, the same pair who had interviewed him about Dr. Levine. They stood by a tall bank of windows overlooking a panoramic view of the Boston skyline, dressed in suits with shiny badges hanging from lanyards draped around their necks.

Also present were Knox Singer and Amanda Nash. Singer, dressed sharply as always, not a hair out of place, looked ready to pounce. Nash looked utterly drained. Her coloring was off, and her glasses magnified the dark circles around her eyes. Standing near Nash was Carl, looking angry as ever.

Rounding out the guest list were Annabel Hope and Jill Mendoza, both of whom Zach recognized from his day in court. He wondered if the police had examined his phone records, which he believed required a warrant and would be hard to get so fast. If somehow they did get those records, they'd find a call to his cell phone from Becky, who had his private number. She had called not long before the breakout, but only to vent about Kelly London's betrayal, nothing more.

Carl turned his attention to Zach, balling his hands into fists at his sides. Zach half expected everyone to circle around them, chanting: *Fight! Fight! Fight!* Thankfully, Carl's jab was verbal.

"Hope you're happy with yourself," he said.

"Carl," Zach answered simply. "Blaming me isn't going to help get Meghan back."

"No, it's not," he said. "But I'm going to sue the shit out of you, Fisher. I'm going to ruin you."

Zach responded with a wan smile. Color rushed to Carl's cheeks as he whispered something into Nash's ear. Maybe he was asking her to be an expert witness in his forthcoming malpractice suit. What did Zach care? Lawsuits were the furthest thing from his mind.

"Let's all sit down," Singer said.

There was muted talk as people found their respective chairs. The two cops sat near the whiteboard at the front of the room. Knox took a middle seat at the table, flanked by Nash on one side and Carl on the other. The team from DCF sat a few chairs away from Zach, as if the physical separation would underscore whose side they were on.

After introductions were made, Singer said, "Listen, Zach, we've been meeting all day, trying to sort this out. We need to get this girl back."

"Understood. Not sure how I can help. I'm just a doctor."

"We need to get a bit creative here," Detective Spence said.

"What about the Amber Alert?" asked Zach. "Doesn't that usually work?"

"Usually, yes," said Capshaw, the more sturdily built of the two detectives. "But we've canceled the alert."

"We found a hair in the food cart that services the floor Meghan Gerard escaped from," said Spence. "Everything was well orchestrated — the mother created a distraction while Meghan hid in that cart. What that tells us is that Meghan was an active participant in her escape, not a kidnapping victim, which means we no longer consider her to be in immediate danger."

"She's sick and needs treatment for her disease," Zach said. "I'd say she is in danger."

"Oh, for God's sake!" Carl spat out. "Can we please not go there?"

"Zach, not here," Singer joined in.

"Actually, that's why we've asked to meet with you," Capshaw said. "From our interviews, we understand that this disease, mito, whatever that is, is at the heart of the matter, and that Becky believes her daughter needs treatment for this condition. Is that correct?"

"Yes, that's right."

"It's not a fast-moving disease. Is that

right?" Spence asked.

"In a normal presentation, no, it's not," Zach said. "But Meghan has experienced several unusual flare-ups: an intense, rapid-onset of various symptoms that are atypical for mitochondrial disease."

"You should know that those flare-ups Dr. Fisher speaks of had no correlating physical cause," Nash said. "In fact, we strongly suspect Meghan is afflicted with a somatic symptom disorder."

"What's that?" Spence asked.

"It's when a person feels extreme anxiety about physical symptoms, such as pain or fatigue. The patient isn't faking the symptoms per se. To them, the pain and other problems are real, but often, as is the case with Meghan, no physical cause can be determined. And I, for one, believe that the mother has contributed significantly to Meghan's developing this medical condition."

Zach was not sure what he believed anymore. He harbored doubts about Carl, Becky, even himself, but no way would he admit that to this group.

"The mother believes Meghan has this disease," Capshaw said. "And that's what matters."

"How so?" Zach asked.

"Our goal is to get Meghan safely back to the hospital, where she belongs," Spence said.

"Again, what can I do to help, Detectives?"

Spence and Capshaw glanced at each other. Nash eyed Zach with trepidation. Carl looked away. Knox Singer wore a steely expression. Zach's mouth went dry. Something told him he was not going to like what he was about to hear. And when they described exactly how he could help, Zach did *not* like it, not one bit.

"I can't do that," Zach said after giving the matter careful consideration. "I'm a doctor, not the police. What you're asking of me is way out of my comfort zone."

"We need your help because she trusts you," Spence said matter-of-factly.

Zach eyed Singer with some contempt. "Yeah, well, we've given her plenty of good reasons not to trust anybody here."

"Are you saying you agree with what she did?" Capshaw asked his question with arching eyebrows. "Breaking Meghan out of White and all?"

"I'm saying that she thinks her daughter needs treatment for a disease, and I don't disagree."

"She's not innocent, Zach, don't fool

yourself," Spence said.

"Innocent until proven guilty, isn't that the American way?" said Zach.

The detectives exchanged knowing glances before Spence said, "We recovered a diamond earring in Dr. Levine's apartment that had Becky Gerard's DNA on it."

Zach took a moment to let the news sink in.

"Oh," he said, feeling a little light-headed. "Well, then, I guess that changes everything."

Chapter 44

Meghan

I chickened out. I couldn't do it. I couldn't bring myself to tell her the whole truth and nothing but the truth. I think I knew that once I did, it would be over. My little fantasy of us becoming a family again would be done with for good. I may have been angry and disgusted with my dad, but he was still my father. In my heart of hearts, I didn't want him gone from my life forever. I wanted to believe things could be different. But if I opened my mouth, they couldn't be. So I told her only part of the story.

Dad hit me. Hard.

It was an open-handed smack on my right cheek, forceful enough that it left a mark on my face. Mom was horrified, of course, when I told her. "Why would he do that?" she shouted. "Why would he hit you?" I gave some bullshit answer about calling him an asshole for not believing me.

"You called your father an asshole?" Mom said, almost smiling, sounding proud of me.

I nodded.

"I know your father. He wouldn't hit you, no matter how angry you made him."

That's when I got nervous. She was right, of course. Dad wouldn't hit me for calling him that name. I needed to up the ante, and I needed to think of something fast.

"I said he wanted me dead. That's why he wasn't supporting you or believing me. He wanted me to die from mito or whatever it is I have. I said that he never wanted kids and that he was probably glad when Sammy died."

That lie came out faster than I was thinking. I made it sound like I was irrational at the time, and that I'd given him good reason to hit me, which Mom seemed to think I did.

"I'm sorry," I said, tears blurring my vision, because I couldn't face the truth. It wasn't a total lie. My father had hit me, and it was a hard smack on my face with his open palm. But it wasn't because I said anything about Sammy.

"Sweetheart, that's an awful thing you said to him," Mom told me as she pulled me into her arms. She shushed and soothed and did what only my mother could do — make me feel better. She was my hero, my champion. I couldn't believe the allegations against her. How could someone with that kind of power to heal intentionally be making me sick? I couldn't reconcile it. But then I thought of the secret I was still carrying and wondered if Mom might have secrets of her own.

I pushed the doubt aside — again. Mom and I were in this together, and there was a chance Dad could join us so, for now, I kept what I knew to myself. As far as being here in this Airbnb and not at White, well, that was a million percent better. No, make that a hundred million percent. There were no weird noises. No grunts. No tantrums. No group therapy. No blaring TV. No horrible lunches. This place was cool. Whoever lived here had awesome taste, and I wanted to be like her — arty, hip, and chic. But we were cool, too, kind of like outlaws now. I'd seen *Thelma & Louise.* We were like that: two best friends having the adventure of our lives, on the run from the crimes we'd committed — minus the super-hot Brad Pitt part. It was a thrill. And I'd never felt so close to my mother before.

There were some big drawbacks to this new lifestyle of ours, including having none of my things from home. I also couldn't go for a walk outside, because Mom was freaked out about us getting caught. There was a rooftop where I could go for fresh air. I'd sit for an hour or two on a chair, reading books Mom bought for me at the supermarket.

The sun felt incredible on my face but, sadly, it didn't make me feel any better. That good feeling I had when I first broke out of White had gone away like a short-lived adrenaline rush. The old Meghan had returned. Switches inside me started going off again. The fatigue was back with a vengeance. Going up the stairs to the rooftop was like a mountain-climbing excursion. I slept away most of the three days we'd been on the run.

We were still the hottest news story in town. *Where is Meghan Gerard?* I bet my friends at school were talking about me nonstop — Shelly Stevenson, Lily Beauport, Cecilia Montgomery, all of them. Too bad I couldn't send them anything. In fact, I couldn't send them anything ever again. It was like I was entering Witness Protection or something. I bet someday they'll make a TV show or even a movie about me. That would be unbelievably cool. I could come out of hiding to do the talk show circuit. I'd probably get a book deal. Then I'd be able to get in touch with my friends and tell them everything. We'd hug, and it would be just like old times, only I wouldn't be sick anymore. I'd be cured. And Mom and Dad would be together, and all would be forgiven. And I wouldn't be burdened anymore.

I was in bed sleeping (nothing new there) when Mom called me into the living room. There was breaking news on the TV: Dr. Zach Fisher was giving a news conference outside the front entrance to White Memorial. His dark hair ruffled in the steady breeze. Reporters gathered around, shoving their microphones into his face. My dad stood next to Dr. Fisher, looking sad, as if he were attending my funeral. I saw Dr. Nash there, too, looking prim and proper, her hair tied up in a bun, glasses in place.

Mom turned up the volume. Dr. Fisher had finished whatever he had to say, so the reporters all started shouting questions at him. He ignored them, thanked everyone for coming, and then Knox Singer stepped up to the mic to announce that the news conference was over. This wasn't like in the movies, where we happened to catch the news report right at the critical moment. We'd missed it all. But lucky for us, it was breaking news, so they reran the entire press conference about fifteen minutes later. This time we caught every word of it, including the most crucial part.

"I'm speaking directly to Becky Gerard," Dr. Fisher said, his chocolate-colored eyes boring into the TV cameras. "Becky, please bring Meghan back to White. We found something in Meghan's labs that's very concerning to us. I won't go into detail on TV, but please listen to me. She's sick — very sick. You need to bring her back to White immediately so she can be treated for this new issue we've discovered. Everyone here at White Memorial — including the police — we all just want Meghan to come back so she can be cared for properly. I know you want what's best for Meghan. It's urgent, Becky. You must act now."

Mom shut off the TV. She stared for a long time at the blank screen. I said nothing. My stomach was the size of a walnut.

"What could it be?" I asked.

"A trap," my mom said. "It could be a trap."

"But what if it's not?" I asked. "What if there's something truly wrong with me?"

I told Mom how I'd been feeling — the switches going off inside me, one by one, sensing that every day was bringing me one step closer to the last switch getting flipped.

484

"What do we do?" I asked Mom.

"I don't know, sweetheart," Mom said, stroking my hair. "I really don't know."

CHAPTER 45

Becky

Of all the holes in her plan — and there were plenty — she'd never contemplated the possibility of a new diagnosis for Meghan. She'd broken her daughter out of White because she had feared what would happen without continued treatment — thoughts of Will Fisher had propelled her into action. Now she feared what might occur if they stayed in hiding.

A pressing need demanded Becky risk a brief shopping excursion. She spent extra time on her disguise to make sure no strands of blond hair spilled out from underneath her brown wig. She walked with purpose, head down, careful to avoid all eye contact, until she came to an electronics store not far from Inman Square. According to the salesperson, a chipper young man of Indian descent, the LG TracFone would allow her to make calls without being traced.

He went on to describe plenty of other features, but untraceable calling was her only purchase criterion. As he talked, Becky wondered what use a person would have for a TracFone outside of criminal activities. Then the salesperson asked if she was selling something on Craigslist, which made sense to her. Becky told him yes, she was in fact selling some furniture through Craigslist, and left the store with the phone in a bag and sixty fewer dollars in her wallet.

She walked back to the apartment in a hurry, mindful not to touch the wig, which was irritating her scalp. Bright sun filtered down from a nearly cloudless sky. A warm spring breeze bathed her face, scenting the air with the fresh smells of blossoming trees and flowers. She could not enjoy the fine afternoon weather, however, as every step was marked with fear. Did that person recognize her? What about that woman across the street? Or that man on his phone? Was he calling the police? Each worry served to quicken Becky's strides, and soon she was winded from exertion.

Back in the apartment, she found Meghan asleep in the bedroom. How many hours had she been sleeping? It had to be at least twelve. She was sleeping all the time. In the two days since Dr. Zach Fisher had made his televised plea, Becky had kept a close watch for signs of Meghan's deteriorating health, for any proof that Dr. Fisher was telling the truth.

At Walgreens, she had purchased a thermometer, a wireless blood pressure monitor, and a device to read Meghan's glucose levels. Those instruments told her nothing. Whatever was wrong with her daughter — whatever had been wrong all along — had always lurked below the surface, impervious to detection. She was foolish to think two hundred dollars' worth of medical devices available in aisle four at the local pharmacy would tell her something the doctors could not.

Becky fixed herself a mug of green tea and slumped on the futon to watch the five o'clock news. Instead of the lead story, she and Meghan got a mention ten minutes into the newscast. With no updates, no leads, and no developments from Dr. Fisher's press conference, there was little for the reporters to discuss.

Becky sipped her tea as she debated her next move. Her head told her Dr. Fisher's plea was a trap somehow, but her heart was saying something else. Her heart told her that Meghan was direly ill.

It's cancer . . . it's a rare form of cancer . . . she needs treatment, not a bus ride to California . . . she needs help . . .

Try as she might, Becky could not pull out from her thought spiral.

She slumped on the futon, letting Meghan sleep while her tea went cold. She held the phone in her hand. One call might answer the question she'd been chasing for years, the question that had inspired her to create her Facebook group, that had brought Veronica into her life, that gave her filing cabinets full of medical jargon, and had ultimately ripped her and Carl apart. One answer was all she sought: What was wrong with Meghan?

Becky returned to the futon, where she stared at the phone as though it were going to tell her what to do. If she called Zach, he'd want to see Meghan right away. He'd arrange a meeting place and time. He'd take Meghan back to White, not to the crazy floor, but somewhere she'd be treated properly for her illness — finally. *It's not mito; it's cancer,* Becky thought again.

But what would happen to me? Becky wondered. That had to be a consideration. In addition to jail, Carl would fight her for full custody — a hardship of an entirely different sort. Judge Trainer would take away

489

her parental rights. Jill Mendoza would be back in the picture. Kelly London, too.

Becky saw herself standing at a fork in the road, but there was no good path to take. Go to California and possibly delay treatment for too long, maybe even past the point of no return. And that's even if they could get to California. Becky had yet to figure out how to make fake IDs. Then they'd have to find a new doctor, one who might reconfirm the mito diagnosis, or maybe not. Maybe he'd say, *I wish you'd gotten to me sooner. I'm so sorry, but there's nothing I can do.*

Becky powered on the TracFone. The keypad illuminated in white light.

A chorus of *it's a trap . . . it's cancer . . . it's a trap . . . it's cancer* looped in Becky's mind.

She dialed a number from memory. The phone rang. She heard a click. A voice.

"Hello?"

"Hi, Sabrina," Becky said.

CHAPTER 46

Becky heard a gasp, followed by a deep inhale, and then, "Becky? Is that you?"

"It's me, Sis," Becky said, stretching out her legs on the wood coffee table in front of the futon. "Long time no talk."

"Oh my God. Oh my God. Becky, where are you?"

Her sister had a scolding tone, as if Becky had missed curfew. Once again, Sabrina was playing the parent, a role that had been thrust on her all too often.

"I'm safe," Becky said. "And Meghan is, too. We're okay. That's all I can tell you."

"You need to go to the police."

"I thought about coming to see you," Becky said matter-of-factly. "How's Mom?"

"She's alive, nothing new there."

"Tough old lady," Becky said coldly. "What's she hanging on for?"

"I don't know. Maybe she's waiting to see if her youngest daughter is going to spend twenty years in prison for kidnapping."

"Does Cora even know what's going on?" Becky asked.

"Thankfully, no. She's too out of it to understand much of anything these days. But everybody else in the country knows what you've done."

"They didn't give me a choice," Becky said. "They took my daughter. Took her illegally and then took my rights as her parent."

"As I understand it, they took her quite legally," Sabrina said, always the logical one. No wonder she had gravitated toward a career in numbers, Becky thought to herself.

"That's not the point," Becky said. "The point is, they had no business taking her in the first place. I'm her mother. I know what's best."

"They obviously felt otherwise."

"She needed a second biopsy," Becky protested. "But Carl paid off the Court Investigator so the judge would rule against me."

"You have proof of that?" Sabrina asked. "The bribe, I mean."

"No. If I did, I'd have gone to the police instead of going on the run with my daughter."

"Point taken," Sabrina said. "So what now?"

"Did you see the news conference?"

"The one where the doctor told you to bring Meghan back to the hospital because they found something?"

"Yeah, that one," Becky said. "What do you think?"

"Is that why you called? To get my advice?"

"Yes, and to ask about Mom."

"You know what I think."

"That I should meet with Dr. Fisher?"

"That you should turn yourself in," Sabrina said succinctly. "Throw yourself on the mercy of the court. Tell them you were temporarily insane. Apologize profusely. Do something, but you can't stay in hiding."

"Because Meghan might be sick," Becky said, feeling encouraged by the thought that maybe Dr. Fisher hadn't betrayed her.

"No!" Sabrina shouted. "Because what you've done is wrong. It's wrong for everyone. You have to undo this, Becky. You have to undo it now!"

"Why? And let them stuff Meghan back in that psych ward? Have them not treat my daughter for her disease?"

"What disease?" Sabrina said, exasperated. "There's been no diagnosis. None."

"She has mitochondrial disease," Becky answered defiantly, "or are you forgetting that? And she might have something else now, something Dr. Fisher found. What I need help with, what I'm asking your advice about, is if I should try to get to California and find a new doctor for Meghan, or if you think I should get her seen by Dr. Fisher right away. But I'm worried it might be a trap."

"Your mind, Becky, is the trap," Sabrina said cuttingly.

"What's that supposed to mean?" There was rising anger in Becky's voice.

"It means that you grew up with a mother who faked her disability for years, who didn't give you the attention you craved, that you deserved, except when you were helping support her scam."

"Same applies to you. What's your point?"

"My point is that I think something in your life changed, that you became deeply insecure, needy, something, and the only way you knew how to fill that void was to bring sickness back into your life. You're reliving your childhood through Meghan. She's not sick, Becky. You are."

"No, no," Becky said, her voice sharpened. "You haven't been here, Sabrina. You haven't come to see us, not once since

Meghan became ill. I've been dealing with this for years."

"I haven't come, because I can't stand to see it," Sabrina said in a shaky voice that sounded on the verge of tears. "It hurts me, it physically hurts, to see what you've become. You've turned into Mom. Don't you get it?"

"No, I have not," said Becky assuredly.

"Our mother was very damaging, and you learned at her feet. For God's sake, Becky, you learned to make up illnesses to please her. Yes, she did it to feed us, but she did it to feed herself as well. She craved the attention that she got. She needed it. She used it to try to fill some bottomless hole in her. And you're doing what she did because it's what you know how to do and it feels right and rewarding. But it's not right. Not even a little."

"I am not making up anything. Meghan is sick. She's been diagnosed. She's here with me, in this apartment, sleeping twelve, fourteen hours at a time. Does that sound healthy to you?"

"No, it sounds like a girl who's craving her mother's attention and getting it by acting sick. She sounds like someone I used to know, a little girl who'd do anything for her mother's love."

"That's not fair."

"You're not well. Ever since Sammy —"

"Don't," Becky warned. "Don't bring him into this."

"Ever since Sammy died," Sabrina continued, undeterred, "you've been struggling, understandably so. Look, I think Meghan did get sick. Okay? I think it happened, some strange, weird illness that came and went. But it triggered something inside you — a fear, out-of-control anxiety, I don't know what. I think Carl didn't give you what you needed, and I suspect you became desperately lonely. You never had Mom's love, and you didn't have Carl's support, so what did you have? You had Meghan. She is your world, your whole world."

"What's your point?" Becky said, annoyed.

"My point is that when you suffer a terrible loss, as you have, and you have attachment issues like we both do, it can mess with your head. When Meghan first got sick, it all came flooding back. Then she got better, but you couldn't see it. You were still afraid something bad would happen to her, like it did to Sammy. You needed reassurances that nothing would happen to Meghan that you weren't getting. But you knew just where to get those reassurances because Cora taught you how to play the doctors. And when you started doing that, you filled some empty place inside you, that place Sammy used to occupy, that space Meghan's mystery illness took over."

"Fuck you and fuck your fucking two-bit psychoanalysis," Becky snarled. "How dare you! You're not here. You don't know."

"Goddamn you!" Sabrina yelled. "I lived it, too! I lived it, too, and I didn't run away from her. I stayed. I stayed because somebody had to look after our screwed-up mother."

"So that's what this is really about, isn't it?" Becky said curtly. "You're angry that I left."

"No, I'm angry that you *never* left," Sabrina said with venom.

Becky's throat tightened. "You . . . you have no business judging me like this. You never had children. You never got married. You never took those risks. You don't know."

"No, you're right, I didn't do any of that." Sabrina sounded wistful. "And I regret it, or a part of me does. A part of me is jealous of what you have, that you've been willing to open yourself up to hurt, to loss, to pain, when I haven't been that brave. So it's not about judging you, Becky. It's about loving you. It's about seeing you hurt, and suffer,

497

and me wanting to help end that pain."

It was this rare display of her stoic sister's vulnerability and honesty that forced Becky to lower her defenses.

"What should I do?" Becky asked.

"You need to take Meghan to White and turn yourself in," Sabrina said.

"But then I'll lose her," Becky replied. "Carl will fight for custody. And he'll win. Who is going to advocate for her health then? She's sick, Sabrina. You have to believe me. There's something wrong with Meghan."

Sabrina fell silent. For a moment, Becky feared she'd ended the call.

"Then you just answered your own question, didn't you? Get her to the doctor," Sabrina said.

CHAPTER 47

Zach

The four-door Toyota Camry was parked in the breakdown lane near the high-traffic entrance to Storrow Drive, directly across from the iconic Boston Sand & Gravel Company. The lights of Boston twinkled all around Zach like tiny stars cast down from the clear night sky. He checked the time. Ten o'clock. Becky should be arriving any moment now. But how would she get here? Was she coming by car? On foot? She did not say. Her only instructions to him had been where and when to meet.

Zach had been at work, pulling a late night as usual, when he'd received Becky's call. At first, he thought it was another prank. He'd received about a dozen of them since his widely publicized press conference. A few of those calls were obviously men, but a couple could have been Becky. Zach had prepared for that possibility. He asked any

499

caller he could not easily rule out a simple question: What was Meghan most afraid of? He heard all variety of answers — spiders, heights, clowns — but only one person said needles.

Becky.

She had given him thirty minutes from the time of her call to get to the meeting spot. He understood why. She was being careful, not wanting to allow the police enough time to set up an ambush. Clever. She had also picked the highway breakdown lane because it would allow her a quick escape if she were to spot any police. But there'd be nothing to spook her. No helicopters hovering overhead. No police cars or undercover types in the vicinity. There was no reason for Becky not to show.

Guilt ate away at Zach, but what choice did he have? The earring had changed everything. It was not enough evidence for the DA to bring Becky up on murder charges, but it had been enough for Zach to agree to cooperate with the police. Even so, he had refused to do anything until he got assurances from Singer and Nash that Meghan would be treated for mito. That was the Faustian bargain he'd struck. He suspected he was doing it for Will as much as for Meghan. He'd get proof she had the disease, and then provide treatment to slow the progression until, hopefully, a cure could be found. As for Becky — well, Zach had no idea what was in store for her. If she had something to do with Levine's death, then she deserved punishment. But in terms of breaking Meghan out of White, while Zach did not exactly condone what she had done, he damn well respected it.

"What's wrong with her?" Becky had asked him on their brief phone call.

"I won't tell you," Zach said. "I can't tell you. Not until we have her back. That's the agreement I made with the police."

"Just tell me if it's a rare kind of cancer. Tell me you can save her."

"When we meet," he had said.

Damn you, Zach Fisher, he had thought, then and now.

Becky had called the office while Zach was reviewing medical charts for Baby Sperling. The child was doing remarkably well despite his breathing abnormality, but only because he was being cared for properly. Meghan deserved the same, he told himself.

Five minutes had passed since Zach last checked the time. He was starting to think Becky might be a no-show. Maybe she'd rethought her plan. Per her instructions, Becky was going to hand Meghan over to

501

him, then go back into hiding. Zach was to send her updates on Meghan's treatment and prognosis. That was all Becky wanted, that and a promise Meghan would not be locked up again. Once she knew her daughter's medical regimen would continue, she'd willingly turn herself in to the police.

Yes, he respected her immeasurably.

At twenty past the hour, Zach was sure the rendezvous was off. Becky had had a change of heart. Just then, bright lights flashed in his rearview mirror. He heard a car door open and shut. A moment later, the rear door to Zach's Camry flew open. Becky and Meghan slipped inside.

"Drive," Becky said.

Zach had kept the car running while he waited, per Becky's earlier instructions to him. He pulled the car into traffic, following signs for Storrow Drive — another of her demands. At this hour, the traffic moved briskly.

Glancing in the rearview, Zach assessed Meghan's health as best he could. She looked pretty much as she had when she'd first come to his office — maybe a bit frailer, a bit thinner, but in general good health, at least on the outside. She did not look malnourished. No visible signs of trauma. Becky seemed healthy as well, but was visibly strained. And the worst was yet to come. Once this was over, Zach knew Becky Gerard would never speak to him again.

"How are you, Meghan?" Zach said. "It's good to see you, even under these crazy circumstances."

Meghan laughed sweetly. "Hi, Dr. Fisher," she said. "I'm fine. And yeah, it's been a bit crazy."

"You two pulled off quite the disappearing act. Everyone is looking for you."

"Mom's pretty smart," Meghan said proudly. "She thought of everything."

As if on cue, Becky produced something from her purse. For a second, Zach worried it might be a gun. But it was something else, an object he did not recognize.

"Plug this into your cigarette lighter," Becky said, handing Zach the device.

"What is it?" Zach asked, glancing at the road as well as the rearview.

"My friend at an electronics store sold it to me," Becky said. "It jams GPS trackers."

"You think I have a tracker on the car?"

"Please, Zach. Plug it in."

"Very well," Zach said, pushing the device into the car's electric lighter port. It was an adapter with a small antenna attached.

Becky peered out the window. "Where are the police?" she asked.

"No police. That was our deal."

Becky leaned over the backseat, placing her hand on Zach's shoulder. "Please don't double-cross us, Zach," she said, whispering in his ear, her voice soft and pleading. Becky's hand brushed up against the nape of his neck, raising bumps on his skin. "Just tell me if it's cancer." Her hand caressed him, touching him in a way he had not been touched in years.

Zach told himself: *She's playing you, she's been playing you,* and his guilt lessened, but only somewhat.

"Tell, me, Zach. I need to know. Is it cancer?"

"It's not cancer," he said.

"But it's something," Becky said.

"It's something," was all Zach could say.

Becky leaned over and kissed Zach gently on his cheek. The spot her lips touched felt on fire. "Thank you, Zach. Thank you for not lying to me. You're the only one I trust. The only one I've ever trusted."

Zach did not know what to say.

"Get off here," Becky told him.

Zach exited at Storrow Drive and headed for Beacon Street in Downtown Boston.

"I'll call you later tonight," Becky said. "I need to know when Meghan gets settled. I have a bunch of phones, so you won't recognize the number."

"Okay," Zach said.

Becky kept her hand on Zach's neck. Her touch burned him with shame. "Pull over here," Becky said, pointing to an empty parking space in front of a fire hydrant.

Zach did as he was told.

"Meghan, give a look," Becky said. "Do you see anything? Any police?"

"No, all clear here," Meghan said, peering out her window.

Becky did the same, then turned to Meghan. "You'll be okay, sweetheart," she said, hugging her daughter tight. "Zach will take care of you. Don't worry about me. It'll all be fine."

Meghan sniffled but stayed composed. "Please stay safe, Mom."

"I will," Becky said assuredly. "You have nothing to worry about. I love you very much."

"Mom." Zach picked up on Meghan's hesitation. "There's something I should tell you."

"What is it, sweetheart?" she asked.

"Be . . . be careful."

Zach heard the stutter and was sure Meghan had intended to say something else.

"You have my word. I have to go now. Trust Dr. Fisher. Okay? Do as he says, and

505

everything will be all right." Becky kissed the top of Meghan's head. "I love you so much," she said.

"I love you, too, Mom," Meghan said with a quake in her voice and tears in her eyes.

Becky leaned over and kissed Zach on the cheek for a second time. "Thank you," she said. "Thank you for everything you've done for us."

"Becky —" Zach stopped himself because there was no changing what was about to happen.

Becky exited the car, closing the door behind her. She bent down to blow a kiss to Meghan, who blew her a kiss back. She straightened, took two, maybe three steps, and then the Camry's trunk popped open. Zach did not have to engage the latch. A safety mechanism allowed it to be released from the inside.

As the lid went up, Detective Richard Spence uncoiled his thin frame from where he'd been hiding all along. The movement drew Becky's attention. She glanced back at the car, focusing on Zach, noting his confusion.

Spence climbed out with his gun drawn. He shouted, "Becky Gerard, freeze, right where you are! Hands up! Hands up now!" The plan had been for Spence to use his cell phone's GPS to keep the police in-formed of their whereabouts, but Becky's jammer had required the detective to take action on his own.

Becky glanced back over her shoulder at Spence, who came at her with his gun in one hand and his police radio in the other. Zach could almost see Becky's thoughts in motion. Should she run? Could she run? Becky stood frozen, body tense, like a sprinter waiting for the starting gun, but there'd be no running today.

Blue lights exploded from the cross street ahead of them, and more strobes arrived on the scene.

"Get down on the ground, Becky," Spence said, aiming the gun at her chest. "Let's not do anything stupid."

Meghan fled from the car, screaming. "Mom! Mom!"

Zach got out as well. The blue lights were closing in fast.

Becky shot Zach a look so hard, it could have broken a bone. "You lied," she said, her voice raw with emotion. "You son of a bitch, you lied."

"I'm so sorry," Zach said. "I had to do it, for Meghan."

Meghan ran to her mother as the blue lights closed in.

Spence kept his gun on them both. "Meghan, move away from your mom," he commanded. "We will take care of her and you. Okay? She's going to be safe. But you have to move away."

Meghan would not let go. She held on to Becky as if she were a life raft in the ocean. "Leave us alone!" she screamed. "Just leave us alone."

Zach came forward. "Becky, don't make this worse," he said.

She looked at Zach again as half a dozen police cars screeched to a stop. A moment later, the street was full of police. The night burst with color.

Becky's shoulders slumped. She pushed Meghan gently away. "It's okay, baby," she said. "It's all okay."

She raised her hands above her head in a show of surrender. The police closed in.

Meghan sank to her knees on the hard pavement, her body racked with anguish. Her hands covered her sobs.

Zach stayed close to the Camry as Spence approached.

"I have to handcuff you now," he said to Becky, his voice gentle, compassionate even.

Zach watched Becky get crammed into a police car as two other officers escorted Meghan to an ambulance that had arrived on the scene.

Zach crossed the street to the car where Becky sat with her head slumped forward. A police officer near the cruiser kept him back several feet. "I'm going to look after her," Zach said in a loud voice so Becky could hear. "I promise we'll resume the mito treatment. That was the deal I made with Spence and Singer."

Becky lifted her head, turning to face Zach, and strangely enough, she looked relieved.

Chapter 48

Becky

In the same Boston courthouse where Judge Trainer had sided with Kelly London, a court officer, as big and intimidating as a professional wrestler, directed Becky to a microphone at the front of the courtroom. Standing before a silver-haired judge who sat high up on his bench, Becky felt her legs shake slightly.

She was dressed in street clothes, not the prisoner's attire she had had to wear for the past two days. Friday, she'd found out, was an inopportune time to get arrested, as courts did not conduct arraignments over the weekends. The delay did give her time to make arrangements, including hiring Andrea Leers as her defense attorney, who had dropped the custody case so that she could represent Becky for the criminal charges. It also gave Becky a chance to relive the trauma of her arrest, to hear Meghan's cries echo in her ears, and let her anger over Zach's betrayal simmer like a toxic stew.

As for jail, it was as horrible, dehumanizing, and terrifying an experience as she had imagined it would be. It was Meghan's psych ward all over again, only with gray cement walls, worse smells, more screaming, and a host of hardened female prisoners who took to calling her Blondie. She was propositioned, offered drugs, and threatened with violence. Becky kept to herself as much as she could, leaving her cell only to eat. The rest of the time she spent waiting until Monday.

Attorney Leers stood beside Becky as she faced the judge, and even helped her raise the microphone up to her level. Carl was one of the few people watching the proceedings. They had exchanged glances, but no words. A prim court clerk, seated at a desk below the judge's bench, read the charges aloud: parental kidnapping, obstruction of justice, and conspiracy.

"How do you plead?" the clerk asked Becky.

"Not guilty," Becky said after a whispered conference with Ms. Leers. That's all there was to it.

"Is there a question of bail?" the judge asked.

"There is, Your Honor."

Andrea Leers had warned Becky that the assistant district attorney would be tough on her.

"Proceed," the judge said.

"Your Honor, these are very serious charges against Mrs. Gerard. In addition to the kidnapping and obstruction charges, Mrs. Gerard has lost custody of her daughter, Meghan Gerard, to DCF for reasons of medical child abuse."

"Objection, Your Honor," Leers said into the microphone. "That case is under investigation and there's been no formal ruling, so the conduct the ADA is referring to is alleged only."

"Counselor, I'm listening to everything, and I'm going to make my evaluation based on the entirety of the matter."

The ADA continued her argument. "Thank you, Your Honor. In addition to the DCF investigation, Becky Gerard is a person of interest in the death inquiry of Dr. Peter Levine, who was Meghan Gerard's staff psychiatrist at White Memorial Hospital. Detectives Richard Spence and Howard Capshaw of the Boston Police Bureau of Investigative Services Homicide Unit, who were both instrumental in apprehending Mrs. Gerard, are heading up that investiga-

512

tion. For these reasons, the state is recommending that bail be set at two hundred thousand dollars."

Becky had to stifle a gasp. Where was she going to get that kind of money?

Ms. Leers quickly countered. "Your Honor, my client has no criminal record and, as I've said, there's been no court verdict in regards to the accusations of medical child abuse or any death investigation. Becky Gerard is an upstanding citizen who until recently has had no troubles with the law. And, if anything, she's shown a very strong desire to be close to her daughter, which makes her not at risk for flight. Bail should be set solely on flight risk, risk of committing other offenses, or interfering with a witness — none of which apply to my client."

"Bail will be set at fifty thousand dollars," the judge said. "With the conditions that Mrs. Gerard not set foot inside White Memorial or have any contact with her daughter."

Becky's heart sank at the thought. The judge set the trial date for January — after the custody hearing, which Becky suspected she was now destined to lose because of the charges against her. All Becky wanted was to see Meghan, but first she had to figure out how to make bail. At least that worry proved short-lived: Carl paid the full amount.

When Carl and Becky emerged from the courthouse together, there was a crush of reporters waiting to pounce. Carl was acting as her protector again, reminding Becky of that day at White when they'd first learned Meghan had been taken into DCF custody.

He shielded her from the onslaught of news people, microphones, and cameras, which were snapping so many pictures, it sounded like cicadas in mating season. Carl held the car door open, and Becky slid by her husband to climb into the passenger seat of his Mercedes parked curbside. He went around the front of the vehicle to get into the driver's seat, pushed a button to start the engine, checked the rearview mirror, and pulled away with a squeal of tires while Becky stared numbly out the window. As they sped away, Carl put on his sunglasses to battle the midday glare. News vans tried to follow them, but Carl was an aggressive driver when pushed, and easily put distance between them and the reporters hunting for a scoop.

"Thanks again for bailing me out," Becky said as Carl maneuvered his way through the heavy stop-and-go traffic.

"I'm just glad you're safe," he said. "Where am I taking you?"

"Let's try the Copley Plaza Hotel."

"You know, at five hundred dollars a day, that's not a long-term solution," Carl said.

"I understand that, but I needed — I need — the space. Just take me there, will you?"

"As you wish," Carl said.

"How's Meghan?" Becky asked.

"She's . . . she's struggling."

"*Where* is Meghan?" she asked.

"Becky, let's not —"

"Where is she, Carl?"

"She back in the Behavioral Health Unit at White," he said.

"Fuck!" Becky screamed, smacking her hand on the car dashboard with a thunderous pop. "Fuck! Fuck him! He promised! He promised!"

"It wasn't Zach's fault," Carl said.

"The hell it wasn't." Becky's eyes were ablaze.

"He tried to help . . . well, help you, anyway," Carl said.

"What's that supposed to mean?"

"It means Zach resigned from White."

"He did what?"

"You heard me. Zach quit. Yesterday, in fact."

"How do you know?"

"Amanda . . . Dr. Nash told me."

"Why?"

"Because he thought Meghan was going to resume her mitochondrial treatments, but Jill Mendoza and DCF had other plans — and, thanks to you, they're still Meghan's guardians, not us."

Becky looked away. They were silent for a time as Carl navigated the Mercedes to the freeway entrance.

"We've sure fallen a ways, haven't we, Becky?" he said.

"I'm not harming her," Becky said. "I'm not. And I never have been."

"Well, it doesn't matter now, does it? You're in real trouble. God, what were you thinking?" Carl sounded disgusted, horrified, and baffled all at once.

"I was thinking that you must really have given Kelly London the goods to get her to turn against me like that," Becky said with bite. "What was it, Carl? How much did it cost to buy her off? Or were you giving her something *else*?"

"Kelly came to that decision on her own," Carl said. "I had nothing to do with it."

The look Becky sent him implied that his lies needed more work than their marriage.

"The kidnapping charge is going to send

you to prison — my lawyer says you'll get seven years and do two, maybe one and a half. Maybe the judge will make it a suspended sentence."

"I don't give a shit about me right now," Becky said. "I care that my daughter is right back where she started — on that floor, *not* getting the care she needs."

"Funny, I thought she was *our* daughter," Carl said.

"You know what I mean," Becky said.

"What about our marriage? Do you give a shit about that?"

"I didn't think you'd care."

"I bailed you out, didn't I?"

"What do you want me to do, Carl? I thanked you. I *thank* you. I honestly can't do more than that."

Carl drummed his fingers on the steering wheel. "What about our 'get through this together' pep talk we had at Andrea Leers's office? Or was that just a bunch of BS?"

"It wasn't BS until you turned against me. She needed that biopsy."

"And you need professional help," Carl said cuttingly. "I don't claim to understand what's gotten into your head, but I do know that you're not well."

"Is this your pitch to win me back, sweetheart? Because I'll tell you, it could use some polish."

Carl smiled. "Can I win you back?" he asked.

"It's all about Meghan right now. I can't think about us — I don't even want to."

"Fair enough," Carl said. "But I still think it's all about you."

"Which is why I'm moving out," Becky said.

"We don't need to be like this," Carl said.

"Like what?" Becky answered coolly.

"Like enemies. I still love you. You're still my wife."

Becky glared at him hard.

"What?" Carl asked.

"Why did you do it?" she asked.

"Do what?"

"Hit Meghan. Why would you ever do that?"

"What are you talking about?" There was a notable unease in his voice.

"Why did you hit her?" Becky asked again.

"That's . . . that's utterly ridiculous," Carl said. "She told you that? What did she say?" Again, Becky heard the tremble that betrayed his anxiousness.

"She said it's been hard for her that you don't believe she's sick, and that she confronted you about it. The only explanation she could come up with, which she told you, is that you wanted her dead. And that's when she said you must have been glad Sammy died because you probably never wanted children. And then you hit her, open palm, against her cheek. Is it true?"

Becky fixed Carl with a fierce stare, expecting him to rage, even to strike her but, to her surprise, his whole body seemed to relax.

"She said all that?" His faint smile would have been imperceptible without decades of marriage for her to reference.

"Yes. So, did you do it? Did you hit her?"

"No," Carl said with certainty, and this time Becky detected no deception from him. "I never did. I never hit her and I never would. And yes, she did say all those things to me, but you have to believe me, what she told you never happened. Don't you see?"

"See what?"

Carl shifted the Mercedes over to the fast lane. He glanced in the rearview, perhaps to make sure no news vans were following.

"Meghan is so desperate for your approval, for your love, that she's going along with your delusions. You're re-creating the same dynamic you had with your mom. Your daughter is trying to reconnect with you, to reach you, which is why she's inventing things that never happened."

"I'm *not* delusional," said Becky, striking a defiant tone.

"She's making up stories about me that are as crazy as the ones you're inventing about her. You're *making* her sick, Becky — physically, emotionally, mentally sick. And you need to stop. You need to stop right now before it's too late."

Becky brushed strands of hair away from her face. On her wrist, she could still see a trace of red where the handcuffs had been, but the real scars were invisible. Those were scars from Cora, or Sammy, the ones that Carl and Sabrina seemed to think had driven her mad.

The phone rang. The number on the in-car display came up as WHITE MEMORIAL. Carl answered the call using Bluetooth.

"Carl Gerard here, you're on speaker."

"It's Dr. Nash."

Becky's stomach clenched at the name of the woman she blamed most for her ordeal.

"I'm with Becky now," Carl said. "Is everything all right?"

"Hello, Becky," Nash said with a touch of disdain.

"Is Meghan all right?" Becky asked, feeling the sting of the court order barring her from White.

"Well, that's why I'm calling," Nash said.

Becky gripped the car armrest with grave anticipation.

"Meghan saw the news, meaning she saw you, Becky."

"I thought the children weren't allowed to watch the news," Carl said.

"One of the patients smuggled in a cell phone, which we've confiscated."

"And?"

"And she's been struggling since coming back here. She hasn't been eating. She's been extremely depressed. Agitated. And seeing you on the news has only made things worse for her."

Becky felt a surge of anger toward Zach.

"What can we do?" Carl asked.

"I think Meghan needs to see her mother, see that she's okay, that she hasn't been hurt. I've spoken with Meghan's new psychiatrist, who agrees the visit would be beneficial."

"Well, that's impossible," Becky said, "because the judge has ordered me to stay away."

"DCF is working on that as we speak," Nash said. "They should be able to get that condition lifted."

"Could you please contact the kitchen staff right away," Becky said to Nash.

"Why?" she asked.

"Well, I'm not showing up without some chicken soup."

CHAPTER 49

Meghan

At first, I couldn't believe my eyes when Mom walked through the door to Charlotte's Web. I did a double take before leaping out of my chair. I ran to her, not my dad, at a full sprint, forgetting all her warnings about exertion. Maybe everything was going to be all right.

Our emotional reunion had an audience. We weren't going to be left alone, for obvious reasons. All the key players were there: that annoying lady from DCF, Annabel Hope, who I suspected cut her bangs with a ruler; Jill Mendoza, my oh-so-charming guardian ad litem; Knox Singer; Dr. Nash; and my new shrink, who shall remain nameless because I don't care about her one bit. There were also a bunch of orderlies and nurses in the room in case things got out of hand.

My fellow inmates (okay, okay, patients)

weren't around to witness the joyous reunion, but they were nearly as excited as I
was for Mom's visit. Mom was a legend on
this floor, and I guess by proxy (get it?), so
was I. I got a huge round of applause when
they brought me back. Even Bathtub Girl
started acting nice to me. In fact, she was
the one who showed me the news footage
on her contraband cell phone of Mom leaving the courthouse.

But Mustache Man didn't seem all too
pleased with my return. The same went for
Loretta, who everyone said hadn't ventured
so much as five feet from her food cart since
my escape.

Mustache Man was guarding the door
with four other orderlies — four instead of
the usual two, just in case there was trouble.
But there wouldn't be any trouble. My spirit
was broken. *I* was broken. Maybe I was
broken *and* crazy. Maybe my mom had
planted the idea that I was sick in my head
and it had sprouted into a forest where I
couldn't find my way out. Crazy or not, I
could almost hear the switches inside me,
each click a symptom of something wrong.

Fatigue. Muscle aches. Weakness. Headaches. But there was never anything major
— no seizures, no cancer, no blood disorder,
nothing medically amiss, at least nothing

524

Nash could find.

But I forgot all about those symptoms, real or imagined, when Mom showed up. I swear there was like an angel's halo surrounding her. She came running over to me, thermos in hand. We hugged and cried. I could tell she was trying to hold it together for me, but it was no use. We were both a hot mess, the full waterworks. I swear even Jill Mendoza got a little teary.

My new shrink, aka she-who-shall-remain-nameless, looked on with curiosity, studying us like a field scientist watching animals in the wild. To be fair, she was a nice lady — harmless, I supposed. She and Dr. Nash were the ones who had pushed hard for my mom to come here, so I guess I couldn't think too badly of her.

Still, I wished Dr. Levine were around — or, let's be honest, still alive. I could have sworn he was starting to have doubts about his original diagnosis before he died, the medical child abuse and all that. Maybe those switches I kept talking about weren't in my head. But my new shrink wasn't going to entertain that notion, not for a second. In her mind, my mom had filled me with so much nonsense that I couldn't tell delusion from reality.

"We know what's wrong with me," I told

my shrink during our last session. "It's mito. Dr. Fisher told me I was going to resume my mito treatment."

"Dr. Fisher is not treating you anymore, Meghan. We are." To my ears, she sounded a lot like a grief counselor. That flicked a new switch in me — the one that stopped caring about anything she had to say.

But now that my mom was here, I was feeling better already.

"Baby, it's so, so good to see you," Mom said, stroking the same cheek where my dad had struck me.

"I didn't think I was coming back here," I said to Mom as we broke apart.

"Let's talk," she said.

We sat on colorful plastic chairs at a round table in the back of the room, just my mom, my dad, and me, with everyone else keeping watch from afar. Being here with Mom made me miss the apartment we had shared — more than I missed my bedroom, even. I loved the cool furniture and the hip neighborhood I could explore only from the rooftop. But mostly what I had loved was being with my mom. I wanted us to be on the run again. Thelma and Louise back in action. I wished we'd gone to California and forgotten all about Dr. Zach Fisher. Forgotten about my dad, even.

"We're going to get you out of here," said my mom.

Dad sent Mom a nasty look. "Becky, don't."

"Don't what, Dad?" I said with attitude.

"We don't need to go there, is all," Dad said.

"Go where, Dad?" I asked.

"The doctors told us to keep it positive."

For the first time in a long time, I could feel switches going on, not off, firing up my anger at my father. He had backed Dr. Nash, and she had backed my new shrink. Just because he had paid Mom's bail didn't mean he was on our side.

"You look so thin," Mom said, unscrewing the thermos lid to the chicken soup. "Eat something. I made it special for you."

"Please eat, Meghan," Dad said.

I took one whiff and wanted to gag. In truth, all I wanted to do was sleep. I wanted to crawl under the covers of my bed and sleep the day away, sleep away the night, my life. I wanted to close my eyes and never wake up, not unless I was magically transported somewhere else. Mom screwed the lid back on the thermos. Dad looked disappointed, but Mom knew there'd be no convincing me.

"Dr. Fisher quit," Mom told me. "Did you

know that?"

"Why?" I was genuinely surprised by the news.

"Because he thought you were going to be treated, not returned," Mom said.

"Becky, please, this isn't the conversation —"

"No?" I said, fixing my father with the kind of "leave me alone" look he must have grown accustomed to seeing by now. "Are there *other* things we should talk about?"

I looked at him piercingly, assuming Dad would get the hint. He looked over at Mom, and I knew they had talked about "the Slap," which is how I'd come to think of it. Hit or slap, it was still assault — it was child abuse. It was also kind of ironic that my mom was accused of abusing me when, in fact, it was my father who'd hit me.

I guess that's what finally changed things for me, why I decided to tell her the truth. *Will the real abuser please stand up!* I didn't even care about being a family anymore. I'd come to a new realization after the police took my mom away: she's the one I needed in my life, and it wasn't fair that she didn't know the truth about my dad. I'd been trying to protect everyone, but I could see now how strong my mother was, how much she could handle. Finally, I could get rid of the weight I'd been carrying because I had nothing more to fear. But, of course, I couldn't say anything in front of my father.

"Dad, could Mom and I be alone for a minute?" I asked.

Dad looked unsure. "I don't think —"

"Carl, please," Mom said with force. "Just give us a minute to ourselves if that's what she needs. Don't worry. I'm not going to run off with her again."

Dad sized up the situation. He knew he was outnumbered, outvoted. He groaned as he stood. It was his way of voicing disapproval. He jabbed a finger at the thermos of soup. "Get her to eat something, will you?" he said. "She looks emaciated." He stormed away.

Mom took hold of my hand and squeezed it. A tear leaked out of my eye. The truth was hard. It hurt. It had a crushing weight. But keeping secrets, well, that had weight, too.

"What is it, sweetheart? Talk to me. Did someone hurt you?"

I lowered my head because I couldn't look her in the eyes. "Remember what I told you about Dad?"

"Oh yes," Mom said, her blue eyes darkening. "He had a very different story to tell."

I'd always adored and idolized my father.

I had always wanted his approval, wanted him to notice me on the soccer field, anywhere. He was my hero. I knew he was charming, attractive, that women noticed him. Hell, some of my friends noticed him. But I wished I could bring back the image of him I'd had when I was a little girl. I wanted that feeling of pure awe, of sweet love. I wanted to adore him again. But I knew too much to ever go back.

"Well," I said, my gaze shifting to the floor. "He's lying, and I wasn't entirely honest either."

"He didn't hit you?" Mom sounded perplexed.

"No, he did hit me, but not for the reason I told you. It wasn't about Sammy."

"Why, then?"

"Well . . ." My leg was bouncing with nervous energy. "A few months ago, I figured out the password on his cell phone. The code was my birthday. I was just goofing around to see if that was it, and it was."

"And?"

"And I saw some messages on his phone."

"Oh no . . ." Mom's coloring went paler than mine.

"And they were . . . they were really explicit."

"Who? Who was it with?"

"Her name is Angi," Meghan said. "Spelled *A-N-G-I*, so it's kind of trendy, nontraditional, maybe she's young, I don't know. I told Dad I was going to tell you, and that's when he hit me, hard across the face. He told me I had no business looking at his phone. He said I didn't even understand what I was seeing, and that if I told you, it would be the end of our family. He was so angry; I thought he was going to hit me again."

"That son of a bitch," Mom said through clenched teeth.

"I read the messages . . . a bunch of them at least, and I think . . . I think they're in love."

There. That was it. I had nothing more to say.

And — surprise, surprise — I did feel better.

Chapter 50

Becky

Numb.

She had never felt so utterly, completely, devastatingly numb in all her life. Carl was with her, on his phone, talking loudly to his lawyer about Becky's case. She glanced at him occasionally. It was hard to look for too long. In her mind she kept seeing the open-handed slap against her daughter's face, heard the hard smack of skin against skin, felt that sting of betrayal as much for Meghan as for herself.

By the time they got settled in the car, the numbness had receded, leaving Becky shaking with anger. Questions came at her like bullets from a gun. *Who is she? How long has the affair been going on? Are there others? Is Kelly London one of them?* Carl pushed the ignition button on his car. Becky was so upset she had rushed out and forgotten to give the thermos of soup back to

532

Nash. Now it rested at her feet, and she thought about unscrewing the lid and pouring it on Carl's lap, but that would be a waste.

"Meghan didn't look well," Carl said, backing out of the parking space.

"I've been saying that for a long time now. Funny how you picked this moment to finally start hearing me."

"You don't look so well, either," Carl said, sending her a sideways glance.

Becky felt her heart rev faster than the car's engine. "I'm fine," she lied.

Carl navigated the Mercedes into the flow of traffic. "How about we both go home," he said, sounding a hopeful note.

Becky gave it some thought. That's where she needed to go, where she'd be staying now.

"That would be fine," she told him.

Carl's smile broadened. He placed his hand on Becky's leg just above the knee, giving it a gentle squeeze before traveling up a bit higher. "I've missed you," he said. "I've missed us. This whole ordeal's made me realize how much I love you and Meghan, our family. I know we've had our problems, but you and Meghan mean everything to me."

Becky kept tight-lipped. She wanted her

first words to be the right ones, to deliver the kind of shock and hurt Meghan must have felt when he'd hit her.

How dare he! How dare he!

On the drive home, Carl talked about her legal case, and what his lawyer thought, and why Andrea Leers was not a good fit, and other things Becky only half heard.

There were reporters camped out in front of the house when they arrived — three news vans and a couple of cars. Carl told them all to go away; there would be no statement. Cameras filmed Carl parking in the garage, which must not have been enough for the evening news because some of the news crews stuck around.

Inside, Carl headed to the living room to close the curtains on other reporters who might wish to pay them a visit. Becky went to the kitchen, where she set the thermos of soup on the granite counter.

"The media are vultures, don't let them bother you," Carl said upon rejoining his wife. He reached for Becky's hand, perhaps thinking of leading her to the bedroom to supplant a bit of pain with pleasure. Becky pulled away from his touch as though it were a hot coal. He looked wounded. *Good.* She eyed him with disdain.

"What's wrong?" he asked. "I know you're

worried about Meghan, but she's where she needs to be. You and I, we somehow need to get to that better place, too. And we *can.* If you get the help you need, I believe we can."

Becky stood in the center of the kitchen, hands on her hips, a fierce look in her eyes. "She told me," Becky said flatly.

Carl groaned, looking away. "I told you that never happened. I'd *never* hit her."

"No, she told me about the phone, the texts, she told me everything — the truth."

"Becky, none of that —"

"Stop." Becky held up her hand like a traffic cop. "Just stop. Don't debase yourself any more than you already have. Who is she, Carl? Angi, right?"

When he made eye contact, Becky thought her husband looked more upset at getting caught than at what he'd done. "It's not what you think."

"Please," Becky said in an exasperated tone. Bitterness rose up in her throat.

"Okay, it *is* what you think, but it's over. It happened, and it's done."

She had long suspected Carl might have been unfaithful, but her need for stability in one part of her life had made it easy to accept his feeble assurances.

"Meghan thinks you're in love. Are you?"

535

"No," Carl said, but in a way that could not have sounded convincing even to him.

"Who is she?"

"She's nobody," Carl said. He took a single step toward Becky while she took one in reverse.

"Who?"

Carl dragged a hand through his thick hair, nervous and agitated. "A girl in the office," he said.

"A girl or a woman?" Becky asked. Meghan was probably right — Angi spelled with an *i* was a trendy, young person's name.

"You know what I mean."

"I know that you demean everyone, including yourself."

"I swear to you, Becky, it meant nothing. It *was* nothing."

"And that's supposed to make it better? That you'd throw away twenty years of marriage for something that meant nothing?"

"It was just . . . just something that happened, that got out of control. You have to believe me. But it's over now. I know I shouldn't have done it."

"Done what? Fuck your coworker or hit your daughter?"

Carl looked away. "Neither," he said.

"Get out," Becky told him.

She was surprised to see that Carl looked

surprised. What did he think she'd do? Go back to her hotel so as not to inconvenience him?

"You heard me," Becky said. "You disgust me. Get out. Get out now!"

"Becky, please, you're being —"

Becky picked up her cell phone. "Get out, or I'll call the police." Becky showed him the phone like she was leveling a gun to his chest. "I'll call the police and tell them that you hit me."

Carl scoffed. "Oh, because making up stories comes easy to you, doesn't it?"

"And hitting comes easy to you," she said. "Go. We can make arrangements to get your things later. You'll be hearing from my attorney — Andrea Leers, by the way, whom I am *not* going to fire."

Carl pursed his lips and hesitated before striding up to Becky. He came to within striking distance, but Becky held her ground, fighting the urge to flinch. It felt good to show no fear, no emotion whatsoever.

"I may have screwed a coworker, but you screwed up our daughter something good," he said with menace. "Just because you believe something doesn't make it true. And I will do everything in my power to make sure you can never harm her again."

"Get out!" Becky screamed. Her shrill voice sounded foreign to her ears. "Get out now!"

Carl stormed away.

Becky stayed in the kitchen. Her fingers gripped the counter as she listened for the sounds of his departure, so familiar that they normally went unnoticed: the garage door rising, the crunch of wheels backing up, engine noise growing fainter as the fast patter of her heart quickened.

Becky got a spoon and carried the thermos from the granite counter over to the kitchen table. She unscrewed the lid, unleashing the aromatic scent of chicken soup. She figured something warm might help ease the cold dread whirling through her.

She took a few tentative sips of soup, then, closing her eyes, tried to forget what Carl had said. But she could not forget. She was going to jail. She was going to lose custody of Meghan. All of that seemed inevitable now. But a seemingly unanswerable question troubled her the most: Was her daughter sick, or was she the one making Meghan sick? Had she created an illness out of nothing? Had Meghan bought into her delusion?

Those were the questions dancing around in Becky's head when the doorbell rang. She hurried to the front door, expecting to confront a determined reporter. She opened the door with anger in her eyes, which did not go away when she saw who it was standing on her front step.

Dr. Zach Fisher.

CHAPTER 51

Zach

Zach had heard from a nurse at White that Becky Gerard had come to the hospital, gone up to the BHU to visit Meghan, and then left with Carl. He knew Carl had paid her bail — that was all over the news — so it was a gamble going to her Concord home. It was also a gamble to try to make amends. But Zach felt as though he had nothing more to lose.

The moment Becky opened the door, he sensed he'd made a grave mistake. Anger leaped off her like an electrical discharge. She tried to slam the door shut, but Zach got his foot in the way.

"Please, Becky . . . please just hear me out."

"Why should I?" Her blue eyes smoldered.

"Because I'm the only one who's ever believed you."

Becky kept her hand on the door. Zach

was unsure if she'd open it or try to kick his foot away. To his surprise and relief, she opened the door. Zach went inside, trying not to let his jaw hit the floor. His studio apartment was the equivalent of an upstairs closet in this house.

"Nice place," Zach said, noting how his voice carried in the cavernous home.

"It's got a lot more room than I need," Becky answered coolly.

Zach followed Becky into the kitchen, where again he tried not to gawk. Pediatrics was a calling, but never a path to riches.

"Do you want something to drink?" she asked.

"Water would be fine."

Becky retrieved two glasses from a cherry-wood kitchen cabinet, filled them with water from the sink faucet. She handed one glass to Zach, and the other she set on the kitchen table, next to an open thermos.

"I hope you don't mind if I eat," she said. "It's been a long day, and I haven't had a bite."

"No, of course not," Zach said. He waited while she took a spoonful of soup, and another after that, until it seemed half the thermos had to be gone.

"I'm sorry, Becky," Zach eventually said.

"Nothing we can do about it now," she replied.

"They promised me they weren't going to bring Meghan back to that floor. We were going to resume the mito cocktail. I was going to push for the Elamvia clinical trial."

"The only thing I know is that you lied to me," Becky said, shaking the spoon at him.

"I misled you," Zach countered, "because I knew there was no other way you were going to bring her back. I had to do it. For her safety, and for yours."

"Well, I should be very safe in prison, thank you very much," Becky said curtly.

"Not if I prove she has mito," Zach said.

Becky shot him a hopeful look. "Can you redo the biopsy?" Quick as her excitement had come, Zach watched it fade. "You quit," she said, remembering. "Carl told me that you had resigned."

"Knox and Nash reneged on our deal. I had no choice."

"So you can't help," Becky said.

"I'm not going to abandon this case, or you," said Zach. He thought about reaching across the table to take hold of her hand in a comforting way, but worried about how the gesture might be construed. "I may not be at White anymore, but I'm still a doctor; I can still advocate for you in court. I want

542

to keep trying to help."

Becky inhaled deeply. "Thank you," she managed in a whispered voice. "You're the only one who seems to believe me. Guess you should know that Carl and I are getting divorced."

Zach was sorry to hear the news, but he was not the least bit surprised. "Was it your *Escape from Alcatraz* routine that dealt the final blow?"

Even though Becky managed a strained smile, Zach immediately regretted his attempt to bring levity to the situation.

"No. I had pretty much made up my mind to leave him when he blocked the second biopsy. Then I wanted to kill him when he bribed or screwed Kelly London. But I'd say the last straw was when Meghan told me that he hit her after she found out he was having an affair."

Zach grimaced in sympathy. "Becky, I'm so sorry. I can't even imagine how enraged you must be. What now?"

"Now I get my lawyer involved and —"

Becky stopped mid-sentence. Zach thought she was getting emotional, but she looked strange. She was blinking rapidly, taking in short, sharp breaths.

"Becky, are you all right?"

All she could manage was a wheezing

gasp. Becky clutched at her stomach, teeth clenched from what appeared to be a sudden, sharp pain in her belly. She made a groaning sound, slumped forward, righted herself, groaned again, and kept blinking.

Zach got up, knocking over his chair with a loud clatter as he stood. "Becky, are you okay? Are you choking?"

He was about to perform the Heimlich maneuver, but Becky had the wherewithal to shake her head. Air seeped into her lungs like she was taking it in through a straw crimped at one end. She groaned and gurgled something wet and viscous up her throat. Panic and the fear of death overcame her as she tried to take deeper breaths. She made an effort to stand but was wobbly on her feet, dizzy as though drunk. Zach studied the too-rapid rise and fall of her chest. She braced her hands against the table, her body racked with another spasm.

Zach's mind clicked through health conditions that could cause breathing problems, recalling all possibilities as fast as any Google search. Asthma. Heart failure. Respiratory infection. Pericardial effusion — fluid around the heart. Pleural effusion — fluid around the lung. None of those quite fit what he was seeing. Becky seemed suddenly and inexplicably ill.

Suddenly ill . . .

A thought tugged at the back of Zach's mind as Becky's color began to change, from moonlight pale to a touch of blue. Traces of spittle frothed at the edges of her mouth. Each breath sounded like she was choking on air.

Zach got Becky back in the chair before she toppled over. Placing his index and middle fingers on her neck, just to the side of her windpipe, he felt the rapid pulse over the carotid artery.

His eyes went to the thermos on the table, and to the spoon, spotted with remnants of the chicken soup.

Suddenly ill . . .

Zach had no monitors to check blood pressure or oxygen saturation. He could not administer medications through IVs. There were no labs to inform him of blood gases, potassium levels, or levels of creatinine, bicarb, sodium, or any of a multitude of readings he'd want to know. There was only Becky's continued wheezing, her evident disorientation.

Zach made his calculation based on Becky's alarming coloring, her continued respiratory distress, and the viciousness of the spasms that shook her body. Zach decided to call 911 on the way to the hospital, knowing every second counted, and praying he could get there in time.

CHAPTER 52

Becky

Somehow she was in a car, and they were moving.

How did that happen?

She didn't remember leaving the house. She did not remember much of anything. She could think only of how sick she felt. Her vision had gone out of focus, as though someone had taken steel wool to her eyes and scratched everything blurry. Her stomach cramped severely, worse than labor pain, squeezing her insides like a balloon compressing to the point of rupture. Her body prickled with the needle-like sensations of every muscle going to sleep all at once. All she wanted was air, sweet, precious air. She could feel her throat tightening, choking her.

She felt the car swerve sharply, heard the violent scrape of tires fighting for traction.

Oh . . . God, give me air, please, please . . .

"Becky, can you hear me?"

She may have felt a hand on her shoulder or her face. Her body burned and froze simultaneously, making it hard to feel anything. The voice, though, that was familiar — Zach, he was with her. He was driving.

"I just drove past the Village Pharmacy on Sudbury Road. I'm going to stop there. Have the ambulance meet us there; I've got to try something to help her breathe." Did she see him put his phone away? Who was he talking to? "Becky, can you hear me? Stay with me, okay? You're going to be all right."

That was a lie. Becky knew it in her heart, her head, her soul. She was going to be anything but all right. She understood right then and there that she was going to die. It was about to happen. Minutes, maybe not much longer. Her lungs felt useless. The world was growing dark. But she wanted to see clearly, even for just a moment. She wanted one last look at the world before everything went black.

"We're almost there. You hang on, now."

Almost where? Becky wondered. With Sammy, perhaps. At least she'd get to hold her baby again. And maybe Cora would be there as well. Maybe she could finally make peace with that. Peace. Becky could feel and

548

hear her heartbeat slowing. She stopped struggling for air. There was no point. But Meghan . . . what would happen to her? Who would care for her?

She's not sick. She's not. You're sick. Carl's voice came to her from deep in her subconscious. *You're sick and need help. You've done this to her because of your mom — history repeats, it repeats.* It was Sabrina's voice she now heard. *Stay true to yourself, to your beliefs.* Veronica. Her friend. Her helper.

She's not helping; she's not your friend. It was Carl's voice she heard again, his doubt.

"Who's not your friend?" That was Zach's voice. But somehow Becky knew it was not in her head. She must have been speaking aloud.

"Zach . . . Zach . . . help . . . help me . . . can't . . . can't breathe right . . ."

"We're here. We're here," Zach said, and she felt the car come to a hard stop.

A moment later, her door opened. She felt herself being dragged from the vehicle. Her legs were useless. Her body was shutting down.

Can't breathe . . . no air . . .

Becky was a rag doll in Zach's arms. The light changed, so she knew they'd gone from outside to indoors.

"Ipecac syrup!" she heard Zach shout. "Do you keep a bottle behind the counter? I'm a doctor. This is an emergency."

"Yes, I think so," someone said nervously.

Becky felt her feet leave the ground. For a second she thought she'd passed and was floating to the special place where Sammy would be, maybe Cora. But it was Zach lifting her, holding her in his arms. Soon she was on the ground again. She felt a pinch on her nose as a firm hand forced her head to tilt back.

"Get me a bucket and water, too. You're going to hate this," Zach said.

A foul-tasting liquid poured into Becky's throat. For a moment, it felt as if she were drowning, but moments later the contents of her stomach gurgled before shooting back up her esophagus like an erupting volcano. Vomit poured from her mouth in a thick stream. She gagged, lurched forward, and vomited again and again. Her body quaked with each violent expulsion. A putrid smell filled her nose. But her lungs, those were filling with air now. She heard disgusted groans from nearby people, heard sirens blaring in the distance. Hot bile shot up her throat again. But none of that mattered, because she could finally breathe.

Zach held Becky's head, keeping the hair

from her face as she vomited. "You're going to be okay, do you hear me, Becky? You're going to be all right."

The sirens grew louder. She heard him, and this time she believed him, even as more poison shot out of her body.

Consciousness returned to her along with a flood of bright lights. She heard hushed conversation mixed with strange noises. Her head felt stuffed with cotton balls. Her vision was blurred but clearing. A moment or two of hazy disorientation passed as she came more fully awake. *A hospital . . . I'm in a hospital.* Her eyesight continued to improve until shadows morphed into recognizable shapes. Bed. IV. Door. Window. Monitors. Tray. One blurred shadow transformed into a face that she recognized: Zach Fisher stood at the end of her hospital bed.

"Welcome back from the abyss," he said.

"Where — ?"

"White Memorial," Zach said. "ICU. I had the ambulance bring you here. I figured you'd want to be close to your daughter."

"What — ?"

"Some kind of poisoning," Zach said. She was glad he kept preempting her questions. Swallowing was near impossible and her dry, raw throat made talking feel like an endurance sport. It was then she became aware of a tube stuck up her nasal passage, which felt as though it ran all the way down her throat to her stomach.

"It's called 'nasogastric intubation,' " Zach explained as Becky tugged ever so gently on the tube inserted up her nose. "Your doctors used it to administer activated charcoal to absorb any residual poison in your gut. They're also treating you symptomatically with Valium to control your muscle twitching."

Zach came around to the side of the bed, where he checked the pulse oximeter attached to Becky's index finger. She was quite familiar with the medical apparatus due to Meghan's countless hospitalizations.

"Your O2 levels are in the eighties — what we docs call 'hypoxemia' — which is why you're probably still feeling some uncomfortable shortness of breath."

"I thought you'd quit being a doctor here," Becky said as a spasm returned to her belly.

"I'm here as a friend, not a physician," Zach said. "The police were here as well — those two detectives, Capshaw and Spence."

"What for?"

"To get a statement from you, but you couldn't give them much of one. You've been in and out of consciousness for hours. We still don't know what got into your system, but Dr. Lucy Abruzzo here in pathology is testing your chicken soup."

"My . . . my soup?"

Becky's stomach lurched again, maybe from the memory. She felt her world tilt, but thankfully her equilibrium returned quickly. Her vision had improved considerably in the short time she had had her eyes open. Now she could see the tubes sticking out of her arms, could follow the trail of wires attached to monitors reading her vital signs. The bright fluorescents overhead were harsh on her eyes.

Zach must have noticed her agitation, because he turned off the room lights, providing Becky with instant relief.

"You became violently ill while you were eating the soup," Zach said. He went on to recount a terrifying ordeal that involved a frantic race to the local pharmacy and him force-feeding her a bottle of ipecac syrup.

"In hindsight, I really screwed up," Zach said.

"Why?"

"I shouldn't have induced vomiting. Your breathing was already compromised and you could have aspirated, which could have been fatal. And with the poison already having been absorbed, making you throw up was dangerous at that point. I made a spur-of-the-moment decision when I drove past the pharmacy. I panicked, and my judgment was wrong, plain and simple. That seems to happen to me with people I care about."

Becky knew he was talking about Will — and surprisingly (and yes, flatteringly), her as well.

"The doctors wanted you intubated and sedated," Zach continued, "but I told them no, you'd want to be awake so you could help the police."

"I was so sick," Becky said as horrible memories flooded her, the intense pain in her belly, the blinding fear of death. "Meghan . . . my God, Meghan. It must have been what she felt like."

Zach's expression blended curiosity and concern. "Why do you say that?"

"Because she was sick like that . . . suddenly and intensely," Becky said in a weak, raspy voice. Zach helped her drink water from a cup on the tray beside her bed. "It happened once when we were home and twice here at White. It was why we brought her to the ER that day, when you referred us to Dr. Nash. The last time I visited her, I didn't give her soup, because I wanted her to eat the hot lunch that day. It was part of our escape plan."

"So three times it's happened," Zach said.

"Three, yes," said Becky. "Four, if you count me."

A dark look crossed Zach's stubble-covered face. He looked worn and exhausted, as if he, too, had swallowed something deadly. "Becky . . . have you ever wondered . . . if Carl could have something to do with it?"

"Carl?" There was a pull on the nasogastric tube as Becky lifted her head slightly off the bed pillow to fix Zach with a confused look.

"I brought up the idea of Carl's involvement earlier in a rather unpleasant exchange with Nash and Knox Singer. It's not common for the father to be behind a case of Munchausen by proxy, but it's not unheard of either."

"You think Carl poisoned my soup?"

"He's been present for every instance where a possible poisoning took place. At your home, and here at White."

"He was with me every time . . ." Becky's voice trailed off.

"I should call the police," Zach said.

"Wait!" Becky pulled on the tubes again as she held up her hand. "Carl's powerful and determined. He's also the cosigner of my bond."

"And?"

"And if he revokes it, I could end up in jail."

Zach seemed to share Becky's concern. "What do you want me to do?"

"Let's see if we can get proof," Becky said. A fresh jolt of adrenaline masked the discomfort of her nasal tube, making speech less effortful. "I kicked him out of the house. I don't think he took his computer with him. I know the password. Maybe we can find his secrets before he thinks to cover his tracks."

CHAPTER 53

Zach

It was just after sunset when he pulled into the driveway of Becky and Carl's Concord home. The posse of reporters — who had followed Zach to the pharmacy and later to the hospital — was no longer camped out front, because the story was not here anymore. The story was in the ICU at White, where Becky was recovering, and in the Behavioral Health Unit, where Meghan was locked up. But soon enough, the story could be with Carl, whose whereabouts remained unknown.

Carl had not come to the hospital, either to check on Becky or to visit with Meghan and offer reassuring words about her mother. If he were anywhere near a cell phone, TV, or radio, he'd have known his soon-to-be ex-wife had nearly been fatally poisoned. His absence drew the interest of the two detectives, Capshaw and Spence, who viewed any unusual behavior as cause for suspicion.

Zach had his own hunch about Carl. Pieces of the puzzle began to fit together in unexpected ways. Carl did not have the psychological makeup typical of someone committing Munchausen by proxy, but that did not mean he had no role to play. Zach kept returning to the idea of a somatic reaction in Meghan — that it wasn't mito, and it never had been mito. Meghan had developed various symptoms that just happened to mirror mito because of some sort of external stress, something related to her father.

It was entirely possible that Zach had embraced the mito diagnosis because it was his proclivity to do so, and Becky had jumped aboard seeking a clear answer, while it may have been Carl pulling the strings all along. Was his plan to manipulate Meghan in order to wage psychological warfare against his wife? If that theory held water, it would mean that Carl had intentionally poisoned Meghan, had killed Levine for reasons still unknown, and had planted the earring to cast suspicion on Becky. While the narrative had some logic to it, the big question Zach could not answer was why.

Becky had told Zach where to find the

house key — under a fake rock next to the wooden bench on the side of the house overlooking the stone patio, in what looked to be a professionally landscaped garden. He entered through a side door, half expecting to hear the warning chirps of a house alarm, but Becky had supplied him with the numeric code to deactivate it. There were no sounds of any kind. He found the lights in the kitchen after feeling for a switch plate on the wall. The chair he had knocked over had been righted. The thermos of soup was gone, bagged and tagged for evidence.

Zach located the staircase, which Becky had said would lead to Carl's office. He ascended the carpeted stairwell, wondering what he would do if he encountered Carl there. He did not think Carl would be eager to hear any of his prepared explanations. From the moment they'd met, the man seemed itching to dish out a good pounding. Or was the bullying part of Carl's personality all part of his act?

As Zach turned a corner on the stairwell, he spied a sliver of light spilling out from underneath the white painted door at the top of the landing. Zach listened intently for any sounds beyond but, hearing none, turned the brass knob, opening the door a crack to peer inside. He half expected Carl to be standing there, ready to pounce. Emboldened, Zach opened the door fully and went inside.

The office was ransacked.

Zach's gaze traveled first to the books spilled onto the floor, then to a pile of papers that appeared to have been angrily swept off the expansive desk. While the framed pictures of Carl's many showpiece homes and family photos of Meghan and Becky remained secured to the walls, the drawers of the desk had been pulled free of their slots, the contents within — pens, pencils, papers — dumped haphazardly onto the floor. It was then that Zach noticed the body, dressed in faded jeans and a navy polo, lying facedown, as still as the tipped-over chair beside him.

Carl.

Zach rushed to Carl's side, knowing in his gut there was no need to hurry. The skin was cool to the touch as he checked for a pulse, finding none where none had been expected. The muscles were stiff, suggesting that Carl had been dead for some time. The top layer of skin had already begun to loosen and had a telling sheen of early-stage decay.

Near Carl's body, Zach spied an empty whiskey tumbler. He picked up the glass to examine it, using his shirt as a glove to preserve any fingerprints for the police. Inside the glass was the residue of something green, leafy, not unlike tea leaves. Zach was no botanist, but he very much doubted this was Carl's favorite Earl Grey. He took a whiff inside the tumbler. He could smell the remnants of whiskey, but not the plant. It was odorless, probably tasteless, too, but he was certain it was the same substance that had sickened Becky.

A scene formed in Zach's mind: Carl ingesting a fatal dose of some poison, knocking over bookshelves and papers as life was leaving him, then collapsing to the floor, dead. Was it suicide? Had he feared that his secret would be revealed in the wake of Becky's inadvertent poisoning? Zach scoured the floor with his eyes, searching for answers, when he spotted what appeared to be wrapping paper torn open in haste, not far from Carl's inert form. Near the crumpled paper was a small open box, colored the distinctive aqua blue that comes only from Tiffany.

As he glanced back at the body, Zach saw that Carl's right hand was balled in a fist. In his hurry to check for a pulse, Zach had failed to notice the glint of a silver chain barely sticking out from between the fingers of his clenched hand. Zach pried open the fingers, suspecting that what had been inside that jewelry box could very well be the object in Carl's dead grasp. He unfurled the fingers to reveal a diamond-encrusted silver pendant shaped in the form of a heart. He turned the pendant around in his fingers to examine it — forgetting for a moment the need to preserve what may be a crime scene — and saw the name *angi* engraved on the back.

Zach called 911 and informed the dispatcher he could not stick around for the police. He had to get back to White Memorial. He had to let Becky know what he'd found, because something told him that Carl had sent her a message from the grave.

CHAPTER 54

Becky

What should she feel, knowing her husband was dead? Why weren't there any tears? Where was the ache? The wailing? The flood of grief? When Zach broke the news about Carl, she felt none of those emotions. Instead, a strange sense of relief washed over her. Now the man who had shared her bed, her life, could not hurt her or Meghan ever again. The realization came with a perverse sense of justice. Carl had gotten what he deserved, because Becky now believed, as did Zach, that he had poisoned Meghan. It was entirely possible he could have killed her had Becky not consumed the soup meant for their daughter. The man Zach had found dead in his home office was not the man she had married and once loved. More than a stranger, he was a monster, and his motives were now as clear as the liquids being pumped from the IVs into her veins.

This was not about Munchausen's, Becky now believed. This was about Carl.

He wanted out of the marriage, out of his obligations, out of his life so that he could start a new one with this Angi person, whoever she was. To do so, he was willing to kill his sick daughter and use Munchausen's as proof of Becky's instability when he set her up to take the fall for his crime. With one devilish act, both Carl's anchors would be cut free so that he could sail away into the glory of his new life. Becky would go to prison and Meghan into the ground, while Carl and Angi would get to live out their days on some tropical beach, brushing each other with suntan lotion and imbibing mango rum smoothies.

But Angi — that whore, that bitch — apparently had a plan of her own. Becky and Zach had a new theory, which they shared with Capshaw and Spence, who had come to the hospital to take a statement. At some point, Angi had decided to do away with Carl, poisoning him the way he had Meghan. Carl was not the type to take his own life, which was why Becky suspected his paramour had staged the suicide, which would be entirely believable, given what he'd been doing to his daughter. In the aftermath, Meghan would live, Becky would avoid jail, and Angi would vanish, along with her reasons for double-crossing her lover.

Maybe Carl had set Angi up financially. Maybe he'd funneled money to her in the same secretive way that she believed he had to Kelly London, using his corporate account as a personal piggy bank. All would be revealed soon enough. Carl had indeed sent a message from the grave, and the police were now out looking for Angi. With such an unusual name, she would not be too hard to track down, Becky believed.

What Becky wanted now was for the tube shoved up her nose to be taken out. She wanted the IVs removed as well. She wanted to be back on her feet so that she could visit with Meghan, to tell her in person that her father was gone before she heard it from someone else. Even though her father had committed an unfathomable act of pure evil, he was still part of her history and an integral part of her. In Meghan's time of sorrow, she would need the comfort only a mother could provide.

"See if you can get her down here," Becky said to Zach as he checked the drip flow of her IVs. It was pitch dark out her window, but the ICU bustled with its typical degree of chaos. The sounds from the hall beyond her cubicle, the incessant beeps and buzzes, so hard to ignore at first, had morphed into white noise akin to the dull din of a Vegas casino. Zach's cell phone rang. He answered, a grave look soon coming to his face.

"Are you sure?" she heard him say. His eyebrows were knitted together, while deep creases stretched across his furrowed brow. Becky's gut told her the call had been about Carl.

"That was Detective Spence," Zach said, putting his phone away. "They spoke with the COO at Carl's company. Apparently, there's no Angi who works there, and there has never been one."

"That's . . . that's not possible," Becky said, stammering. "Carl told me she was someone he worked with."

"Carl lied about a lot of things, didn't he?"

"Well, who the hell is Angi, then?"

"I wouldn't imagine it's someone's initials, not with that many letters," Zach said, thinking it through. "A nickname, perhaps?"

"Maybe."

"Or it could be a first and last name put together," Zach said. "The first letters of each."

"Perhaps," Becky said. She thought about

names that begin with *A-n.*

Anne . . . Angela . . . Anita . . .

But those were just names, not people she knew. Maybe Carl knew her. Maybe she *was* someone at work whose identity he was protecting. The police could search every An/Gi name pretty quickly, she thought.

God, how she wanted that tube pulled out. She wanted to stand, to pace, to think clearly without being all doped up. *Who the hell is Angi?* Because that's the message Carl had sent, wasn't it? There was a reason he had ripped open that package and held on to the necklace, the same kind of diamond-encrusted pendant with an engraving on the back that he'd once bought her.

Angi . . . Angi . . . Angi . . .

Becky thought of what Zach had said, that the engraving was a set of initials, first and last names. In her mind, she split the letters again. *AN-GI . . . AN-GI.*

A surge of terror raced through her body. *AN-GI.*

"What kind of doctor is Amanda Nash?" she asked, knowing the answer already.

"Gastroenterologist," Zach said. "Why?"

Becky had only to answer with four letters. *"AN-GI,"* she said.

CHAPTER 55

Meghan

When I heard Dr. Amanda Nash's voice, I thought I was dreaming.

"Meghan . . . Meghan, are you awake?" she called out.

My eyes opened. Slowly, my foggy vision cleared. I propped myself up on my elbows to see her standing just inside my room. She came toward my bed, calling my name in a gentle, motherly tone.

"Meghan, wake up, sweetheart. I've something to tell you."

I became instantly alert. My body tensed as a terrible feeling came over me, a gnawing knowing that something awful had happened.

Dr. Nash sat on the edge of my bed and placed her hand on my shoulder, the way someone does before they break bad news. "Meghan, sweetheart, there's been some trouble."

"What . . . what kind of trouble?" I asked in a shaky voice.

"Your mom is in the hospital. She's here at White. She came in and was very sick, but she's okay now. She's going to be all right, and she wants to see you."

My heart began to jackhammer. "What . . . what happened to her?"

"She had some . . . breathing difficulties. But we treated her quickly, and she's making a terrific recovery. Why don't you get dressed and I'll take you to her."

I was on my feet in no time. I didn't have to get dressed, since I was sleeping in sweats. One look out the window told me it was night. I got the sense it was late.

I slid my feet into a pair of slippers Mom had brought me from home. My mouth had that gross taste of sleep, but I wasn't about to take the time to brush it away. As we walked down the hall toward the locked exit, Dr. Nash gripped my arm like she had that first day, the day I came and never left, holding on like I might try to escape. I guess I'd given her good reason to be cautious.

Dr. Nash paused at the front desk. "I'm taking Meghan to see her mother," she said.

Nurse Amy, who often worked the overnight shift, gave a nod as she typed something into the computer. A moment later, the door clicked open, and Dr. Nash escorted me out of the BHU for the first time since my inauspicious homecoming.

"What happened to my mom exactly?" I asked.

"I told you, breathing troubles."

There was a funny edge to her voice, an anger I hadn't picked up on before. I figured we'd take the elevator to wherever my mom was, but Dr. Nash took me to the stairwell instead. I didn't even think to question it; I just went with her as she led me up floor after floor.

"Where is she?" I asked again, my voice echoing in the stairwell like I was calling up from the bottom of a well.

"She's here, up a few floors. Just keep walking."

"Why didn't we take the elevator?"

"What's the matter? You don't like exercise?" Maybe she was trying to be funny, or cute, but her voice sounded strangely menacing to me.

"No, I'm fine," I said, even though I felt fatigued because I hadn't exerted myself in ages. We went up four flights . . . and then five . . . then six, and so on. With each step, I could feel my cells starving for air, each of them dying slow, painful deaths. I slowed my ascent, but Dr. Nash gripped my arm tighter, all but pulling me up those stairs.

"Hurry," she said darkly. "Your mom is eager to see you."

But where is she? I wondered. We were near the top of the stairs, and yet Dr. Nash took me even higher.

My uneasiness increased with every step. I knew I wanted to go down, no, had to go down — now. A surprise burst of adrenaline gave me a spurt of energy I hadn't felt in ages. I spun like I was dodging a defender on the soccer field, quickly putting two steps between Dr. Nash and me. But before I could make it to step three, Dr. Nash grabbed my arm with crushing force, pulling me back toward her with a violent yank.

I screamed, "Help!" loud as I could, my voice bouncing off the walls. Dr. Nash let go of my arm to cover my mouth with her hand, and at the same time I felt cold, sharp steel pressed against my throat. Terror coursed through me when I peered down to see what looked like a scalpel clutched in Dr. Nash's hand. The blade was hidden from my view, but I could feel it digging into my flesh. I became as rigid as a block of ice.

"You think needles are bad, Meghan?" Dr. Nash hissed in my ear. "Try having your throat sliced open. That's as bad as can be.

Now, keep walking."

"Why . . . are you doing this?" I asked.

"Walk or bleed — those are your two choices."

I headed up the stairs, because it really wasn't a choice at all.

CHAPTER 56

Zach

He had his cell phone out, and within moments was connected to the duty nurse on the BHU. He put the call on speaker so Becky could hear the conversation.

"This is Dr. Zachary Fisher," he said with the authority of someone who still worked for the hospital. "I need to speak with Meghan Gerard right away, it's urgent."

There was a pause that made Zach's stomach turn over with worry.

"Meghan left a few moments ago with Dr. Nash. She's bringing her to see her mother in the ICU."

"How long ago exactly?" Zach's tone was sharp.

"I don't know," the nurse said, clearly shaken. "Five minutes, maybe more."

"Get this tube out!" Becky screamed. "Get this damn tube out now!"

"Call the police!" Zach shouted at the

duty nurse. "Lock down the Mendon Building. Tell them to find Dr. Nash. Tell them to find her now!"

"She's got her," Becky said, her voice a tremor. "She's got Meghan. Get me unhooked. Do it! Do it now!"

Zach gave it a thought, just for a moment or two, where he contemplated the consequences of complying, then realized that if he were in Becky's position — if it were Will and not Meghan in jeopardy — he'd rip the damn tube out of his nose himself.

Zach quickly donned a pair of disposable gloves retrieved from the shelf behind Becky's bed, forgoing the usual hand hygiene. Instead of a towel, he used his jacket to catch the fluids that would soon spill out. Without alerting the nursing staff, Zach separated the tube from suction. Normally, he'd have used a syringe flush with ten milliliters of normal saline, but he did not have one at the ready. He instructed Becky to take a deep breath and hold it. Clamping the tube with his fingers, doubling it up on itself, Zach began to pull. Becky's face contorted in discomfort as the tube came up her nasal passage. Clear fluid poured out her nose and onto the jacket as the tube came free.

Zach went to work on the IVs next, disconnecting them with practiced efficiency, while Becky blew residual fluids into a tissue. As he removed the hookups connected to various monitors, alarms began to ring out. A team of nurses, as well rehearsed as any Broadway troupe, stormed into the cubicle, ready to take action, looking shocked to find Zach helping Becky out of her bed.

"Get me a pair of scrubs," Zach said, putting his arm around Becky to help keep her upright.

"Where are you taking her?" a perplexed-looking nurse asked in a panicky voice.

"I'm taking her to her daughter," Zach said.

CHAPTER 57

Meghan

Walk or bleed.

Those were my two options as I opened the door marked ROOF ACCESS — AUTHORIZED PERSONNEL ONLY and stepped from the stairwell into a cool night. City lights from the surrounding buildings battled back the dark like an artificial dawn. A breeze blew my loose hair in front of my face, setting a chill against my skin.

Nash half dragged, half shoved me onto the roof. All was silent except for the sounds of traffic below and a steady hum emanating from big metal boxes dotting the rooftop. I tried to find my composure, strengthen my resolve, but my heart was lodged in my throat while my knees knocked together like castanets.

Dr. Nash held the scalpel to my neck, pressing the point into my skin. In my mind, I saw the blade sink into my flesh, felt it

576

tear across my throat, ripping open a grisly gash in the shape of a wicked grin.

"Please . . . please let me go." My weak voice quaked with fright. I thought of my father, how he'd hate that voice. He'd want me to stand up to Nash like he'd wanted me to stand up to my mother. He'd want me to be strong, to fight back.

"Walk," Nash said.

It was the damn scalpel — the needle to end all needles — that made my legs move.

"Why are you doing this?" I asked.

A voice in my head shrieked at me: *Run! Fight! Scream!*

But my body wouldn't obey. I was moving in slow-motion, taking one step after another, shuffling forward like a sleepwalker. For years, I'd been pushed around, told what to do, where to go, what to eat, when to sleep, what doctor to see, what pill to swallow, so taking another step toward the roof's edge seemed simply like something else I had to do. But my feet slowed, giving me hope that a bit of fight might bubble up from deep inside me.

"It all fell apart," Dr. Nash said, mumbling to herself, as though she were trying to sort out what had happened. "I had to do it. . . . I had to."

Nash gave a second hard shove from

behind to hurry me along. I stumbled forward, my arms flapping for balance, feet skidding for traction, no more than twenty steps from the drop-off. I couldn't tell how high up we were — ten stories, twelve? What did it matter? If I went over, I'd never get up again.

I felt another hard push from behind.

Fifteen steps now.

Off in the distance, I heard the wail of a siren, and for a brief moment allowed myself to believe it was a rescue team coming for me. But that wasn't possible. Dr. Nash had told Nurse Amy she was taking me to see my mother. There was no way to know we'd gone up a stairwell. The only way they'd find me was if I hit the pavement. I didn't know how Dr. Nash would get away with my murder. I didn't much care.

"Please don't hurt me . . . please, please don't."

I tried to sink to my knees, but my sudden movement caught the scalpel and it sliced into my flesh. Nash yanked me up as blood snaked down my neck in warm, wet rivulets. It was hardly a gush, so I figured the slice could not have been too deep, just a nick, but it awoke something inside me. The sting had come and gone. It wasn't so bad, was it? I *could* take the pain. I didn't have to be afraid to the point of paralysis. Not if I wanted to live.

To save myself, I had to channel the strongest person I knew — my mother. Real or imagined, I'd have to fight back the way she had fought my disease.

"You said it all fell apart. What did you do? Just tell me that. I deserve that much."

Nash pulled me to a hard stop but kept the scalpel against the side of my throat. A trickle of blood continued to ooze from my neck. One swipe of her wrist, one quick pull across my skin, and it wouldn't matter what I was sick with.

"What I did?" Nash's cold voice cut through the air. "I killed your father, Meghan. That's what I did. I killed him because I had to."

The world tilted. It seemed to stop. The wind no longer bit at my face. All noise became a loud ringing in my ears. My throat closed up like I was being choked.

"My father? Dead?"

I sputtered out the words. I didn't want to believe it. I *refused* to believe it. But something told me it wasn't a lie. My father *was* dead, and Nash *had* killed him. But why?

"He told me, did you know that?" Nash said. "That you went snooping on his phone. That you found out about us."

I couldn't believe my ears. "You're . . . you're Angi?"

"We were so, so good together . . . so good."

My thoughts tumbled as though the floor had given way. "If you loved him, why would you hurt him?" I was shaking with anger and fear even as a horrible emptiness swelled in my chest.

"You're too young and stupid to understand," she said.

The pressure of the scalpel against my throat lessened. My mother's voice, her face, her strength came to me like a guiding light.

Before Nash could say anything more, I jumped forward, and with agility mastered on the soccer field, spun around, driving my left foot into Nash's shin in a move that most certainly would have earned me a red card. Nash cried out in pain as I brought my right leg, my kicking leg, into her knee the way I would send a ball to the goal from twenty yards out. The kick dropped her to the ground. Nash tried to roll away, but I pounced on her, pinning her beneath my arms.

I tried to hold her down, but she was far stronger. She hadn't been confined to a hospital room, didn't have switches clicking off inside her. She rolled me onto my back as though moving a sack of laundry, but somehow, I kept the momentum going, causing us to roll over a second time. As we did, Nash's cell phone spilled from the pocket of her lab coat. I heard it clatter, but couldn't reach it.

Nash swung her free arm in a wide arc. In pure reflex, I attempted to block the strike instead of dodging it. A slice opened in my sweatshirt, and an instant later I felt blood filling my shirtsleeve. I fell off Nash in a sideways tumble that brought me within a few feet of the discarded cell phone. Scrambling forward on my hands and knees, I sent a donkey kick into the side of Nash's head. Nash groaned. The kick bought me enough time to reach the phone, which I picked up as I clambered back to my feet.

I pressed the word EMERGENCY.

"Nine one one, what's your emergency?" I heard a woman say.

"I'm on the roof of White Memorial Hospital!" I shouted into the phone. "She's going to kill me. Help! Hurry!"

But before I could say another word, I felt a sharp sting as Nash plunged her scalpel into the small of my back.

CHAPTER 58

Becky

Terror swam through her veins. She raced for the elevator as fast as her rubbery legs could move. Nearly twenty-four hours spent in a hospital bed had stiffened her muscles and drained her endurance. A painful stitch formed in her side, slowing her gait. She hurried her steps to keep pace with Zach, who gripped her arm to hold her upright. A crowd gawked as she and Zach waited for what seemed an eternity for the elevator to arrive. Blood oozed from beneath a hastily applied wad of tight gauze and tape that covered punctures where her IV ports had been. The steady ache in her throat served as an unpleasant reminder of the nasogastric tube, but she found the discomfort easy to ignore.

Becky donned the scrub bottoms a nurse had supplied on her ride down from the eighth floor to the fourth, leaving the floral-patterned hospital johnny for a top.

"What if she's not even there?" Becky said as she and Zach raced along the glass walkway connecting the Mendon Building to the main hospital. "They could be anywhere. We don't know if they're even in the hospital."

"We're going to find them," Zach said reassuringly. As proof, he gestured to the chaotic scene swarming outside the locked doors to the BHU. The bedlam involved dozens of security personnel, along with orderlies, Boston Police, nurses, and doctors, all of whom had assembled with startling rapidity, crowding the narrow hallway. Radios crackled. Phones rang. Voices rose above the din. Becky heard sirens blaring outside and watched with widening eyes as the commotion intensified. The noise was utterly disorienting, enough that the room began to spin.

Without warning, a blue tide of police moved toward the stairwell with frenzied purpose. Uniformed officers danced in and out of her field of vision, but nobody recognized her as the mother of the missing girl until Detective Spence gripped her shoulder forcefully.

"You shouldn't be here," he said. "We'll handle this."

Becky thought she saw Detective Capshaw in front of his partner, both men in blazers, not blues.

Zach waited until the two detectives were out of sight before he pulled Becky into the stairwell into which they had vanished. He kept a tight grip on her hand as they ascended one floor after the other. The stairs were cacophonous with shouting, the echo of fast-moving footsteps, and the click of gun holsters unsnapping.

At the top of the stairwell, the pace slowed as a crush of bodies jammed the exit to the roof. Becky heard police officers shouting "Put down your weapon! Drop it now!"

"Where is the mother? Get her up here, fast."

Becky recognized Capshaw's husky voice as her fatigue fell away, replaced with a renewed resolve to push her way to the top of those stairs.

"I'm her mother," Becky implored those in front of her. "Please let me through . . . please."

The blockade of bodies formed sliver-size gaps through which Becky and Zach pushed their way to the top of the stairs. She emerged into the chilly night, feeling as though she had stepped into a dream. A line of police stretched out in front of her, many with guns drawn, some standing, some kneeling. Powerful flashlights blazed across the rooftop, which was already aglow from the light cast by the many surrounding buildings.

Amanda Nash stood in front of the line of police, close to the building's edge. She held what Becky believed to be a surgical scalpel against her daughter's throat. Blood dripped from a gash in Meghan's neck and from a cut to her arm, visible through a long slice in her sweatshirt.

Pulling free from Zach's grasp, Becky rushed forward, frantically calling Meghan's name. Some police turned. Spence and Capshaw waved Becky over to them.

"She's here," Spence called out to Nash. "You've been asking to see Becky Gerard, and she's here. Okay? Now, put down your weapon."

"No!" Nash's voice was loud and clear even over the steady whapping of an approaching helicopter.

Becky took a tentative step forward, putting a couple of feet between her and the two detectives.

"I'm here, Amanda," Becky said in a plaintive voice. "Please, please don't hurt my daughter. Please —"

"She ruined everything!" Amanda

shouted. Spit flew from a mouth misshapen in rage.

Meghan's blank expression showed she was in a near-catatonic state. It took all the restraint Becky could muster not to run to her.

"It wasn't supposed to end like this!" Nash continued. "She was going to jump. She was supposed to kill herself. Now we're both going to jump. But I wanted you to watch. I want it to hurt."

"No!" Becky shrieked as she took a single step forward.

Nash smiled wickedly and pressed the scalpel harder against Meghan's throat. A spotlight from the hovering helicopter illuminated them like stage lights as the rotors kicked up powerful winds that blew Meghan's long hair every which way.

"You think I wanted to kill Carl? I loved him! I loved him more than anything."

Becky dared a few more steps. The police stayed back.

"You don't have to do this," Becky said, continuing her approach, holding her hands up to show she was unarmed.

Get her talking, Becky thought. *Distract her.*

"Carl's not dead," Becky said.

Nash's eyes went wide. "No, that's . . . that's not possible."

Becky dared another step. "It's true. Zach saved him, just as he saved me. But Carl still loves you, Amanda. He told me so himself. He confessed to everything, even poisoning Meghan."

Meghan flinched at the mention of her father's betrayal, while a strange look crossed Nash's face.

"You're lying," Nash said.

"No, no, I'm telling you the truth. He's alive. He wants to see you."

"He didn't poison Meghan," Nash said, her expression one of disgust. "You think he'd do that to his own daughter? How stupid are you? You don't even know him. All you care about is your precious Meghan. And that's why I'm going to take her from you." Nash moved backward, positioning her and Meghan closer to the drop-off. She craned her neck to peer over her shoulder, perhaps calculating the number of steps to a fatal plunge.

"No," Becky said. "Let my daughter live. Please. You don't have to do this."

"Stay back," Nash said.

"Some good can still come from this," Becky said, moving closer, getting to within five or six giant steps away. Meghan lifted her head so she could lock eyes with her mother as Zach came forward.

"Amanda, please," Zach said. "There's another way."

"You really screwed this up for me, Fisher," Nash said to Zach. "You just couldn't let it go. You had to keep pushing for that diagnosis; you just had to keep pushing. Well, now you and Becky can have a happy life together, mourning your dead kids." Nash took another step back, taking Meghan with her.

One more step, one lean too far, and they'd both be gone.

The air stilled. The persistent *whap-whap-whap* of the hovering helicopter seemed to stop. Becky watched in horror as Nash leaned her body back, her toes coming up high enough to reveal the bottoms of her shoes. Meghan leaned backward as well, forced to follow Nash, who kept a tight grip on her. They were going over any second.

As she tilted, Meghan drove her elbow hard into Nash's stomach. Stunned, Nash let the scalpel fall from her grasp as she stumbled away from the ledge. Police moved forward as a blue wave, piling on Nash before she could scramble for her weapon. But Becky darted forward, her focus on Meghan, who teetered off-balance at the roof's edge.

There was a second when Meghan seemed

suspended in midair, but she soon lost her footing and started to go over. Becky lunged, closing the gap between her and Meghan in a single stride. Becky's feet left the ground as she stretched out her body, reaching for the blur of motion in front of her like an outfielder making a diving grab. She latched on to the sleeve of Meghan's sweatshirt as she went over the edge.

Becky fell to the ground with a thud, somehow without letting go of her hold. Momentum and body weight dragged her perilously close to the ledge. She thought for a second she was going over, too, before someone gripped her ankles hard, arresting her forward slide. Becky spun her head to see Zach, hands latched to her legs, his feet braced against the rooftop, his contorted expression showing the strain of a weight lifter.

In the next instant, the burning, unyielding ache in Becky's arm lessened as a group of police, Spence and Capshaw joining in, clambered over the ledge to pull Meghan up to safety.

A moment after that, Becky was on her back, chest heaving, eyes fixed on the night sky. Noises swirled around her like hurricane winds. Meghan broke from the crush of police to reach her mother. She landed on Becky's body like a blanket, tears streaming down her face, blood dripping from her wounds. Becky hugged her daughter tightly, stroking her hair. She gazed disbelieving into Meghan's eyes, awash with relief. It was then that Becky became aware of something wet and sticky painting the palm of her hand. Feeling around the small of Meghan's back, Becky watched in horror as her daughter's eyes rolled white.

The scream rising in Becky's throat spat out a single word. "Medic!"

Chapter 59

Meghan

I visited my father's grave two days after his funeral. He didn't have a tombstone yet, but one was coming. Mom and I got a bit lost trying to locate his plot, but the guy who ran the place helped us out. The dirt covering Dad's casket was like a scar on the green earth. I couldn't believe he was six feet underground. Weeks later, it still seemed surreal to think he was gone forever. Mom and I put a bouquet of flowers on his grave — daisies and marigolds as bright and sun-filled as the cloudless sky. I asked Mom for some time alone, and she agreed to wait for me in the car, but only after I assured her I could find my way back.

That is how I found myself alone, on my knees, talking to my dead father, smoothing the dirt covering him with a lazy brush of my hand.

"Hi, Daddy . . . it's me, Meghan."

I laughed — who else would call him Daddy? I wondered if he could hear me. Was he watching? Was he one of the birds flying overhead? Was he the butterfly that flittered near my face? Or was he just gone?

"I hope it's okay down there," I said, struck by a rush of emotion that made the wound on my back flare up. "I got stabbed, in case you didn't know — I'm assuming you don't know — by your girlfriend, of all people. That bitch."

I laughed again awkwardly. I was never comfortable cursing in front of my father.

"The scalpel cut only muscle. I'm going to have a nasty scar but, besides that, I'll be fine. My injury wasn't the reason it took so long to bury you, though.

"Sorry you had to be in the morgue, but the medical examiner had to figure out what killed you first. Turns out it was this thing called heartbreak grass — a fitting name because, you know, lots of heartbreak here. It's a kind of Asian vine or something, and it's, like, super poisonous. You have to test for it specifically, which is why it took so long to confirm what Nash said she gave you. I guess she bought it at an herbal shop in Chinatown, or at least that's what she told the police. In small doses, it can be used for medicinal purposes, but she didn't give you a small dose, did she?

"Looks like she was as crazy in love with you as she was crazy. It kind of broke my heart — there we go again with heartbreak, right? — when I found out you didn't actually do any research on doctors who specialize in mitochondrial disease. I wanted to believe you thought I was sick enough to go searching on your own. But nope. It was Dr. Nash, your gal pal, who told you all about mito, and Dr. Fisher, and you just went along with it, not having a clue that she was going to try to set Mom up.

"Anyway, I figured you should know Dr. Nash's plan in detail so that if you still have any feelings for her, you can let those go, because she is one evil bitch — oops, there I go with my mouth again. Sorry!"

I smiled, because I wasn't sorry at all.

"So here it is in full, straight from her police confession, and that's what I came here to tell you, because I think you deserve to know the whole story. When you described all my symptoms to Dr. Nash, she latched right on to mito and Dr. Fisher. She knew Dr. Fisher would diagnose me with mito because he did that a lot, I guess. She *wanted* Mom to think that I had a serious illness because she was eventually going to tell her the exact opposite.

"That's where the heartbreak grass came in. Those strange and sudden symptoms I had at home happened because Dr. Nash put some extract of that heartbreak grass in my flask of vodka that I thought I'd done a good job of hiding. The police told me she found it one afternoon when you two were having a rendezvous at our house, which you cleverly timed around Mom's workouts. God, Dad, how could you?

"Anyway, those new symptoms that didn't quite fit with mito gave Dr. Fisher a reason to get a GI consult with her — which she knew he'd do. Now Nash could set up the whole Munchausen's thing by telling Mom that my issues, everything I was feeling, were all in my head. She knew Mom wouldn't buy it, and would refuse to believe a less dire diagnosis is a sign of Munchausen's, which I suspect you already know.

"When Mom freaked, Nash's plan got rolling. She got DCF to take me into custody, child abuse and all that, and then she'd poison me, just a bit every time Mom came to visit, by putting some heartbreak grass extract into the chicken soup. That was her way of establishing a pattern. Nash was going to tell the police that mom must have smuggled in the poison, you know like how they sneak drugs into prisons. She'd say there were plenty of chances for mom to have spiked the soup without anyone noticing. It's also why Dr. Nash did the exam every time I got sick. I had plenty of real symptoms that could be measured by real medical instruments, but she lied and said I didn't. She even forged the lab results so the bloodwork would come back normal. How crazy is that?

"Mom's final visit, the one after you bailed her out, that was supposed to be my last day on earth. The soup would have killed me, too, but Mom ate it instead — and, lucky for her, the dose wasn't fatal, because she weighed more than me.

"If it had worked out the way Nash wanted, if I'd died, the soup would have been tested and found to be poisonous. Eventually the police would have found the heartbreak grass Nash planted at our house, the same stuff she used to poison you, and Mom would have been put in prison for my murder. The motive? Munchausen by proxy. People cause illness or injury for their own weird needs, so that's the only motive the prosecutor would need. They'd say that Mom messed up and put too much poison in my soup one day, and that's why I died. She'd be charged with manslaughter, maybe. But Mom would be gone twenty-five years, I'd be dead, and then you and Nash could live happily ever after, because you weren't going to leave us for her. That's what you said to her. You couldn't do that to your family. That's why she took matters into her own hands.

"But you didn't know what she was doing, did you, Dad? You didn't know DCF was going to take custody of me. Which is why you broke it off with Nash. Which, by the way, was in Nash's confession. It made me happy to hear, and it's one of the reasons I'm still talking to you. I guess she figured you'd come around eventually, even though I know you wouldn't have.

"But when Mom got sick, you got suspicious, so I'm proud of you, Dad. Nash told the police you invited her over to our house to confront her, but somehow, she got to your favorite whiskey and, well, you tried to warn us. Mom figured it out — Angi and all — but that came a little too late.

"Your Angi was going to tell the police that I'd broken away from her as she was taking me to see Mom, and that I'd run up the stairs like a crazy person and jumped off the hospital roof because I was emotionally damaged. She wanted me dead because she wanted Mom to suffer for messing everything up."

Tears poured out of my eyes. My shaky breath came in sputters.

"But I want to tell you something else. Something Mom said was important to say. It's something she needs to say to Grandma Cora, who miraculously is still alive.

"I want to tell you that I forgive you. I know you never meant to hurt me. I know that you loved me. And I love you, Daddy."

I got up, brushed the dirt from my hands, and used them to wipe my eyes dry. I walked away feeling better until I realized there was one last thing I'd forgotten to tell him.

I got the results from that second biopsy.

CHAPTER 60

Becky

Waves lapped against the sandy edge of the Pacific Ocean. Becky and Sabrina sat on a plaid blanket, sipping beer from red plastic cups, watching the shimmering sun descend gently into an endless horizon. Sabrina had on a white sweater and light-colored jeans, clothes Becky remembered borrowing a dozen years ago. With Sabrina's dark hair and olive complexion, a passerby would have no reason to think the two were sisters. But hours earlier they had been at the Wayside Funeral Home, paying their last respects to Cora — dear Cora, who had clung to life far longer than any doctor had thought possible.

"What now?" Sabrina asked, taking a sip of beer.

"Now we treat her," Becky said. "And hope for the best. There's a drug that might help. We're going to try to get her into a clinical trial."

" 'We'?" Sabrina's eyes twinkled.

"Yes, Zach Fisher and me."

"Are you two . . . ?" Her sister's voice trailed off.

"Sabrina, please, I just buried my husband. The last thing I need is a man. But if I were to try one out again, I'm pretty sure it would be someone like him."

"Take your time. You've been through quite a trauma, not to mention your husband's betrayal. How did they meet, anyway, Carl and Amanda? I've been meaning to ask you."

"Believe it or not, he renovated her apartment," Becky said with notable sadness.

"Isn't that how you two met — when you sold a place he built?"

"Yeah," Becky said, now with a slight smile. "I guess I'll have to talk to my therapist about that one."

"She's one crazy lady," Sabrina said. "I read in the paper that she confessed to killing the psychiatrist — Dr. Levine, I think his name was. But the article didn't say why."

"She did it because Levine started to believe that Meghan might be sick with something, which would have screwed up everything," Becky said. "If Levine suggested Meghan get treated for mito, and if the tests came back positive, it would have meant I didn't have Munchausen, and Nash's big plan would go up in smoke, so she took care of him by, you know, killing him. And then she got one of my earrings so the police would focus on me. I guess Carl had shown Nash where the damn key was and never changed the locks after the two of them broke it off.

"That might have been it, her last hurdle, but Zach got his biopsy thanks to Meghan, and so she had to go and sabotage that. I guess she messed with the data entry so that the lab techs would do the wrong stain or something."

"So twisted."

"Tell me about it."

"But I thought Carl didn't want the second biopsy done?"

"He didn't. He had broken things off with Nash after the kidnapping, but he still trusted her medical opinion because he didn't trust me. He had no idea what she was up to, but somehow she had convinced him that for Meghan's mental health, he had to do anything and everything in his power to prevent that second biopsy from taking place. That's why he paid off Kelly London from his corporate account and told her to betray me. I guess everyone has a price, even lawyers."

"How's Meghan taking it?"

Becky knew Sabrina was talking about the results from the second biopsy that showed the ragged red fibers that were a clear marker of mitochondrial disease.

"She's doing remarkably well given her diagnosis, not to mention all that's happened," Becky said. "But we have a long road ahead of us. Mito is a terribly, terribly debilitating disease. We're still not sure how many of Meghan's organs are affected. A lot depends on the severity; we just don't know yet. But she's taking it all in stride, going day by day, because that's all we can do."

"Meghan's an amazing girl."

"You don't know the half of it," Becky said.

"I *should* know," Sabrina said tellingly, and Becky understood. Sabrina needed to come east. They were family. They were all each other had now.

"Can I confess something?" Becky said.

"Anything," Sabrina said.

"I'm not sure they were wrong."

"Who?"

"Nash, Singer, Carl, the whole lot of

them. There's truth to what they said about me."

"What do you mean?"

"I've been talking a lot to Veronica, a friend from my online group, about my past, what happened, and it got me thinking. Part of me wanted Meghan to be sick."

Sabrina did a poor job of hiding her "I told you so" face. "That's not easy to admit," she said.

"No, it's not," Becky replied assuredly. "When Meghan got sick, I think I understood Cora better than I ever had. She didn't just get money faking her disability. She got attention. That was how I connected with her. Attending to her fantasy. With Meghan, I felt like . . . like . . ."

"Like you got to be Cora? You got the attention finally, not her — is that it?"

Becky nodded. "I think you were right, Cora's cancer brought up a lot of issues for me. With Sammy, you know. There's a lot of loss in me, and as I was losing Mom, a part of me felt that loss of Sammy all over again, which made me hold on even tighter to Meghan. So I think part of me secretly wanted her to be sick. I think what Carl said was true, that I thrived on it. I became like Mom, filling up on the attention."

"Our mom was not a healthy person," Sabrina said, stating the obvious.

"Maybe I wasn't healthy either."

"Honestly, I think you were confused, struggling, but I don't believe you have Munchausen, if that's what you mean," Sabrina said. "At least not a typical case."

Becky exhaled a weighty sigh. "Maybe I do, maybe I don't. But I am sure I don't have it now. With Cora gone, I feel like I can finally move on. I feel a million pounds lighter — and before you judge, I know that's a terrible thing to say."

"Don't feel bad for not feeling bad," Sabrina said. "It's unbecoming of you."

Becky leaned in so that their shoulders touched. "Ironic, isn't it, that Nash's plan to use Zach to get me out of the picture might have helped to save Meghan — that is, if the doctors can ever find a cure for that damn disease."

"They will. Have faith."

Becky fixed her gaze on the rolling waves. "Cora loved the ocean. It was one of the gentlest things about her."

"You can let go now," Sabrina said. "She's gone."

Becky focused on a seagull lazily riding the draft of the steady ocean breeze. "Nobody is ever really gone," she said. "We leave marks on this world, as invisible as the trail of that bird out there. Cora, Carl, even Amanda Nash, will always be a part of me. But there's a difference between letting someone into your life and letting them define it. I know that now. And, yeah, I finally feel free."

EPILOGUE

Zach

Dear William:

Dad here.

I'm writing you on what would be your nineteenth birthday to let you know that I'm getting married. I met her two years ago, through some rather unusual circumstances. You'd love her, Will, and I know you'd approve.

I want you to know that I miss you every single day. I never stopped fighting for you, same as I never stopped blaming myself for your death. But I have to stop now. If I'm going to be a husband again — and a stepfather to her amazing daughter, Meghan — I have to move forward with my life. I can't stay stuck in limbo anymore. So that's why I'm writing you this letter, which I will put in an envelope but sadly never mail, to let you know that while I'll never forgive myself for what happened to you, I won't use it as an excuse to stay trapped in the past. You were dealt a bad hand in life — the worst. Sometimes life simply isn't fair. But good can come even in the darkest times if you keep your heart open.

So that's what I'm doing. I'm opening my heart again. I'm moving forward, one small step at a time. Your mom is going to be at the wedding. She's married, too, did you know? And I hope that you'll be there as well, a smiling angel looking down on us all. I love you always.

— Dad

ACKNOWLEDGMENTS

Writing is said to be a lonely profession, but publishing could hardly be considered a solo endeavor. With that sentiment in mind, I offer thanks and gratitude to the multitudes of people who lent their time, talents, and expertise to help bring this work of fiction to the printed page.

I'll begin with a heartfelt thanks to the team at the Jane Rotrosen Agency: my agent Meg Ruley; Rebecca Scherer and Jane Berkey, who have stuck by my side through the years, encouraged me to dig deeper when I felt I'd already reached bottom, and to trust the process, which has yet to steer me wrong. Thanks also to Danielle Prielipp, for giving my stories a global reach, and Christine Prestia and the rest of the team at JRA, for keeping the business side of the operation running smoothly.

A special thank-you goes to Jennifer Enderlin, my editor, who has been a constant source of encouragement, a wealth of wisdom, and a steadfast advocate. I'm one grateful writer. Jen, you've done more for my family and me than I can adequately convey, so a simple thank-you will have to suffice.

Thanks also to my mother and Zoe Quinton, who read each word with a thoughtful eye toward how I could write it better. Dr. David Grass, my uncle and a dear friend, helped me conceptualize this story, provided medical expertise, and worked with me as I juggled the plot, characters, and various storylines in the semiartful, often fumbling quest to bring verisimilitude to the novel. To that end, I extend my gratitude as well to Dr. Jay Woody, who, thanks to a chance encounter at a watering hole on a Caribbean vacation, agreed to read the manuscript in draft form and discovered some issues that I was more than happy to correct. Thanks also to Dr. Joel Solomon, who helped me plan a daring escape, and to Patrick Fitzgerald, who acted as my legal eagle.

While this is a story about what can happen when parents go up against a hospital, it is really about family and the power of love. To that end, I thank with all my heart my family: my wife, Jessica, and my children, Benjamin and Sophie, who are a constant source of inspiration and a guiding force that gives my life shape and meaning.

Lastly, I thank you, dear reader, for whom I am here to entertain, enthrall, and thrill, and to that end, I hope I have exceeded your expectations — wildly so at that.

— D. J. Palmer, New Hampshire

ABOUT THE AUTHOR

D. J. Palmer is the author of numerous critically acclaimed suspense novels, including *Delirious* and *Desperate*. After receiving his master's degree from Boston University, he spent a decade as an e-commerce pioneer before turning his attention to writing. He lives with his wife and two children in New Hampshire, where he is currently at work on his next novel.

The employees of Thorndike Press hope you have enjoyed this Large Print book. All our Thorndike, Wheeler, and Kennebec Large Print titles are designed for easy reading, and all our books are made to last. Other Thorndike Press Large Print books are available at your library, through selected bookstores, or directly from us.

For information about titles, please call:
(800) 223-1244

or visit our website at:
gale.com/thorndike

To share your comments, please write:
Publisher
Thorndike Press
10 Water St., Suite 310
Waterville, ME 04901